WE
ARE
HERE

Also by Michael Marshall

The Straw Men
The Upright Man
Blood of Angels
The Intruders
Bad Things
Killer Move

As Michael Marshall Smith

Only Forward
Spares
One of Us
The Servants

WE ARE HERE

MICHAEL MARSHALL

MULHOLLAND BOOKS

LITTLE, BROWN AND COMPANY

NEW YORK   BOSTON   LONDON

In memory of Ralph Vicinanza:
Agent, mentor, friend.

Copyright © 2013 by Michael Marshall Smith

Mulholland Books/Little, Brown and Company
Hachette Book Group
237 Park Avenue, New York, NY 10017
mulhollandbooks.com

First North American Edition: February 2014
Originally published in Great Britain by Orion Books, an imprint of the Orion Publishing Group Ltd, March 2013

Mulholland Books is an imprint of Little, Brown and Company, a division of Hachette Book Group, Inc. The Mulholland Books name and logo are trademarks of Hachette Book Group, Inc.

The publisher is not responsible for websites (or their content) that are not owned by the publisher.

The Hachette Speakers Bureau provides a wide range of authors for speaking events. To find out more, go to hachettespeakersbureau.com or call (866) 376-6591.

Library of Congress Cataloging-in-Publication Data

Marshall, Michael
    We are here / Michael Marshall.—First North American edition
        p. cm.
    ISBN 978-0-316-25257-7
    1. Male teachers—Fiction.   2. Mind and reality—Fiction.   3. Stalking—Fiction.
4. New York—Fiction.   5. Psychological fiction.   I. Title.
    PR6069.M5225W4 2014
    823'.914—dc23   2013038912

10 9 8 7 6 5 4 3 2 1

RRD-C

Printed in the United States of America

In the realm of the emotions,
the real is no different to the imaginary.
André Gide

Prologue

He drove. There were times when he stopped for gas or to empty his bladder or buy cups of poor coffee out of machines, selecting isolated and windswept gas stations where no one was doing anything except filling up and staring vacantly at their cold hand on the pump as they waited, wanting to be back in their warm car and on the road to wherever it was they had to be. Nobody was looking or watching or caring about anyone who might happen to be doing the same thing. Nobody saw anything except another guy in bulky clothing getting into a big car and pulling back out onto the highway.

Sometimes it was raining. Sometimes there was sleet. Sometimes merely the wind coming across the great flatness. He did not listen to the radio. He did not consult a map. He didn't know where he was going and so he did not care where he was.

He just drove.

He had barely slept beyond nodding out for short stretches in the driver's seat, the car stashed behind abandoned farmhouses or in the parking lots of small-town businesses that would not open for several hours after he was back on the road. Other than bags of potato chips or dusty gas station trail mix, he hadn't eaten since he left what used to be his home. He already knew he wasn't going back there. He was light-headed with hunger but he could not eat. He was exhausted but he could not sleep. He was a single thought in a mind no longer capable of maintaining order. A thought needs somewhere to go, but flight does not provide a destination. Flight merely shrieks that you have to be somewhere other than where you are.

keep going, too, but first he had to stop.

the third day he passed a sign for a motel

on practice in parts of the country where

hout seeing anything of consequence, the

y of warning to think about it and check

be it was time to call it a day. He had

out registering them. This one looked

where forty years or more, from when drives cross-country

were everybody's best hope of a vacation. It showed a basic-looking mom-and-pop motel with a foreign-sounding name. It was still thirty miles ahead at that point.

He shook his head and looked back at the road, but he already knew he was going to stop. He'd said no to a lot of things in his life, especially in the last month.

He'd gone ahead and done them anyway.

Half an hour later he pulled up outside a single-story L-shaped building down a short road off the highway. There were no cars outside the guest rooms, but a dim light showed in the office. When he went in, an old man came from the room out back. The old man looked him up and down and saw the kind of person who arrives alone at out-of-the-way motels in the back end of nowhere; he had never been a curious person and had stopped giving a shit about anything at all when his wife died three years before. The man paid him in cash for one night and got a key in return. A metal key, not one of those credit card swipers found everywhere else these days. A real key, one that opened a particular door and no other. The man looked at it, becalmed, trying to remember if he'd locked the door to his house when he left. He wasn't sure. It was too late to do anything about it. He asked the owner for the nearest place to get something to eat. The old man pointed up the road. The driver took a handful of matchbooks from the counter and went back out and got in his car.

Fifteen miles away he found a small store attached to a two-pump gas station that had nothing he wanted to eat but did sell things he could drink and smoke. He drove back to the motel and parked in front of Number 9. The rest of the lot remained empty. It was full dark now.

In the room he found a frigid rectangular space with two double beds and an ancient television. He locked and bolted the door. He shoved the closest bed over until it blocked entry. Years ago the bed had been retrofitted with a vibrating function — no longer working — and was extremely heavy. It took him ten minutes and used up the last of his strength. He turned the rusty heater on. It made a lot of noise but gradually started to make inroads on the cold.

In the meantime he lay on the other bed. He did not take off his coat. He stared up at the ceiling. He opened the bottle he'd bought. He smoked cigarette after cigarette as he drank, lighting them with matches from matchbooks. His face was wet.

He wept with exhaustion. He wept because his head hurt. He wept with the self-disgust that permeated every cell of his body, like the imaginary mites that plague habitual users of crystal meth, nerve misfirings that feel so much like burrowing insects that sufferers will scratch and scratch and scratch at them until their arms and faces are a mass of bloody scabs, writing their affliction for all to see.

His affliction was not thus written, however. His was a text only he could read, for now. He still appeared normal. To anyone else he would have looked like a chubby man in his early thirties, lying on a motel bed, very drunk now, sniveling by himself.

In his mind, however, he wept. There was majesty to it. A hero, lost and alone.

Sometime later he started from a dream that had not been a dream. He'd been getting a lot of these since he left home, waking possessed by shadows he wished were dreams but that he knew very well to be memory. The wall in the back of his head was breaking down, wearing out like something rubbed with sweaty fingers too hard for too long. His mind wasn't trying to mediate through dramatization any longer. It was feeding up the things it had seen through his eyes or felt through his fingertips. His mind was thinking about what had happened even when he was not.

He didn't lie to himself. He knew he wasn't innocent, and could never be again. He knew what he'd done. He wouldn't have done it alone, maybe, but that didn't mean it hadn't been done. By him.

The other man had suggested things, but he had done them. That was how it had always been.

He'd waited and watched down alleys and outside bars and in the late-night parking lots of the town he'd called home. He'd made the muscles in his face perform movements that looked like smiles. He'd selected forms of words that sounded helpful and charming. The other man planned the sentences, but it was he who'd spoken them aloud. The other had researched what would work best, but he'd been the one who slipped the ground-up pill into the wine he'd made available, offered casually, as if it was no big deal, and oh, what a coincidence—it just happens to be your favorite kind.

The other man invented the games he and his guest had played until she suddenly got scared, despite how drunk and confused she had become. Who had then raised his hand for the first blow? Impossible to tell. It didn't matter, when so many others had followed.

All he'd ever done was follow, but he'd wound up at the destination anyhow, and of course it's true that when you submit to someone's will then it's you who gives them power. You follow from in front. You can follow a long way like that. You can follow too far.

You can follow all the way to hell.

He rubbed his eyes against the last shards of the memory and sat up to see the other man was sitting in the armchair. He looked smart and trim and presentable as always. He looked strong. He was holding one of the motel matchbooks, turning it over in his fingers.

"I don't want to do it again," the man on the bed said.

"You do," the other man said. "You just don't like that you do. That's why you've got me. We're a team."

"Not anymore. You're not my friend."

"Why don't you have another drink? It'll make you feel better."

Despite himself, the man on the bed groped blearily for the vodka and raised it to his lips. He'd almost always done what the other man said. He saw two necks to the bottle. The alcohol had caught up with him while he dozed, and he was far drunker than he'd realized. Might as well keep drinking, then.

"You left a trail," the other man said. "Deliberately?"

"Of course not." He wasn't sure if this was true.

"They'll be turning the house upside down tomorrow, or by the next day at the latest."

"I cleaned up."

"They'll find something. Then they'll come looking. Eventually they'll find you. Wherever you run." The man's face turned cold. "You fucked up, Edward. Again. Always. Always with the fucking up."

The man on the bed felt dreadful fear and vertiginous guilt mingled with relief. If he was caught then he could not do it again. He would not find himself returning to the same Chinese restaurant night after night, hoping for a glimpse of one of the other customers, a young single woman who worked in the bank across the street and sometimes came to grab a cheap bite at the end of the workday, though with infuriating unpredictability. He would not gradually come to know where she lived—alone—and where she went to the gym, where and when she shopped for groceries, or that her basket always included at least one bottle of wine.

The man on the bed shrugged, trying to feel glad that something like this could not happen again, though he knew every single moment of it had held a terrible excitement and that there could be other such women in other towns, if he chose to keep driving down this road. "They catch me, they catch you."

"I know that," the man in the chair said. He opened the matchbook. With effort he managed to get one of the matches out. After a couple of pulls along the strip, he got it lit.

The man on the bed noticed, too late, that he'd piled all the other matchbooks on the bedspread of the bed that now blocked the door. The bedspread was old, not to code, flammable. Very flammable, it turned out.

"I'm not going to jail," the other man said as he stood up from the chair. "I'd rather die right here."

He dropped the burning matchbook on the pile.

It didn't happen fast. The man on the bed, whose name was Edward Lake, had a little time to escape. He was far too drunk now to move the heavy bed from the door, however. He was too drunk to understand that the dead tone from the phone by the bed was because the other man had unplugged it while Edward crashed out.

By the time he got around to trying, he could not get past the flames to the window. He was too scared, and the truth is that the only real and meaningful thing Edward had done in his entire life was kill a woman, and there's no good way forward from that. So it's also possible that, deep inside, he did actually just want to die.

As his former friend burned alive, the other man watched from the parking lot. He knew the moment when Edward died, and was surprised and awestruck by what happened next.

The death of the girl back home had felt powerful. But this . . . this was completely other. This was something else.

He felt altered, very different indeed, and knew in that moment that he was finished with following, even if by the end he and Edward had been traveling side by side and hand in hand.

People who walk alone travel faster. It was time for new horizons and bigger goals.

Everything would be better now.

To mark the occasion, he glanced up at the motel sign — lit by flames as the remaining rooms of the structure caught alight and the owner choked to death in his bed — and renamed himself. Then he turned from the blaze and walked away up the road into the darkness, savoring with every step the solid feel of the earth beneath his feet.

Even with the immense degree of will at his disposal, it was a long and very tiring walk. The dawn found him sitting exhausted by the side of the road. A passing salesman, who'd risen early after a bad night's sleep and was running early and of a kindly disposition, stopped and gave the man a ride. The man realized what it meant to have been seen by a stranger, and he got in the back of the car with a faint smile on his face.

After fifty miles the salesman glanced in the rearview mirror to see that his passenger had fallen asleep. In this rare moment of defenselessness, the man looked pale and worn through.

But this all happened five years ago.

He is much stronger now.

Part One

The number of people here who think alone, sing alone,
and eat and talk alone in the streets is mind-boggling.
And yet they don't add up.

Jean Baudrillard

America

Chapter I

It should have been a wonderful day — a day to photograph and frame, to Facebook and tweet, an afternoon to cut out and save in that album of updates and keepsakes you return to in daydream and memory; the pressed flowers of our lives that we'll hold up to God or his gatekeeper when our moment comes, to prove we are worthy of entrance and have not merely been marking time.

It should have been one of those days.

And until the very end, it was.

They arrived at Penn Station just after ten, on the kind of fall morning when it's warm in the sun but chill in the shadows of the skyscraping monoliths; when the city feels pert and alert and struts with head high, marching to work with tightly specified coffees and a bounce in its step as if someone loosened everyone's bolts in the night. David was in town not as some sightseer or nostalgia seeker, either, but for a meeting followed by lunch — the Lunch of Legend that people conjure in their minds to keep them strong through the months and years spent doing lone, heroic (or merely stoic) battle against the Blank Page of Infinity and the Blinking Cursor of Doom.

Suddenly, David was going to be published.

No, seriously.

He'd assumed they'd take a cab uptown, but the streets were so traffic-tangled — not to mention they were very early, Dawn having selected a departure time that allowed for everything from minor delays to a full-scale terrorist attack on the line — that they strolled the twenty-some blocks instead. David was struck by how unfamiliar it all seemed. It wasn't merely that everywhere was much cleaner than ten years ago, or that he felt less likely to get attacked on any given street corner (though both were true). During his long-ago five months living in the city he'd simply been very unadventurous, he realized, sticking to the same haunts in a way that struck his older self as appallingly cautious. But when you look nostalgically back from thirty it's easy to forget how much of your twenties were spent feeling awkward and lonely, weaving a cloak of familiarity around you like the armor it eventually becomes.

They spent the last half hour in a Starbucks on Madison, perched at the window counter withstanding bland jazz and fiddling with stirring sticks. Dawn kept quiet. David didn't chatter in the face of anxiety, she knew, but gathered troops behind invisible walls. She people-watched instead, wondering as always who everyone was and where they were going.

At a quarter to, she escorted David the final block, kissed him, and wished him luck—and told him he didn't need it. She waved as she left on a lightning strike up to Bloomingdale's, a wide, proud smile on her face.

For a moment, as he watched his wife disappear into the crowds, David felt nervous for her. He told himself it was merely his own anxiety.

At 11:55 he took a deep breath and strode into reception. He told the guy behind the desk who the hell he was and who the dickens he'd come to meet, speaking more loudly than usual. The receptionist made few bones about not giving a crap, but a few minutes later someone young and enthusiastic bounced out of an elevator, shaking hand already outstretched.

David was whisked upward many floors and finally got to meet his editor, Hazel, a gaunt fifty-something New Yorker who proved fractionally less intimidating in person than via e-mail, though still pretty scary. He was given a tour of untidy offices and book-infested cubicles while a selection of affable strangers told him that his book was great, that *he* was great, that everyone was unbelievably excited and that it was all going to be just...*great*. A lot of hand-shaking and smiling took place, and people stood around with notepads clasped to their chests as if ready to jot down anything significant the moment it occurred, though evidently nothing of the sort happened, because nobody did.

Then suddenly they dispersed like birds startled by a rifle shot, and Hazel took his elbow and steered him firmly toward the elevator. "Lunch," she muttered darkly, as if warning him not to put up a fight.

Dawn had just arrived back outside, and stood hurriedly. David's agent, Ralph—another character he was meeting in person for the first time—was already in position at the restaurant two blocks away, an old-school grill and steak house that prided itself on serving cow by the slab in an environment of white linen, low lighting, and disconcertingly formal service.

David realized how nervous Dawn really was only when he saw her beaming glassily at the waiter, unable to comprehend a query concerning her desired genre of mineral water (fizzy or not). David squeezed her hand under the table, realized he was smiling at Ralph in exactly the same way, and tried to relax.

He'd told himself he wasn't going to drink wine with lunch, but when it became clear that his editor sure as hell was, he relented, combating the effects with so much water that he had to visit the bathroom three times. Meanwhile, he and Dawn watched as the professionals gossiped about people they'd never heard of—feeling like a pair of venturesome kids, a Hardy boy and Nancy Drew on joint reconnaissance, ears pricked for intel about the curious new world they'd been told they would become a part of—if the capricious gods of market forces, key bloggers, and the zeitgeist willed it so.

Eventually the stupendous check was paid with reference to some protocol David didn't understand but knew wouldn't involve him. Everyone reemerged blinking into the sunlight, to part on excellent terms. Graphic artists were at work on a jacket design. Cover copy would soon be e-mailed for David's approval. David had never "approved" anything before and was looking forward to the experience. He thought he might wear a special shirt for it. Everything was going perfectly, he was assured, perhaps even a little better than that.

"It's all good," Hazel kept telling him sternly, as if he were well known for championing an opposing school of thought. "David, it's *all good*."

By then he was in no mood to disagree.

They wandered down Park Avenue until David had an idea and cut across to Bryant Park. Back in the seventies it had by all accounts been a place where, should you wish to score drugs, get laid on a commercial basis, or have the living daylights mugged out of you, the locals would have lined up around the block to oblige. By the time David spent his few months in New York, it had turned around to become one of the most amenable spaces in Manhattan—and he'd spent hours sitting in it with a notebook and dreams of a future that were only now coming true. The intervening decade had kicked it up further still. Not so much a park as a grassed plaza lined on all sides with trees, it now held coffee stands and walkways lined with planters, an upscale grill and bar to the rear of the reassuring bulk of the New York Public Library, and the only mugging going on involved the prices demanded for crab cakes and sauvignon blanc.

They took glasses of the latter to a table on the terrace and spent an hour excitedly going back over lunch. A voice in David's head seemed intent on convincing him it was a mirage, that there were twenty other authors having the exact same experience this afternoon and all would be back to working their day jobs (and bitterly grateful for them) in eighteen months' time. He even glanced around the park, a little drunk now, in case he could spot any of his fellow hopefuls.

He couldn't, and this wasn't an afternoon for doubt. It was for listening to the babble of conversation and to the warmth in Dawn's voice as she told him how wonderful everything was going to be, and finally the muttering voice retreated to the cave in the back of David's soul where it had lived for as long as he could remember.

Eventually it was time to leave, and that's when it happened.

They were leaving the park and David maybe wasn't looking where he was going — wrapped up as he was in the day and with yet another glass of wine inside him. The sidewalks were a lot more crowded now, too, as the end of the workday approached and people set off for home.

It wasn't a hard knock. Just an accidental collision of shoulders, an urban commonplace, barely enough to jolt David off course and provoke a half turn that had him glancing back to see another man doing the same.

"Sorry," David said. He wasn't sure he'd been at fault, but he was the kind to whom apology came easily.

The other man said nothing, but continued on his way, quickly becoming lost in the crowds.

Penn Station was a total zoo, epicenter of a three-way smackdown between baffled tourists, gimlet-eyed commuters, and circling members of the feral classes that make transit depots their hunting grounds. Twenty minutes before departure Dawn elected to visit the restrooms, leaving David to hold a defensive position near a pillar. He felt exhausted, eyes owlish from unaccustomed alcohol, feet sore. He experienced the passing throng as smeared colors and echoing sounds and nothing more.

Until he saw someone looking at him.

A man wearing jeans and a crumpled white shirt. He had dark hair, strong features, and he was looking right at David.

David blinked, and the man wasn't there anymore. Or he'd moved on, presumably. He'd barely been visible for a second, but David felt he'd been watching him — and also that he'd seen the man before.

"What's up?" Dawn returned, looking mildly shaken by the restroom experience. David shook his head.

They made their way toward the platform via which they'd arrived at the station that morning. This turned out *not* to be where the train was departing from, however, and all at once they were in a hurry and lost and oh-my-god-we're-screwed. David figured out where they were supposed to be and pointed at Dawn to lead the way. She forged ahead with the boisterous élan of someone having a fine old time in the city, emboldened by a bucketful of wine, clattering down the steps to the platform and starting to trot when she saw their train in preparation for departure.

As David hurried after her, someone appeared out of the crowd and banged into him—hard, knocking David back on his feet and getting right in his face.

Untucked white shirt and hard blue eyes.

The same man again.

"Hello, David," he said. Then something else, before stepping around the corner and out of sight.

Winded and a little scared, David tried to see where the man had gone, but Dawn was calling him urgently now, and someone blew a whistle. He hurried along to where his wife stood flushed and grinning.

"We made it," she said, as they clambered onto the train. "See? The gods are on our side now."

Dawn started to crash within fifteen minutes, head on David's shoulder, hair tickling his neck. David sat bolt upright, trying to be distracted by the view as the carriages trundled over the river and out through urban sprawl. It wasn't working.

So he'd banged into some guy.

And so that man had evidently then followed them to the train station, watched David from across the concourse, and tracked them through the crowds to bang into him again.

Why would someone do that?

Because he was crazy, that's why. New Yorkers were famous for taking a hard-line approach. Even the well adjusted and affluent appeared to conduct human interaction as a contact sport. Insane people all the more so, presumably.

That's all it was. Big deal.

And yet...

As Dawn slipped into a doze and the train began to pick up speed into the hour-long journey to Rockbridge and home, there was one thing that David couldn't get out of his mind. It was what the stranger had said before he melted back into the crowd. Not the fact that he'd known David's name—he'd realized the man could have overheard Dawn using it, maybe.

It was the other thing. Just two words. Words that are usually framed as a question but this time sounded like a command. Or a threat.

"Remember me," he'd said.

Chapter 2

When I stopped by the apartment to drop off the groceries, Kristina was still in bed. It had been a late night — they generally are, five nights out of seven at least — but I like to begin my days early, with a long walk. Kristina prefers to deal with them sprawled under the sheets like a pale, lanky spider that has been dropped from a very great height.

I finished wedging things into the tiny fridge (all we had room for, in a kitchen that's basically a specialized corner of the living room) and strode into the bedroom, an epic journey of three yards. The top of the window was open, proving Kristina must have groped her way out of bed at some point. It's shut at night or we'd never get to sleep on account of the racket from drunken good times in the streets below. The heater was ominously silent. The unit had been ailing for weeks, wheezing like an old smoker. Though the fall had so far been mild, finding someone to take it up a level from my own feeble attempts at repair (glaring at the machine, once in a while giving it an impotent kick) was high on my list of things to do today.

I put the massive Americano by the side of the bed. "Beverage delivery. You have to sign for it."

Her voice was muffled. "Fuck off."

"Right back atcha. It's a beautiful morning in the neighborhood, case you're interested."

"Christ."

"By the way. This woman later, Catherine. She gets that I'm just some guy, right?"

Kristina laboriously turned her head and blew long strands of black hair off her crumpled face. "Don't worry," she mumbled. "I made a point of saying you were nothing special. Matter of fact, I went so far as to imply you were something of an asshole."

"Seriously."

She smiled, eyes still closed. "Seriously. No biggie. And thank you for doing it. And for the coffee."

"So I'll see you there. Three o'clock?"

"If I don't see you first."

I looked down at her and thought it was disquieting how much you could come to like someone in only six months. Shouldn't our hearts be more cautious? A child or puppy learns after straying too close to a candle to hold back next time. It seems that emotional calluses are not as thick or permanent as they appear, however.

I bent down and kissed Kristina on the forehead.

She opened her eyes. "What was that for?"

"Because I like you."

"You're weird."

"It's been said."

"That's okay. Weird is good." She stretched like a cat, all limbs pointed in the same direction. "And you'll think about the other thing?"

"I will."

"Good. Now scram. I need more sleep."

"It's ten thirty."

Her eyes closed. "It's always ten thirty somewhere."

"Very deep."

"Really, John, I mean it. Don't make me get up out of here and kick your ass."

I left her to it, jogged back down the five flights of stairs to street level, and stepped out into the big, strange city that lived — in all its train-wreck glory — right outside our door.

*   *   *

The rest of the morning was spent covering Paulo's shift at the restaurant's sidewalk window, hawking pizza and bottles of Poland Spring to passersby. This task is usually reserved for someone barely able to stand unassisted on their hind legs (currently Paulo, fresh-off-the-boat nephew of someone or other and an earthling so basic it's a miracle he can work out which way to face the street), but I didn't mind. Paulo's a sweet kid, eager to please, and was off trying to find somewhere to improve his English. Also, I kind of enjoy the job. There are only two styles of slice available—plain or pepperoni—and one drink. Each costs a dollar. It's hard to screw that up, and it's pleasant to lean on the counter exchanging banter with locals and making strangers' days better in straightforward ways. When your life has been overly complicated, simplicity can taste like a mouthful of clear, cool water. Available, this lunch hour, from me, near the corner of Second Avenue and 4th. Price—one dollar.

When my stint was over, I chatted with the owner, Mario, and his sister Maria—evidently the children of parents with either a sense of humor or a dearth of imagination—over a coffee at one of the sidewalk tables. The Adriatico has been holding down its patch—snug between a venerable Jewish bakery and a thrift store with pretensions of funkiness, a few minutes' walk from the dives of St. Mark's Place and side street legends like McSorley's—for forty years, largely due to the family's willingness to embrace change, however bad-temperedly. In the time Kristina and I had been on staff (me waiting tables, Kristina running the popular late-night basement bar), the owners had replaced the awning, repainted the picket fence around the sidewalk tables a (much) brighter color, and tried adding the word "organic" to everything on the menu: briefly offering an organic ragù with organic pasta and organic béchamel, oven-baked in the traditional organic manner—aka lasagna. I'd eventually convinced Mario not to pursue this (it made announcing the specials tiresome, and was moreover absolutely untrue), but I had to admire the ambition. It was certainly easier to understand why this restaurant was still in business than the last place I'd worked, on the other side of the country, on the Oregon coast.

I left with the customary mild buzz. The Adriatico's coffee is celebrated for its strength, to the point where there's a water-damaged poster in the restrooms (badly) hand-drawn by some long-ago college wit, suggesting it should be cited in strategic-arms-limitation treaties. Nobody can remember why the standard cup has three shots in it, but I'd come to learn that's how New York works. Someone does something one day for reasons outside their control and beyond anyone's recollection—and then winds up doing it for the next fifty years. The tangle of these traditions floats through the streets like mist and hangs like cobwebs among the trees and fire escapes. Tourist or resident—and it wasn't yet clear which I was—you're forever in the presence of these local heroes and ghosts.

I did my errands, including visiting the heater place. They promised they'd get to ours real soon. As both engineers were regulars at the bar I had reason to believe it.

With an hour still to kill, I took a long stroll down through the Village. There's always something to see in our part of town, and I liked watching it and walking it, and for the first time in some years I liked my life, too. It was simple, contained, and easy.

But I got the sense that was about to change.

What Kristina wanted me to consider was the idea of a new apartment. There was much about the East Village that we enjoyed. The remnants of the old immigrant population, their pockets of otherness. The leafy side streets and crumbling prewar walkups, the area's determination to resist gentrification and order, forever tending toward chaos like some huge silverware drawer. The fact that if you came shambling out of a bar late at night waving your iPhone around then you were likely to only get robbed, with brisk efficiency, rather than killed.

At times, though—with roving hordes from NYU and Cooper Union, plus all the young tourists who wanted to show how cool and not just about Banana Republic and the Apple Store they were — it could feel like being shacked up in the low-rent end of a college town. There had been a spate of odd muggings recently, too — people having their bank cards stolen and their accounts immediately emptied at ATMs with mysterious ease.

I never got a chance to do the student thing — having spent those years and more in the army — and I was open to a second adolescence. Kristina was wearying of the locale, however, perhaps because she spent her evenings at the sharper end of the Asshole Service Industry. I'm thirty-seven, old enough for sketchy to have a retro charm. She's twenty-nine, sufficiently young for the idea of being a grown-up to remain appealing. She'd started talking about moving to SoHo or the West Village, for the love of God. I kept reminding her that she ran bar and I served circular food in a fiercely down-market restaurant. She'd counter with the observation that I had money from the sale of my house in Washington State after the split from my ex-wife. Feeling old and dull, I'd observe that we weren't bringing in much *new* money, and nobody tied themselves to loft rentals under those circumstances, though I'd be willing to consider subletting somewhere tiny, as an experiment, if we committed to not eating for the foreseeable future — and anyway, it took less than half an hour to walk from our front door to the streets she was talking about, so what was the big deal?

And so on and so forth. The subject would eventually fade into abeyance, like a car drifting out of range of a local evangelical radio station, and I'd be left feeling like the patriarch who'd decreed that instead of eating in the lovely seafood restaurant with an ocean view, the family was going to make do with sandwiches in the parking lot. Again.

An hour later it would be like it never happened, however. Kristina did not study on things. She hit you between the eyes with the full payload, all at once. When that was spent, the storm was over — at least for now.

Two days ago she'd asked if I'd do her a favor, though, and I'd agreed because I felt I was letting her down in other ways. That meant a change was coming. If you're with a strong woman (and they're *all* strong, whatever they may have been told to the contrary; women have backbone men can only dream of), then once you've given ground you'll never be off the back foot again.

I was on the way to do that favor now.

Chapter 3

The café was on Greenwich Avenue. I deliberately walked the last forty yards on the opposite side of the street, and when I spotted them at one of the rickety tables outside I slowed down to take a look.

Kristina was wearing a skirt and jacket I hadn't seen before. It was probably only the second or third time in our entire acquaintance, in fact, that I'd seen her in anything except head-to-toe black. Opposite her sat a trim woman in her midthirties, attractive in the way that owes less to bone structure than to upkeep and confidence. Her hair was sleek and blond and impregnable, cut in a style that announces that the wearer will have valuable intelligence on the relative merits of local schools. I couldn't tell much else from a distance save that, judging from her clothes and bearing, the woman could probably afford an apartment more or less wherever she wanted.

I crossed the street. I was introduced to Catherine Warren and shook hands. We chatted about the weather and reprised background I already knew, like how the two women had met at a weekly reading group held at Swift's, an independent bookstore in what we're supposed to call Nolita these days but is just a boutique wedge between SoHo and Little Italy. We agreed that Swift's was a swell little store and deserved our fervent support, and I elected not to mention my impression that the staff there always watched me as if they suspected I was about steal one of their hand-made gift cards, holocaust memoirs, or chunky anthologies of short stories about growing up poor but wise in Brooklyn.

When these subjects ran out of steam — and the wizened old gay couple from the next table had shuffled away up the street, bickering all the while — I put my cigarettes on the table. Now that you can barely smoke anywhere in the city, this is an effective shorthand for "I'm not going to be here forever, so let's get to it."

"Kristina said there was something you might want advice about."

The woman nodded, looking diffident.

"And she explained to you I'm not a cop, right? Or private detective?"

Kristina rolled her eyes. "She did," Catherine said. "She said you're a waiter."

"That's true," I agreed affably. "So, what's up?"

She looked at the table for a while, then raised her eyes like someone being forced to make a confession.

"I think," she said, "that I'm being stalked."

I'm not sure what I'd been expecting. Problems with a neighbor. Vague suspicions about her husband. A younger sister with an unsuitable boyfriend.

"That's not good. How long has it being going on?"

"On and off, nearly ten years."

"Whoa," Kristina said. "Have you *reported* this? Haven't the police —"

"I've never told anyone," Catherine said quickly. "Apart from Mark. My husband," she added. "It hasn't been happening *all* that time or I would have. That's what's strange about it. Part of what's strange."

"Tell me," I said. "From the start."

"Well, I can't remember the day, not like, the actual date. It was around the time I met Mark, or a month or two before. We've been married nine years."

"What does your husband do?"

"He's with Dunbar & Scott?" She delivered this as though I should have heard of the company and been impressed. I had not, though I doubted her husband was familiar with the Adriatico either.

"So how come you don't remember when it started? I would have thought that would be somewhat memorable."

Kristina shot me a warning look across the table.

"Of course. But..." Catherine raised her shoulders in a pantomime shrug. "Where do you draw the line? If you walk the city at night—or even during the day—once in a while you're going to get spooked. There's all these people around you all the time and you don't have a clue who any of them are, right? People at bus stops. In parks. In delis or diners or outside bars or reading magazines between the stacks at Barnes & Noble. Runaways. People *hanging around*...or heading down the same street as you are. Sometimes you wonder if they're genuinely on their way somewhere, or if they're walking with you in mind. Or women do, anyway. Maybe you're not aware of it."

I could have observed that the vast majority of random street violence happens to men, but I let it lie. "I know what you're talking about."

"So. There'd been *that* kind of stuff, but I put it down to urban living. But then I'd been out for a drink with girlfriends this one time, and afterward I took the subway home. Back then I had an apartment on Perry, on loan from my aunt."

"Good deal," I said. Perry is a leafy enclave of brownstones in the heart of the West Village, and somewhere I have no expectation of living in this lifetime. This time Kristina gave me a covert kick under the table. I moved my leg out of reach. "And so?"

"I got out at 14th and Eighth and walked. After a while I realized I could hear footsteps. But when I stopped, I couldn't anymore. I know once you start listening to things they sound strange even if they're really not, but there was just...there was something weird about it."

"What did you do?"

"Got home. That's the idea, right? Get inside, lock the doors, and if you can't see a psycho on the sidewalk holding a machete, you forget about it. Which I did."

"But it happened again?"

"Not for two, three weeks. Then one night I was walking back after dark, taking the same route from the same subway, and...yes, it happened again."

"What, exactly? I'm cloudy on what was actually taking place here."

"I knew I was being followed. Isn't that enough?"

"Of course," I said. "But in terms of—"

"I turned to look a couple of times, didn't see anyone, but I had this *really* strong sense that someone I knew well was close by, watching me, trying to get closer. At one point I even thought I heard someone softly say my name. Then, as I was turning into my street, I caught a glimpse of someone on the corner of Bleecker."

"What did he look like?"

"Average height, slim build. He was only there for a second, and it was dark. I couldn't see his face."

"Any idea who he might have been?"

It seemed to me that she hesitated. "No."

"No guy across the hall who was always there to say good morning? No one at work who could have misunderstood the colleague/potential boyfriend boundary?"

"I don't think so. Though I suppose you never know the effect you have on other people."

"And this has been going on for *ten years?*"

She glanced at me irritably. "Of course not. I met Mark soon after, and we just clicked, and within a month I was effectively living at his place in Murray Hill. The feeling of being followed stopped when I moved there. And I forgot about it. I got married. Our daughters were born; they're six and four now. We moved to Chelsea five years ago. Everything was great. *Is* great."

"Until?"

She exhaled in one short, sharp breath. "We live on 18th. It's nice, quiet, close to the school, and you got all the restaurants and stuff on Eighth Avenue—though it's not exactly knee-deep in culture, right?

Hence I've been going to the reading group at Swift's, which is how I met..." She gestured across the table.

"Kristina," I said.

"Exactly. Until a few weeks ago I was taking a cab home. Now it's warmer, so I walk. I go via the market on Seventh—Mark's addicted to their shrimp salad, so there's domestic brownie points to be earned right there. But the last two, three times I've turned onto my street...someone's been back at the corner."

"Eighth is busy, especially in the evening."

She spoke sharply. "Right. Which means people tend to *keep moving*. Going where they're headed. Not standing on the corner, looking down my street."

"You've never got a good look at his face?"

"No."

"So what makes you believe it's the same person?"

"I just *feel* it is. You...wouldn't understand."

"Maybe not." There are women who believe they have recourse to intuitive powers beyond the understanding of male kind, and what they "feel" supersedes information available to the more conventional senses. This can be irritating, especially if you happen to be one of the dullard male robots who apparently can't see past the end of his own unspeakable genitals. In my own woman's case, I had reason to know such a belief could be justified, however, and so I didn't call Catherine on it. "And it's never been more than that? This impression of being followed?"

"No. Though two weeks ago I was drawing the curtains in the girls' room and I saw someone on the sidewalk below. I *know* he was looking up at the window. But Ella started fussing and I had to deal with her and the next time I got a chance to look...he'd gone."

She trailed off, looking at me defiantly. I didn't know what to say, and so I didn't say anything, which is generally my policy.

"I *knew* this was going to sound ridiculous," she muttered. "I'm sorry to have wasted your time."

"You said you'd mentioned this to your husband?"

"I get the impression he thinks the same as you."

"Which is?"

"I'm a woman, being silly."

I was taken aback. "I don't think that, Catherine. The question is what you can do about—"

"Assuming any of it is actually *happening,* right? That it's not an attack of the vapors or some other charmingly feminine malaise?"

"I'm just trying to be practical."

"Absolutely. Men are good at that." She pushed her chair back decisively. "My friend's looking after Ella and Isabella. She's going to need to leave soon."

"So, John—what should she do?" Kristina's voice was clipped. She was pissed at me, and not hiding it.

I shrugged. I'd been intending to follow that up with something more helpful, but wasn't given the chance.

"Thank you for your time, John," Catherine said.

After telling the waitress to put the drinks on her account, she gave Kristina a peck on the cheek.

"See you tomorrow night," she said. "Nice to meet you," she added to me. I've heard more convincing lies.

As the two of them headed out to the sidewalk together, I got out my wallet and covertly put a five-dollar bill on the table.

Chapter 4

When Catherine had disappeared up the street, Kristina turned to me. She had a look in her eye that I've seen her use on men in the bar, optimistic drunkards who've mistaken professional courtesy for a ticket to bed. The look works. The guys always elect to buy their next drink someplace else. Often in a different city altogether.

"What?" I asked, though I knew.

She kept glowering at me.

"I just don't get it," I said. "All she has is a vague impression of *maybe* being followed. So she got spooked walking home on a few occasions a very long time apart—there's not a woman in the city who couldn't say the same. And a few guys."

"That doesn't mean she's—"

"I'd be more convinced without the big gap, to be honest. I don't know much about stalkers, but my impression is they tend to stick to the job at hand—not get distracted for a couple of presidential terms. What'd he do, set an alarm to remind himself to act crazy again after a decade-long vacation in normality?"

"You were being snippy before she even got to that part."

"Possibly," I admitted. "She's not my type. You can't dismiss every disagreement with a male as institutionalized sexism. And who has an account at a coffee shop, for Christ's sake?"

"Lots of people."

"Really?"

"Around here, yes."

"Christ. Either way, you tip the waitress. Plus . . . her daughters' names rhyme."

Kris cocked her head and stared at me ominously. "What?"

I wasn't sure what I was trying to say and didn't want to keep trying to say it. "Let's walk."

For a moment it seemed like she wasn't going to follow, but eventually she did.

After fifteen minutes of silence we wound up in the streets on the other side of Bleecker. Close, in fact, to where Catherine had been living in the late 1990s and where she claimed to have first sensed someone following her. I didn't try to get Kris talking. I used to have two young sons. Still do have one, though I've seen him only once in the last three years, for reasons that are not entirely under my control. One of the few skills I'd started to develop before my marriage and family fell apart was the diffusion of unproductive conversations. Kids have far more focus and persistence than adults give them credit for, and may get a buzz out of the attention that conflict gains. Back them into a corner and they'll go at you toe-to-toe, and so the trick is to stop banging that drum and try something else instead. It works with grown-ups too. I use the technique on myself, when the conversations in my head threaten to become repetitive or obsessed with events that I cannot go back and change.

So rather than returning to Catherine Warren's problem—about which I wasn't sure more could be said—I wondered aloud how much the apartment she'd mentioned would cost to rent these days. After a *very* slow start, this led to discussing the area semi-seriously from a residential point of view, and back toward life in general, and finally to the fact that it was approaching time for us to get ready for work.

"You'll be changing your clothes, I take it."

Kristina's skin is very pale, and when she flushes you notice it. "There's no law that says I have to wear black jeans and a rock chick shirt all the time."

"I know that." I didn't mention I'd noticed she'd been drinking tea at the café, which she never does at home. She would reasonably have said there was no law against her drinking tea, either. "I just thought maybe I could help. With the changing process."

She was surprised into a reluctant laugh. "I'm not sure you deserve that honor."

"Perhaps. It's just I've heard that skirts can be challenging. For those unaccustomed to their ways."

"Is that right?"

"I'm just saying. If you need a hand when we get home, I'm there for you." I left a beat. "Of course, if we were living *here,* we'd be home already."

She smiled and looked away. "It's not so far," she said. "I'll race you."

We got slammed that evening, the restaurant packed out the entire night. This wasn't enough to distract me from feeling like an ass over the discussion with Catherine Warren. So she'd rubbed me up the wrong way. It couldn't have been easy to talk about her concerns, and I hadn't provided a considerate audience.

When I took a cigarette break midevening I called an old friend on the other side of the country. Bill Raines answered promptly.

"Well, hey," he said. "How's tricks, pizza boy? Still keeping it thin and crispy?"

"Always," I said, leaning back against the wall to watch people ambling the sidewalk, looking for the cheapest way to feel like shit tomorrow. "How about you? Still lying through your teeth in pursuit of clients' claims, however mercenary and indeed fictitious they may be?"

"It's how I roll. S'up in your so-called life?"

"Wanted to pick your brain."

"Shoot."

I gave him the bones of Catherine's story. He listened without interrupting until I was done.

"I don't see you selling the movie rights," he said. "As jeopardy goes, it's kind of blah, right? Plus, what does she think *you* can do about it?"

"I'm not sure," I said, realizing that the more I thought about it, the less I understood why the meeting had even taken place. "Just hoping for some advice, I guess. I didn't have any. So I'm trying you."

"I'm sure you haven't forgotten everything you knew about the law, John. The cops need probable cause. The sense you're being followed isn't enough, and an attorney's going to need a lot more for a restraining order — like knowing who the alleged perp is. You can't get those things filed 'To Whom It May Concern.'"

"The cops won't help in the meantime?"

"I'm not saying that. These days they take this stuff pretty seriously. Thousands of people every year believe they're receiving unwelcome attention, and most women who get murdered by ex-partners are stalked by them first. Your friend's not going to get a 'Hush, girlie; run along,' but you'll require actual evidence before they can do more than advise buying some Mace. Doesn't sound like she has any."

"Nothing like."

"Sensing you're not her biggest fan, either."

"Christ. Is it that obvious?"

"You've always been a heart-on-the-sleeve kind of guy, John. Least, I assumed it was your heart, though it was kind of shriveled. Could have been an unusually large raisin."

I asked if he was intending to be in the city any day soon. "If I am," he said, "I'll warn you. Give you plenty of time to get out of town. We done here?"

"Always a pleasure, Bill."

"Liar."

* * *

As I slipped the phone back into my pocket I felt someone plucking at my sleeve. I turned to see Lydia looking up at me with anxious eyes.

"Have you seen Frankie?"

"'Fraid not," I said. "But I'll keep an eye out."

The old woman smiled, sending a car crash of deep lines across her face. "Would you, dear? I'm *sure* I saw him earlier. Just by here. I *know* it was him."

Within hours of starting work at the Adriatico I'd been told about Lydia. A long time ago she'd been an actress/singer/dancer in shows on (or within a cab ride of) Broadway, by all accounts talented and beautiful. Then one night thirty years ago someone close to her — her brother, lover, or just a friend, accounts varied — was murdered outside a bar on First Avenue.

That's what the police told her, anyway, though she refused to believe it — refused adamantly, no quarter given. She remained convinced that this guy, whatever he'd been to her, was still alive; that she saw her Frankie sometimes; that she called out to him, but he never heard or never stopped. She had a brusque way with outreach volunteers who tried to boss her around, because she knew she was not crazy. She still turned heads on the streets, though nowadays that was because of her multilayered outfit of castoffs. She slept in Tompkins Square Park, holding her corner and snarling at runaways. Her hair was white, and decades of cigarettes had filled her throat with glass. When she hollered a show tune, which happened occasionally, it did not sound good.

"Need to get back to work, Lyds," I said, slipping a few bucks into her hand. She would not accept money proffered in plain sight. "Take care tonight."

"I will. You're a good boy."

I wasn't sure about that. But most of the time, I try.

*   *   *

After service ended, I went downstairs and propped up the bar until one thirty, lending a hand as required. Afterward, as often on lively nights, we went on to prop up a corner of someone else's bar in the company of cooks, waiters, and allied miscreants from other local dives. By the time we were walking home, things felt good between us again.

"She didn't say anything, did she?" I said.

"Huh?"

"Catherine. You guessed there was a problem. You talked *her* into speaking to me. She never asked."

"You're smarter than you look," Kristina said. "I mean, you'd have to be."

"And you've got an eye for bad things."

"Does this mean you're taking her more seriously?"

"There's *something* up in her life. That I believe. It's also obvious you care about her, which means that I should too. So when you see her tomorrow at the book club, tell her that your boyfriend can be a dickhead but if she wants him to help, he'll try."

"My boyfriend?"

"That would be me."

"I see. 'Course, if we moved to the Village, you might rate being upgraded to 'partner.' I should add that comes with additional benefits."

"Which are?"

"Oh no. My mother may have been a lunatic bitch, but she at least taught me not to toss away the farm."

"You don't give up easy, do you?"

"I don't give up *at all*. You should know that about me by now."

I put my arm around her shoulders and she looped hers around my waist and we walked the rest of the way listening to the sound of distant others shouting and laughing, a solar system of two spinning quietly home through the universe.

*   *   *

I was standing peaceably in the kitchen pouring glasses of water to take to bed when I heard Kristina padding quickly back out of the bedroom.

"I missed a call."

"And?"

She jabbed a couple of buttons. "Listen."

Catherine Warren's voice came out of the speaker, tinny and hesitant.

"Kristina, it's me," she said. "I'm so sorry to call, but I don't know who else to talk to."

There was a pause, and when she spoke again her voice was cracked. "Someone's been in my house."

Chapter 5

The man got to Bryant Park at eleven o'clock, the time the informal morning gathering started. There weren't many friends present — more made the effort to attend the gathering on Friday, and Union Square had become more fashionable recently — and nobody he wanted to talk to. He kept on the move. It wasn't long before people started to drift back out to the streets. He knew she would appear eventually, traditionally arriving from the Sixth Avenue side. He sat halfway up the steps that looked down over the central grassy area and waited.

He had no idea what her reaction was going to be. In general she preached acceptance, making the best of their situation. Might she feel differently about this?

He didn't know.

Three days he'd waited. Three days and three long nights of trying to live normally while a thought drummed in his head like a migraine. As a Fingerman he couldn't just up and leave. He had obligations. Some were arranged on a schedule — his services could be booked — but it was also his time on call. He was required to make himself available in known locations (including this very park) for set periods, ready for requests relayed to him by local Cornermen or friends presenting in person. He did not consider abandoning his post. The rotation had been in place for many years, legacy of Lonely Clive and others. His skills put him in a privileged position, and responsibility came with it. If *they* couldn't man up and do the right thing by each other, then they could hardly criticize others for failing to do so. Thus the Gathered had said, and on this — if not everything else — he agreed. And after all, if he hadn't happened to be holding his post in Bryant Park at the right moment on the right day, this chance to reconnect would never have been born. (Though hadn't he also felt a peculiar pull to the park that afternoon? And hadn't he lingered for more than an hour after his slot had finished? Yes, he had.)

Either way, though the language of the fates is often garbled and obscure, when they speak it pays to listen. He didn't buy the "everything happens for a reason" mantra so beloved of the girl he was waiting for, but when life drops a boon in your lap, you pay the fee.

So he'd waited, stoically, growing more and more tense, finding sometimes that his fists were bunching without him realizing it, knowing however that the important thing was that he was now in possession of information that could change his life.

"Hey," said a voice.

He turned to see the girl, up on the top step. "You came in the other way?"

"I like to remain mysterious."

In silhouette she looked even more ethereal than usual. The sun hung behind her as a halo of gold against long, dark hair. As always, she was wearing dark red under a black coat. If you glimpsed her flicking through old LPs in a thrift store you'd assume she was merely a tall and unusually fine-featured Goth. "What's up?"

"How do you know something's up?"

She smiled. "I know everything, remember?"

He told her everything as they walked around the park together. It had always been that way with them, since they first met in a stinking, moldy room above a boarded-up porno theater soon after he'd come to the city. When he'd finished — it didn't take long — her face was unreadable.

"How wonderful," she said. "Lucky you."

"What do you think I should do?"

"What you're going to do."

"I should . . . do whatever's in my heart?"

She laughed. "No, but bless you for making the effort to speak in my language. I just mean you should do it. You're *going* to, regardless, and as it happens I think it's the right choice."

"Really?" He studied her face. All he found was what he always saw. Pale, open features that were symmetric and strong and yet delicate, and blood-red lips. "Why?"

She shrugged her narrow shoulders. "You could have done something without talking to me. You didn't. What's important to you is important to me. You've waited a long time for something like this. We all have. So do it."

"Thank you, Lizzie."

"*De nada.*" She looked as though she was about to say something else, but stopped.

He turned to see a figure approaching across the grass. Stocky, balding, pugnacious even from a distance. Coming up behind were three other people he recognized — two guys, one woman. Very tall, very thin. "Christ."

"Looks like someone's heading your way."

"It won't take long to say no to whatever it is he wants. Will you wait?"

"Can't. Got things to do and wonders to perform," Lizzie said, taking his hand and squeezing it briefly between her long, pale fingers. "Will you have a phone number?"

He reeled it off to her.

"Be careful, Maj," she said, before drifting away across the grass. "And don't hurt anyone."

As usual, Golzen was wearing a suit styled in the mode of the 1930s — double-breasted, with wide chalk-colored stripes and extravagant lapels. Maj had no idea why he did this. He didn't care.

"I'm in a hurry," he said when the man reached him. The other three stayed well back, thirty feet away, in a huddle in the middle of the grass.

Golzen smiled, a thin, straight line that looked as if it had been drawn on his face and then just as quickly erased. "I'm sure. Interesting business?"

"Not to you."

"I have a proposal."

"Same as usual?"

"Pretty much."

"Guess my answer will be the same, too."

"And I'll ask again, why?"

"Because he's a thief."

"We're all thieves."

"He's different."

"Just more organized, which means better returns—for us. I don't see the difference between him and the lamer you're associating with. Except for the lameness, obviously."

"Jeffers doesn't take anything."

"Everybody takes something, Maj. Some do it more subtly, that's all. Sometimes just by looking."

"What's that supposed to mean?"

"You'll work it out. My point is that with Reinhart the terms are clear and the rewards material."

"You're wrong about him. You'll realize that sooner or later."

Golzen seemed to swell, turning up prophet mode. "No, *you'll* realize a change is coming. Perfect is calling, and it is nearly time to heed its voice."

"You know I don't believe in that bullshit."

"That's immaterial. Perfect believes in you. The question is whether you want to be on the winning side."

"Since when were there sides?"

"Are you kidding? *Everything* has at least two sides. Even a single individual. You know that."

"May be true for you. It doesn't have to be that way among the friends."

"Jesus." Golzen stared at him with open contempt. "You spend far too much time with that hippie chick."

"Like I said, I'm in a hurry. This all you got?"

"Just don't be gone too long. I'd hate for you to miss the excitement."

Maj stared at him. Golzen smiled. "There may be one more chance to change your mind," he said. "We're saving a place. We'll need friends like you, with skills, character, strength of mind. Assuming you can finally see where your best interests lie." He walked away.

Maj watched him go. How could Golzen know he was planning on leaving town? Only by talking to the sole person Maj had discussed the matter with: a Journeyman he'd gone to for advice. Even so, it could only be guesswork, as Maj had been careful to appear to be conducting his inquiry out of hypothetical interest, and the Journeyman would never have talked.

So it was pure luck, that was all. It showed how widely Golzen's influence spread, however, and how determined he was. Maj had already suspected these things. For the time being, it didn't matter.

But consider it logged.

He stopped by the churchyard and tried to talk to Lonely Clive. Though he was able to get a few words out of him, he had to take his former mentor's blessing on trust, or decide to take it implicitly. He left unclear as to which it had been, but it didn't matter.

He was going to do it anyway.

Chapter 6

At a little after eight on Monday evening I was in SoHo. I'd been in the area for two hours already and I was cold and bored. I'd watched Catherine and Kristina arrive at Swift's ten minutes apart, and then I'd walked the neighboring blocks in a grid pattern. After I tired of this, I took a covert pass through the store and then wandered back out and eventually into the grounds of Old St. Patrick's Church. An eight-foot-high brick wall surrounds most of a small block, augmented on one side by the tall, white side of another building. Inside the wall stands an unassuming sand-colored church, well-tended grass, and a clean graveyard arranged in orderly lines. It is a calm place and a good spot to stand for a while even if you do not believe in God. But also . . . very cold.

I emerged in time to observe as the reading group wrapped up and to see the two women buying coffees from the bookstore café before bringing them out to the concrete bench outside. This being, as I knew, their custom. They didn't hurry over their drinks.

I stood across the way, in the shadow of the wall around the church, and waited some more.

It had already been established that someone had *not* entered Catherine Warren's house the evening before — nobody who wasn't supposed to have, anyway.

Kristina tried calling right back, but it went to voice mail. Catherine's message had been left at eight thirty and it was after three a.m. by the time we found it. Kristina was awake and on her feet before me the next morning, for once. Catherine called early, to be fair, and was apologetic and amusing at her own expense. She'd called after noticing things had been moved in the office nook of their house. This had subsequently been explained. Her husband—who'd stopped by en route to a business dinner—had been told to drop everything and attend a meeting at the London office the next day, taking the oh-my-god-that's-early flight out of JFK. (This is something you don't have to put up with if you work in a pizza restaurant.) He'd been searching for his passport—neatly filed by Catherine somewhere else entirely—and hadn't tidied after himself. Some people wouldn't even have noticed, but Catherine evidently ran a tight ship, and so she did.

Panic over.

After the call, Kristina seemed embarrassed on her friend's behalf. Perversely, though I had to refrain from wondering aloud whether Catherine couldn't have made a second call to Kristina's phone to let her know everything was okay, the incident made me take her more seriously. My ex-wife, Carol, had been prone to anxiety even before the truly bad things happened to us, notably the death of our older son, Scott. I know from experience that anxiety is a very powerful force, as close to malign possession as makes no difference. It may not sound like much—so someone gets worked up over little things? Big deal. They should try coping with *real* problems, right?

Wrong. Real problems are easy. They have real solutions. Anxiety turns the world into an intangible and insoluble crisis and transforms every doubt into a rat intent on devouring its own tail. It is like being caught in a trap in the dark forest when you can hear big, hungry animals closing in on every side.

The confident, sleek woman I'd met outside the coffeehouse on Greenwich Avenue hadn't presented like someone so close to the edge, but that could mean she was hiding some problem a little too well, or else that there *was* something going on—something sufficient to have her putting two and two together to make twenty-five. I wouldn't have cared much either way except that the woman I loved evidently wanted to regard this person as a friend—and friends were something Kristina was generally willing to do without. I'm far from gregarious, but she can make me look positively needy. Catherine's presence at the reading group had kept her attending. If the other woman flipped out, it would stop.

That's why I was there, getting cold. Having made a bad job of being someone's man in the past, I was open to the idea of working harder at it this time around.

Eventually they finished their coffees and went separate ways. Kristina did not glance in the direction of the church because she didn't know I was there. I hadn't wanted her to convey inadvertent signals to Catherine. I was probably doing nothing more than wasting my evening off work (the Adriatico is closed on Mondays, to everyone's relief), but in that case I wanted to make doubly sure I got something out of it. If I followed Catherine home and saw nothing, I would have demonstrated that—on a night when her movements were predictable, and therefore an alleged stalker's ideal opportunity—there had been no one on her tail. I could choose whether or not to convey this to Kristina when I got home.

I stayed back as I followed Catherine up into the Village. I had a good idea of what route she'd take and so gave her plenty of space. She walked confidently, with the brisk stride of someone who knew the area and had lived in the city a long time. She lingered in front of a couple of stores but never came to a halt. From Bleecker she skirted Washington Square Park and took the predictable left onto Greenwich Avenue. From here she'd likely head up past the Westside Market. With her husband across the ocean, it was possible she'd give this a miss. I doubted it, though. If she'd fallen into the practice of going to the deli for his shrimp salad, chances were she'd do it tonight and find a reason while she was there. Humans are creatures of habit.

I kept an eye on other pedestrians. The young, the old, professionals and the half-dead homeless, the weird-looking and the painfully vanilla. New York is a place where you'd have to hail from the planet Zog and sport three heads to really stand out, though if you kept those heads down and didn't smoke in a public place you'd still have a chance of passing without notice. Of course, if Catherine *did* have a stalker he'd be going to some trouble not to attract attention. But by the time we were crossing 14th I was confident this was a bust.

Fine by me. I'd left a note for Kris saying I'd gone for a walk and would be home by nine bearing food. I'd shadow Catherine to her door in Chelsea — ten minutes from where we were now — then double back via Chong's.

Catherine slowed as she came up toward the Westside Market. She hesitated, then headed in.

I swore wearily. I was tiring of the game and wishing I were back at the apartment already, but I gave it a moment and then followed her inside.

I'd been there before and knew what to expect. Beautiful food at belligerent prices, a store that was large for the neighborhood but kept intimate by the height of the stacks and a layout dotted with islands of especial fabulousness. Increased proximity to places like this was one of Kristina's expressed reasons for wanting to move, and here I had no disagreement.

I realized I was reaching the limits of my competence. As I'd wanted to be sure that Catherine understood, I've never been an undercover cop or a detective. My years in the army were spent at the grunt end, where you generally want to ensure that people *do* know you're around, in the hope this will stop bad things breaking out in the first place. Skulking is therefore not one of my core skills. I caught a break as I entered the market, however. Catherine was heading toward the produce section. This meant I could head right, the problem being this would obscure her from view. Doing the opposite would make it more likely she'd spot me. Belatedly I realized what would have made much more sense was staying outside and waiting around the corner to pick her up again as she left. Duh.

I was about to act on this when I caught another glimpse of Catherine, in front of a cooler of prepared foods. The famous shrimp salad, of course. Her husband was going to get his treat after all.

Then I noticed someone.

I couldn't see his face or head, as it was obscured by hanging goods, but he stood a little over average height, slim build, wearing a long, dark coat and standing near the end of the aisle behind Catherine.

She moved away from the cabinet, and I stepped back into my aisle to keep out of view. I gave it a beat and leaned forward, catching a momentary glimpse of the other figure as he walked off down the distant aisle.

I hadn't seen him clearly and there were maybe fifteen, twenty other people in the store. But none of them had made me feel the need to see them a second time.

Catherine was heading for the checkout counter.

I skirted around the back. There was no sign of the other person. I returned to my original position and waited, glancing across to check on Catherine's progress. She was nearly done at the register, tucking a frequent-buyer card back in her purse.

I decided on an abrupt change of tactics and headed down the far aisle and out the side door instead.

Back outside, I walked a few yards down the street. The deli was on the corner, at the intersection. If I hung here and waited for Catherine to emerge, I'd be in a perfect position to see anyone following her.

Three minutes later Catherine emerged with an environmentally friendly hemp bag over her shoulder. The lights were in her favor and she strode straight across 15th. I held my position, watching for the figure in the coat. No sign. Maybe he was still inside. Maybe he'd already left. Very likely he'd never been more than some random guy come to score coffee and cat food.

I crossed the street and followed Catherine up the avenue, keeping close to the buildings. There were lots of people around, and Catherine looked relaxed. At the next intersection she did something I hadn't antic-ipated, however, unexpectedly cutting across the road.

I got caught behind a gaggle of French tourists who were laughing and shouting and clearly very lost but having a whale of a time. One of them picked at my sleeve, but I shrugged him off. Catherine was nearly at the other side of the avenue by then, heading toward 16th.

A figure in a dark coat was standing in a doorway on the other side.

It was too far for me to be sure it was the same guy, but he sure as hell looked similar. I still couldn't see his face, as he was turned away from the street and the collar of his coat was turned up.

He remained motionless as Catherine reached the west side of the avenue—and then moved to follow, entering the side street only about twenty yards behind her.

The lights had changed and it seemed like every car in the city had business that took it past my face, fast. I tried to weave my way through them, realized some asshole was going to run me down if I kept it up, and was forced to step back onto the sidewalk.

Catherine meanwhile had disappeared from sight, along with the fig-ure that was either following her or just happened to be walking in the same direction.

I finally saw a gap in traffic and darted across the road. I got to the other side accompanied by loud honks and abuse in at least three lan-guages, but kept going into the side street, where I slowed to a fast walk. It was quiet, residential, dotted with trees, and very still.

Catherine was fifty yards ahead. She was striding quickly now—faster than before. It could be that the cold had gotten to her or she'd realized she was going to be late for the sitter, but I didn't think so.

She glanced behind. She didn't see anyone.

How do I know? Because there was no one there.

I stopped dead in my tracks, confused, stared up and down the street. I'd seen the figure turning onto this street. He hadn't come back out before I got here—I would have seen him—but...he wasn't here now.

I saw houses. I saw a brick church with ornamental staircases leading up to a wooden door on either side. I saw cars and trees. I didn't see any people at all.

Catherine was moving even faster. Once she reached the corner she'd be two short blocks from her own street. It seemed like she wanted to cover the distance quickly. It looked as if she felt someone was after her.

But she was wrong.

There was no one there.

I followed her the rest of the way home. I even waited for half an hour at the end of the street, standing in shadow. Eventually I walked back to my own home, picking up food on the way.

I told Kristina what I'd done—I had to, I was so late—and got a big, tight hug for it. I didn't mention that I thought I'd seen a nondescript individual in Catherine's orbit in the Westside Market, or that he'd followed her afterward. I said I hadn't seen anyone, because as far as I could tell, that was true.

As I lay in bed later, however, listening to Kristina's breathing and waiting for sleep, I knew that when she glanced back, I'd seen genuine fear in Catherine's face.

I realized also that, for the first time, I was not convinced she was wrong to feel that way.

Chapter 7

The next morning I was up early. Kristina remained in bed, refining her impersonation of someone who'd passed away in the night. An idea struck me as I stood in the kitchen, provoked by the sight of her phone on the counter. I picked it up and went to her incoming log. Catherine's number was there. I made a note of it and went into the shower to think about the idea.

When I walked out onto the street half an hour later, I made the call.

We met at the café on Greenwich Avenue. Catherine looked warily up at me when I entered. All I'd said on the phone was that it would be a good idea if we talked alone.

"Here's the thing," I said, sitting opposite her. "I followed you last night."

"You did *what?*"

"I walked the blocks around the bookstore during the reading group and shadowed when you left for home."

"Kristina didn't say—"

"She had no idea it was happening."

"Why did you do it?"

"You left a message on her phone the night before. A message that freaked her out. Kristina is not easy to freak out."

"I called and explained all that."

"The following morning."

She looked impatient. "I didn't know what time you went to bed. I didn't want to wake anyone."

"Do you recall Kristina's occupation?"

"Of course I do. And I don't like your attitude."

"It's never been popular. So — what does Kris do?"

Catherine looked flustered. "She . . . She works in a restaurant. Like you."

"She runs a late-night bar."

"That's right. So . . . Okay, so probably you would have been awake. I get it. I'm sorry. But once I'd worked out no one had been in the house I wanted to forget about it. I didn't realize it would be a big deal."

I didn't say anything.

"I'm sorry," she said again, eventually.

"I didn't see anyone last night until you went into the Westside Market," I said. "I'm not sure I saw anything there either. One person caught my eye, though."

Catherine's eyes were watchful. "And?"

"I saw him a few minutes later, hanging around the entrance to 16th. When you went up it, he followed."

"I knew it," she said dully. "Did you . . . Did you get a good look at him?"

"No, but it means I'm inclined to take your fears more seriously, which in turn means I have to ask you the obvious question. Again."

"What question?"

"Who is it?"

"I don't *know.* Like I told you last time."

"I remember. I still find it hard to believe. If you think this is the same guy from a decade ago, then it's not random and you must be able to come up with a name or two if you think hard enough."

"I really don't —"

"Bullshit," I said calmly. "In a past life I spent a lot of time in small rooms with people who were not telling the truth. I believe I'm sitting opposite one again now. You've got two minutes to alter that impression or I'm out of there and that's the end of it."

For a moment she looked furious, or as if she was going to cry. Then she started to talk.

I told Kristina about the meeting as soon as I got back to the apartment. I could tell from her body language that this was several hours too late.

"So who is he?"

"Ex-boyfriend. They went out for six months way back. She decided it wasn't working and let him down gently. She's now saying he could be the guy, maybe. Their relationship ended right before the first night she thought she was being followed. She 'feels' it could be the same person now."

Kristina looked out of the window onto the rooftops. "Drop the quote marks, John. People feel stuff. And it's women who do, more often, and sometimes they're right."

"I know," I said.

"So why didn't she mention him before?"

"Didn't believe him capable, she says. Or didn't want to, anyway."

"So what are you going to do?"

"What makes you think I'm going to do anything?"

"The fact that you're you."

I had to smile, and after a moment, she smiled back. It looked underpowered. "I'm sorry," I said. "I should have told you about arranging to meet her."

"Yeah, you should have. You should have told me last night you thought you saw someone following her, too."

"What's my punishment?"

"Don't know yet. But it's going to be severe. In the meantime, what's the plan?"

"This Clark guy lives in the back end of Williamsburg. Works there, at least."

"Am I allowed to come?"

"Of course," I said. "I'm hoping you will."

I'd been back and forth on this, in fact. I did want Kristina to come. Partly because she had skills when it came to assessing people—far better than I, and drawing on deeper wells—and also because it would make a nicer trip of it. Assuming the guy didn't become violent when confronted. In that case I'd prefer it to be just me and him.

"Well, I can't," she said. "The heater guys are coming, finally." She looked cranky, but she often does, and I knew I'd said the right thing.

"So?"

"So be careful. And I want to know what happens. And not just the nonexecutive summary this time."

I don't enjoy the subway. I know I should, that it's part of the fabric and texture of the city, and come, let us behold urban kind in its glorious variety, but I prefer to get that kind of experience aboveground, where you can walk away from it when you want. On the L line urban kind is like a too-tight, unwashed coat, and by the time I emerged in Brooklyn I was low on temper and pretty convinced that this was my second dumb idea of the day.

I'd traced Clark via Facebook. I'm not on it, but the restaurant is, courtesy of some nephew who thought it might shift more pizza. You can go like the Adriatico online if you want. I cannot imagine how that would help anything. It sure as hell will not get you a free pizza.

There were plenty of people listed under some variation of "Thomas Clark" but only one who lived in the area Catherine had suggested and who showed other likely characteristics. When they'd dated, Clark had been a decorative fine artist with a high opinion of himself. It was evident from his page that he now co-ran a small gallery instead. The gallery had a website with its street address all over it. As a job of hiding, it sucked.

Assuming he had reason to hide, of course.

The gallery was at the far end of the hipster pocket and I arrived just after two o'clock. The entire width of the store front was glass, a single large, square painting on an easel in windows on either side of a central door. I have no idea what they were paintings of. Apparently that's not the point. In the back of the white-walled space beyond stood a minimalist white desk. A man sat behind it, slender in build. There was no long black coat with a high collar hanging on the wall. Life doesn't hand things up that neatly tied.

When I pushed the door open, a discreet bell chimed three times. The man looked up and smiled generically. He had longish but tidy dark hair and a pair of neat round spectacles. "Good afternoon."

I looked around the walls. Further large, square paintings — or canvases with paint on them, at any rate.

"Can I help you, or are we just browsing?"

I kept silent long enough for him to register something wasn't right with this encounter. Then I turned to look at him. "Are you Thomas Clark?"

"Yes."

"Catherine says hi."

He looked confused. "I'm embarrassed to admit this, but I don't think the name sounds familiar..."

"Back then you were going to make it as an artist yourself. Fancy handmade pots, she said."

He blinked as the penny dropped. "You mean...Catherine *Warren?*"

"I do."

"But...I haven't seen her in years."

"Really?"

"Ask her."

"I talked with Catherine three hours ago. She gave me your name."

"Why? Who *are* you?"

"My name is John Henderson. Someone's been following Catherine. At night. She thinks it could be you."

"*What?* Why would I do that?"

"I have no idea," I said. "And your question doesn't answer mine."

His eyes flicked to the side. A smart-looking middle-aged couple were drifting to a halt outside. I could not see the painting that had caught their attention, only their eyes and a desire to acquire.

I walked over and flipped the OPEN sign to CLOSED. The guy outside stared at me. I stared back. They went away.

Clark meanwhile remained at his desk. "I haven't seen Catherine since I moved out of Manhattan," he said. "We split up and I called her a couple times afterward, I'll admit, but—"

"Why did you call her? Were you uncertain why she was ending the relationship?"

He laughed. "Uncertain? Oh no. At first it was all 'It's not you, it's me,' but it became clear she was leaving me for this guy she'd met. The marvelous Mark."

That struck an off note, but I kept drilling. "You remember his name?"

"Of course I do. I was *in love with her.* Then one night over the phone it's bam—she's with this other guy instead. My services are no longer required; could I please let myself out of her life."

"Why did you try to contact her afterward?"

"She'd always said we'd be friends forever. It had been this big thing of hers. She didn't mean it, though. Once you stop being useful to Catherine you're cut out of the script for good. I called a few times. I sent her a letter... and two cards. I sent..."

He trailed off, memory dulling his face. "I sent her a bunch of irises. They were her favorite. That was something I'd known about her back when we'd been friends, before we started dating. It was supposed to signal, you know, that we could go back to that, if she wanted. There was no response. I gave up."

"When did you move out of Manhattan?"

"Eight years ago."

"Do you go back?"

"Of course. I used to have an agent there, but he let me go about the same time I realized people were using the pots I'd slaved long hours over . . . to keep flowers in. I visit an exhibition once in a while, see friends, and, well, yes—obviously I'm there sometimes. But my real life is here now."

"Where were you last night?"

He gestured around. "Hanging these. If you need witnesses you'll have to find someone who happened to walk by. It's a busy street at night and I'm sure there were some, but I don't know their names."

"I don't need witnesses. I'm not a cop."

He cocked his head. "Then what right do you have to be asking all this?"

"None. I apologize if I've been intrusive."

"So what happened? Did Catherine dump Mark? Is she with you now?"

"No. They're married. They have two kids."

"Huh. Guess at least I can tell myself that I lost to the winning team."

"If that helps. You got any message for her?"

"Seriously?"

"If you do, I'll pass it on."

He thought about it. "Sure," he said, looking down at the papers on his desk. "You can tell her to go fuck herself."

Chapter 8

It was twenty-four hours before Golzen had a chance to speak to Reinhart. The man's movements were wholly unpredictable, and his presence could not be guaranteed even at the club he owned on Orchard, in the ratty, crumbling backstreets of the Lower East Side, south of the Village and east of anywhere good, above which Golzen and others laid their heads at night in exchange for services rendered.

He slipped in through the street door. It was ajar, as often in the mornings, in a vain attempt to clear the stale, secondhand air inside, a stealthy, underhand odor that seeped up from the crumbling building's foundation. The area beyond was empty, cavernous, and dark, a wide central space with black-painted walls shading off into low-ceilinged, shadowy little corridors and booths where the small hours would find the bar's racier patrons taking drugs and advantage of one another.

Golzen walked across this, past the bar along the right-hand wall, and into the office in the back. Reinhart was sitting behind his desk. The space was otherwise empty. No filing cabinets, no computer, no pictures on the wall. No second chair, even. Just a boxy old 1970s-style phone, positioned to line up neatly with the corners of the desk. As always, Reinhart was wearing a coat, as if he'd recently arrived or would be leaving almost immediately. He was watching the door as Golzen entered, as though waiting for him.

He didn't wait for Golzen to speak. If you needed that kind of fluff, you did business with someone else — the problem being, so far as Golzen knew (and his contacts were indeed good, and situated far and wide), there was no one else working this game in the entire city. It was Reinhart or nobody.

"Did you talk to him?"

"I tried."

"The fuck is up with that guy?"

Golzen considered his response. Idealists who cleave to different ideals seldom mix well. His view was that Maj was unpredictable, full of himself, and basically an asshole. Moreover, a dangerously volatile asshole. He'd expressed this opinion more than once. Reinhart evidently saw something else in the guy, however, and wouldn't let the matter drop.

"He learned at Lonely Clive's knee."

Reinhart grunted, irritable and dismissive combined. Golzen knew the man got what he'd meant — some of it, at least. Reinhart had taken the trouble to understand the world inhabited by the people he now did business with. He knew Golzen meant that when Maj arrived in the city he'd been taken under the wing of a member of the old guard — the ones sometimes called the Gathered, before the term became loosely applied to all of them. Originally it had referred to a cabal of friends who'd started introducing structures and systems into their lives. The Jesuits declared that if you gave them a boy, they'd give you the man. It had been the same with the Gathered, or the few that were left. The Scattered would be a better name now. They'd done good in the way back, for sure, dominating the scene for fifty years or more — but had been fading in authority even before Reinhart arrived. It had happened much faster since, and good riddance to them. They'd never listened to Golzen's ideas either.

"Keep on it," Reinhart said. His hair was cropped short and the single bulb above caught the top of his hard, square head. "Get your buddies to stick to him, too. Like glue. Any sign of an angle, tell them to work it. Hard."

"Okay."

Reinhart smiled. It was pitch perfect as a coordinated movement of muscles, but once you got to know the guy, his ability to do this only made him even more unnerving. "Don't worry — you'll always be my number one. I'd simply prefer to have that guy inside the tent pissing out, instead of the other way around. Get it?"

Golzen shrugged. Talk of Maj bored him. "Sure."

"Good. Because we're getting close, my friend."

No longer remotely bored, Golzen looked up. "For real?"

"The time for change is upon us."

Golzen felt his stomach flip. "How soon?"

Reinhart closed his eyes, as if listening to something beyond the hearing of normal men, perhaps simply the dark workings of his own mind. "I don't know. But *soon.* Maybe even within the week."

He opened his eyes. "Put out a broadcast to the chosen. Encourage readiness."

"Saying...?"

"I'll leave that to you. Just hold the date. There *is* no date yet, but... hold it anyway."

Golzen grinned. "You got it."

"And bring me fresh blood. I'm going to lose some of my best stealers on this. We need replacements in training before I can open the door to Perfect and let us walk the road to our brave new world."

"I'm on it."

"Not while you're standing here."

Golzen walked quickly out through the bar and onto the street. He already had ideas for friends to turn, clueless wanderers to bring into the fold: people who could learn to do what he and the others had been doing for Reinhart, while the chosen left on a mission Golzen had been preparing (and advocating and prophesying) for years. He had no problem with performing this task for Reinhart. Relished the prospect, in fact. He'd tell his buddies to sniff harder around Maj, too, if that's what Reinhart wanted. Why not? It wouldn't be much longer that he had to work with the man.

Golzen was built to hold impulses in check, most of the time. He'd been very patient, working every opportunity to bind the other eleven of the chosen to him through the treats and advantages he'd gained for them. The relationship between him and Reinhart had been very useful in this, symbiotic.

But such relationships end.

Chapter 9

As he entered Roast Me, David confirmed—with a sinking feeling—that Talia was working the counter. He considered turning around, but not seriously.

"Hey, Norman," she hollered, as she cranked through the orders of those ahead of him in line.

He sighed. Yesterday it had been "Ernest." Couple days before that, "F. Scott." The previous week they'd been more contemporary—Richard, Don, and Jonathan (two or three guys she could have been shooting for with that last, the handle of choice for today's nascent Great American Novelist). She evidently believed she'd found a rich seam of comedy and was determined to mine it out.

And that was okay. He'd always liked Talia, a big, cheerful woman in her fifties who cussed freely and had been holding down the Gaggia in the town's only coffee shop since it opened. Very occasionally they let Dylan have a turn for light relief, but basically if you wanted a latte in Rockbridge, Talia was the go-to gal. She was fiercely resistant to the term "barista" and happy to remain—as she was prone to tell their rare, easily intimidated tourists—just "the fat chick who makes the fucking coffee."

When David had been working in an office up the street he'd often passed the time of day with Talia, content that in Rockbridge everyone knew everybody else along with a fair portion of their business. He was aware that Talia lived with nine cats in a trailer on the other side of town near the creek, was long-term single but had once been the lover of a man called Ed who'd died under tragic circumstances, and that she possessed a strong creative urge, manifest in prolific journaling and collage-making and a vast novel of epic fantasy on which she'd been working for at least five years.

And therein lay the problem.

While he'd been holding down a day job David had been happy to shoot the breeze with Talia. They'd been hobbyists, engaged in the same struggle. Since he got his deal, things had changed. Talia seemed to believe David had breached a citadel — like one of the characters in her forever-in-progress novel, perhaps, a book David really, *really* did not want to read — therein defeating the dragon who had guarded the How To Get Published Spell. Instead of something they could enjoy gossiping about, it had become a matter on which Talia wanted *clues*. She wanted to be sold the magic potion that put you onto the bestseller lists forever and stopped people from seeing you as just that big, noisy woman who had way too many cats.

David would have given her the secret if he knew. He was not a selfish man. The problem was he didn't have a clue what it was, and on mornings like this he almost wished he were back where he had been six months ago.

"So!" Talia bellowed, hands already in motion toward his customary drink. Her tone was partly due to the coffee machine doing something hectic, but mainly because she habitually addressed people as if across a field and against a heavy wind. "How many of those bastards you caught in your net today?"

David shrugged mysteriously. He knew Talia would interpret this as coyness over how many words he'd nonchalantly hammered out that morning, instead of realizing it meant *None. No words at all.*

She laughed raucously. "You dog."

They chatted, Talia filling him on some "consultant" she'd met on an Internet forum and passing on the advice he'd granted her, which — as far as David could tell — was total nonsense. When she told him, in hushed tones and all seriousness, that the guy had revealed it was best not to sign submission letters on the grounds publishers employed teams of graphologists to divine the worth of your manuscript from tells in your signature, he had to cough to cover a laugh—a desire that quickly faded when it became clear this asshole had gotten Talia to PayPal him a hundred bucks before he handed up this and other pearls of wisdom.

"You know what, Tal?" he said. "I'm not sure about that. Can't see them doing that when it'd be simpler to get an intern to flip through the manuscript."

Talia looked at him. "Could be."

David wasn't sure she meant it. It seemed to him she might actually be saying, *Yeah, and what do you care, big shot? You've already got it made.*

But the moment passed, and David realized that envy was something he might have to get used to. In time, that seemed possible. The problem was going to be convincing himself he deserved it.

He'd been intending to take the drink home to consume virtuously at his desk, but as he turned from the counter he realized he couldn't face it and headed to a table instead. He'd carried a notebook all the time since he was thirteen years old. He could sit and think and jot *bons mots.* Be that kind of writer. Live the lifestyle.

Right. Except it turned out the lifestyle...kind of sucked. He didn't mind spending every day by himself. He'd always been a solitary person (or, as his father had once put it—to his face and in public—"a total loner geek"). Since giving up his job, however, he'd written fifteen pages all told. When he'd been writing at the end of eight hours of wage slavery that had seemed okay. As the product of fifty full days' labor, it was not.

There was another problem, too.

What he'd written *wasn't any good.*

His first novel had been about someone rather like David. An everyman forging a life in a small town, blessed with big dreams and a bigger heart. The raw material had come easy, but it had taken two years and seven drafts to make it feel like he'd written it. The characters were well drawn and mildly interesting things happened to them and there was a crisis that got semiresolved and some people lived happily ever after while others did not. Nobody was expecting it to storm the bestseller lists when it came out in six months' time, but it was the kind of book that genteel reading groups might take to and David's editor was confident it would get good word of mouth. It had a chance, in other words.

It had also, unfortunately, said just about all David had to say about what it was like to be David.

The publishers wanted another. David wasn't sure he had one, and the last month had done nothing to convince him otherwise. He'd started and scrapped three story lines already. It seemed possible that he could keep coming up with ideas and pushing them around the screen before abandoning them . . . *for the rest of his life.*

Which was why he was here, in the coffeehouse, trying to do something else. It wasn't working. Like their increasingly quiet and desperate attempts to get pregnant, there seemed to be some kind of block. Something invisible but real. Something they couldn't get past. Something *in the way.*

He turned from his notebook — to which he hadn't added a word — and looked out the window, summoning up the energy to go home.

Outside, people wandered up and down. Some seemed like they had pressing goals, others like leaves being blown nowhere in particular. It seemed for a moment like there was someone on the opposite side of the street, looking at the coffeehouse, but then he or she was gone.

"How's it going? Really?"

Talia had appeared on the other side of his table. She seemed diminished when not behind the counter.

"Not great."

She sat, plunking her big elbows down and supporting her chubby face in her hands. "Must be tough, huh?"

David couldn't tell how much irony this carried. "What do you mean?"

"Dreaming dreams is easy. Living them, not so much. That's why they're called 'dreams' instead of 'lives.' "

"Nice. I may write that down."

"Check the copyright position. Think I heard it in a country-and-western song, which is how the eternal truths are most often revealed." She smiled. "You'll get there, David. You done it once, you can do it again."

"Got proof?"

"I feel it in my bones. And I got heavy bones."

There was a loud clattering, and they turned to see the door to the coffee shop had swung open by itself. They stared at it together, and laughed.

"Huh," David said, getting up to close the door. "Doesn't even look that windy out there."

Talia looked enthused. "That reminds me! You know George Lofland, right?"

"Works at Bedloe's? Not really. By sight."

"Well, he was in here at the crack of dawn, like always—that guy actually drinks *too much* coffee—but he looked a little whacked, so I asked if he was okay."

"And?"

"*And* so early yesterday evening he's driving back from his mother's on the other side of Libertyville—she's rocking Alzheimer's big-time—and he's coming home through the woods and he sees this guy by the road. It's cold and windy with a pissy little drizzle on top and George decides to take pity on the asshole. He pulls over, asks where he's going. The guy says Rockbridge and George tells him to hop in, but the passenger seat is full of work files so he should get in the back if he doesn't mind. George drives on and they talk about this and that, though not much—George ain't no great talker when he's not selling something, never has been—but then he pulls over on the street here to let the guy out...and guess what?"

"I have no idea."

Talia leaned forward. "He wasn't there."

David laughed. "*What?*"

"For real, and like, O-M-fucking-G. George says, 'Okay, here we are'—there's no reply. He looks around and...dum dum DUM: the backseat's *empty,* dude. He jumps out of the car and goes around to check. But there's *no one there.*" She sat back and folded her arms. "Freaky, no?"

"But...you realize that's a classic FOAF story, right?"

"FOAF? WTF?"

"Stands for 'friend of a friend.' As in 'This weird thing happened to me, well, not to *me,* actually, but to a friend...In fact, it wasn't even a friend. It happened to the *friend* of a friend of mine. But it's totally true and...' and so on. It's a way of making a story seem real without taking responsibility for it."

"Gotcha," Talia said. "Though, like I said, this actually happened to George, or so he says."

"But I don't know George," David said, "so...he's a friend of a friend, to me."

Talia worked this through in her head, and smiled—a dazzler that took off thirty years. "I see what you done there, smart boy. Guess that's why you get paid the big bucks."

David spread his hands in mock self-appreciation. "When genius strikes."

"Uh-huh. So why don't you take those smarts and go home and do some actual work?"

David laughed. "Good advice, as always."

"Right. It's on account of me being so fucking wise. Now push off. It's easier for me to steal cake if there's only Dylan around."

Just before he opened the door, David turned back. "Talia," he said. He hesitated. "Your novel?"

"You want to help me set fire to it? I got matches."

"It's not like I know much, but if you wanted me to take a look...I'd be glad to. For what it's worth."

Talia blinked. Never mind losing thirty years; suddenly she looked about fifteen. "Oh, David, that would be *so* cool. I'll e-mail it to you tonight, soon as I get home. I know there's a lot of work to do on it, but . . . It would mean a lot to me, really."

"Can't guarantee how quickly I can get back to you, is the only thing."

"Oh, I understand, totally. And I won't bug you about it. I promise. David, that's so kind. Thank you."

He nodded, feeling shy. "What are friends for?"

He walked home knowing he was going to regret the gesture but telling himself you had to pay it forward or sideways or whatever the hell it was. He owed Talia for picking up his mood, not least because the old chestnut of the phantom hitchhiker was working at him, becoming an itch in the hard-to-define area in the back of his brain from which the ideas came (when and if they did).

He went straight up to the bedroom that had been designated his study. As he settled at his desk, the phone rang. He grabbed the handset while reaching for the keyboard. Once something started working at him he had to start typing it *right now,* or it would fly away.

"Yes?"

Nobody said anything. "Miller house," David said irritably. There was silence; then he heard a noise down the line. It was quiet, as if coming from a long way away. "Can you hear me?"

Silence, then a distant, muttered sound that might have been words, but was impossible to make out. There was something about the tone that did not sound friendly.

David put the phone down. If it was important they'd call back or try his cell, and either way he didn't care.

He started typing, slowly at first, and then faster, and the next few hours disappeared to wherever they go when the page opens up like a six-lane highway, for once.

Chapter 10

I have never been good at walking away from things. This is not a boast, a declaration that I'm the kind of guy who will by God get things done and rah-rah for me in particular and testosterone in general. Quite the opposite. There have been times when I've manifestly failed to do the right thing, when I've hidden from problems and let my life degrade and rust. I suspect the truth is when I do try to leave a situation I'll run, not walk — but in a circle. I believe I'm escaping from the problem but spin around it instead, maintaining orbit until a gravitational change plunges me back into the center. This is what happened after the death of my son. There was a period in the wilderness of alcohol and then a spell of affectless calm working at a restaurant in Oregon. But after that came a return to a small town in Washington State, where it turned out I had unfinished business. People died during the resolution of this business. I might have thought I was walking away from something, but it wasn't so. I'd merely been killing time before pulling the pin out of the grenade.

Put more simply, Catherine's stalker was beginning to annoy the hell out of me.

Rather than take the subway, I'd elected to walk back from Clark's gallery, which was doubtless good for my heart but took a very long time. I didn't like the fact that I'd spent the whole way back thinking about Catherine's stalker. I didn't like that I was mad at myself for losing the guy when I'd tracked Catherine — and for undertaking that without telling Kristina. Something that was supposed to have been a quick favor had gotten under my skin, and I wanted the situation gone.

By the time I arrived weary-footed back at our apartment, Kristina had left for work. I turned straight around and went to join her. As we walked home hours later, I filled her in on the discussion with Clark. I could see her wishing she'd been there to take her own reading.

"You really don't think he's the guy?"

"No."

"So...?"

"So I don't know. I guess I should call Catherine, tell her that he's probably not the man. Probably she should talk to the cops. Log her suspicions, so if the situation ramps up it's a matter of record."

"But you said Bill felt they probably wouldn't do much."

I shrugged. I had said that, and he had said that, and I didn't know what more there was to add.

As we turned onto a side street that we customarily used on our journey home, there was a noise from up ahead that sent a chill down my back. It was a sound that said someone was in pain, or needed help, and badly. Half the lights in the street were out and it was impossible to see what might be happening.

We trotted up until we could tell the noise was coming from someone standing in the middle of the street. It was a woman, not young. She was shrieking, apparently at a brick wall on the other side of the street.

It was Lydia. Her body was rigid, arms held down hard and straight, as if in face-to-face confrontation with someone. I'd never seen her like this.

I covered the last yards cautiously, walking in an arc so I came around the front and she got a good chance to realize someone was approaching, and who it was.

"Lydia?"

She stopped screaming as if someone had punched a mute button, but maintained the same position, every stringy tendon and underfed muscle taut.

"Lyds? It's John."

She turned her head and slowly seemed to recognize me. "Is that you?"

"Yes. It's John. From the restaurant."

"For real?"

"Yes." I held my hands up in a way that was supposed to be reassuring. "Was somebody giving you trouble?"

"It was Frankie," she said. Her voice was even more of a rasp than usual. "And he was *close*."

She grabbed me with hands that were bony and surprisingly strong. "I tried to catch up to him. But . . . he ran away from me. He saw it was me, and *he ran*. He didn't want to see me."

She started to cry, irrevocably, the tears of a child, the worst kind of all: the tears of someone who feels all the hope in the world disappear at once.

Kristina waited a few yards down the street, sadness in her face. "Lydia," I said, but I didn't know where to go afterward. The things it made sense to say — that the person hadn't really been there, or was some random stoner or thief taking a back route home and who ran because he'd been startled by being chased by an elderly street person — were not explanations she was going to accept.

Instead I put my arms around her shoulders. She did not smell good and I knew there would be a significant community of small, unwelcome insect life about her clothing, so I made the hug tight but quick.

"It's been a while," I said, stepping back. "Maybe he was just surprised to see you. Or maybe he feels shy or embarrassed that it's been so long."

She gave this some thought. "You think?"

"I don't know. But it could be. Right?"

She looked up at me hopefully, as if I'd told her that the pet we'd just buried together was absolutely *definitely* going to heaven. "Maybe you're right."

"You going to be okay?"

"Of course," she said, old again. She stomped to the sidewalk to retrieve her bags. "Why wouldn't I be?"

We watched as she headed off into the darkness that nests in the shadows of tall buildings in the night.

The next morning I called Catherine. I outlined my conversation with Clark but didn't pass on his interpretation of her behavior, or his final message. I suggested she talk to the cops. She uttered a sound that made it seem unlikely she would follow this advice — and perhaps it was this kind of thing that caused her to rub me the wrong way. She considered her options and made selections rather than drifting along highways of least resistance. Yes, she'd dropped Thomas Clark after she'd met Mark (I hadn't failed to notice that, in her version of events, it had happened that way around), but that made sense too. It's a cute idea that you can remain buddies with ex-lovers, but woefully adolescent. Love is not a charm that pops into the world from a better place to bless two individuals before flitting back home, leaving the couple broken back in two parts and forlorn but fundamentally unchanged. Love is a fire that burns in the soul, sometimes for good, sometimes just for now, sometimes hot enough to scorch and sometimes with a low and sustainable glow. Either way, it leaves the original constituents permanently altered. After the fact everything is different — not just the relationship, but the people involved. I didn't blame Catherine for what she'd done, but I was glad it wasn't me who'd fallen in love with her.

"Thank you," she said.

"No problem," I said. "You've got our numbers. You get the sense something's up, then call, okay?"

I was about to add something designed to sound upbeat, but the line went dead. I realized that was something else that pissed me off about her. Always having to be the one in control.

Whatever. I was done. I made a cup of coffee and took it over to the rear window of the main room. I opened it and climbed out onto the ten-foot-square patch of roof outside, which I had colonized as my personal smoking domain. There's not much competition, to be honest, what with it being inaccessible from any other building and half submerged under bits of wind-blown debris and discarded material from long-ago roof maintenance. A few birds perch there once in a while, but even they don't seem to like it much. Soon after we moved into the apartment— disinclined to trudge down a billion stairs every time I wanted to fuck up my lungs—I semi-civilized the area with a battered chair I'd found on the street and a heavy glass ashtray from a thrift store. It's the little piece of New York that I can call my own.

I sat and looked out across the rooftops and listened to the street noise from below, sipped my coffee, and smoked a cigarette, and I told myself the Catherine Warren story was over.

I tell myself a lot of things.

Chapter 11

Meanwhile, Bob stands on the corner.

He is on this corner every day except weekends. He stands there between the hours of ten in the morning and four in the afternoon, and he waits. There's always someone here. Most corners are covered only a few hours a day, to a schedule written by a Fingerman in chalk on the sidewalk or low on a wall nearby, someplace you wouldn't notice unless you were looking for it. If by chance they caught your eye, you might assume they related to a scheme of public works. They don't. A circle means daylight. The figure to the left indicates the start time, the one on the right, the number of hours it will run. A crescent works the same, but for night, obviously. At these corners you have to get there within the correct time frame or no one's going to be around and you're neither going to be able to leave a message, nor pick one up.

Bob's corner is in business twenty-four-seven and three-sixty-five. There are only five like it in the whole of Manhattan, and this one at the southern point of Union Square is the oldest of all. It's said that someone has been manning the spot for over sixty years. It could be longer, no one's sure, but word of mouth (the testimony of trusted friends among the Gathered, be they ever so hollow now) puts it back to the late 1940s without a doubt. Before that it gets cloudy, but if you come now, someone will always be there.

These are the Cornermen, and Bob is proud to be one of them.

The first qualification is the ability to keep in movement — the right *kind* of movement. Most people don't see past their own eyes, but there's always someone who does, or might. Children, animals—cats especially—plus the old and the slightly crazy. You have to keep in flux or a dog might start barking or madman try to strike up a conversation. Bob's corner is set up for movement, which might account for its longevity. There's a lot of foot traffic. Four days a week there's the greenmarket, plus the Strand Book Store and the B&N and Whole Foods. Even without those banner destinations it'd constitute the major crossroads at this point in town. The most noticeable features in a river are the rocks that stand their ground. And so you move.

The second requirement is a good memory. Nothing gets written down. Most couldn't, anyway—anybody with that kind of skill would be promoted to Fingerman, which even Bob acknowledges is the premium role. Many of the messages are straightforward instructions or pieces of information. Others are more personal. When a message is given to a Cornerman, he or she will hold it in confidence until it's passed, after which they'll forget it. Bob doesn't make moral judgments. It is not his place nor in his nature. Make the job any more complicated than it already is and the system would break down fast.

You need a memory for faces, too. Some will have made an arrangement ahead of time, but with many the message will be left merely in the hope the intended recipient will happen to pass. With those it's Bob's job to keep an eye out for the friend in question. When he sees them coming, he will move into their path and tell them what he's been asked to tell, before moving on, glancing back to make sure the message got across.

Then Bob forgets the message, to free up space for the next. At any given time he has maybe forty in his head. Twenty percent are broadcasts—"Mention to everyone you see that..." Seventy percent are personal, one-to-one "asks"—as in: "Ask Rose to meet me at the corner of x and y at eight o'clock this Friday night."

The remaining one in ten are the messages Bob doesn't like. They're the ones that never got where they were supposed to go. Once recently he happened to walk past old St. Patrick's and saw someone against the interior wall of the boneyard there. Bob had been holding a message for this guy for over six months, but when he saw him slumped against the wall in twilight he knew it was too late. He went in and passed the message anyway, whispering it into the friend's ear. The Hollow slowly raised his head. There was no recognition in his eyes (though Bob had passed him perhaps a hundred messages down the years) and no suggestion that he'd understood.

Now and then you'd hear someone had gone for good — getting the Bloom and burning out, or much more rarely flicking off the light by themselves. Bob wasn't a romantic person and his expectations of life were low, but holding that last message in his head, for a person who'd passed on, was a way of giving them longer in the world, prolonging a life that had likely been full of neglect. He'd heard it was a tradition among retiring Cornermen to get a Fingerman to write down these orphaned messages, a representative word or two of them at least — on a wall or under a bridge — so they never died.

Bob didn't know if that was true, but that's what *he* was going to do. He'd ask Maj, probably. Maj had skills and was friendly, most of the time.

Everybody deserves to be remembered. Without that you're nothing.

It was almost three, only an hour before he would be relieved of his post and could go somewhere warmer, when Bob saw someone heading purposefully toward him.

He immediately felt tense. This friend often had messages. Recently they had been getting more frequent. They'd stopped making sense, too, and Bob was smart enough to know that implied they were in code. Since when did friends need code? Code said there were messages that were for some ears and not others. Bob didn't like the feel of that. They were supposed to be pulling together. That's what his job was about and why the Gathered had always stressed its importance — doing something for the greater good. Messages for the greater good do not need to be obscured, surely?

"Hey, Fictitious," Golzen said. He looked even more self-important than usual. "Got a broadcast."

They always were, with Golzen. He didn't speak — he proclaimed.

"I'm listening."

The two men kept walking, not looking at each other, in slow circular movement, like an eddy of wind.

"Broadcast runs: 'For the twelve. Be ready. Follow signs until Jedburgh appears.' Message ends."

"That it?"

"That's all it needs," Golzen said. "You got it?"

"'Course I got it."

Golzen walked away. Bob ran the message through one time to lock it in his mind, and got ready to tell it to everyone he saw. That was his job, and he was going to do it the best he could, as always.

He had no way of knowing how many people would die.

Chapter 12

David happened to be passing through the hall when Dawn got home. He felt guilty when he heard her key in the lock, as if he should be at his desk typing instead of self-indulgently larking about voiding his bladder.

"Just been to the john," he said.

"Thanks for the status update." She kissed him on the cheek. "I'll be sure to like and retweet."

Then she turned him around and felt up his ass. "Well, hi," he said, surprised.

She kept exploring his right buttock. "You keep it here, don't you?"

"Actually, it's around the front," he said, deadpan. "I've been meaning to talk to you about that."

She swatted his chest. "Funny. Your loose change, I *meant*. You keep it in your back right pocket."

"Well, yes. Though there's none at the moment."

"Right. It's here." She held up her other hand. Cupped in the palm was a couple of dollars' worth of quarters. David made like a question mark.

"It was lying on the step outside," she said. "I assumed you had a hole in your pocket and it fell out."

"No. I put it in the pot like normal."

"And there *is* no hole in your pocket. Which is what I was establishing, for the avoidance of doubt."

As she plunked her bag on the chair and took off her coat, she peered into the pot on the table. The pot was squarish and unevenly glazed in unfashionable colors, the product of some long-ago creative urge or spasm of suburban boredom on the part of David's mother, and one of the few mementos he had of her. It held small change leavened with buttons, paper clips, and a couple of dollar bills. "So what was this doing outside?"

"No idea. Where was it, exactly?"

"Top step. Right in the middle."

As Dawn headed kitchenward to begin assessing her charges' entanglements with the mysteries of basic math, David looked back at the three steps that led down from their door to the path and then out at the street.

There was nothing to see except a cloudy, darkening sky and the branches of trees that were starting to shiver from the top down.

David read a little more of Talia's book while putting together a pasta/salad dinner. The novel was...surprisingly okay, in fact. He'd already lost track of who the characters were, who they were in conflict with and why, but he decided to let it wash over him on the assumption that it would probably become clear. In the meantime it was easy to read and occasionally pretty funny or moving and in general starting to freak David out, through demonstrating he wasn't special after all and clearly *anyone* could write—and look, Talia wrote a *lot* more than he did, every day and all the time, without making such a big song and dance about it.

When supper was on the table, they ate in companionable silence, listening to the world outside. The wind was now buffeting the house with serious intent. Local news said it was going to be a big storm.

"That was nice," Dawn said, setting her fork aside. There were a couple of mouthfuls left, but David had come to believe this was not a negative review but an ingrained nod toward keeping an eye on her weight.

"We aim to please."

"You didn't come by the school today, did you?"

"No. Why?"

"Angela thought she saw a man standing outside the gates, midafternoon. When she went to see what he wanted he'd gone. She said it could have been you."

"I've been here all day."

"Working hard."

"Right. And why would I come to the school anyway?"

"That's what I said. I also reminded her of the existence of cell phones. I like Angela, but I'm amazed she can find her way out of the house every morning."

"Maybe she leaves a paper trail. Of unmarked art assignments."

Dawn didn't reply. Normally the good-hearted dissing of her coworkers was something she enjoyed. She was not the kind of person to ever be rude to their faces, and didn't really *mean* most of it, but it was her low-key way of letting go of daily frustrations.

Not tonight, evidently. David tilted his head. "You okay?"

"Yes, why?"

"Seem a little preoccupied, is all."

"I'm fine."

But she wasn't, quite. "So...everything's okay?"

"Yes, worry-guts. Apart from the dumb-ass questions, anyway. And the weather. *Listen* to it out there."

The wind got a lot louder and more violent, peaking in occasional mournful howls. As they watched a final chunk of random television, there was a banging sound out in the yard. They looked at each other, eyebrows raised, and David got up and went to the back window.

"Wow," he said. "It's the end times."

Rain was lashing down from what appeared to be all directions. A newspaper appeared, in several installments, blown over the fence. It spun chaotically around the yard before reversing direction and rocketing toward the bench that stood in the middle. An austere wrought-iron two-seater, this had been a moving-in gift of Dawn's parents. It stood in the middle of the yard because that's where Dawn's father liked to sit when he came to visit. David found the thing uncomfortable.

"What's happening? Is anything down?"

David was distracted by the newspaper. It looked like it was stuck on something. It could only have been the strange flicker light caused by branches moving back and forth in front of the moon, but it seemed almost as if the paper had become plastered around a shape on the bench, as if someone was sitting there.

Two seconds later it was yanked back up into the sky. The bench was empty. Of course.

"Nothing," David said. "Just the wind."

Dawn was out long before he was. Sleep was Dawn's buddy and welcomed her with a warm smile and open arms. Sleep got a little goddamned fresh with Dawn, as a matter of fact. It was different for David. Sleep was the soul sister to his muse, and treated him much the same way. Sometimes she would be all friendly and hey-how's-it-going. At others she looked at him sideways, and with disdain, as if he'd suggested playing Twister, just the two of them.

After lying patiently on his right side and then his left, as was his practice, he wound up on his back listening to the wind. He tried to empty his mind, but after a while he made the decision to think about work instead. He could feel it stirring tendrils of panic but he kept focused on this for as long as he could, though he knew it was generally a one-way train to insomniaville.

Pretty soon he found himself running over the very thing he'd been attempting to avoid, however. The money Dawn had found on the top step.

It bugged him. He didn't understand why it bugged him quite so much. Sure, it was odd, but there could be mundane explanations. He'd already come up with several. Each had checked out for credibility, but then been dismissed. Why was that? Why did he think there was something more, something that he should know, and be taking seriously?

He couldn't remember, and that made him uncomfortable.

*   *   *

A while later it seemed like he'd managed to fall asleep after all, or at least be on the verge. He was distantly aware of the sound of the wind outside, sprays of rain thrown like gravel over the roof and windows, and the sound of some small metallic object cartwheeling down the road outside. Probably a stray soda can.

Then someone knocked on the door.

David lay rigid, listening so hard that the blood in his ears sounded like footsteps in the attic space above. He didn't hear anything else for a while. But then . . .

Yes, there it was again.

Someone was knocking on the front door of the house.

He got up and pulled on his robe, quietly left the room, and went downstairs. The noise had stopped. Now that he was up and about, David felt he'd better check, in case . . . in case . . . *what?* He wasn't sure. For whatever reason, you checked these things. He'd thought he'd heard a knocking and that could mean a neighbor was outside, desperate after an accident or a branch had come crashing through their roof. Either way, you checked out a noise. That was what grown-ups did, grown-up men in particular. It was the law.

As he unlocked the door, David realized how unconvinced he was that he *was* a grown-up after all.

Buffeted by the wind, the door flew open so hard that he had to use both hands to stop it swinging around to crash against the wall. Once he got it stable, he stepped forward to take a better look.

There was no one outside.

The lamp that hung above the doorway cast a light unequal to the conditions. It did enough, however, to show that on the top step, where Dawn had found the small change, something small and flat and square now lay.

David picked it up, squinting against the rain being driven into his face. It was a matchbook.

Plain white on the outside, with the name of a bar—Kendricks—in red, and an address on the back.

It *could* have been dropped out on the road and blown across the yard to here.

David opened the matchbook. At first he thought the inside of the flap was plain too, and unmarked. As he moved it against the light he saw something. He held it up and looked more closely.

It was hard to tell if the marks had been made with a pen whose ink had run dry, or a fingernail, or toothpick. There were just three characters.

$$5_P M$$

David thought it likely that the time and the name on the outside of the matchbook were supposed to be a message. The message could be a reminder for whoever had dropped the matchbook, in theory, the hypothetical person for whose existence he had no proof, only hope.

He didn't think so, though.

He slipped the matchbook into the pocket of his robe and went back inside and up to the bedroom.

He lay on his back, hands down by his sides, until an overcast morning finally arrived.

Chapter 13

This time it wasn't so cold, but it was raining, a persistent drizzle that reminded me of summer in Oregon. The upside was this empowered me to wear a workman's jacket with turned-up collar, which I borrowed from the thrift store near the restaurant. As I was likely to be in close proximity to Catherine for at least some of the afternoon, this could help keep me from being spotted too quickly—by her or anybody else. Wearing the coat made me feel ridiculous, but no more than being there in the first place. At least I wasn't alone this time.

The "walking away" approach hadn't worked out. I didn't know whether this was down to the unhappiness I'd heard in Catherine's voice before she put down the phone or if I was an asshole who couldn't let things lie, but Kristina and I wound up talking about it and it became clear I was looking for ways of refining the investigation rather than ending it. Kristina hadn't helped by pointing out that (probably) removing Thomas Clark from the picture had made the situation *worse,* rather than better, for Catherine. What's more unsettling than being followed by someone you know? Being followed by someone you *don't* know. The threat level of a stranger is much harder to gauge. The only thing you can be sure of is their intentions are unlikely to be good.

Mario had been annoyed when I'd told him I wouldn't be able to cover for Jimmy that afternoon. Not as far as I was concerned—there are squirrels who can do my job—but because of Kristina and the bar. I reassured him we'd be back in plenty of time for evening service, and he was mollified, but gave me a lingering look as I left. It made me realize this was becoming too much of a hobby. We'd spent a lot of the last week talking about it—so much that it had even taken the idea of moving to the Village out of the picture. I wasn't sure what our joint obsession said about us or our lives. Perhaps, though I'd thought I was content to be a waiter living in a tiny apartment, the reality was I'd allowed myself to float downstream into a pleasant backwater that part of me knew was insufficient. I also had the feeling I was pandering to some unwholesome impulse—and not just to my own.

As we reached the sidewalk after leaving the apartment, I stopped and looked meaningfully at Kristina. "This is it," I told her. "If nothing comes of this afternoon, I'm done. So are you."

She cocked her head, but saw my face and nodded. She knew we were getting fixated too. "You're the boss."

"Yeah, right."

The idea—Kristina's—was to observe Catherine picking her daughters up from school, on the grounds that this was another predictable routine in her life. Once again, Catherine would be unaware we were watching. The Gower School is small and boutique and stands on the north side of 15th between Ninth and Tenth, sandwiched between town houses on a quiet and leafy Chelsea street. It had a cute hand-painted sign declaring that it specialized in the methods of Montessori or Steiner or some other educational haute cuisine. That made sense. Catherine Warren wasn't going to just go ahead and trust the New York school system. She'd have spent time researching the alternatives and debating the issue with husband and friends and selecting first the ideology and then its outpost, yet another existential choice in her life. I envied her this level of constant self-determination while knowing that I simply didn't have the energy.

We got to the street at 2:40. School got out at three o'clock. Early birds were spread along the sidewalk, chatting or consulting smartphones, some huddled under umbrellas, others braving the drizzle without.

"How are we going to do this?"

"We take opposite ends of the block," I said. "I'll call you when I get down there, and we keep the line open. Holding the phones will give us cover, too."

Kristina nodded. "Nice."

"When one of us sees Catherine, we say so, and stay put. The person at the *opposite* end drifts toward the school on the other side of the street. The other holds their position on the assumption Catherine will leave the street the same way she came in. When she comes back past with the kids, that person follows at a distance. The other walks parallel a block away, taking the third man role. This is assuming that—"

I noticed Kristina was grinning. "What?"

"Can I buy you one of those slouch hats to go with that coat?"

"That won't be necessary."

"Oh, go on. Once we solve this case, can we set up a private detective agency?"

"Ain't going to happen. And it's not a 'case.' And remember what I said about this being the end of it."

She pouted and walked over to stand on the corner.

I walked briskly down the street and past the school. Weaving through the scattering of women near the school gate, I was confident they were all mothers. Mothers are the backbone of reality and the ether feels different around them. They broadcast a signal, even the ones that are convinced they're doing a lousy job. There was one male present, but he had a very tidy beard and was chatting earnestly with two women who might as well have had the word "parent" tattooed on their foreheads, so I was content to assume he was someone's telecommuting/creative/unemployed dad. When I got to Tenth, I looked back along the street and got out my phone.

Kristina answered quickly. "Nothing?"

"Nothing," I said.

"So now?"

"We wait."

"That's all we *can* do now...wait," Kristina intoned solemnly, and giggled.

"I hope you're taking this seriously."

"Absolutely."

"Good."

"By the way, I've never been more attracted to you than I am right now."

"Could be because we're eighty yards apart."

"You know, I think that might be it."

"Great. Now shh. Concentrate. If you want to diss me you can do it later, at leisure, in the comfort of our own ratty little home."

And so we waited, in silence. Meanwhile the clouds got darker and the tips of my fingers started to go white.

"I'm hungry," Kristina muttered. "And cold."

"Shh."

At five minutes to the hour the street got a lot busier—many mothers evidently operating a just-in-time policy. They came toward the school from both ends like hordes of exceptionally well-groomed zombies. I panned my gaze across the throng, phone still up to my ear, walking in a circle as if in conversation. I didn't see anybody odd. Just mothers. En masse.

"Got her," Kristina said. "Brown coat. Walking fast, north side of the street."

I started to head back along the sidewalk opposite the school. When I was fifty yards away, I slowed and stepped out into the street, skirting around the back of the main knot of people but keeping close enough to the fringes to remain part of the crowd.

Seconds later I spotted Catherine cutting through the gathered with the air of a woman who was by God going to be at the gates by 3:00:00. She got there with moments to spare and exchanged a businesslike nod with the teacher in black pantsuit who was manning the gate, clipboard in hand.

"Catherine's at the gate," I said, cutting through the women to aim toward the sidewalk on the school side of the street, a decent distance from Catherine, so I could covertly look back through the crowd in the hope of spotting anyone taking an interest in her.

"And the condor flies tonight," Kris intoned.

"Shut up."

Before I even got to the sidewalk I noticed someone back in the mix, obscured behind the bearded man and two women. A knot of umbrellas prevented me from seeing the newcomer's face, but I saw enough.

Tall, slim, in a long black coat.

"Got him," I muttered into the phone.

"You sure?"

"Same guy. Even the same coat. Hold your position—I'm going to try to get around back."

I started moving away, attempting to keep a line of people between me and the man. This was hard to do without banging into people, and there was a certain amount of maternal muttering.

"What's he doing now?"

"I don't know," I said.

"What do you mean?"

The truth was, I'd lost sight of him. I started trying to arc through the crowd toward the back, near to where I'd seen him last. Over at the gate Catherine was waving at two little girls running across the small playground on the other side of the fence.

I looked back across the press of women focused on the school gate. I caught a glimpse of the dark coat through a gap. He seemed to be heading away. To leave? Or to get in position so he was ready to follow?

Catherine was leading her daughters away, but coming in my direction. I hurriedly turned my back.

"Change of plan," I muttered. I gave Catherine twenty seconds and set off after her, trying to remain discreet. "She's coming this way."

"So now what do I do?"

"Head up Ninth. No, actually . . . come up this way too."

Catherine was near the corner of Tenth now. The man in the coat was still following her, about forty yards back. I got a clear enough view of him from behind to confirm that the coat was very long, almost floor length, and he had thick, dark hair.

I had to turn away for a moment after banging into a mother with three apparently identical boys, but looked back in time to see one of Catherine's daughters disappearing around the corner holding her mother's hand.

But now I couldn't see the man in the coat. Kristina arrived at my shoulder, breathing hard. "What's he doing now?"

"I've lost him again. Catherine just left the street. Come on."

I started to trot. When we turned onto Tenth, I fanned wide to the edge of the sidewalk and saw Catherine hurrying her children up the block. "I still don't see . . ."

"Is that him?"

Kristina was pointing across the avenue. "It can't be," I said, peering at a figure up at the next intersection on the other side. "There's no way he could have . . . But yes, that's him."

"What are we going to do?"

"Follow Catherine. I'm going over there."

The traffic along the avenue was heavy but slow, snarled by the rain. I threaded across the street between cars and yellow cabs, glancing back to see Kristina heading up the other side after Catherine, and doing it right, not closing the gap too much.

By the time I got to the other side, the figure had crossed 15th and was heading up the next block. I hurried after, trying to work out how to play the next few minutes. The chances now looked high that the guy was going to track Catherine to 18th Street and her house. She'd told me she'd thought she'd seen someone on her corner, so he evidently knew where she lived. The question was if he'd go further today—and follow her right to her door—or if he'd hang back as usual. I had to make a judgment call and I didn't want to get it wrong, because something told me we were seeing a ramping up.

Following a woman on her own is one thing. Doing it when she's got kids with her is far more serious.

We were closing in on 18th. I saw Kristina slowing so as not to be too obvious. The person in the coat was a block ahead of me now, walking fast with his head down, but showed no signs of crossing the road—and so I signaled to Kris to abandon Catherine and come to my side instead, waving to indicate she should go on half a block before she crossed so the guy in the coat would be stuck between us.

She got it, taking a diagonal course across the road, jogging up between the two lanes of traffic.

I started walking faster too, closing the distance with the man ahead. When Kris reached the sidewalk, she was sixty yards in front. She caught sight of the guy in the coat, glanced back for instructions.

I pointed at him and mouthed the word "Now."

We started to run toward each other, matching pace so he would be trapped between us. It struck me that we hadn't established a plan for what would happen at that point. I hadn't really believed it would arise.

"Hey," I said loudly when I was down to ten feet. "I want to talk to you."

The figure stopped dead and turned.

It was a woman.

Slim and tall with thick, dark hair and strong features, eyes the gray end of blue.

She stared at me like a cornered animal, body tensed for flight. Kristina faltered ten feet away on the other side, seeing the same as me and not knowing what to do.

Disbarred from throwing myself at the person and tackling her to the ground, I hesitated.

It was enough. The woman darted away from us and across the street with disconcerting speed.

I lunged across the street just as the lights went green. Kristina got stuck, so I left her to it and ran. On the other side of the avenue I slipped on the wet curb and went careering across the sidewalk. By the time I got my balance, the woman was half a block down the avenue, headed back the way we'd just come, looking like she was going to take the turn onto 16th street.

I ran after her. She'd gotten a head start, but I'm pretty fit and was gathering speed fast. I hurtled around the corner and onto 16th, confident that somewhere along its hundred-yard stretch I'd be able to catch her.

I got twenty yards down the street before realizing I couldn't see her anymore. I kept moving, looking both ways, at passing doorways, even up at first-floor windows, convinced I was somehow just being dumb.

By halfway along I knew it wasn't so. The street was deserted but for a man at the bottom of one of the redbrick staircases I'd noticed a couple of nights before. He was middle-aged and dressed in a brown corduroy suit and watching me with an amused expression.

When I got closer I realized that he was wearing a priest's collar. I stopped running.

"Is everything okay?" His voice was calm and friendly.

I tried to catch my breath, looking back and forth up the street. "Did you just see somebody?"

He raised one eyebrow eloquently.

"A woman," I said. "Long coat. Must have come past here about a minute before I did."

"I'm sorry," he said. "I've just this moment come out. Is something wrong?"

"No," I said. "Everything's fine."

I saw a winded-looking Kristina turning onto the street, and walked irritably away from the priest.

Kris was panting. "Any sign?"

"No," I said. "She vanished."

"But it *was* a woman, right?"

"Yes."

"That changes things, doesn't it?"

"Yes."

"So now what?"

"I don't know."

Chapter 14

When David walked into Kendricks at a quarter of five, he realized how long it had been since he'd gone to a bar outside Rockbridge's downtown area. Bars downtown make an effort. There are napkins with logos, the staff were perky, and high chairs are available. They downplay the alcohol side of things and pitch themselves as no big deal, a place you can go as part of a perfectly sane existence and enjoy an afternoon from which you will not emerge on all fours or married to someone deplorable.

Bars outside the city limits are different. Plenty are decent businesses who chose their position on the basis of zoning, convenience to the highway, or any number of reasonable criteria — including the one that says this is where the bar's always been and who knows why or cares, and look, do you want a beer or not, pal. Their clientele will be more varied, however, and many of these people (and bars) aren't going to a lot of trouble to hide the bottom line: they're here because they don't need to be anyplace else and because liquor is served and they want a big old glass of it, right now, with a peace-and-quiet chaser.

Situated just outside Rockbridge by Route 74, Kendricks was firmly in the latter camp. It had been in business forty years and had an unusually large metal sign over it that once sported an apostrophe before the "S," but it blew down long ago and nobody had given enough of a crap to do anything about it, including Ryan Kendrick himself. The rusted punctuation mark was believed to still be around someplace, possibly in the overgrown creek that ran along the back of the parking lot. Once in a while the more intrepid sort of drunkard might amuse himself by having a look for it before lurching home.

Kendrick died in 2008, following a short, bare-knuckle fight with lung cancer, and after a couple of years during which the bar seemed to change hands almost nightly, it had found its level once more, settling back into bleary, boozy equilibrium. Battered furniture, a pair of battered pool tables, a battered wooden bar, and some pretty battered regulars—these last in low numbers and staking out the corners with their backs to the door. Music played in the background, not too loud. Some guy earnestly advertised something or other on the TV screen above the bar, pointlessly, the sound off.

David tried to remember the last time he'd been in the place. It had to be five or six years, soon after he started seeing Dawn. Kendrick himself had still been alive, though a shell of the hulking bad-ass he'd once been. It had been a sketchy bar then. It was a sketchy bar now.

David got a beer from a barman who looked like he'd just received bad news about his dog. He took it to a table in the darkest corner and sat with his back to the door. It was unlikely he'd see anyone he knew, but the drinking-in-the-afternoon look was one he'd prefer to avoid. He hadn't wanted alcohol at all, but the barman didn't look like he'd respond positively to a request for a low-fat latte, extra shot or not.

David took a cautious sip of the beer and looked at a poster for a long-ago gig on the wall. Why was he even here? After a long night without sleep, he wasn't sure. However hard he'd tried to work, his mind kept returning to the change left on their top step. For some reason that was working at him even more than the matchbook. It reminded him of something, but he didn't know what. He kept trying to push it out of his head. It kept coming back. Each time it returned it felt as if someone was gripping his guts a little tighter in their fist.

He'd decided that he would come here and sit for half an hour. Dawn had a staff meeting and wouldn't be back until nine, so that was covered. He had the matchbook in his pocket and intended to leave it on the table when he went, along with any notion that there was something he was failing to remember.

If you spend your life trying to make things mean something, it can be hard to stop when you get up from your desk at the end of the workday. That was all this was. Some unexplained change. A few scratch marks. Big deal.

In twenty-five minutes he was walking away.

"Hello, David."

David looked up, heart thumping. A man was standing over the table. He was lean and wearing jeans and a white shirt under a dark coat. His skin was tan, chin stubbled, and he had sharp blue eyes.

It was the man David had seen in Penn Station. The man who'd followed him. Seeing him again was like hearing a phone ring in the dead of night.

"Who..."

"Is this chair free?"

David stared dumbly up at him. The man grinned back, a little too wide. "But then—are *any* of us truly free?"

"What?"

"You used to say that. It was funny."

"I have no idea what you're talking about."

The man sat in the chair opposite. "It'll come."

"What are you doing here?"

"I came to see you, of course."

David put the matchbook on the table. "I bumped into you in New York. It was an accident. I saw you again at the train station. That's all I know."

"No. That's all you *remember.*"

"Look, is this some kind of scam? Because—"

The man held a finger up to his lips. "Don't talk so much. You'll learn more that way. And it'll look less weird while you remember how things are done."

Despite himself, David lowered his voice. "What are you talking about? What things?"

The man picked up David's beer and took an unhurried sip, before placing the glass back exactly where it had been on the table.

David stared at him. "Are you *kidding* me?"

The man settled back and folded his hands behind his head. "Look around, friend."

David did so. The barman was watching an advert for a barbecue set. The other drinkers were staring into their glasses or space or, in the case of one throwback, reading a paperback novel.

"I didn't choose five o'clock by accident," the man said. "Afternoon shift's wandered home or too drunk to care. The evening crowd isn't here yet. In the meantime, everyone's giving each other plenty of space."

"So?"

"Nobody saw what I did. So it didn't happen. Nobody sees, nobody knows, right? Does *that* ring a bell?"

David swallowed. It did, though he didn't know why. "How did you find out where I live?"

"I saw the train you left the city on. 'Course that wouldn't have led me to this bump in the road, except I also overheard your wife mention somewhere called Rockbridge. It wasn't hard and I'm not dumb. I usually get what I want. You should remember that."

David felt the hand tighten around his guts — this time far worse than before, as if long fingernails were digging in. "I'm going to leave now."

"Don't. We've got a chance here, David. We can be friends again. That almost never happens."

David tried to sound calm and firm. "Look, I don't have much money. I don't have *anything* you might want."

"You're so wrong," the man said, leaning forward earnestly. "Just being here like this, seeing Dawn . . . you have no idea of how much that means. And she's wonderful. You did well, my friend. Congratulations."

David stared, chilled by the way the man had casually dropped his wife's name. "This is going to stop," he said. *"Now.* Or I'm walking out of here and going straight to the—"

There was a rasping noise.

The man swore and pulled a cheap cell phone out of his jacket, the disposable type that comes with prepaid credit and no contract. The kind, David gathered from watching cop shows, that are called "burners" and are favored by the criminal fraternity because they're easy to come by and dispose of. Was that what this guy was? Part of a group who'd singled him out for a complex shakedown—some real-world version of an e-mail phishing scam?

"I have to take this," the man said. He looked torn. The phone vibrated again. "You'll stay?"

His tone made David realize this encounter was more inexplicable than he'd realized. There was no threat in it, rather a kind of entreaty.

The phone rasped once more and the man got up and walked away, gesturing for David to stay where he was.

When he heard the door to the bar open and shut, David let out a shuddering breath. His hands were shaking. What should he do? There was only one way out of the place and if the guy was in the lot he'd be bound to see him. If David walked, would he follow? If so, what then? The man hadn't done anything overtly threatening. If anything, his mood had been one of off-kilter good cheer—albeit the kind of dark cheer that sometimes escalates into pulling out a concealed weapon.

David wanted to put distance between them. Leaving the bar was the only way. Walking out—and then talking to the cops. He'd seen too many movies where the hero kept quiet about some whacked-out situation for too long. He wasn't going to be that guy—especially now that he remembered Dawn saying Angela had thought she'd seen David outside the school gates.

She hadn't seen David, but perhaps she had seen *someone*. A man who'd just dropped Dawn's name into the conversation as if he knew her.

Or as if he had been watching her.

There was a coughing sound. David quickly turned, convinced the man had somehow slipped back in without him hearing. It was a man in his midfifties, however, heavy in the gut, with a broad, fleshy face. He stood a few yards behind David's chair, beer in hand.

David realized it was George, the guy who worked at Bedloe's Insurance up the street from his old office at It's Media.

"Hey," the man said.

David nodded cautiously. "George, right?"

"You're the writer guy. Friend of Talia's."

"Yes." One out of two, at least. It was the first time someone had referred to him as "the" or even "a" writer. It didn't feel a close fit. Meanwhile, the other man kept looking oddly at him.

"You okay, George?"

"It's been a strange week," the man muttered.

David got the sense that George was a couple beers down already. Also that what he probably meant was the story he'd told Talia, about the hitchhiker who disappeared. David didn't know whether he was supposed to know about that. He was only a friend of a friend, after all.

"Huh," he said, in the hope this would cover it.

"You here alone?"

"Yes," David said, fighting the impulse to glance toward the door. Right now that was the truth. It occurred to him this might even be some kind of come-on, but if so he had no idea of how to respond.

"Really?"

"You see anyone?"

"No. Thought I did, though. Couple minutes ago. Sitting opposite you."

The back of David's neck twitched.

"Didn't see him leave," George went on thoughtfully, as if to himself. "Did you?"

"I'm not here with anyone," David repeated.

George looked at the chair opposite a moment longer. "Yeah, well, okay. Sorry to have bothered you."

He wandered back toward the far corner. David waited until George settled at a table there, and then he got up and left the bar, taking care not to catch anyone's eye.

Outside it was dark with storm clouds and the wind was picking up. Cars and trucks stood at discreet distances from one another, like people awaiting the results of blood tests that would not reflect well on their lifestyles.

Down at the far end of the building David saw a shadow beneath the dim corner light. After a moment he heard a voice, too. It sounded like someone on the phone.

He marched toward it. The man must have heard him approaching, because he slipped around the corner into deeper shadow, presumably to protect his privacy. This was the final straw for David, who felt that *his* privacy had been plenty invaded.

"I don't know what you want," he said loudly as he rounded the corner to confront the man. "But if I see you again, I'm going straight to the —"

There was nobody there. The side of the bar was a graveyard for broken wooden crates. There were a few battered and rusting gas canisters and some old sacking too, tangled in the long grass like brown ghosts.

Nothing — and nobody — else.

The man must have slipped along the side.

David picked his way through the debris and grass toward the back, where the lot shaded into the edges of the creek that ran past the rear wall of the bar. Holding on to the wall to stop himself from sliding into muddy water, he looked along it.

No one there. David stared at absence, his guts now screwed so tight that it felt like he was going to vomit, then made his way back to the parking lot.

He noticed a shape drawn in the dusty gravel, a rectangle that tapered toward the bottom. It didn't mean anything to him.

He dragged his feet through it nonetheless, until the shape was completely gone.

Chapter 15

"Because I'm an idiot," David said.

"Roger that, but you're always an idiot. This doesn't explain the specific omission today."

They were in the kitchen and the discussion concerned supper. He always looked after what they ate. It was his job. Hunter-gatherer of words, and also food. Today he'd forgotten. That was because of going to Kendricks, of course, which wasn't something he wanted to discuss. When he got back, he'd gone to his study to work but wound up reading more of Talia's book instead. It was easier than working on his own. Easier than thinking, too, and easier and better than trying to work out whether to go to the cops. Doing this had been Plan A for the entire walk home, but it ran out of steam when he got indoors. What could he tell them? That a stranger was bugging him in a way that seemed too genial and unobtrusive to count as stalking? That there was an excessive familiarity in his manner that made David feel not attacked but guilty, as if the situation was his responsibility? That David believed this stranger had subsequently vanished out of a parking lot (yes, Officer, I had been drinking, just a little bit)?

No. Talking to the cops wasn't going to work, at least not yet, and the real reason was that David couldn't seem to think clearly about what had happened. The encounter felt intangible. Or like a daydream. Something he'd made up. Nothing real.

But not unreal, either.

Eventually lack of sleep and an unaccustomed afternoon beer caught up with him, and he'd nodded off at his desk, waking at the sound of

Dawn getting back to the house after her meeting. He felt bleary and caught out even though she wasn't giving him a hard time.

She laughed at the look on his face. "No biggie, little boy lost. We can rustle up something from the cupboards, I'm sure. How did the day go otherwise?"

He was momentarily wary. "In what way?"

"The *writing,* darling. Remember that?"

"I'm not a writer, babe. I just sit up there to keep the computer company."

She smiled, but it looked a little forced. "Actually it's going a lot better," he said. Apart from that afternoon, this was broadly true. Although he hadn't written many actual *words,* the phantom hitchhiker thing still felt like it might pay off. "Got a new idea."

"That's great," she said, much more warmly. "Don't suppose you'll tell me what it is?"

He shook his head, as she'd known he would.

"I'm very proud of you, you know," she said.

Taken aback by her seriousness, he struggled for a response. "Well, let's see how the first one—"

"No," she said. "I'm *not* going to wait and see how it sells. You wrote it, and it's great, and it's going to be published. Everything else is out of your hands. I'm proud of what *you* do, not for what fate throws your way."

"You probably won't be so proud of the fact I fell asleep at my desk this afternoon."

"Oh, I already knew that."

"You did?"

"You looked like the lurching dead when you came downstairs. No big deal. You didn't sleep well."

"How do you know?"

"You were tossing and turning all night. It's okay. I'm proud of you anyway. Just don't make a habit of it."

"Copy that. Look, I'm going to grab a shower, wake up properly, okay?"

"Please do. You smell *viiiile*," she drawled, an old joke between them, as she bent to start looking in the cupboards. Then, as he headed out into the hallway, she straightened up again. "Oh, and by the way."

He turned. "What?"

"I'm pregnant."

At first he didn't believe it. He didn't think she'd be lying or joking, but after the last couple of years it was like being casually informed that black was, in fact, white—look, here's a picture to prove it. When he sat for five whole minutes, gripping the printed-out results in his hands and staring at them, he finally got it. And it blew everything else away.

"This is it," he said, folding her in his arms. She was crying, and felt both bulky and fragile, though there was no difference from the woman he'd hugged that morning before she left for work. "This is the one. I can feel it. You've done it."

"*We've* done it."

"No," he said, burying his head in the smell of her skin and hair. "*You* did."

They foraged supper out of the cupboards, snacks at the counter as they talked and talked. "There's still a long way to go," she said. "Nothing's ever sure. We've got to take it one day at a time."

He couldn't. David knew this time it was going to work, and the prospect filled his head. It didn't matter how much you assumed you'd gotten a handle on human reproduction nor how steely-eyed and unromantic about the process you'd become after hours spent in doctors' waiting rooms glumly listening to the money meter ticking away, it was still a *total mind-fuck*. Somewhere deep in a hidden crucible in Dawn's body, magic had occurred. Things invisible to the naked eye had conjoined and as a result something real was growing inside her. An entirely separate being. It had Dawn within it—and David too—but wasn't merely their product or the sum or averaging of their souls. This wasn't two plus two making four. It was two plus two making lilac. It was different. It was other. It was — or would be — purely itself.

For the time being it might be attached to her by blood and tissue, but one day it would sit opposite David and call him dad, hopefully with a smile on his or her face rather than a snarl (though both would doubtless happen at one time or another), a being with words and emotions all of its own. And one day it would announce it was getting married. And then — assuming it took matters in the traditional order — announce a grandchild was on the way, yet *another* being, a further step along the road to infinity. Every act of creation only ever apes the *real* one: the creation of a new being that one day will walk away from you out into the world to do its thing, forever linked to you by history but the center and sole inhabitant of its own universe. Who cared about the imaginary, when reality could be so magical?

When they went to bed — earlier than usual, with much joking about how Dawn had to sleep for two now — she drifted off quickly, crashing out on her side. David lay next to her in the dark, for once happy to be awake, savoring the experience, in fact — though the sluggish shadows around his internal eye told him that tonight his sleep siren was going to come across for once, and soon.

He turned cautiously, slipped his hand under Dawn's arm, and placed it gently on her stomach. The shadows gathered, deep and warm, and soon he was asleep.

Chapter 16

It was Kristina's idea to call Catherine. It came to her after we'd been sitting in a bar in the Village for a couple of hours, which tells its own story. I could tell from what I overheard that Catherine wasn't wild about the idea of us dropping in, but she agreed if we'd wait a couple hours so she could get to the other side of the dinner/bath/bed routine. Kristina seemed impatient about this, but she'd never had her own kids to debrief and shut down, and didn't realize how badly the unscheduled arrival of strangers could derail the process. So we waited in the bar some more, during which Kristina called Mario at the restaurant and promised she'd be at work by nine, cross her heart and hope to die. Mario has no defenses against her and said, "Okay, that's fine, Miss Kristina. See you later."

Eventually we stepped out into the dark and made our way to Catherine's house. She opened the door looking well dressed and grown-up. I trooped in behind Kristina feeling like a teenager being let in by someone else's mom. It was one of those very vertical town houses with black-painted railings and cream detailing around the windows, like the dwellings you'd see in a child's illustrated tale about life in a big city. There were books everywhere and posters for recent exhibitions and well-framed black-and-white photos of family and relatives and everything looked like it had been tidied recently by a professional. At one point I thought I saw a mote of dust lurking under a chair but then realized it was just a trick of the light. I didn't have to watch Kristina's face to judge her take on the house, or see her thinking how jolly nice it must be to live there.

Catherine led us into a kitchen with eating space that took up half of the raised first story. It was bright and airy and the kids' art on the fridge was better than anything I could have done. A door at the end led onto a sitting room with stripped brick walls, a fireplace on one side and a television of judicious size on the other.

"The girls are in bed," Catherine said brightly, as if briefing a new au pair. "But Mark's due back from the airport in about an hour, so..."

Kris glanced at me, but I didn't say anything. I wasn't sure we should be here and had said so. So as far as I was concerned, this was her gig.

"We followed you this afternoon," she said.

Catherine blinked, and I was reminded of an incident from childhood. I must have been about twelve, wandering around town with a couple of buddies, and we'd climbed up the big tree at the back of the library, as we sometimes did. Once there, we realized an older girl we kinda knew—she worked Saturdays in the general store, a regular stop on our wanders-around-town—was studying at the desk in the window, about ten feet away. So we hooted and waved and eventually she looked up and saw us.

I guess we'd been expecting...I'm not sure *what* we'd been expecting...that she'd be pleased or flattered or at least amused to see us. She evidently did not feel this way. She responded in a fashion that in retrospect made absolute sense. She reacted like a girl realizing she was being spied upon by a bunch of younger boys to whom she was polite in the store but whom she possibly somewhat dreaded seeing; boys who (and she was old enough to get this, even if we were not) would one day, and maybe soon, become even *more* interested in her.

Her face showed shock at first and then anger. We didn't wait to see what happened next. We scooted down the tree and walked away talking loudly about other things. We felt dumb and embarrassed and as if we'd had something revealed to us about ourselves that we hadn't previously understood. There'd been no harm in what we'd done. None intended, anyway. But we cut the store out of our Saturday routine for the rest of that summer.

When Catherine looked at us, I felt the same way.

Kristina didn't seem to notice. "We've been worried about you," she said. "And then it looked like Thomas wasn't the guy after all..."

"Yes," Catherine said. Her voice was clipped. "So?"

"Well, we thought we'd take another look today, see if we could see anyone."

"When were you doing this?"

"After you picked up Ella and Isabella."

"You waited outside the school? Hiding?"

"Well, not exactly hiding, but...yes."

Catherine stared at her. "Excellent," she said. I was baffled Kris wasn't picking up on the atmosphere. She's preternaturally sharp. Right now she was failing to read Catherine on even the most basic level.

"I'm sorry if that was inappropriate," I said. "My fault. I felt bad after I spoke to you yesterday. I wanted to give it one more try. Macho pride, I guess."

Catherine seemed to soften. "Sorry," she said. "I've been tense all day and Isa did not go down easy. Do you want coffee?"

We said we did, and she got to work with an expensive-looking machine on the counter, and it seemed like all was going to be okay.

Though in fact it got worse, and pretty fast.

Kris and I didn't speak all evening at the restaurant. I understood why I was pissed at her, though not why she was pissed at me, but I guess that's the bottom line in most disagreements and she probably felt the exact same way. Wrong though she was.

The idea of her follower being a woman evidently hadn't occurred to Catherine. She asked what she'd looked like. We told her. She frowned, trying to make something of this, but gave up, looking a little scared.

"Was she pretty?"

"Yes," I said.

Catherine stood nodding, eyes turned inward. Kristina apparently didn't have anything to say, so I asked Catherine the obvious question. "Are you going to talk to your husband about this?"

Two minutes later Kristina and I were back out on the street. Catherine had abruptly realized there were a *lot* of very important things she simply had to get on with and while she was *very* grateful for our efforts she needed us to go, right now. She'd be in touch with Kris.

Real soon.

As the door closed firmly behind us, Kristina hissed at me and stomped down the steps. I followed, not understanding what the hell her problem was. She apprised me of it soon enough. She ranted at me all the way back to the East Village, in fact.

"What kind of an *asshole* question was that?"

"About talking to her husband?"

"Yes. I mean, Jesus, John. What the *fuck?*"

"A young woman stalking an older married one — do you have a better explanation?"

"Of *course* he's not having an affair. Christ, John, you can't go around making assumptions like that. I know you don't like Catherine, but I *do* and I've spent a *lot* more time talking to her."

"Yeah, so?"

"So I know her marriage is solid and that Mark's a good guy. For God's sake — you saw that house."

"Kris, that's the most naive thing I've ever *heard.* Yes, it's a lovely house. So what? Having expensive taste and an efficient maid doesn't mean everything's immaculate underneath the water line."

"Don't judge people by your own mistakes. Just because you fucked up a marriage doesn't mean everyone else is busy doing the same dumb thing."

There was enough truth in this — after Carol and I fell apart I entered a liaison with Bill Raine's wife, which he knew about, and we'd worked through, but it remained the most damaging thing I'd ever done in my life—to make me as angry as Kristina.

This led me to snap that she was not experienced enough in long-term relationships to know what the hell she was talking about. She shouted back that she had more experience than I knew and furthermore was tired of me treating her like a kid all the time, which was so out of the blue I'd had *no* idea it was coming, and I didn't handle it well, and after that...

Well, CNN didn't actually cover the rest of our stomp back to the restaurant, or give us our own logo, but it was *loud*.

In the end I got tired of sitting at the bar being ignored by Kristina while she was bright-eyed and charming to everyone else. I left, reasoning that she knew where we lived and also, well, fuck, whatever.

As I stomped out onto the street I saw Lydia at the end of the block. She was facing traffic and, to be honest, I tried to slip past without her seeing me.

"Don't worry," she said, however, without turning. "I ain't seen him."

"Okay," I muttered. "That's good."

"See a lot of others, though," she added thoughtfully. "Lot of people on the streets tonight."

I looked around, confirming what I already knew—if anything, it looked quiet for the small hours of a Thursday night. "Okay," I said again.

She looked at me, a wistful smile on her face. For a moment her eyes were clear and I got the sense that, were it not for the lines and layers of grime, I'd be seeing in her what a man might have forty years before.

Then they went dead. "Frankie was a dad bitch whore."

"What?"

"What? What? What?" She took a fast step toward me, raising her bony fist to wave it in my face. "Fuckers everywhere, that's what," she snarled. "You ain't going to steal from me, motherfuckers. I'll cut you bad."

"Whatever you say, Lyds."

"Fuck you, asshole. I'll fuck you up too."

"Okay then. See you tomorrow."

I walked away, simply not in the mood for New York tonight.

Kristina got home at two thirty. We talked. We did not kiss and make up—neither of us regards sexual intercourse as an effective means of arbitration in matters of serious dispute—but we did start to laugh at ourselves, and she eventually fell asleep in my arms. I lay waiting to follow her. The city below seemed quiet, far away, as though we were in a tiny room at the top of a stone tower in some other world. The wind was strong. We're always aware of it here up in the garret, but this was rowdier than usual. It sounded as though someone was bouncing little objects across the roof.

I don't like arguments. They always feel like a failure, which I presume must be mine. Pretty soon my head began to feel crowded, and it felt like a fight not to open my eyes.

Then I heard a real noise, from out in the main room. I carefully lifted Kris's arm off my chest and slipped out of bed.

The source of the sound was obvious and mundane. Kristina's cell phone lay on the counter, as usual, and the screen was glowing. A little red number on an icon in the dock said she had e-mail. At this time of night it would only be spam and so I put her phone facedown on the cushion on the sofa instead, where further vibrations wouldn't make the thing rattle so audibly.

I stood aimlessly for a moment before deciding to enact the only ritual that's ever helped me to sleep—a weak coffee and a cigarette. I know two stimulants taken together should do the opposite, but... they don't.

I made the drink on autopilot, trying not to worry about the problem of Catherine's follower. There was now only one credible explanation and it was down to Catherine to chase it down. I still found it hard not to keep thinking about, though. It was this that had been keeping me awake, along with dregs of the adrenaline occasioned by arguing violently with a woman whom I knew, increasingly, that I loved pretty hard.

The image that kept coming into my mind was the face of the girl in the coat when we'd cornered her. So much of our experience is mediated and cushioned. Car crash–style interactions are unnerving, cracking the paper-thin shell around our lives. Who *was* this woman? What did she want? Was she basically a good person, or a certifiable whack-job? What did she think would come from stalking Catherine, even if there *was* something going on between her and Mark? Was being confronted on the street going to make her back off, cause her to be more stealthy, or possibly escalate her behavior? Where was she now?

Abruptly I shook my head.

Whatever. I was done. For real this time.

I took the coffee and a cigarette over to the window. It was the middle of the night and so I wasn't going to actually climb out onto the goddamned roof, but I'd at least open the windowpane and blow the smoke out.

As I started to pull up the sill, something happened outside. I don't know what it was, but it was fast and large and dark. It was as if a huge crow had been roosting on the roof area and took sudden, chaotic flight. In the fraction of a second in which I saw it, it seemed to split into two, maybe even three shapes—twisting shadows that disappeared or dispersed like a storm cloud ripped apart by the wind.

I heard noises, too—more of the pattering sounds I'd heard while in bed, the sounds I'd put down to the wind clattering objects over the roof.

My chest beating hard, I pushed the window up the rest of the way. I stuck my head cautiously out and saw the scrap of flat roof. The wooden chair. My heavy glass ashtray. The chair had been knocked over. It was windy, but nowhere near enough to have done that, nor for the ashtray to have somehow been upturned or broken in half.

"What's happening?"

Kristina's voice nearly gave me a heart attack. I whirled around to see her yawning in the doorway to the bedroom. "What are you doing up?"

"Heard a noise," she mumbled, turning on a table lamp. "You opening the window for a crafty smoke, it seems. Couldn't have done it a *little* more quietly?"

"Sorry," I said, pulling the window back down again. "But...something weird just happened."

I was about to say more but realized she was no longer looking at me, but at the window.

"What the hell is that?"

I looked where she was pointing and saw there were marks on the glass, revealed by the light now on in the room. I leaned closer and ran my fingers over the pane. The marks were on the other side of the glass, spidery tracks through layers of dust and airborne dirt that neither we nor the last ten sets of tenants had made any effort to clean.

Kristina was standing beside me now. I think we realized at the same time that the marks on the window, though faint and jagged, were letters, and that they spelled out three words.

They said:

LEAVE US ALONE

Chapter 17

David never saw how they began. He watched for the beginnings like some Midwest stormchaser, but they were invisible to him. He was learning with most things that you could observe cause before effect. Careless elbows knocked cups off tables. Mouthing off to teachers got you exiled to stand in the corner, head lowered, the shame of punishment evenly balanced by the welcome change it made from sitting at your boring desk. Shouting at Mom got you smacked—and in this case effect came lightning fast on the heels of cause, and hurt a lot. Cause and effect often came so close together there, in fact, that from time to time the order seemed reversed.

The fights between his parents stood outside this process, however. They just happened. There was no beginning and so, presumably, no end.

He tried to see it this way, at least, but couldn't ignore the fact that most of the time his mom and dad seemed happy together. So happy that they didn't need him, in fact. They would laugh and drink their special drinks from the cabinet, their conversations conducted in looks and implications that excluded him. If he was naughty or lazy, they'd gang up on him, two against one, and after he'd retreated—or been sent—to bed, he'd hear them on the deck, their voices calm and relaxed once again, now that he wasn't around to cause trouble.

Then some afternoon—for no apparent reason—he would hear the distant sound of the whistle coming out of the woods on the other side of town, and he'd know the train was on its way. He understood it wasn't a *real* train. He knew what he was hearing wasn't even a real *sound*, but an itch inside his head. A sign that, sometime soon, there was going to be a fight.

But why? There was no track leading to their house. So how did the train always know how to find the way? The child had come to believe that the reason he could not see the cause was that he *was* the cause. He was the nail on which they snagged themselves. He was the station the dark train was trying to find.

It was his fault. It had to be.

And sooner or later, the train reached town.

This time it happened during dinner. It took place at the big old wooden kitchen table, one of the few things the family had wound up with after the death of his mother's father. There hadn't been much to pass on, which had been something of a surprise to all concerned. When they'd visited Grandpa in the old days, Mom always put on something smart and Dad grumbled in the car and seemed smaller all the time they were in the big old Victorian house on the better side of town. Then Grandpa died and it turned out there wasn't much money in the house after all (in fact, there was *minus* money, though that didn't make sense). The child remembered his father's slow smile at this discovery. His face had radiated a warm, uncomplicated pleasure that the boy would have given anything to have caused.

After it had all been sorted out and bills paid and the big, grand house hurriedly sold, Grandma went to live with Mom's sister in North Carolina and they got two small, ugly paintings and some silverware they never used, and the vast table in the kitchen. It was too large for the room—even the child could see that—but that's where it went. He didn't mind the table at all—it was great for spreading art things out on and made an ideal fort, especially when the big white tablecloth was in place, as it reached down almost to the floor on all sides—but his father did. He complained about it a lot.

In fact...Yes, that's how the fight had started this time. It had been the trigger, at least.

The child had been finishing the last of his pasta with red sauce — his default fuel at the time — and in a vague world of his own, making up a story, as he so often did. Slowly he began to realize the weather system in the room had changed. He raised his head to listen.

No, his father declared, he was not prepared to work at this table. It was a big, dumb table and would not be convenient. The study was his domain and was going to stay that way. The subject was closed.

The child glanced at his mother and saw the subject was *not* closed. He was familiar with his father's study, a tiny room on the upper floor. His dad had a typewriter set up there on a little desk and sometimes spent a while sitting at it. There was a pile of paper on the left side of the desk, sheets on which his father had typed words. They lay facedown. The pile didn't ever seem to get bigger. That wasn't surprising, as there would be weeks and months in which his dad didn't go into the room. This appeared to be his mother's point. The room would be better deployed as a closet, she believed, than indulging his father's futile "hobby." The child wasn't sure what a hobby was, but gathered it was a Bad Thing.

He swiveled his gaze from his mother's face, saw the way his father looked, and turned hurriedly back to his cooling pasta. He loved his father, but sometimes his face changed. His jaw clenched and his eyes went flat. Usually this was a fleeting condition, but sometimes it would settle in, and it made the child feel scared. His father was looking at his mother that way, and that could only mean one thing.

The train was pulling into the station.

Right now.

Things were said. Many things, with increasing volume. The child tried not to hear.

His father stood, banging the table with his thighs. He shouted, his face red, the fighting vein standing out on his forehead. His mother jumped up too, shouting back. His father stormed out into the hallway.

His mother followed. Even though they were farther away, the noise got louder as they spiraled up into the thundercloud.

The child slid off his seat and slipped underneath the table. It always seemed safer under there, the big white tablecloth forming a barrier to the outside world — though the shouting remained perfectly audible. He heard his parents storming back into the kitchen, shouting over each other. He learned, or was reminded of, some facts:

His father was a loser who never completed any task. His mother was a bitch who complained all the time. His father was an asshole who looked at other women, which is not allowed. His mother was a bitch who thought she was better than everyone because of Grandpa, who it turned out wasn't the man everyone thought. His father was a liar and drank too much. His mother was a bitch, and was also a pot calling the kettle black.

The child closed his eyes and put his fingers in his ears. It wasn't enough. The shouting went on and on and on. His mother was better at coming up with different rude words to call his father. But his father...

Yes, there it was.

The sound of the first slap.

His father was better at that part, though Mom was pretty good at throwing things. If it hadn't been his parents doing this to each other, it might have been interesting to watch these evenly matched players hacking and sawing at each other's weak points. But they *were* his parents, and the boy loved them, and so it made him want to push pencils into his ears until he could not hear. It made him want to disappear, forever.

His mother's feet hurried past one end of the table as she moved to put the piece of furniture between her and the man at whom she was screaming obscenities. And...

Yes, there was the sound of something smashing on the wall. A plate or bowl. Possibly the child's bowl. It wouldn't be the first time his things had been used as ammunition. It would be replaced tomorrow, with hung-over but heartfelt apologies. The apologies made the child feel angry and numb.

He screwed his eyes up tighter and pressed his hands harder over his ears. It helped, but not much. He tried to fill his head with light in the way that sometimes also helped, a white light of non-thought and non-hearing and non-seeing. He tried to find a place inside that was calm and the opposite of the dark woods from which the first sounds of the train whistle came.

Meanwhile the fight above him raged on, like arcs of red lightning. Did the opposing troops, these mythic armies, have any idea he was under there? Would they care? The child had never been sure whether he was his mother's fault or his father's — he'd heard arguments for both sides — but he was *someone's* fault, that was for sure. Best to keep out of the way, then. To lie low. To fade into the background, or further still.

Better to not be there at all.

But then...

Gradually the boy became aware of a prickling sensation on the back of his neck. It was a bit like the feeling he got when he heard the first echo of the faraway train, but it couldn't be that — the train had already arrived.

He opened his eyes, but the feeling didn't go away. He moved his hands from his ears — causing the sound of the fight to leap in volume — and lowered them to his lap, frowning. What worried him most was the idea that this might be some new kind of sign, a yet more ominous version of the train whistle: a warning that the fight was going to get more than usually out of hand, and that someone — his mother, probably, though that couldn't be for certain — was in danger of getting seriously hurt this time.

The feeling expanded, seeping downward from his neck until it felt like gentle pressure was being applied to his upper back, along his shoulders, and down the spine.

He turned and saw that a boy was sitting under the table behind him. The boy was sitting neatly, legs crossed, hands in his lap.

The child blinked, unable to speak, at first incapable even of working out what question he might ask.

The boy smiled — a bright, sunny smile that said he knew the boy and liked him very much, and wanted nothing more than to hang out and have fun together when the silly fuss raging around them had blown over, which at some point it would, as it always did, and so in the end everything would be okay.

"Hello, David," he said.

"Who . . . who are you?" David whispered.

The boy's smile got broader, shining up into his sharp blue eyes.

"I'm your friend."

David woke, rigid in the dead of night with his pregnant wife beside him, and finally knew where he'd first seen the man in the blue jeans and white shirt.

He remembered his name, too.

Maj.

Part Two

I believe that the human imagination never invented
anything that was not true, in this world or any other.

Gérard de Nerval

Aurélia

Chapter 18

My name is Billy, and in the mornings I wake up. The first adventure of the day is finding out where I am. It may be on a bench in a park. I may be propped against the wall in a backstreet or sitting in the bakery section in a grocery store. I may be on someone's floor.

I try to make it happen somewhere different every day, but sometimes when I open my eyes I realize I have woken there before. You'd think in a city as big as New York that would be impossible, but when it's time to turn in I'm so worn out these days that sometimes I end up doing what I've done before without realizing. Everybody's the same, I suppose. You get up, you go to work, you come home, you eat food that's very similar to what you had yesterday or last week, you sit in front of the shows you always watch, and finally you go to the same old bed. If you could retreat up into the sky like some alien or god and watch any given person, day after day, you'd see that however complex and variable their days might seem to them, they follow tracks. Once in a while this angers or saddens them and they make a big deal of changing something. They leave their job, they move house, they screw somebody slightly different from their partner, and they get divorced.

Then, before too long, they find themselves rolling along a new set of near-identical tracks.

I have tracks of my own. They run to different destinations: sites of memory or places that have proven useful for killing time. There are some of us, Journeymen and Angels and Cornermen, who have found methods of spending their days that do not seem like a waste. I tried to find something too. Once I started to get the picture, however, I felt something break.

There was a period before all that when I used to be delighted with the whole deal, I'll admit. The Dozeno Phase, as the Gathered call it, otherwise known as dumb ignorance. There was an incredible sense of freedom. Nothing I had to do. Nowhere I had to be. An endless Friday night, one long freshman year or an endless spell in your early twenties, when it feels like infinity is there to play for, that no doors will ever close, and the only way life will change is by getting even better.

I didn't notice when it started to change, only that one day I didn't feel the same. I went through a period of feeling listless, depressed. Eventually one of the others took me to one side and explained the score.

Was it a surprise? Well, yes. Though... maybe I'd had some inkling. I'd known there was something missing, some point to life I hadn't been able to find. But everyone feels like that, don't they, from time to time?

Everything was basically fine. Everything was sort of okay, though I couldn't seem to find the place I was meant to be. I knew people, counted some as friends, but they didn't feel as if they were the ones I'd been waiting for. I did things, and I had a life, of a kind. It just didn't feel like what I'd had in mind.

Time passed, years went by, but I never got the sense that I was getting closer to anything that I recognized from the dreams of the future that I'd once cherished. Assuming they were dreams and not memories.

Now I know what I am, but I cannot get it to sit right. I cannot accept this is all there is, all I can ever be. I was loved once — can it *never* be that way again? Can't things go back to the way they were, when we meant more to each other than anything in the world?

I guess not. It's never happened before that anyone knows of. That doesn't stop some from trying, of course. Rapping on windows. Living in their friend's house. Hiding their keys. Constantly on their shoulder, always a few steps behind. I heard recently that one of us has made real contact with his friend, even spoken to him. The guy's called Maj, and I counted him as a friend before I stopped caring much about that kind of thing. I still see him around. Maj is a very forceful person, though, one of the most accomplished Fingermen. He's got solidity and heft. If he can't pull the thing off, I doubt any of us can. Certainly not me. My heft was never strong, and I can feel it deserting me. Every morning I look at my hands. Each day they look less substantial.

Sometimes I can smell the odor of hospitals and hear the whisper of people shuffling down corridors in thin, papery gowns they will never take off.

I'm not sure I've got it in me to fight.

At night I stand in the street outside the house where I think I'm supposed to live. I recognize everything about it — the shape of the front and the color of the bricks, the arrangement of the lintels and the roof, the positions of the trees outside on the street. I know how it looks inside, too, though the glimpses I sometimes get through the windows suggest either that I'm not remembering it correctly or parts of it have changed — different color curtains, different color walls.

Several times it's gotten to be too much and I've walked up the steps to the door, four stone steps I remember running down so many times as a child — or think I do — and try to knock or ring the bell. Nobody ever comes, and the door never opens. I can touch things, but I can move almost nothing, so perhaps that's the problem. Maybe they just don't hear. I hope that's the answer. It's better than thinking that they hear but choose not to open the door, choose not to allow me to come home.

That's why I try to find somewhere different to spend each night. In the hope that when I wake in the morning, everything will be different, that I might even find myself in a bed in that house, in a life that makes sense. Lately I have begun to dream of that less, however, and find it harder to believe.

*   *   *

Lately I have also found myself looking at graveyards and thinking of cellars. There's one I know, under the control of a man who doesn't understand the world as well as he thinks. A number of us already nod there. I've started to wonder if perhaps it would be comfortable to go down into it and sit with my own back to the wall.

To go in there and never come back out.

Chapter 19

David stepped off the train at the exact time he and Dawn had arrived the previous Friday. He'd climbed on the first available service from Libertyville — the nearest town to home with a train station — and hadn't even realized it was the same one until he saw the clock at Penn Station. This made him feel very guilty, even guiltier than he'd felt throughout the journey and in the shower and ever since the idea had first dropped into his head as the two of them sat eating cereal together.

But that was dumb, right? He was a grown-up. He was allowed to leave the house, and the town.

He set off for the escalator — still feeling guilty, and confused, and more than a little scared.

He'd waited until Dawn had left for school and then written a note explaining that the novel idea he'd been nurturing had given unexpected birth in the night, presenting him with a litter of sub-ideas and plotlings that he needed to bottle feed with fact. One of these story lines was going to unfold in New York. He needed to check out some locations, and sure, he could fire up Google Maps and get Street View on it, but he thought it might be cool to go check in person, soaking up the atmosphere and letting the city do some of the work. He hoped that was okay.

This last sentence, seeking permission, disappeared in the second draft. He didn't need her to say it was okay. This was the kind of thing writers did.

It went back for the third draft. It made him feel better. As he stood in the kitchen giving the note a final read, marveling at the unusual neatness of his handwriting, he was relieved to see the contents came across as credible and plausible and not-at-all-crazy.

Even if they weren't. He wasn't going to New York to research. He was going because...He didn't know why he was going. He was just going. And if he was going then he might as well go, instead of standing in the kitchen dicking around redrafting an excuse that wouldn't be found until after he was gone, or perhaps even back home.

He left the note in the center of the kitchen table — the one that, long ago, had graced the big kitchen in Grandpa's house, one of the handful of possessions he'd shipped to Rockbridge when he'd moved. It was a big, sturdy piece of furniture and (propped against a bowl full of wholesome red apples, and with a smiley at the bottom) the note looked like the most reasonable thing in the world.

He was careful not to look under the table, however.

It was colder than the last time. Overcast and windy, too, far more like he remembered it from his period living in the city, a time that included the tail end of winter and during which he'd been colder than ever before or since. The weather — and being by himself — made the streets feel more familiar, like a stranger in the street turning to resolve into an old acquaintance. New York was a place he associated with being alone.

He went into the first Starbucks he came across. While in line he texted Dawn, deciding to let her know he'd come to the city right away rather than waiting for her to find the note. The text was upbeat.

There was no immediate reply, which didn't surprise him — she'd be in class, knowing she now carried inside her the genesis of one of the little beings that sat around her. Remembering this gave David the same pang of bewildered hope and fear, and more than anything else he believed this was why he was here. There was something that needed to be put right, even if he was not sure what it was. There was unfinished business.

When he got to the counter, the barista did not know what he wanted before he asked for it and betrayed no obvious sign of caring about his day. David missed Talia for a moment, and realized he was actually looking forward to getting back to reading her book.

For want of any other plan, he walked the coffee up to Bryant Park, where he sat on a bench and stared across toward the library and the terrace where he and Dawn had taken celebratory glasses of wine. He recalled that for the second half of the nineteenth century, this site held the Croton Distributing Reservoir, a block-sized behemoth with fifty-foot walls for storing water transported down from Westchester County by aqueduct in an attempt to stop the citizens dying of cholera and yellow fever quite so enthusiastically. It was now impossible to imagine. But it was hard to remember being twenty, too, to imagine himself in the head and life of that former person, to recall who he'd been when he'd sat in this park then. Do we grow older by dint of additions and remodeling, or through knocking ourselves down to the foundations and rebuilding from the ground up? David supposed it was meant to be the former, but the latter had more of a ring of truth.

He left the park and headed east along 42nd. Two minutes later a text came in, Dawn bubbling with enthusiasm and telling him to take his time and she'd look forward to hearing about his adventures when he got home.

He kept walking east for a further few blocks and then turned to head downtown. The sky grew gray as he trudged, the wind more persistent. He tried — for whose benefit he wasn't sure — to maintain the pretense that he was here for research, peering meaningfully at the buildings and people he passed.

He walked for hours, crisscrossing back and forth as if searching for something he couldn't recall. Until eventually he arrived at the top of Union Square — and found himself slowing down.

Union Square runs from 17th down to 14th between Park and Broadway — the only major street that ignores the grid and carves on the diagonal, turning the park into a wedge. It's a block wide, the top four-fifths arranged in areas of grass and trees with a kids' playground way at the top right, half hidden behind high bushes. Tree-shaded paths paved with hexagonal bricks wander through all this, the grassy areas easily accessible on the other side of low metal fences. The bottom of the square is a major downtown pedestrian thoroughfare.

David wandered down the central path. It was almost three o'clock by then. People perched on benches, talking on the phone, meditatively working through late sandwiches. He remembered the park well. He must have crossed it a hundred times on the way to the Strand Book Store, where he'd picked up most of his secondhand reading when he'd lived there, selling the books frugally back again afterward. This afternoon something about the place felt off. Had they changed it? Altered the layout? He wasn't sure. It *looked* the same, but his memory had started to feel like a jigsaw where he had all the pieces around the outside and nothing in the middle at all.

Traffic coursed noisily back and forth across 14th. A pair of Japanese women wandered by, cheerfully consulting a city guide. A handful of business types strode past, deep in conversation, pant legs flapping in the wind.

David slowly got the feeling he was being watched, or at least observed. He turned to see a man standing in the center of the area. He looked about forty, with ginger hair, wearing the upper and lower halves of two quite different gray suits. The shades did not match and neither did the styles. The pants were too loose, the jacket too tight. He was watching David with an odd expression. Part cautious. Part curious.

David looked away, and then back. The man was still watching him. Everybody else was in transit, a mutating, rotating backdrop of water-color hues. They were the only two people who were motionless.

Finally the man strolled over to David.

"What's your name, then?"

He spoke in a low tone. His accent was distinctive, with a strong hint of London Cockney. Too surprised to come up with an evasive response, David told him.

"Nice." The man nodded. "David. Good name. A *proper* name." He winked. "But then it would be, wouldn't it?"

"What . . . what do you mean?"

"I know what you are, David."

The back of David's neck felt hot. "You do?"

"I do. And . . . welcome, *welcome*. You want to be back up there in the trees, though, really."

"Why?"

"Well, who are you here for?"

"Here . . . for?"

"His *name*, David. I'm assuming it's a 'he,' anyway. Usually is with guys. Not always, though. *Could* be a 'she.' Could be a kangaroo, for all I know, right?"

David stared at him.

"So. *Is* it a he?" The man had an unusual odor, like the memory of cotton candy on a fall afternoon. He was leaning forward expectantly, conspiratorially, eager to help. David felt as if he'd wandered into some dark club and been greeted as a regular by a doorman he'd never seen before.

"I . . . don't know what you're talking about."

The man winked. "Fair enough, mate. Understood. I'll bugger off and leave you to it. Good luck, eh?"

He held up both hands, fingers crossed, and walked away, glancing around as if already on some other mission entirely. He curved around a group of Europeans wearing bright anoraks and seemed to fail to come back out the other side — presumably having crossed the road.

David felt scared now. Plain, downright scared, deep in his guts, seized with the certainty that whatever impulse had brought him to this place was faulty, and this wasn't somewhere that he should be. It was as if he'd come to a park and found himself standing up to his neck in a reservoir of dark water instead.

It was only then that he realized that the park, if seen from above, probably looked rather like a shape he had seen etched out in the gravel of the parking lot of Kendricks. That realization made being there feel wronger still. As if he had followed instructions that he hadn't even realized he'd been given.

It was half past three. If he was intending to walk back to the station, he ought to be setting off. Or maybe he should get a cab. But...he thought he should be leaving, either way. Leaving felt like a good plan. Getting on a train. He could be home in time for dinner.

Just...*be home.*

He was halfway back up the central path when he heard an intake of breath and glanced to the right to see a homeless man sitting on a bench. His skin was nicotine brown, thin black hair plastered across a mottled scalp, tatters of an old suit swaddled around a skeletal frame. He was glaring past David into one of the grassy areas. He screwed up his face and flapped his hands spastically, as if to ward something away from his face.

"No, not again. Fuck off, fuck off, fuck *off.*"

David turned to see what he was looking at and realized the park was full of people now.

Many seemed to be on their way somewhere, striding along the paths. They flowed on either side of David, eyes ahead, as though he were a rock in a fast-moving stream.

Others were gathered in knots on the grassy areas, apparently in conference, but even these were not static. Each person within these groups was constantly on the move, walking in small circles, or in slow, weaving patterns among one another that left the basic shape of the groups intact. They were dressed in just about any outfit you could imagine, from a teenage girl in a gray hoodie to a plump woman of about fifty wearing a strapless ball gown in dark blue. There must have been two, maybe three hundred of them. There were animals, too. A few large dogs, a bright orange cat, and... for a bizarre moment, David even thought he saw a bear. Then they weren't there anymore.

None of them. The park was empty again.

David turned to the man on the bench. He smiled, revealing a mouth with hardly any teeth in it.

"You saw them?"

"I saw *something,*" David whispered, looking around, skin crawling. Everything was as it had been two minutes before. The paths and grassy spaces were empty but for fallen leaves. He spotted the two Japanese women he'd noticed earlier, sitting together on one of the benches now, consulting their guidebook and laughing.

"Where... where *did they all go?*"

"Nowhere," the man on the bench said. "I don't ever see them anywhere but here." He stood, gathering his plastic bags. "But *I'm* leaving. You should too. They don't like it if you can see them. I got bitten once."

He walked away up the path.

David stood his ground, knowing now what he'd been feeling ever since he'd first come into the park. There was a disparity between the way it looked and the way it really was. It was... too *full.*

On impulse, he stretched both arms out to the side. The women on the bench looked at him strangely, but that wasn't the only effect. Something backed off a little, as if he'd become a bigger rock in a hidden stream.

He put his arms back down and hurried up toward the children's playground. At the heart of this was a castle-like construction with wooden walkways and turquoise turrets, planks and rope bridges connecting the different sections. Only the under-tens were allowed on this, a sign clearly stated, but there were adults on it now. Perhaps thirty of them. In pairs and threes and fours. Most of them dressed in black or rich colors, drapey, goth-style clothing that looked cobbled together from remnants. They were all moving, constantly. Back and forth, around and about. David got glimpses of pale faces in conversation, but most of the time it was as if you could see them only from behind.

If they were here, then...

He turned and trotted back to the center of the park. Yes — they were back here, too.

David ran toward the largest grassy area, off center in the park, sixty feet around with a fountain off to one side. He could barely see it now for the mass of people. There were no children — and only a handful under eighteen — but otherwise every age group was represented. Old, middle-aged, with a big peak in early to mid-twenties. Black, white, Asian. Most in casual clothes, a few in suits. Again, the thing that looked like a bear but surely had to be a man in a costume.

And then — they were gone again.

Except...they weren't. David couldn't see them, but he could *feel* them. There were people here in the park, people he couldn't see. There was no doubting that.

Unless I'm losing my mind.

The two Japanese women had gone back to giggling over what had to be the funniest NYC guidebook ever. A muscular guy walked past with a pair of very tiny dogs. Two men sat on a bench, both on the phone, presumably not to each other. All of these people seemed too far apart, like a scattered handful of books on a shelf.

"Hello, David," said a voice.

He turned to see a man in battered jeans and untucked shirt, the one he'd last seen in Kendricks. The man was grinning, and this time it seemed more sincere and less threatening. Behind him stood a slim woman in a long black coat. She was smiling too.

The man took a step forward and put out his hand. "Welcome back," he said.

Chapter 20

"This what you had in mind?"

I looked up from a sidewalk table outside the Adriatico. Kristina stood outside the fence dressed more or less as I'd suggested: raggedy black jeans and sweater under a cheap coat, hair pulled back in a ponytail, the whole outfit topped with a pair of sunglasses nondescript enough not to look like obfuscation.

"Perfect," I said.

"For what?"

"Thinking of entering you in this 'Hottest New York Bag Lady' pageant everyone's talking about."

"Careful," she said. "We may not be back at the openly-mocking-each-other stage just yet."

"Yeah, we are," I said, coming around to kiss her on the cheek. "It was a dumb argument and I've said I'm sorry. That's the end of it."

"I see, master. So — what's the plan?"

Something had been nagging at me since I'd gotten up that morning. It nagged as I walked to work. It nagged when I took a break to go thank the heater guys for fixing our unit, watching their faces while I did so and seeing nothing untoward. It nagged as I stood chain-drinking strong coffees and pushing pizza to passersby, and even while being patient with Mario's sister, who'd picked up on the coldness between Kristina and me the night before and was taking an excessively maternal interest.

The nagging didn't amount to much more than the idea that there was something I was missing, dots I was not joining up. Which was no help.

But finally, halfway through selling someone two slices of pepperoni, I'd realized what the connecting line might be.

"We're going for a walk," I said.

The message on our window could have been put there at any time in the last however many years, some previous tenant's thigh-slapping attempt to freak out a roommate that we'd never noticed simply because the lighting conditions hadn't been right and it hadn't ever occurred to us to clean the windows. I didn't believe that, though. Neither did Kristina. Together with the overturned chair and the broken ashtray out on the apartment roof, it didn't ring true — never mind the sensation I'd experienced when I opened the window, of someone (or perhaps more than one person) in sudden movement.

The message had been put there recently. It had to have been sometime after the last time I'd been out in my rooftop aerie to smoke, which was only the night before and so kept the timeframe tight.

"Face it," Kristina said. Her pupils looked big and pale, green edging out the gray for once. "You know this just happened. *Tonight.*"

Against Kristina's wishes I reopened the window (after taking a picture of the message on my phone) and climbed out. It was dark and the wind was strong and it felt like being on the battlements of a tottering castle tower. I confirmed what I'd suspected. If you were light and nimble — not to mention insanely reckless — you could probably access the scrap of flat roof from over the rooftops. By leaning against the nearest of these and standing on tiptoe, I got a glimpse over to the next building. Presumably if you kept going then somewhere there'd be a means of dropping into a gap and ultimately down to ground level. The tiles were wet and mossy and I wasn't going to get any more intrepid about the investigation than that, certainly not in the dark.

I climbed back in. "There's another possibility," Kris said.

"Yeah, I know. Our window wasn't locked. They could have got out there from our apartment. But that raises too many questions. Like how they'd have gotten in *here*."

"Heater guys were here day before yesterday. They took forever and I had to leave for work, so I gave them a key to lock up. They shoved it back under the door, but I guess they could have made a copy and—"

"Nope. If Dack or Jez had tried to scrabble away over that roof, we'd be listening to the sound of ambulances right now and there'd be blood-drenched dents in the sidewalk the size of two small cows."

"They could have done it while they were here. We wouldn't have noticed until now."

"But why? We pay them money and they drink in your bar and neither of them has a sense of humor that I've ever noticed."

"So who did it?"

"You know who it's got to be. What I don't understand is why it says 'us.'"

Kristina and I live a small, contained life. We hadn't made any enemies in the city—one tries not to—or many acquaintances outside the restaurant and staff from others nearby. We'd barely seen the other people in our building. They had normal jobs and lived different hours. "Maybe it *was* a guy you saw the other night after all," Kristina mused. "In the market, and afterward. Maybe there's more than one person following Catherine."

"That would help, sure. But in that case, who are we dealing with?"

"You got me. The question is whether *Catherine* knows."

I thought about it. "I don't think so. If you're a woman being followed, you'll assume it's a man. She looked genuinely surprised when we told her we'd seen a girl. And I'm sure that was the same person as the one I saw the other night. The height and clothing were exactly the same. I just didn't see a face then and so I made the same wrong assumption that Catherine had."

Kristina nodded. "Okay. But here's the thing. A person or persons unknown evidently not only realizes we've been tracking them, but also knows *where we live*. Either someone followed you back the other night . . ."

". . . or he/she/they were outside Catherine's tonight and followed us back to the restaurant."

"Which would not have been hard. Raised voices were involved."

"I recall. But what — then they kicked their heels for a few hours before following one of us back here?"

"This is a *stalker*, John. That shit's what they do."

She had a point. I thought back over my solo walk home. I hadn't been aware of anyone following me, but I'd been in an irritable frame of mind and the incident with Lydia had deflected my attention too. Nonetheless, I believed I would have noticed someone trailing me. That meant if they'd done it tonight they must have waited and followed Kristina as she walked home later. It wasn't far, and I knew Kris was capable of looking after herself — otherwise I'd never have considered letting her walk it alone, regardless of how bad a fight we'd had.

But still.

I locked the window and we went back to bed. I don't know who went to sleep first, but we were both awake, listening for sounds on the roof, for quite some time.

We walked quickly over to Chelsea, retracing in reverse our steps from Catherine's the night before. It was a nicer walk this time — except for being cold and cloudy — but there was no denying we were tense.

"I realized something," I explained as we hurried west along 14th. "The two occasions on which I or we saw someone started in totally different locations — the Westside Market and outside the girls' school — and at different times on different days of the week. It may have been the same person, it may not. But there's a constant I should have noticed right away."

"The way they were dressed?"

"Yeah, well, that too—but that's not notable if it's the same individual both times. I'm talking about the fact that I lost her/him/them in the same place. Somewhere along 16th."

Kristina frowned. "That's not much."

"It's all we've got," I said. "And this is now our problem, not Catherine's. Someone was outside our window last night. I want something done about that."

We arrived on 16th Street without a plan. We walked along the north side and back on the south. Houses. Cars. The church. Trees. All in midafternoon mode with no one around. We stood halfway along the street for ten minutes. A car holding a woman and a child drove down the road and out the other end. Kristina was getting cold and cranky.

"If I pass out with all the excitement, leave me where I fall."

"You were the one talking about setting up a detective agency. When I was a lawyer I dealt with private investigators, and this is how their lives are. You go somewhere and wait. For hours."

"So their life sucks. But this is a nice street, John. We loiter here, someone's going to call the cops."

"You got a better idea?"

"Going home. Going for a beer. Going to Hawaii. Pretty much any sentence showcasing verbs of movement in a nonmetaphoric sense."

I heard the sound of a door opening and turned, looking as bland as possible in case it was an eagle-eyed local making sure we weren't casing out their house. Thirty yards up the other side of the street, the door on the right-hand side of the church was now open. The man I'd seen the previous afternoon stood in it, talking to someone inside.

"It's the priest," I said. Kristina was frank about not finding this an arresting development.

After a moment the man closed the door and trotted down the stairs. He let himself out the gate and closed it before setting off at a brisk pace.

I gestured to Kristina.

"What — we're going to *follow* the guy?"

"No," I said. "You are."

"Say again?"

"I spoke to him yesterday. He'll recognize me. You're going let me know where he goes."

"John, he's a fucking *priest.*"

"He was here when we lost that girl."

She started walking reluctantly. "What are *you* going to do?"

"I'm not sure yet."

She rolled her eyes but got on it, scooting up the street after the priest's disappearing back.

I walked back to take a look at the church. The central portion was three stories high, the width of two of the houses that lined the rest of the street. The ground level held a row of small windows with darkness beyond, suggesting that they fronted office space or storage. The two stories above had bigger glass, though they still looked to have been designed with little more than a protractor and ruler and as if to withstand impact rather than to inspire spiritual fervor. On either side stood a staircase leading up to a wooden door at the left and right extremes of the second level. All of it looked dusty and city-grimed and weightily functional.

I let myself in through the gate and walked up the steps on the right. I knocked on the door, which was heavy and large and made of wood. Nothing happened, so I knocked again, this time using the brass knocker.

After a minute I turned the handle and pushed. The door swung open to reveal a short, tidy corridor with a wooden floor and white walls and an area on the left designed to hold coats. At the far end was another door.

"Hello?"

I stepped inside. I called hello once more, then opened the second door. I wandered into a big room that tapered upward toward a pointed roof with exposed beams. The walls were paneled too, somber paintings dotted here and there. It was dark and gloomy and gothic without anything in the way of richness, the domain of a faith that didn't pander to its audience by adding unnecessary pizzazz. Rows of battered chairs sat facing a single one, which faced back the other way. Behind this was a plain altar, surmounted by a simple metal cross. An unloved-looking upright piano stood to the side.

Turning, I was confronted with the street-side wall. There was a notice board with sheets of paper thumbtacked to it. Three big Palladian windows and five smaller ones above. The glass in each was a different shade of muted—blue, green, pale red, pale purple. Each had been protected from street-side vandalism by close-fitting sheets of chicken wire. As a spectacle of light it would not make you want to glorify anybody's name unless you'd already been of a mind to do so.

My phone rang. It was Kris. "Where are you?"

"Heading back along 15th. He went into a deli. Came out with a bottle of water. Do you think that's significant? Should I get a picture with my spycam?"

"Kris..."

"Okay, okay."

She hung up. I wandered out into the middle of the room along the aisle between the two groups of chairs. I noticed a plain, narrow door at the end, behind the altar and painted the same color as the wall. It seemed likely that it led to the lower level. I considered finding out but decided that would be taking this too far, especially as there was presumably somebody still in the building. Also...I have no strong views for or against organized religions, but their structures possess a certain psychic weight. If you're alone in a church they can make you feel you shouldn't be. Church doors are often left open, but that's for the faithful to come in and do their thing. I was not faithful and I wasn't here in the hope of finding God or even myself. I'd seen—or thought I'd seen—the priest stopping to exchange words with someone on his way out. That person must still be here. If they appeared and asked my business, I didn't have an answer.

As I was bringing my phone up to call Kris off the chase, it rang again in my hand. "Okay," I said. "You're right. This is a waste of—"

"Get over here," Kris said. "Union Square."

"Why?"

It sounded like she was running. "Just come, John. *Now*."

Chapter 21

Kris hadn't given me anywhere specific to head for and so I dropped south a couple blocks to hit Union Square at the most obvious entry point, the paved area at 14th.

There was no sign of her when I ran across the street. I called her phone. She picked up right away but didn't give me a chance to speak. "Where are you?"

"The bottom," I said, out of breath. "Where are you? You okay?"

"Look around."

I turned in a slow, winded circle. "I don't see the priest, if that's what you mean. Or you."

"Okay. Wait there."

A minute later Kristina came walking quickly toward me along the central path. "You scared me," I said.

She smiled distractedly. "I'm fine. Just...come with me."

She led me up the path into the heart of the park. When we got to where the two main crossways intersected, she stopped. "Stand here," she said. "And be still."

She glanced around and then back up at me. "Are you getting it?"

A father and small child, toddling past, in no hurry and going nowhere in particular. In the distance, a small group of what looked like students in a loose huddle, talking and laughing. Over on a bench, a couple of men in business suits. There was more than this, however. It reminded me of what I'd just experienced in the church. A sense of residue, of spaces not being voids. Two Japanese women ambled in our direction consulting a guide-book. A jogger appeared from nowhere and flashed past, leaving a waft of hot skin and self-satisfaction that seemed to linger longer than it should. I was aware of the sound of traffic and the rustle of distant chatter, but it sounded far away, as if there was something between me and it.

"I'm getting *something*. I have no idea what."

"I lost the priest on the other side of Broadway," Kristina said. "I came to check just in case, and..."

I nodded, not wanting to dispel the atmosphere.

"Try over here," she said, gesturing up the path. "That's where I felt it first."

I followed, knowing there was a conflict between what my senses were telling me, but not knowing which to trust.

"Look," Kristina hissed suddenly. She was pointing at one of the grassy areas, a forty-yard stretch near Park Avenue.

The priest was close to one end. He was standing talking to a woman—a woman who looked a *lot* like the one we'd lost after following Catherine home from school.

"That's *her*," Kristina whispered. "Christ—you were right. That's the woman, isn't it?"

"Could be. Try to get closer."

She walked quickly up the path. I tried to keep myself out of the priest's line of sight while drifting in the same direction.

A moment later Kristina slipped her hand out of her coat pocket and made a fist with her thumb sticking up, down by her side, which I took to mean that it was indeed the same woman. What did that mean? And why was she here now, talking to a priest in a park?

When Kristina got to the next junction she slowed, waiting for me to catch up. "It's definitely her," she said. I took a good look at the woman and saw she was tall, with dark hair. A pitch-black coat with a high collar, edged at the sleeves and hem with black lace. In good light it looked a little threadbare. Underneath it she was wearing a dress made of muted red velvet, trimmed with cream around the neckline.

Two other people were standing just beyond. One was standing, at least — a nondescript man of about thirty, with brown hair. He was in conversation with another who was wearing jeans and a white shirt, and who was moving around in a kind of slow circle. Despite the fact that the second man was the taller and better-looking of the two, there was something more *present* about the first guy.

I glanced toward the priest and realized the same was true there. He was a man in early middle age, blandly decent-looking. The woman talking to him was slim and very attractive. Yet your eye tended to settle on *him* and stay there. I tried to look at the girl, and it happened again — my gaze slipped back toward the priest.

Then they were no longer talking, but walking rapidly in opposite directions.

"Shit," Kristina said. "Now what?"

"Follow her."

She peeled off and strode up the central path. I was about to head after the priest but realized I knew where he'd be going, or at least where he could be found. So I stopped and looked back up through the park.

I saw nothing but trees and grass.

I was still there when my phone rang.

"I lost her."

"Already?"

"Right away. I'm sorry, John. Either I'm crap at this or that girl really knows how to lose people."

"You think she knew you were on her tail?"

"I don't see how. You still on the priest?"

"No. I'm in the park."

"Why?"

"I don't know."

We met where the two main paths crossed and sat on a bench. We waited half an hour but didn't see anything, and soon I stopped expecting to. It just felt like a park once more, and a cold and increasingly dark one at that.

"We'd better head back," Kristina said. "I need to be at work in an hour. So do you."

"Yeah," I said, though I'd already started to think that I'd be spending some of the favors I'd earned through handling Paulo's pizza shifts, and taking the evening off, in order to try to talk to someone.

Just before we crossed 14th to head down toward the East Village and the evening's work, we turned together and looked back at Union Square.

We still saw nothing.

Chapter 22

When David tried to think back over what happened in Union Square he got only fragments. He remembered turning to see Maj. He remembered a beautiful girl in a black coat standing to one side and taking a friendly interest before returning to an intense conversation with another man, who was wearing a brown suit.

"It's *not* Reinhart," she said to him. "It's somebody else."

"Just consider staying at the church," Brown Suit was saying. "For a couple of days, that's all."

She smiled, but it was obvious that meant "no."

There were others, too, including a listless man called Billy, all taking part in some kind of informal gathering or catch-up. Maj appeared torn between wanting to talk to David and having business with the girl and the man in the brown suit — and David overheard enough to gather that it was this that had sent Maj hurrying to the phone in Kendricks and brought him back to the city after that. They were talking fast and urgently. Billy stood off to one side throughout this. He looked ill.

In the back of David's mind a voice kept telling him he ought to be getting to the train station. That voice, the voice that always told him *not* to do things, to be careful, to stay safe, was taking up perhaps ten percent of his mental bandwidth. Thirty percent was insidiously suggesting the opposite.

All the rest was a cloud.

Sometimes he thought he could hear a hubbub of conversation, but it sounded like a combination of traffic around the square and the distant roar of a jet passing high overhead, and so it was possible that's all it was.

If you blinked, everything came into focus. A New York park on a cold afternoon. If you let your attention wander...it became something else. David hadn't spent much time stoned—experiencing his parents out on the deck staring owlishly at him before breaking into high-pitched laughter had been enough to put him off the idea—but it's hard to grow up in semi-rural America and avoid drugs altogether. From his single experience with MDMA he remembered this sensation of being untethered, watching reality peeling off to stand to the side and of being unsure of whether it was you who'd taken this step, or the world—and what it would take to marry you again.

He observed groups of the circulating people, in conversation—some serious, some joking. Individuals and twos and threes walking up and down the thoroughfares. A very large dog came and stood and looked up at him as if waiting for him to say something. The dog appeared to be on his own, without an owner, and after a few moments trotted off. All of this was silent, as if seen through thick and grubby glass—but once in a while there'd be a bubble of noise, like opening the door to a room that held a party to which you hadn't been invited. Similarly, David stood there as if invisible most of the time, but once in a while someone would turn their head to look at him curiously, before turning away again.

Then he was down at the bottom end of the square once more, his head clear, as if jolted out of a daydream. Two women were walking toward him from the pedestrian crossing. He felt a panicky urge to step out of their way. They seemed too big. Not tall, or fat, just too *present*. One glared at him as they passed, as if to forestall him bothering them. He heard the other sniff, and saw rings of red around her nostrils.

Two normal women, one with a cold, but he felt disconcerted and frightened. Was *that* all this was? Some kind of panic attack? Was he seeing normal people, but just responding to them in the wrong way?

He realized belatedly that someone else was looking at him. About forty feet away, on the other side of Broadway, a man wearing a fedora and a dark suit with wide lapels. He was standing with his hands in his pants pockets, staring at David.

His face was hard and unfriendly.

"Let's go," said a voice from behind.

It was Maj, alone now. The other man and the girl had disappeared. David glanced back toward where he'd seen the man in the hat, but he was no longer there either, and all the other people in the park had gone.

"*What just happened?* Who were all those people?"

"Come with me."

"Why . . . would I do that?"

"You came to the city for answers, yes? You're not going to get any standing by yourself in a park."

Maj started walking. David followed. The other man crossed 14th, striding along busy patches of sidewalk, avoiding oncoming pedestrians without ever dropping pace. After ten minutes he finally slowed, somewhere south of the Village, but kept switching in and out of backstreets before popping out opposite a high wall made of stained red brick. To the left was a metal fence, and beyond it David saw a church. It took a moment for his memory to serve up the name — old St. Patrick's Church.

Maj stopped outside. "I want to introduce you to some friends," he said. "But something happened while I was out of town. We've got outsiders taking too much interest. I need to try to talk to someone, get his advice. You can't come with me. He won't talk if you're there. He probably won't anyhow."

"Why?"

"I won't be long. Half an hour. I'll meet you at Bid's. You remember that, at least?"

David didn't, or at least hadn't thought of the place in years, but then there it was — back in his head. A basement bar not far from where they now stood.

"Get a table in back if you can. In the meantime, there's something you should do."

"What?"

"Call your wife," Maj said, and walked away.

It took David ten minutes to get an approach straight in his head. Then he stood on a corner and called her.

"Plus amazingly I ran into someone," he said, low-key, after he'd told her everything he'd done—up to but *not* including whatever he'd just experienced in Union Square. "From when I lived here."

"Would this be a man someone . . . or a lady someone?"

"Man, of course," David said quickly.

"I'm joking," Dawn said, though she sounded a little relieved. "So who is he? I don't remember you mentioning anybody in particular from back then."

"His name . . . he's called Maj."

"Weird name."

"He's . . . kind of a weird guy."

"Do you want to stay there tonight and hang out?"

"Would that be okay?"

"Of course, silly. If you're going to set a book there, this has to be a good thing, right? He should be able to help. With current stuff, atmosphere, what it's like living there now. It's been a while since you were in the city properly, after all."

"Exactly," David said.

"Where would you stay?"

"I don't know. Maybe with him. Crash on a couch or something." There was silence down the line. "What?"

"I wasn't going to tell you," she said, in a bubbling rush. "I wanted you to find it when you got home. But there's a letter for you from Ralph's office. Plus . . . I checked our account. Your advance came through."

David felt exhausted. "Oh, thank God."

"So if you wanted to stay in a hotel or something, it's okay. Nowhere too fancy, though — save that for when we're there together."

"I will," he said, laughing, feeling relief wash over him — mingling with guilt he felt for not being honest with her. "What will you do?"

"I'll muddle through somehow. I'm..." She hesitated. "Maybe it's wrong. But I thought I might start sorting through the spare room."

For a moment David didn't get what she meant — he couldn't imagine what would impel her to tackle the room on the second floor where all the homeless junk in their lives got thrown — but then he did.

"Go for it," he said, momentarily nowhere else in the world except on this phone call, with this woman.

"You don't think it's too early?"

"I think it's a great idea."

"And it won't... you know."

He knew what she meant. That starting to prepare the room for a nursery would anger the gods, causing them to reach down to stir darkness back into their lives.

"No," he said firmly. "We walked a long way down Superstition Road the other times and it didn't help at all. Good things need welcoming too, and that's what we're going to do this time."

"I love you," she said.

"I love you too."

"So go hang out. But get home early tomorrow. Remember what we're doing."

"What?"

"The scan," she said. "I told you."

"I knew that."

"Hmm."

"Be careful, okay? Don't move anything big. Wait until I get back."

"I'll be fine. I'm only a bit pregnant."

"That's like being a bit unique."

"Pedant. Buzz off and have fun. But not too much."

David lowered the phone from his ear, feeling a pang of regret for not being home, for not being able to hug his wife at the moment they'd discovered he'd been paid. He resolved that nothing like this should ever happen again, making it all the more important that he got to the bottom of what was happening right now, and end it.

It took him another five minutes to get to Bid's, down a side street not far from Bleecker. His feet remembered the way even if he didn't. He hesitated on the sidewalk. The door at the bottom of the steps was open and you could smell decades of stale beer from where he stood. He hadn't yet discounted the idea that this was a complicated con and/or set-up—and if so, that getting further into it was a very dumb idea. Right now, a voice was telling him, he could just split. There was no one here to stop him. He could get the hell out and just go home.

That was his rational mind, however.

Another part knew, though it didn't understand, that something else was going on, that even if he didn't remember Maj, he somehow knew him—and that things do not go away simply because you turn your back or run away, and that at least this was a public place.

It was this part that took him down the stairs and into the past.

Chapter 23

The bar was low-ceilinged and narrow and would have felt cramped even if there hadn't been a lot of people already filling it, drinking hard. When David reached the bottom of stairs he was hit with a wave of recollection. He'd stood on this spot a number of times, looking out for someone — usually one of the aspiring artists/writers/whatevers he'd struck up acquaintance with while he lived there, and had never heard from since. The sensation wasn't one of simple nostalgia, however: he also knew that on some of those occasions he'd been feeling much as he was now — trepidation, a sense of duty he didn't want to fulfill. He took faltering steps into the mass of people milling around, propping up the bar, lurking at the few tables at the edges. Bid's made even less effort to be welcoming than Kendricks — took a typically New York pride in this, in fact — and evidently remained the lair of hard-core locals and hipsters.

Finally he saw someone he recognized, a face at the far end of the room. It wasn't Maj, however. It was the man in the ill-fitting suit who'd spoken to David when he first reached Union Square Park.

The man rolled his eyes as if glad to have finally gotten his attention, and beckoned with a small upward nod. When David didn't respond immediately, he gestured him to come over, more urgently. Not knowing what else to do, David started to shoulder his way through the drinkers.

When he got to the other side he saw the man was standing diffidently beside a small table with three stools around it. "Sit down," he said.

"Why?"

"Just do it, mate, eh? Quickly."

His manner was deferential but insistent. David sat. The man immediately followed suit, selecting the stool on the opposite side of the table, so that David was facing the wall when he looked at him.

"Why did you wait for me to sit down?"

"Don't move your mouth so much when you talk, eh?"

"Why?"

"Because you'll look like a knob."

"I don't ... know you, do I?"

"Nah. Didn't know Maj back then, did I? The name's Bob. Fictitious Bob, if you want to be formal."

"What can I get you?"

David looked up to see a straggle-haired girl standing over him with the air of a person for whom this encounter had gotten old and too dull for words before she'd even opened her mouth. "Huh?"

"To *drink.*"

David ordered the first beer that came into his head and watched, baffled, as the girl barged off through the crowd. Bid's had been celebrated for the bad-temperedness of its staff, he remembered. He turned to Bob.

"Why didn't she ask you what *you* wanted?"

Bob shook his head as if every question David asked wrote the word "buffoon" in bigger letters on his forehead.

At that moment Maj appeared out of the crowd and sat straight down at the remaining place. He glanced around as if taking the measure of the room, and moved the stool to be closer to Bob. He looked preoccupied.

"Got your work cut out here, Maj," Bob said, nodding toward David. "Makes your average Dozeno sound like Lonely Clive."

"Being here didn't help? You still don't remember anything?" Maj asked David, exasperated. "I was hoping the fact that you'd come to the city meant something. And we used to meet here often. Before you stopped."

"I ... had a dream last night." David hesitated, looking at Bob.

"He's a friend," Maj said. "And a Cornerman. You don't get any more discreet than that."

Bob nodded with what appeared to be pride.

"What's a Cornerman?"

Bob glanced at Maj as if warning him not to respond, but Maj overrode him. "The closest we've got to newspapers, cell phones, and e-mail. What was the dream about, David? Quickly. It's too crowded here tonight. You won't be able to hold this table long."

"Why?"

"David, seriously. The dream."

"I was in my parents' house," David said, feeling like a kid at school being railroaded into something by older boys who seemed to understand everything he did not. "I couldn't stand their fighting, but I couldn't get away. So I went under the kitchen table."

David had Maj's full attention now, and he realized how familiar the man's face seemed. Not as it was, but as it had been in an earlier incarnation. He'd known this man well. "There was another boy under there."

Maj didn't say anything.

"That was you, wasn't it? And it wasn't a dream. It was a memory."

The man smiled — beautifully, looking in that instant so like the boy from David's dream that he didn't even have to answer the question. Something twisted in David's heart, forgotten joy cut with regret and loss.

"But...how?" David said.

The waitress reappeared, slapped a glass on the table, and barked a number at David. After paying for the beer he took a swallow. A familiar taste flooded his mouth, and he pulled the glass away and stared at it. "This is Brooklyn Lager," he said.

"What you ordered," Bob said. "Good choice. May I?"

"It's crowded, Bob," Maj said.

"Oh, go on. It's been ages."

Maj rolled his eyes. "David, stand up a second."

David did as he'd been told. Nearby drinkers glanced at the table, one couple even taking a meaningful step toward it. Realizing he had to send some kind of signal to hold them off, David hitched up his trousers, as if he'd stood for that purpose.

Meanwhile Maj and Bob ducked their heads toward the table. Bob took a big slurp from the top of the beer. Maj then tilted the depleted glass toward his own face without lifting it from the table and did the same before returning it to the upright position. They leaned back together. The whole thing took three seconds.

"Nice." Bob ran his tongue around his lips appreciatively. "Can't beat your local lagers."

"Sit down," Maj said to David.

David sat, and the seat vultures went back to their conversations, for now. Nobody seemed to have noticed what had happened at the table in the meantime, and David looked curiously at Maj.

"You get good at playing the angles," Maj said. "And misdirection, of course."

"Maj is the best," Bob said. "Famous for it."

"Maybe," Maj said. "But it doesn't pay to get overconfident."

"You get anything out of St. Pat's?" Bob asked, still eyeing David's beer. "Talk to Clive?"

Maj shook his head. "He's not there. Apparently he took himself to the basement two days ago. So...that's the end of him."

"Sorry, mate."

Maj shrugged, but it didn't look convincing.

"Worth checking any of the others?"

"They're even worse."

"Doesn't *have* to be a problem, though, does it?"

"No. It happens all the time. But Lizzie said these people seem very nosy and one might have sharper sight than normal—which is why I came back to the city in a hurry. Not to mention there are a few friends who'd like to capitalize on any outside threat right now."

A shadow passed over Bob's face. "Speak of the devil."

Maj turned. At first David couldn't work out who they were talking about. Then a chill ran down his neck.

Four people were standing next to the bar in a line, their backs up against the wall. David realized with a start that he'd seen one of them before—the short, stocky one was the man who'd been glaring at him in Union Square Park, near the end. The others were thinner and taller, *weirdly* tall, dressed in clothing so dark it was hard to make out details of individual garments. Two men, one with long, gray straggly hair, the other cropped short over a skull that looked like it had been shaped with blows from a shovel. Between them stood a painfully thin woman whose hair was dirty red. All had pale skin stretched over large and bony facial features, and they looked so similar they had to be related.

They were very still—or so David thought at first. Everyone around them was in movement, leaning toward one another, gesturing at bar staff, laughing, talking, looking around for seats. The four up against the wall appeared motionless...except if you looked at them long enough you realized they were vibrating slightly, enough to make their edges look a little blurry.

"Christ," Maj said.

"How does he do it?" Bob asked, with what sounded like awe. "Just *appear* like that—as if he knows someone's been talking about him?"

"Nothing magical about it," Maj said irritably. "Golzen's been sniffing around me for weeks, and his three spooks have been hard on my tail since I got back to the city. Golzen probably told them to follow me. That's all."

Bob didn't look convinced.

"Who *is* that guy?" David asked. "The shorter one? I've seen him before."

"When?"

"In Union Square. He was staring at me."

This seemed to confirm whatever concerns Bob had about the man. "I'm not liking this, Maj," he muttered. "I don't want to get on Golzen's bad side."

"Fuck him. He's just like the rest of us."

"I'm not so sure. I hear a lot of things, remember. People are taking him seriously these days, more and more. There's chatter going back and forth."

"Like what?"

"You know I can't tell you, Maj."

"I meant in general."

"They want to know what he's saying, that's all. And he left a broadcast with me a couple days ago. Sounded like he was telling people to get ready for something. But not everyone. Just them who knew some code."

"What was the broadcast?"

"It was 'For the twelve. Be ready. Follow signs until Jedburgh appears.'"

"What?" Maj laughed. "It's bullshit. He sends out random nonsense to make his acolytes think he knows something. He's crazy. All four of them are."

"So you say. But I'd already been hearing rumors about twelve chosen ones, Golzen and eleven others. What if he's finally found out where Perfect is? I don't want to get left behind, do I?"

"Bob, it's a *myth*."

"I dunno. I'm hearing things. Every day. They say getting to Perfect will be like the Bloom—but it lasts forever. And you get *strong*."

"There's *no such place*. It's Chinese whispers and wishful thinking and the demagogue fantasies of a guy who's not right in the head. The Bloom is the Bloom and then it's done. End of story."

"I'm *hearing* things, Maj," Bob repeated stubbornly.

As the two men argued, David noticed there were a couple of small wet patches on the floor by their stools, as if a splash of water had dropped from the ceiling in front of each of them. When he glanced upward to see where it might have come from, he discovered his view was obscured. Two guys in T-shirts were standing over the table, very close. *Too* close. They had hard faces and the boxy, geometric shoulders of men who paid daily homage to their self-image with repetitive exercise.

"Waiting for someone?" the nearest one asked.

"No."

The other smirked. "You sure?"

For a moment David couldn't work out what this was supposed to mean, then realized the men were looking at him in a way that was predatory and unkind. "Look..."

"No, *you* look. The place is slammed. Either drift or we're going to join you."

"What are you talking about? There's no space left."

"Are you being funny?"

David looked anxiously at Maj and Bob for backup. They weren't there. The stools on the other side of the table were empty.

The first guy squatted down so his face was close to David's. His eyes were very sharp and blue, but there was no depth to them at all.

"So what's the story, princess? You want to make some nice new friends?"

David got up hurriedly. He made his way into the crowd without looking back, but heard the two men laughing together all the same. In the last half hour the room had gotten so packed that he had to shove his way through the crowds. How had Maj and Bob managed to get away so quickly?

When he got to the door he glanced back, but couldn't see any sign of either of them. The other people remained at the end of the bar, however, in a line, their backs against the wall. They turned their heads as one to watch David as he left. The girl smiled at him.

It was not a good smile.

Chapter 24

Maj was waiting on the sidewalk in the twilight, looking distracted. Bob had gone.

"This isn't going how I hoped," Maj muttered.

David stormed up to him. "Look, just tell me *what the hell is happening.* Who *are* you?"

"I'm your friend."

David felt hysterical with everything he didn't understand. "Yes, you *keep saying that,* but how *can* you be if *I don't even know who you are?*"

"There's someone else," Maj said. "He's one of you, not one of us. He's wrong about a lot of things, but he might be able to explain the situation in a way you'll find easier to understand. The most important thing is the opportunity we've got now. This almost never happens, David. I don't know *anyone* who it happened to. Or where it happened and took. It's like . . ." He thought for a moment. "Do you remember third grade science class?"

"*What?* Of course not."

"Yeah, you were never keen on the science bits. I liked it, though. It's like magnets with opposite charges. They *attract,* right? Magnets with opposite charges attract and stick together—and if the charge is strong, they stick *hard.* Pull them apart and they'll try to move back together, to be as one. That's how it was with us for a long time. But then . . ."

Maj stopped talking and started to walk away. David saw no option but to follow, and keep prompting him, in the hope that sooner or later he'd say something that made sense. "Then what?"

"Something happens," Maj said. "The charge in one magnet starts to reverse. The magnet like you. *Always* the one like you." He sounded bitter. "After a while they won't stick anymore. They repel, in fact, so strongly that everything gets forgotten — by you, again, not by us. Cornermen like Bob may have the very best memories, but we're all pretty good at that shit. It's in our nature to look back. To act as custodians of what was."

"But this reversal..."

"It can take place over weeks or months or years. It can happen early or it can happen late. You and I were unusually late, but then it fell apart fast."

"You're saying we were friends," David insisted doggedly.

"Yes. For God's sake."

"But where?"

"From that moment under the table. Here, too, almost the whole time you lived in the city."

"So how come I don't remember you?"

"You grew up. Kids are born without all the made-up rules, but then the world spends the first twenty years of everybody's life drumming the magic out. Training them to draw a line around each individual to separate them from the rest of the universe, turning them into 'I' instead of being part of a cloud of interaction that stretches in all directions. Once the line's been inked around you, the shutters come down. That's what Lonely Clive used to say, anyway, and I figure he was right."

David stuck with it. "Who *was* this Clive?"

"He took me under his wing after you left the city, and he's the only one of us who ever got this close to a reconnect. It didn't work out, and that was the beginning of the end for him. He's hollow now."

"I've tried," David said. "I really have. But I don't understand *a single thing you've said.*"

"You just don't *want* to remember," Maj snapped. "Which proves some part of you remembers *something.*"

"Yo, Maj!"

A teenage girl wearing a gray hoodie over a strange array of other garments came up the sidewalk toward them. David recognized her from the park, the girl who'd been near the woman in the ball gown. She looked like a runaway, about seventeen, and as if she'd selected her wardrobe in a concerted effort to piss off or perplex anyone over the age of twenty-three.

Maj smiled back. "S'up, girl?"

"It's all epic." She grinned. "All the time. We're headed to a party down in 'packing. It's going to be awesome. Wanna come?"

"Love to," Maj said. "But I'm busy right now."

She pouted. "You've *always* got shit to do."

"Shit don't get done by itself, right?"

The girl laughed and went off down the street. She seemed to turn her head a couple of times, as if to talk to someone beside her.

"Okay," Maj said to David, starting to walk in the other direction. "Come meet a guy."

Chapter 25

I'm so loving my life right now. It's amazing. I'm just chilling, doing my thing. I've got some great new girlfriends, and every morning we wake up and it's like, "What are we going to do today?" and we walk out of wherever we crashed without looking back and then we'll hang in a park or go look in stores or whatever. It's all so totally laid-back and at night we'll find somewhere new to sleep and there're always new people to meet, too, and always a party somewhere. Lately I've been meeting a load of these super-cool friends called Angels, who are dressed in black the whole time, and I never thought that look would be for me, but I'm starting to kind of like it, especially as it's not like total goth or anything because they'll wear these bright clothes underneath, like a dress or shirt or whatever. I'm not even sure why they're so friendly to me because I don't really know them and they didn't go to the school or come from the neighborhood, but basically they're these super-nice people and they go around doing epic things and helping people out. Sometimes some of them steal stuff, but not often and only from really big corporations and so it's not a big deal. There're some other people who take a lot more stuff and they steal from normal people. They have, like, this leader or whatever, but they're not like the Angels. They're kind of heavy and scary instead and they don't do good things for other people and they have this idea of a place and it's like their heaven or something. There's twelve of them and I don't really get it, but I don't hang with them anyway because I think maybe it's okay if you just steal something every now and then, but if you're totally doing it the whole time that's so not cool. That's what Lizzie says, and she even says any stealing at all is not good and she doesn't do it anymore. She's one of the key Angels and I agree with her. She's like a big sister to me, and she said if I ever start to feel confused I should go talk to her and she'll explain things. I think maybe I might get into that whole Angel thing at some point, but not yet, because it's too much fun hanging out and partying with my friends even though sometimes it's complicated because they can't remember their names, and I can't either, so it's hard to make arrangements. But it always seems to work out and it's not a big deal.

The only thing that's a bummer is I don't see much of Jessica anymore. I go watch her every now and then, and sometimes if I can get in the house I sleep on the floor under her bed, but she's, like, doing this thing right now where she pretends not to see me the whole time, or even hear me, and she doesn't hang in the places we used to go. If I see her in the evenings, she's out with all these other people she knows from high school and I realize, how freaking long *is* it since we really hung together? And I think, huh, if she's in high school then it's got to be like a year or two or maybe four, but I'm sure it's all fine and she's just super-busy or something. We're so best friends forever and that never dies. It's not like she was with Cynthia Markham, a total bitch she was tight with in the sixth grade but who screwed her over and was like suddenly I'm not your friend anymore, end of story, and I stuck with Jessica through that time even though she wasn't friendly to me at all. That's what best friends are for, right? Okay, so she's got like a boyfriend now, and if it's really five or six years since we spoke, then I've been living in the city a lot longer than I realized, but that's not going to change anything because when you're best friends nothing in the world can change that, *ever.* There was a while when I'd throw things around in the house and try to scare her, but it didn't work and I gave up and it was dumb anyway. She's just going through, like, a phase or something, but it's all good and it'll be okay in the end because true friendship never dies.

It never dies.

Chapter 26

As I walked across 16th I heard the sound of the piano. Once again it sounded like it was coming from one of the upper windows of the town house next to the church. The piece was familiar, measured and sane and beautiful. Bach, in other words. I drew to a halt beneath a streetlight. The player fumbled, stopped, repeated a section with the stress on different hands, then returned patiently to the beginning. Though he or she was not destined for Carnegie Hall they were better than competent, partly because the playing had the freedom of someone who is rehearsing for their own benefit and does not realize they are overheard. There are people for whom an audience is essential, who raise their game and feel more real when observed. The rest of us do much of what we do in an attempt to fill ourselves up, and that is more easily done in private.

I let myself in through the low iron gate and walked up the right staircase to the door of the church. I knocked. As before, there was no response. I tried the handle, but now it was locked.

I was about to knock again but noticed a tarnished buzzer on the side. I pressed it. It didn't sound like anything happened. I hadn't banked on being stymied so quickly and was about to press it again, largely out of frustration, when I heard the sound of a window opening.

I stepped back and looked up to see a head and shoulders sticking out of the window on the second floor of the town house. It was the priest.

He waved. "Just a moment," he said, and disappeared.

I walked down to wait for him out on the sidewalk. He appeared out of the house a few minutes later and trotted down the steps, not looking at all put out.

"Had the bell rewired over to my quarters," he said cheerfully. "If I'm in the church, the door's always open. If I'm not, what's the point of the bell ringing in an empty room?"

"I'm sorry to interrupt your practice."

"Oh, it's not important."

"Bach?"

"Indeed. *The Well-Tempered Clavier,* Prelude Five."

"You're pretty good."

He made a face that was polite but dismissive, the expression you use when someone praises you for something they don't really understand.

"Seriously. Good separation, not too clinical or fast but you don't lean into the bends either. Difficult to guess whether you'd prefer the Barenboim or Angela Hewitt. Certainly not the early Gould."

He raised an eyebrow. "You play?"

"I used to, a little. Back in the day."

"No longer?"

"I lost my audience."

He nodded affably. "I've never wanted one. It's something I do for myself. A kind of meditation, perhaps. It doesn't matter whether anyone hears."

"That's what I used to tell myself. But it matters."

He smiled in a way that remained friendly but was also final, which said I was wandering into territory he knew better than me, and which he had no wish to discuss.

He stuck out his hand. "Father Robert," he said. "Or Robert Jeffers, if you'd prefer."

"John Henderson."

"How can I help you, Mr. Henderson?"

"I was here earlier today," I said. "The door to the church was open then."

"Of course. I was inside."

"I'd just seen you walk off down the road."

I assume priests get a lot of practice in developing a facial expression that says they're listening without judging. "Of course," Jeffers said. His eyes were tired, and his shave that morning, though close, had not been perfect. "I received a call midafternoon, someone who wished to see me urgently. And you're correct—when I got back I realized I'd forgotten to lock up. Luckily nobody entered while I was away."

"Actually, they did. Me."

"Well, you seem like a person of good intent."

"It comes and goes. The funny thing is, I thought I saw you exchange words with someone inside as you left."

"Well, of course."

"I didn't see anyone while I was in there."

He smiled. "I'm sorry. It's a conceit of mine. I meant the Lord. I always exchange a few words with him on entering or leaving the building."

"Does he reply?"

"Naturally. You should try it sometime."

"I will. If I ever think of something to ask."

The priest smiled tolerantly, and it struck me how wearying it must be to work in a profession where people either ask too much of you or else don't believe a word you say. "I've seen you before, haven't I?"

"Yes. Yesterday afternoon."

"Of course. The running man. Did you find the person you were looking for?"

"No. She disappeared. Funny thing is—sorry to use the expression again, but it *is* kind of strange—I think the same woman disappeared in this same street a couple of nights before."

"Are you a policeman?"

"No."

"Then what is your interest?"

"She's been following a friend of mine."

"Following?"

"Tracking her home from social engagements. Waiting when she picks her daughters up from school. Maybe even standing out in the street at night looking up at her windows. *That* kind of following. The not-good kind."

"How unsettling."

I didn't say anything. The best way of getting someone to volunteer information is to leave them hanging. People feel the need to fill awkward space, and while they won't give up what you want straightaway, often they'll show you the beginning of the path.

Jeffers had more self-possession than this, however—or else genuinely had no idea what I was talking about. He merely stood there, looking composed.

"A tall woman," I said. "Young, dark hair, long dark coat, red dress."

"Doesn't sound like one of my flock, I'm afraid."

"You guys really still say 'flock'?"

"I do. I can't speak for others."

"The *other* funny thing—and this really is the last time, I promise—is I'm pretty sure I saw the woman again after I left your church. In Union Square." His face was blank now. "Was she the person you left the church in such a hurry to see?"

"No. That was an elderly gentleman in quite the other direction," Jeffers said. "So I'm afraid you must have been mistaken."

I took out one of the Adriatico's cards and wrote my number on the back. When I offered it to the priest, he looked at it and then at me as if my meaning was unclear. I kept holding it out until he took it.

"Is there anything else?" he asked.

I thanked him for his time and remained where I was while he headed back up the stairs and into his house. He walked more heavily this time, without the personable trot he'd arrived with, but he did not look back.

As I set off down the street I heard him start the second Prelude. It was good—nearly flawless, in fact, at least the portion I caught before I got out of range and the music became buried beneath the sound of traffic. That prelude is a compact little pocket of baroque fury, tight under the hands, and no one's idea of easy. A risky choice to switch from the fifth to that, unless perhaps you knew someone was still likely to be in earshot and might know enough to be impressed.

I thought the priest was kidding himself, just a little. He wanted to be heard.

He was also deluding himself if he believed he'd convinced me. Kristina had followed him to Union Square. I'd seen him there too. Had I learned anything by talking to him tonight? Only that he was willing to lie to me — but from this followed other things. First, there was some connection between him and the woman who'd been following Catherine. Them being together in the park said this, and that maybe she *had* come down this road the day before and he knew where she'd disappeared to.

Second, he was an amateur at misleading people. If someone puts you on the spot, you either avoid saying anything of consequence or tell the truth and dare the motherfucker to make something of it. This made me wonder how he'd gotten himself into a position where he was covering up for someone else.

What makes a priest lie?

I walked to the end of the street and left a message on Kristina's cell. She'd be busy in the bar but get it soon enough. I bought a lousy coffee from the nearest deli and wandered back to the corner.

I'd taken the night off and I didn't have anything else to do. I figured I'd wait a while.

Chapter 27

Half an hour later someone turned onto the street, a nondescript-looking man walking quickly. His movements were a little unusual, and at first I took him for one of those people who endlessly circulate the city's streets, alone, like bugs on a solo trek around a vast windowpane. He turned his head to the side once in a while, as if exercising a crick in his neck. After he'd come twenty yards toward me I caught the sound of conversation, however, and belatedly realized he wasn't alone. I'm not sure how I could have missed the other guy given he was actually in front, and it became clear that the man I'd noticed first was trying to keep up.

Luckily, they were coming up the other side of the street to where I'd been standing, getting cold. I took a step back into the shadows. As they drew level opposite I saw the man in front was wearing jeans and an untucked shirt and realized: these were the guys I'd observed near the priest in Union Square that afternoon.

The one in jeans led the other through the gates of the church. They trotted up the stairs, and the leading man pressed the doorbell.

I turned my head to watch the priest's house. He'd stopped practicing soon after our conversation and it had been quiet from there since, though a light had come on once the night came in.

After a moment the upper window opened and Jeffers stuck his head out. He looked across to the church, then pulled his head back and shut the window.

Two minutes later he appeared out of the front door and walked quickly down the stairs.

"What do you want?" he asked when he reached the men. His tone was polite but less generically friendly than when he'd spoken to me.

I didn't hear what the taller man said, but a moment later the other said "David."

The priest took the other man aside and there was a short conversation. The guy called David stayed where he was. From forty feet away I could tell he wasn't happy to be there, but he waited anyway. At one point he glanced across the street, but I didn't move. Unless you're confident someone's already spotted you, moving is merely the best method of making sure that they will.

The priest eventually got keys out of his pocket and unlocked the church. He stood back to let the other men in, then followed. The door closed behind them with a solid clunk.

I stepped out of the shadows. I don't know much about the lives of priests. I can imagine that tending to the spiritual needs of others is not a nine-to-five job, and requests for guidance may arise at almost any time. I suspect it's still unusual for two guys to turn up together at eight thirty in the evening, however. They didn't look like they'd been in doubt that they would be received, either. The taller of the two had presented as though he felt he had a call upon the priest, or a high level of familiarity at least.

They could just be members of the flock, or perhaps the priest ran some kind of outreach program and these people were cautiously scaling the foothills of recovery.

It was none of my business, of course.

But I kept watching.

Fifteen minutes later someone else turned onto the street, but straightaway I knew there was something different about him. It was partly the way he dressed—a dark suit under an expensive-looking long coat—but mainly in the walk. There's a style of locomotion you see only in a city, the stride of a man—and it's always a man; women have their walks of power, but this is not one of them—who believes himself the dominant animal in his habitat. You never see this walk in the country or in small towns, which are insufficiently similar to the wild. You have to be in a city.

This is my track through this place, and yes, I do own the fucking road.

As he came up the street, heels making tapping sounds on the sidewalk, I was taken aback to realize I'd made the same mistake *again*. Something about the arrangement of the streetlights and shadows clearly made it hard to pick people out. This man was also not walking alone, or at least hadn't been the only person to enter the street at more or less the same time.

Following behind him was a small group of people. One was a short, bulky man in a retro suit who looked like he was trying to walk the other man's walk and not carrying it off. The other three were much taller and thinner, and loped along with heads lowered.

The guy in the coat walked straight up to the church gate and let himself in. The others hung back. I watched the man walk up the stairs, and then glanced back at the second group to see that they'd disappeared.

The man in the coat opened the church door without knocking or ringing the bell. He didn't close it behind him either. It could be that I'd simply spent too long watching strangers do not very interesting things, but I thought that was kind of weird.

It was quiet for five minutes. Then I heard the sound of shouting, and something being broken.

It was still none of my business, but that's never really stopped me.

I stepped off the sidewalk and jogged across the street.

When I got to the church door I could see straight into the hall at the end of the corridor. The man in the long coat was walking up and down, hands on hips and coat flared out behind, like a ham actor delivering a key speech. I couldn't see anyone else and so I kept going.

The priest was in the middle of the hall surrounded by chairs—some of which had been overturned, a couple broken. The second of the two guys I'd seen earlier was behind him, looking totally out of his depth. There was no sign of the other, the man in the untucked shirt, though the door at the other end of the room was ajar.

The man in the coat turned to me. He looked about forty. His hair was cropped and his face broad but the features even. I could feel the power of his presence from where I stood. "Who the fuck are you?"

His accent was flat. Not New York.

"One of the faithful," I said. "I need to talk with the father about something that's been troubling me."

"You shitting me?"

"No. Why do you ask?"

"The father's busy," he said. "I suggest you come back another time." He turned to face the priest.

"That's not convenient."

The man was motionless for a moment. When he turned to face me again there was a smile on his face. It was quite like one, anyway. "Say again?"

"You know how it is with spiritual matters. They crave instant solution. I assume that's why you're here too. Maybe we should go somewhere, compare notes."

He laughed, and turned back to the priest. He liked his body movements, this guy. He was all about owning the space. "Seriously, Jeffers—who the fuck is this person? He a friend of yours?"

The priest said nothing. The man behind him kept glancing at the door, and appeared to be trying to work out his chances of being able to run at it without being intercepted. It looked as though he had nowhere near enough experience of making that kind of calculation to be confident about it, and was aware of the fact.

The man in the coat grew thoughtful. "Wait a minute," he said to me. "I know you."

I hadn't been expecting this. I said nothing.

"Yeah." He nodded to himself. "I don't know where, but I've seen you."

"Could be," I said. "I don't hide."

He came and stood about a yard from me. "Sometimes hiding is a good move, my friend. Running never works. But hiding? Sometimes it's the clever thing to do."

Up close he smelled of cologne and self-confidence. He wasn't scared of me but he wasn't dumb, either. Something random had come into his orbit and he was too smart to do the obvious and throw a punch or pull out a gun — something I was by now pretty sure that he'd have about his person — and I realized maybe I should have sent Kris a message before I came barging in here.

There was a flurry of movement, the clatter of a chair knocked over, and receding footsteps. The scared-looking guy had chosen his moment, and run.

I kept my eyes straight ahead, on coat man's face. He looked at me a moment longer, then stepped back and laughed quietly to himself. The father remained where he was, hands by his side, looking pinched but composed.

"This guy's right," the man in the coat said to him. "I came here for a talk too. But you're busy tonight, it seems. You got all these people coming to you for help at once. Some other time."

He gave me a nod and walked toward the door. Just before he left, he turned back.

"There *will* be another time," he said, but not to me. I'd already been dismissed. "We will talk."

He seemed to be directing the remark toward the door at the other end of the hall. Then he was gone.

Jeffers let out a sharp, hard breath, and ran his hands quickly over his face. "Thank you," he said.

"Who's down there? Through the door?"

"Nobody."

"You mind if I take a look?"

"Yes, I do," he said. "This is a church. But even if I let you, you wouldn't find anyone."

Curiously, I didn't get the sense that he was lying. "I don't know what you've got going," I said, "or who the hell that man was."

"His name's Reinhart."

"Whatever. I've met people like him before. You don't want them in your life."

"Thank you for the advice," he said. "I'll be sure to bear it in mind."

When I got back onto the street I looked for the man in the coat, but there was no sign. I did catch a glimpse of the guy who'd bolted, however. He was right up at the corner of Ninth, head down and hands stuffed in his pockets, walking fast.

As he turned the corner, I thought I saw something else — three tall figures, thirty feet behind him, also hurrying, as if following. The image didn't resolve, however, and I guess it must have been more of the street's strange shadow patterns.

I turned for home.

Chapter 28

After Henderson left, the priest stood for five minutes. He sent up a prayer for guidance, but ran out of steam after the initial formalities. Sometimes it went that way. You picked up the phone and got a dead tone. A lot of people gave up at this point. Jeffers knew some days the plea went to voice mail and that's that. He's a busy guy. Give Him a chance. Jeffers believed this, at least, on good days.

In the meantime he turned to dealing with the chairs that had been knocked over. He picked each up carefully, inspected it for damage, and returned it to its place in the rows facing toward the end of the hall. There were twelve of these, divided by an aisle in the middle. On both sides each held seven chairs. The days of the week, multiplied by two, multiplied again by the number of Christ's disciples, another of the private conceits he entertained in an effort to introduce meaning into his days. With faith, so much of what's important takes place behind the scenes. Not including the single chair at the head, which faced the other way and on which he sat while delivering his informal sermons, the church provided a hundred and sixty-eight places for the faithful to sit, less the three that had now been broken.

Too many chairs.

He gathered up the pieces and carried them to the side. One was damaged beyond repair—the chair that had been on the receiving end of Reinhart's kick. The other two were collateral casualties and had received only superficial damage—legs or spindles dislodged from sockets. Jeffers supposed that they would be relatively easy to repair if you knew what you were doing with hammer or glue. The world of physical objects had never been his domain. Even as a child he'd been prone to playing with ideas rather than things, and had never made much of a distinction. He'd ask Dave to have a look at the chairs. Dave was an ex-alcoholic who'd been coming to the church for years (his conversion an early success of Jeffers's predecessor, Father Ronson) and transitioned more easily than some to the new priest. He functioned as an occasional unpaid cleaner, but from time to time he'd shown himself to be a halfway competent handyman too. Nothing ever quite worked as it should when he'd had his hands on it (the oil heater, for example, which was now discreetly stowed in the basement, along with its fuel, so as not to hurt the man's feelings), but fixing a few chairs would be within his capabilities... pointless though it would be. Jeffers was lucky to see twenty people in the church at any one time. The other chairs were merely there to make up the numbers, and as a statement of intent.

One lived in hope, and worked in hope, and that was the way it should be. Hope is how the idea of faith operates in the world.

Hope is how you make faith do real things.

When Father Jeffers turned from the pile he saw Maj on the other side of the room. Maj didn't look happy.

"Who was the other guy?" Maj asked.

"The one I've told you about."

"The guy who's been tracking Lizzie?"

Jeffers nodded.

"He looks like trouble."

"Your friend ran away."

"He's always had a tendency toward flight."

"You're not going after him?"

"He'll be halfway to Penn Station by now. I know where he lives. Right now I'm more concerned about Reinhart turning up here."

Jeffers sensed this wasn't entirely true and that the man was doing his best to cover intense disappointment. He also knew that Maj, like many of his kind, strongly resisted being told what to feel. Their emotions and memories were all they had. "How do you think that happened?"

"Golzen must have led him here. He's building up to something. Fictitious Bob told me earlier that he's been sending out broadcasts designed to hide something. I had an encounter with Golzen myself before I left town, and he and the three ghouls turned up in a bar earlier."

"Were the messages about Perfect?"

"Not self-evidently. But who knows?"

"If he's preparing to leave on his quest, why would he bring Reinhart here?"

"Could be it wasn't his idea. You met the guy. Does Reinhart seem like someone who lets people do what they choose?"

"I'd like a meeting tomorrow," Jeffers said. "You, Lizzie, Bob, and as many of the others as you can gather."

Maj shrugged. "Lizzie's being kind of . . . I think she's gotten spooked by these people following her. There's something on her mind. I don't know what it is."

"I'd like it if you could try. Especially with her."

When Maj had gone, the priest took a walk around the room, checking that everything else was in place. When he was satisfied, he went to the far end and closed the door there. He locked the church and went around to the house. He paused before going inside and looked up and down the street, half expecting to see someone in the shadows. There was nothing to see, but that didn't mean there was no one there. Reinhart would be back, too. He was sure of that. Though until tonight he'd known the man only by reputation, a confrontation had been inevitable. Black and white, right and wrong, good and evil. They rub along together most of the time, but a battle always comes.

So be it.

Upstairs he stood becalmed in his sitting room. Usually he spent this period preparing for the next day. Planning a schedule of visits for those unable to visit the church in person, which boiled down to reassuring the very old that no, they didn't look so bad and yes, God would be there waiting for them. There was nothing of the sort booked for the next day, however, which left working out what to say to the drop-in group at four and starting to gather his thoughts for the weekend's sermon. He was ahead of himself on the first task, and drawing a blank on the second except for reiterating the bottom line:

God is basically on your side, so if life seems to suck it's probably part of some big plan. In the meantime, pray. And keep coming to church, for Pete's sake. I'm not doing this for the fun of it.

He sat in the chair by the window. It was the single decent piece of furniture in a room that was otherwise Spartan. It didn't have to be that way. Nobody ever came up here. He could buy what he wanted, within reason and the constraints of his salary. He could pimp it out like a gangsta bordello, if he chose, or install a revolving bed with black satin sheets. He'd arrived owning little, however, and remained that way. Everything of substance in the room, excluding the piano, had belonged to Father Ronson. As a child of wealthy parents, Jeffers been brought up in the world of ownership and had found it wanting. Or...was choosing not to acquire merely an easy cop-out, a way of sidestepping the trials and risks of self-definition while appearing to live a virtuous life?

He didn't know. He'd been back and forth on the subject, sitting in this very chair, staring out at the simple beauty of the trees and the streetlights, which he saw as the real decorations of the room.

The results of three years of patient effort stood in the balance. Maj was right. Reinhart could only have been led here by Golzen. Perhaps he should have tried harder to reach out to Golzen. Their messages weren't so different. They preached parallel paradigms, up to a point: the only distinction being that Jeffers's was right, and Golzen's wrong. There were souls to be saved. Souls in danger, lives that had been lived in shadows and untruth but could now be steered toward the light. There was a limit to what Jeffers could do for the regular folks, those who attended because they were old and knew no different or middle-aged and felt they should, as if it was some kind of Book Club with Benefits.

He could make a difference with this other kind. Many were younger. Most lived outside the law, and almost all on the streets. He could bring them home. Through doing this he might also prove to the memory of Father Ronson that he was worthy of his post. Jeffers wasn't sure this would make a difference. That wasn't the point. In the realm of the spiritual, you do things because they're the right thing to do. That is all.

What happened this evening was a sign it was time to step up the campaign. To gather the ones he had influence with and forestall any ideas they might have of allowing themselves to slip into Reinhart's clutches—as so many had done—or following the road to the promised land, for which Golzen claimed to hold the key.

Tomorrow always holds the potential to be the very best of days.

Content to have reached this conclusion, the priest sat in the chair, his mind tending toward a comfortable blank. He started on hearing the sound of a distant thud.

He'd heard the sound more and more recently. He knew the city was loud enough at night that neighbors in the street would either not have heard the noise, or would dismiss it as one of those things, the sigh of a bending branch in the jungle night.

He knew also that when he went into the church tomorrow morning, however, the narrow door at the end of the hall would be hanging open.

Chapter 29

Kris woke earlier than usual. When she trudged yawning into the sort-of-kitchen she found a note on the counter next to an empty coffee mug. It was from John. It said he was going for a walk. There were two arrows underneath, drawn in his confident and surprisingly artistic hand. One pointed to the cup. The other pointed in the direction of the coffee machine, which was loaded and ready to go. She picked up the note and frowned at it.

It was considerate, of course. But that wasn't what struck her. He *always* went for a walk first thing. John went for a walk in the morning in the same way that the sun rose. John going for a walk was not news.

So why the note? The fight after the debacle at Catherine's had blown over. It had been, as John had said, a dumb fight — though possibly not as dumb as he'd made out. It was dumb because fighting never achieved anything, true that, but when two people who love each other bang heads that hard then *something* needs talking about. Kristina was damned if she knew what that was, which was making her twitchy. She suspected John would have even less idea, not least because he wouldn't have a clue that they were at...

The Six Month Suckfest.

It wasn't always literally six months when she bailed — that would be stupid and weird and she could have put a note in her diary in advance saying, "Don't screw things up this week" — but it had fallen close enough on enough occasions that it had become the Six Month Suckfest in her head. She and John had already been together longer than that, in point of fact. More to the point — his stubbornness about moving aside — she was happier than she'd been in her entire life.

And yet... still there was this itch in the back of her mind, an unsettled feeling in her stomach: and a small, shriveled hand starting to reach out for the Bail Switch. She'd never been able to work out whose hand this was. A remnant of her mother, trying to keep her single? Some personification of insecurities she simply didn't feel (consciously, at least)? Pure perversity? She didn't know. In the meantime, the hand kept moving insidiously out of the darkness, its twisted fingers groping toward some agenda Kris didn't understand and wanted no part of.

She shoved it back into the shadows and reached for the switch on the coffee machine instead.

A couple of errands took her up into Midtown, a nice change. The big buildings and overshadowed streets there reminded her of the mountains and forests of Washington State. If you'd been raised accustomed to deep woods, a city was an easier transition than a town (and she should know, having bailed spectacularly from several of those in the past). In mountains and cities you are small in the face of geography and environment. Nobody knows your name, or cares, and that was generally fine with her.

Now it seemed as though some of these strangers were getting too close for comfort, however. More than twenty-four hours after the fact they still had no idea who'd been on their roof and left the message on the window. She wasn't easily unnerved and John sure as hell wasn't either. It was pretty strange, however, as the period yesterday afternoon in Union Square had also been. As John had pointed out, serious people who meant you real harm tended to get on and do it rather than leaving clues — but a warning was still a warning.

He'd said this with a distant look in his eye, as if considering ways of dealing with the situation that might not involve her — steps like taking the last night off from the restaurant and going to talk to the priest, a plan he hadn't told her about ahead of time. Yes, he told her what had happened when he came into the bar later, but he should have told her he was going, like he should have told her about meeting Catherine that time. It probably wasn't personal. Despite what society does in attempting to turn men into team players, they all think theirs is the only name above the title of the movie. She'd met John as a man who'd returned to his previous home in Black Ridge, Washington, to seek an explanation for the death of his older son, who'd perished there in what had appeared to be a freak accident. She'd watched John go at that situation like a bull at a gate, declining assistance until he'd already been shot by people he'd come to believe were implicated in his son's death, and the situation looked to be getting even worse. In the end it had been resolved, albeit messily. So why did it bug her so much that he kept doing these things? Was it because it felt just a little like he was treating her like some young girl?

And had he left the note this morning because he sort of knew he was doing it, too?

The next thing she noticed, she was in Little Brazil, a short stretch of 46th near Times Square, narrow and shadowed and unexceptional, a cut-through between Fifth and Sixth Avenues. Presumably there'd been reason for self-exiled denizens of a South American country to congregate in this corner of the grimy heart of Midtown, but all that remained of their passing — amid a smear of dusty buildings being knocked down or repurposed or ignored and a battered Irish bar — were a couple of small restaurants still flying the green and yellow flag and touting *feijoada* and *caipirinhas* — memories of a community now gone. Near the end of the block, she cut up an alley and onto 47th, the old diamond district, another historic enclave. The street still featured discount jewelry shops and stout men in homburgs but wasn't the separate universe it would once have been. The future homogenizes.

Kristina found herself slowing in front of one of the store windows, in front of tightly filled ranks of metal and shiny stones, arranged to catch the eye of commercial buyers rather than passing individuals. She'd been gazing vaguely at a tray in the center for a few minutes before she realized something.

Was she really looking at *rings?* Was *that* what this was about? It couldn't be. She'd never, in *any* relationship, started thinking along those lines. She sure as hell wasn't going to start now. Even though there was a ring on the left that . . .

No.

As she jerked her head away from the sun-bleached velvet cushions and their rows of expensive I-dos, she saw something reflected in the glass.

She hesitated, unsure what had caught her eye. Then she moved her gaze back down so she'd appear to be looking through the wares in the window again. She kept this up for fifteen slow seconds before allowing her eyes to drift up once more, pulling focus at the same time, so she was looking at the reflections in the glass rather than what lay beyond.

Yes. There, on the other side of the street, someone was standing in front of a boarded-up store.

Kristina held her position, moving now and then to make it look like she was still browsing — meanwhile drifting along the window and watching.

He or she kept in movement. Slow, but constant. Passersby kept coming between them, and it was hard to be sure, but it looked as though the figure was watching Kristina. The figure was tall and slim. The figure wore a dark coat. The figure looked a hell of a lot like . . .

"I give you good price."

The voice made Kristina jump. A man had come out of the shop. He had the cheap charisma of the kind of person that will always be selling something, and offering discounts regardless of whether they've been sought.

"No," Kristina said firmly, heart beating hard.

He reversed back into his store. Kristina took a chance and glanced directly across the street. There was nobody there now except for buyers and sellers of jewelry and a trio of tourists with bright anoraks and a big map.

Had there ever been? Or had she been confused by the shadows of passersby reflected in a dirty store window?

She started up the street and after twenty yards took a right into a narrow alley. It was filled with steam and the complex odors of old garbage. She slowed as she entered, to give anyone behind her a chance to see where she'd gone, and then headed along the alley, casting a quick look back after ten feet.

It was hard to be sure, but it *looked* like someone was now in position on the other side of the street she'd just left, opposite the alleyway, watching her.

It was morning and she was bang in the heart of Midtown. If this person was planning anything, they'd chosen the wrong time and place.

Unless, of course, they crossed the road and followed her up this alley, where there was no one to see anything at all.

She pulled out her phone as if to check incoming, to broadcast to anyone watching that she was plugged into the world and could summon assistance *right now*.

A glance to the left made her heart jump, a heavy double-thump. *Someone was at the other end, in silhouette against the light.*

It could be they were merely pausing on the street, but Kristina didn't think so.

"I'm not afraid of you," she said in a quiet, low voice.

"Huh?" someone said, and she whirled to see a pudgy Asian man in the filthiest chef's whites she'd ever seen, sitting smoking in an open back doorway.

She shook her head, making a mental note to check the name of the restaurant and make sure she never, ever ate there. She walked the rest of the alleyway, not too fast . . . but not slowly either.

Sixth Avenue was reassuringly crowded, people striding up and down and across and back as if fired from a battery of cannons positioned at right angles. She didn't want to stand in a public place and call John, however. It wasn't only that it would make her feel like a damsel in distress, which would suck. She knew that if she pulled John up here, he'd arrive with a strong following wind and scare off her shadow, taking them back to square one.

So instead she walked down the avenue, dawdling at each street crossing, and bought an Americano from the kiosk at the corner of Bryant Park. She kept her eye on the smeary plastic window between her and the server as she waited for her change — just as she'd kept glancing in the windows of stores and banks for the last four blocks — but saw nothing behind her except solid citizens going about their and other people's business.

She took the drink down one of the plaza's side paths, under the trees. She found one of the small, rickety metal tables and sat down at it.

She waited and she watched.

And began to feel foolish. Nobody came into the park that looked like the figure she'd glimpsed. Just office workers with deli boxes, tourists, and some middle-aged guy ten feet away, sitting holding a Kindle that didn't seem to be commanding his full attention. Otherwise it was just a park, and not very warm.

Eventually she pulled out her phone and discovered there was a message on it — left forty minutes before, when she'd been hurrying out of the alley. It was from John, asking where she was and if she wanted to have lunch. She was about to call back when she realized something had changed in her environment.

Someone had sat on the opposite side of the table.

A young woman, tall, with dark hair, wearing a dark coat with a red dress underneath. She had high cheekbones and a strong nose, red lips, and big, dark eyes.

"You can see me, can't you?" the woman said.

Her voice was soft, a little fuzzy around the edges, as if made up of facets of background noise.

Kristina stared at her. The girl seemed curious, but also wary, as if it was Kristina who'd been following *her*. "You can, can't you?" she insisted, still quietly.

"Yes. Of course."

"But . . . you're real."

"Well, yeah," Kristina said, with no idea what she was agreeing to. "Who . . . are you?"

The girl made a puzzled face, as if unwilling to let the first matter go. "I'm called Lizzie."

"I'm Kristina."

"I know."

"How . . . how do you know?"

The girl looked sheepish. "I heard your boyfriend call you that. He is your boyfriend, yes? John?"

"Yes. But *when* did you hear this?"

The girl seemed more nervous, glancing over Kristina's shoulder, and didn't answer.

"When?" Kristina pressed her. "Were you on our roof? Why are you following Catherine?"

The girl stood up. "I've got to go."

She walked quickly away without looking back.

Kristina jumped to her feet to follow but realized someone else was now standing by the table. It was the man she'd noticed earlier, reading a Kindle.

"Hey," he said.

Kristina glared at him. "Yes, what?"

He smiled. "Saw you sitting by yourself, wondered if you might like a little company."

"No," Kristina said.

"You sure?"

Kristina took a couple of steps past, trying to see where the girl had gone. She thought she got a glimpse of a dark coat at the top of the steps at the back of the library, but it could have been the shadow of the trees. The man was still standing by the table hopefully.

"What do you mean 'by yourself'?"

"Hey, it's fine," he said. "I do it all the time. A bit of peace is good for the soul, right? Just, sometimes it means people might want to hook —"

Kristina threw a look that made him take a hurried step backward, and walked away dialing her phone.

"Hey," John said, when he picked up. "Fancy some —"

"They just made contact," she said.

Chapter 30

David and Dawn held hands in the middle of the couch. Dr. Chew sat on the other side of the desk, peering over his glasses at a scattering of papers across his desk. There was silence. David was reminded of the judges on reality television shows and the insufferable way they milk the moments of truth in which (according to prearranged and carefully constructed narratives) one hapless individual is eliminated from the competition, removing them forever from the hungry gaze and fickle affection of millions of box-watching morons. David thought they'd been given the news during the ultrasound itself, but now he wasn't sure. He could feel Dawn's fingers gripping his, and forced himself to breathe.

He didn't need this.

Not this morning. Not ever. They'd sat on this couch in exactly this position eight months before and been told that the woman wielding the ultrasound probe had misread the grainy black-and-white images on her screen — whoops! — and the little blob she'd cheerfully pointed out as showing clear indications of life had in fact been manifesting signs of being rather dead.

Did Chew remember that meeting? Presumably in a technical sense — it must be there in his notes — but did he recall it emotionally, the impact it'd had on this particular couple among the hundreds he saw? No. That style of remembrance wasn't the physician's job. For Chew, news was a subset of uninflected information. Somewhere in his mind there would probably be a formalized distinction between "good" and "bad" types of news — so he could differentiate when events occurred to someone within his own family or tribe — but he evidently didn't allow this to unbalance a dispassionate attention to whatever facts happened to obtain at any given moment. This doubtless made him an excellent physician.

It made him a mighty crappy news bearer, however.

Eventually he raised his head and smiled.

Even this wasn't enough to break the tension or give a clear indication of the direction in which the sheet of glass between their ignorance and his knowledge was going to break. The smile could equally have been one of affirmation of good, or soberness before the delivery of yet more bad. It could betoken nothing more than a fleeting happy recollection of the fact that he was due to get steak for dinner.

David believed he'd give the man maybe three, four more seconds, and then he was going to let go of Dawn's hand, leap over the desk, and beat the guy senseless with his Anglepoise lamp.

"Everything's fine," Chew said.

Dawn remained rigid. David let out an explosive breath, and this time when Dawn gripped his hand it was to give rather than seek reassurance.

Having delivered his showstopper, Chew dispensed with the suspense and got on with it. "As I indicated during the ultrasound, it all looks good and there's nothing in the numbers to make me think, ah, otherwise. It's going to be hard for you, I know, with your history, but right now you should feel happy that things are going well. Really. Happiness and calm are very positive during pregnancy. I believe that."

Dawn started thanking him profusely. Chew waved this off as if it was a common but regrettable misunderstanding of his power, and shuffled the papers into a neater pile. "Have you started thinking about a name?"

Silenced, Dawn shook her head, blinking rapidly. "Well, no," David said for her, and with some surprise. "Not after what happened the last couple of times."

"Of course," Chew said. "Very understandable. And it's early days. Always wise to remain poised in the face of fate. Actually, the question was my clumsy way of telling you something. The ultrasound was unclear, so the technician didn't mention it until I'd had a chance to examine the still images properly. But it's clear to me."

He paused, frowning down at the pieces of paper in front of him, the very picture of someone witnessing a lack of clarity.

Then he looked up and smiled more broadly. "You're going to have twins."

They walked out of the hospital in a dream, still holding hands. After delivering the end-of-episode kicker, Chew had waxed cautious, warning that the passage of twins into the world was more arduous and uncertain and noting that—speculative though it could only be at this stage—though both showed a strong heartbeat, one of the fetuses appeared more developed, a common situation that would hopefully right itself.

This Columbo-style zinger had caused a familiar sinking feeling in David's stomach (nothing was *ever* simple, was it) but he'd decided to take Chew's businesslike delivery of this caveat as a good sign.

"I'm so glad you came home last night," Dawn said, as they drew to a halt at the car.

"Me too." And he was, though he felt bad about positioning this as a desire to make sure he was on time for the consultation. "I still can't believe it."

"Believe it, Daddy-o," said Dawn. "I guess I'll get back to school. Shall I drop you home?"

"Think I'll stop by and get a coffee first. Not sure I'll get much done for an hour or two anyway."

Dawn started nodding, eyes brimming. David nodded back, equally senselessly, thinking how much harder it was to respond to good news. When they'd walked out of this hospital after the second miscarriage, it had been easy. They'd cried and held each other and said this wasn't the end, that they deserved a child and it would happen somehow. With bad news the bad thing has already happened. Hearing something good, or its promise, leaves you out on a limb, even *more* at the mercy of fate. It would be that the Bad Thing is still out there waiting to happen, enjoying its own shitty piece of showboating, waiting for maximum impact before revealing that, I'm so sorry, Dawn and David are out of the reproduction competition for good, but please give them a big hand.

Then David reached out for her, and they held each other and cried. News is news, and our bodies and minds respond much the same whether it's good or bad.

Dawn dropped him off on Main and then cruised off in the direction of the school, driving at about half her usual speed. David didn't think this was conscious caution, more likely that she hadn't stopped running the consultation over in her mind. He watched her to the end of the street and saw her indicate properly and was reassured she'd get to school without sailing serenely off the road into a house.

He hit the late-morning rush at Roast Me, and only as he waited in line did he realize he was going to have to say something to Talia about her book. He found it hard to remember much about it today, except that he'd been enjoying it. Hopefully that would do — along with something he recalled thinking during his last stretch of reading, after meeting Maj in Kendricks, which was that she could rein back on the fantasy elements and present it as something rather more edgy and urban, if she chose. Not that she'd be likely to, but saying this would at least prove that he'd been thinking about it.

When he'd arrived home at eleven the night before, Dawn was still awake. He'd warned her by text that he'd changed his mind and wasn't staying in the city after all, and she evidently felt this constituted a sufficient reversal to require debriefing. She sat up in bed as he told her that he and his friend had had a great conversation and would keep in touch, but he'd decided it was more important to ensure he was there for the scan rather than taking a risk with a tight train schedule the next morning.

She nodded thoughtfully, as if hoping he'd gotten enough out of the trip, but he could tell she was pleased.

His sleep was deep and dreamless. After breakfast, Dawn led him up to the third bedroom and showed him what she'd achieved. Just about everything in the room had been thrown away, put downstairs ready for transportation to Goodwill, or otherwise made to vanish. The only stuff remaining was a small pile of boxes holding things that David had never unpacked since he moved to Rockbridge. He'd agreed to perform triage on this as soon as possible — hoping that he wouldn't be coming back to the house later in the day knowing it wouldn't be necessary.

Now, he guessed, it really was.

"Hey, big shot," Talia said, when he got to the head of the line. "S'up? Finished your book yet?"

"Not so much. I'm enjoying yours, though."

"Really?"

David wouldn't have believed that Talia could look vulnerable. "Really. It's very good. I mean, I don't know the genre, but heck, I'm loving it, so that's probably an even better sign, right?"

Talia tried to look like she didn't give a crap but couldn't pull it off. "Where are you up to? No, don't tell me. Dumb question. It's a big book, I know."

"Dawn's pregnant," he said.

He'd had no idea he was going to say this. He wasn't sure he'd have called Talia a friend, and certainly wouldn't have pegged her as the first person with whom he'd share this news. As soon as he'd said it, though, and seen the look on her face, he realized that yes, she was.

"Fuck me sideways," Talia said quietly.

"Yeah."

"No way."

"Way. It's early days, but..."

She carefully put his cup to one side and then lunged across the counter to grab him around the shoulders with both arms. She was strong and heavy and her grip so fierce that she managed to lift both his feet clear off the floor. "Holy crap," she whispered in his ear. "Chalk one up for the good guys, huh?"

Then she dropped him again, got businesslike with taking his money, and told off the guy in line behind David for grinning at them, though she didn't manage to stop smiling during any of this.

As David turned from the counter and looked for somewhere to sit, he realized he was grinning too.

He chose a table by the window and flicked through the local alternative newspaper, remaining untouched by its demands for his attention and empathy. Usually he didn't care about what the town's handful of hippies felt, but right now he wouldn't have minded a distraction.

He couldn't ignore what had happened the day before, though it felt far less tangible now that he was back in Rockbridge. He remembered being in Union Square and in Dib's. He remembered what happened in the church later, too. He'd barely been introduced to the priest before the guy in the coat had arrived and started shouting. When a *second* unpredictable-looking stranger breezed in, David decided he'd had quite enough weirdness for one day. Waiting for the right moment and then scooting out of the place and all the way to the station was, he believed, the most actualized thing he'd done in his entire life.

And yet none of it seemed real.

In his mind's eye it felt like something he could have made up, a daydream or speculative plot line for which he had no idea of what-happens-next. And he was okay with that. Plot lines, he knew all too well, could be jettisoned. You could decide they led nowhere good and elect to strike them from the story.

That's what he was going to do. He had no need to go back to New

York. Maj knew where he lived, sure, but he evidently had other problems — not least the scary guy in the coat. David could simply decide not to reengage.

They were, as Maj had put it, two magnets permanently set to repel.

While he got these thoughts in order, David watched people out on the street. He wasn't really seeing his environment — more concerned with tidying his thoughts, reexperiencing delight at the memory of Dawn's face after the consultation, and trying to drag his mind back to the idea of doing some *work*.

He did not notice the three tall figures around the table in the back corner. He didn't see the way the red-haired woman looked thoughtfully from David to Talia, as if drawing a line between them, or how other visitors to the coffeehouse chose to sit at other tables even if they were less well positioned or needed the leavings of previous customers to be removed first.

Five minutes later, without apparent signal, the three people all stood together.

Then they were at the door.

Then they were outside, looking back into the coffee shop through the window, standing right over David and smiling down at him. He didn't see them.

Then they were gone.

The sky was gray and cold.

Chapter 31

Sure, I'm a Journeyman. You ask me, it's the only way to live. What—
you want to hang around your hometown your entire life, moping over
what's not there anymore and ain't never going to be? No thanks. Ain't
going to go live in some town, neither. Not a city kind of guy. Never have
been, never will be. Too dark, too noisy, everything too close together. It's
not the way I was raised.

When we were young we roamed the wild plains. If you don't remember, well, I do. We were heroes of the great outdoors, you and me. We
lived in forts and trees and dried river beds. We were free. I can be free by
myself if I have to. Do I go back? Hell no.

What would be the point?

It's not a job; it's a way of life. Wouldn't suit everyone, that's for sure. Seen a
few try and pretty soon go hurrying back to the city or whatever place they
come from. They want predictable. They want routine. There's a few of us
who don't, though. No idea how many—never see us all in the same place.
That's kind of the point. It comes down to constitution. I don't need to
buddy up. I'm good by myself. Those other friends...well, they want company. It's what they miss after the change, and that makes a kind of sense.

Company's what got taken away.

Every little town's going to have people of our general kind. Problem
is...depends whether you happen to like those people or not. In the city—
and I can see the point of this part, I suppose—you got a lot more choice.
You can pick and choose. Find somebody you like, a whole group of them if
you're lucky. Lot of the friends need that, too—they need enough people

around to remind them who they are and keep them strong inside. They got those different things they do there, too. Hobbies, lifestyles, whatnot. Jobs, some of them. I was talking with a Fingerman just the other day, matter of fact, last time I was in New York City for the night. He wanted my advice on traveling on the trains and I told him some of what I know. Don't know why he was thinking of hitting the road, and I didn't ask. Far as I'm concerned, a friend's business is his own, and he — or she — should do what the hell they feel like. Ain't no other damned thing to do anyhow.

This particular friend, Maj was his name, I could see him making this lifestyle work, maybe. He's got substance. Most Fingermen do. Some of the others, well, that's part of why they gather in the cities, I guess. Need a network to make them feel alive.

I see other Journeymen on the trains sometimes. Once in a while we'll sit and talk. Not for long, though. It's not a matter of being unfriendly. It's just — and I don't think some of the city friends realize this — the more of you there are together, the easier it is for other folk to see you and start to wonder what's going on. So if I see a fellow traveler, generally I'll just nod. That's enough to say, "I see you. I know what you are and respect you for it. Travel well, and may your road be ever long."

Some Journeymen walk. Some hitchhike, though that can be a risky business. It's okay if you can slip into a car when the driver's not looking and get out the same way, but sometimes a more inexperienced person will wind up having to absent themselves in a way that's not so subtle, which can look weird to the person who gave them the ride. I would not advise you to take the hitchhiking route unless you know what you're doing, bottom line.

Then there's some of us that head to the coast, walk onto boats or ocean liners, spend their time sailing back and forth. Others go to airports, get on planes, ride the air. Wouldn't neither of those suit me. I like the idea that I can get off at any time, change my mind and go some other way. Freedom. That's what we've got, if nothing else, and if you don't make the most of that then I don't know why you'd stick around.

Any kind of journeying amounts to the same thing. You know that old saying — it's better to travel than to arrive? Well, that's the truth right there, my friend. Traveling is what it is. It's got its own point.

'Specially if there ain't no particular place to go, and ain't never going to be.

I told a white lie earlier, though. I *do* go back, once in a while. You go back to the beginning in your memories often enough — I don't see a problem in going back in body sometimes too. See the places where you used to walk or used to play. I returned only once to the actual house, though, about five years ago. I stood in the street outside and looked at the place. It's been fancied up some since the family left, got extra rooms in back and a swimming pool now, if you can believe that. He would have loved a swimming pool back then. Had to make do with getting our feet wet in the creek. That suited us well enough. Weren't no cowboys in swimming pools, right? And that's what we were, most days. Soldiers sometimes, commandos; then there was a ninja phase, though I never really got behind that. But mainly we was cowboys, every day and every night.

Until some asshole bought him a computer, and that was the end of all that. You don't need a friend to stare at a screen with you, and if you want company I guess there's all those shadow people out there on the Internet. The change came on pretty fast. It does for many of us. Was a time when I used to have a place set for me at the dinner table. Then six months later he couldn't have remembered my name.

Which means neither can I.

Guess the truth is that maybe I *was* a buddy person, way back. I had myself a buddy, but those days are gone and they ain't coming back. I know what I am, and I'm okay with it.

There's a lot of roads left to roam.

Chapter 32

Kristina was pissed when she got home. She was angry throughout her shower—and not just because it kept randomly going hot and cold in the infuriating way it always did. She was annoyed when she stomped out of the bathroom, shivering, and she was furious as she stood toweling her hair in the living area.

When she called John after her encounter with the girl in Bryant Park, she'd expected him to be pleased or excited. Instead he'd given her a hard time about not getting in touch with him *immediately* after she realized she was being followed. He hadn't backed off on this over their subsequent lunch, either.

She knew that he hadn't meant to piss her off. She understood his response came from love, rather than a desire to make her feel inadequate— and yes, when de beast come out of de forest it traditionally be de man's job to stand in harm's way, but John knew she was capable of looking after herself. Reminding him of this had been the last thing she did before stomping away from the sushi bar, leaving him to pay.

He'd texted twice since, and left two voice mail messages. She hadn't replied to any of them.

Slowly she stopped toweling. She was spending a lot of time being grouchy these days. Too much. The story was getting old even to her.

It was time to perk up, to go spend another night in the company of strangers, people she'd either never see again or who were wearily familiar components of her half life, two-dimensional regulars with one-dimensional needs. As she buttoned her shirt, she realized she was sick to death of her job. Sure, you could forge a life in the food and beverage industries, be the best damned barkeep the East Village had ever known, but she couldn't see down that road and she didn't want to. It had stopped feeling real. It didn't make her feel real.

She needed something bigger and wider. She needed to feel her feet on the earth and know that ground was either hers or she had a damned long lease on it. John was good at making mental connections—even when he didn't realize he'd made them—and perhaps he'd started to sense this, had put together that they didn't need a new apartment, but a new life.

They needed a conversation about this stuff, and soon. And she'd start one. When she was good and ready . . . and done with being pissed at him.

She grabbed her keys off the counter and looked around for her phone. She'd thrown it somewhere when she stormed into the apartment, to make it harder to hear the sound of John's texts. That this already struck her as *outrageously* childish proved she was calming down. She swept her gaze over the obvious surfaces before . . .

Aha: there it was, on the couch.

As she picked it up and turned to go, she let out a little scream.

She froze, staring at the window. From this angle all you could see through it was a glancing view of the gable and a patch of gray sky. If you pulled your focus closer, there was the glass of the window itself. The message from the other night was gone. John had rubbed it off the next morning. He'd done it in a hurry, however, leaving smears and blotches and redistributing years of grime rather than removing it.

There was something else written in it now.

Kristina took a cautious step closer, angling her head. As before, the marks on the window could almost have been made by raindrops, or the scrabbling claws of a pigeon blown into it by a high wind. Almost.

LO6

The marks were too close together to be random, however, and gathered right in the center of the pane. There was consistency in their weight, too, as if they'd been scrawled out by the same finger.

Were they supposed to be letters, or a drawing? It was hard to tell. The first mark was kind of like a capital J, though the second upright was shorter than the first, making it look reversed. The third symbol looked a *lot* like a 6. The curves in both were what made it impossible to believe them to be water tracks—there wasn't enough wind to have reversed gravity.

The thing in the middle was harder to make out. It could have been an angular O, or a zero, though she couldn't work out why you'd try to create one of those from a combination of lines rather than one long stroke.

So... it must be a square, presumably.

Reverse J, square, 6.

Kristina stared at it for five long minutes, and then finally got it.

By the time she ran breathless into the bottom of the park—at twenty minutes after six—she'd started to lose confidence in her guess, that the square might mean a square, the reversed J a malformed U, and the U short for "Union"... and the numeral a time.

If someone wanted to leave a message, why wouldn't they have written the damned thing properly? She was well aware that she was behaving contrary to common sense because of how irritated John had made her earlier—and that this wasn't anywhere close to being a good reason.

But still, she was here. The park was emptying out, a handful of people crossing the lower section on their way home or toward an early dinner. Kristina passed them, walking deeper, and felt like she was going the wrong way. During the day, parks are a destination. Come the evening, they get downgraded to cut-through and that-dark-patch-over-the-fence. A chunk of nature in the city turns unsettling after dark. They become home to the homeless, unwelcome reminders that having a place to rest your head is not a given. Even when surrounded by busy streets, parks remind us why we went to the trouble of inventing houses and artificial light. The humans that lurk there become a part of the wilderness, infiltrated by it — shards of the unknown come to nudge us out of comfort. Walking on the other side of the street seems wiser, lest we become infected too.

Nonetheless, Kristina headed up the path. There was no one at the benches or on the grassed areas. The leaves whispered but without any great intent. It took a strong wind to reach down here out of the canyons of buildings.

Kristina drew to a halt, unsure what to do, and whether to stay or go.

"You okay, ma'am?"

A cop stood ten feet away. "Sure," she said. "Just taking a walk."

The cop nodded, and it seemed to her like he took a beat too long over this, as if he was questioning her motives or her right to be there.

She stood her ground. "Which is allowed, right?"

He walked away. Seemed like male kind was determined to present its officious side today. And maybe it was different if you were born and bred in New York City, but it also felt like there was always someone determined to make you feel like a second-class citizen in it, to show how much they belonged here and you did not.

Either that or she was feeling dumb for being here and looking for someone to blame it on.

Yeah, she guessed, it could be that.

So . . . screw this, Kris. Go to the restaurant, make nice with John. Do the sensible thing for once in your bad-tempered and contrary life, huh?

Abruptly deciding she'd misinterpreted the marks on the window or added two and two together and made a billion, she turned toward the main pathway.

She faltered, however. There was something different now. She could feel it, though at first she couldn't work out why. Then something else changed.

There were three people standing in front of her.

Two girls, one guy. All were dressed in tattered black, with highlights of rich colors—blue, purple, emerald green. They stood in an arc, very still, looking at her.

She looked behind.

Two people were behind her, too. Both men, also dressed in black, the clothes so very dark that you couldn't make out what the layers were. There was nothing overtly threatening in the way they stood, except for the fact that they were in a circle and were pale and hollow-eyed and looking intently at her.

Which . . . was pretty threatening.

Kristina took a moment to wish she'd listened to what John had said, and that he was here, but knew she was going to have to deal with this herself. "You going to get out of my way?"

Silence. Nobody moved.

"Who the hell are you?"

Nobody spoke. They were so very motionless that it was as if they were images layered on top of the park. A gust of wind finally made it down out of the trees, moving branches. Though the people in front of her were dressed in rags and tatters of layers and coats, none of these stirred.

"Kristina," said a voice.

Another figure had joined the circle. It was Catherine's follower, the girl Kris had met in Bryant Park that afternoon. She didn't look harmless now, though. She looked like the leader of a small brigade of unknown allegiance and unpredictable behavior and power.

"Lizzie? Who are these people?"

The girl cocked her head to one side, birdlike. "You can see them, too?"

"Two girls, three guys," Kristina said. "Dressed like you. They're freaking me out. I say again: *who are these people?*"

Lizzie looked thoughtful. Kristina was aware of the others glancing at one another now. One of the girls — plump in figure, dressed goth style with dyed white hair — whispered to the man next to her. It sounded like car tires two streets away in the night, or like the door to the bedroom closet falling open an inch in the dark.

"We're Angels," Lizzie said. "Would you like to walk with us?"

Chapter 33

With that, the girl started walking, going from stationary to moving fast with no step in between.

Kristina hesitated, but followed. "What do you mean, you're..."

There was no point — the girl was already too far ahead. Kristina had a hundred questions she wanted to ask, but she had to catch up with the woman first. Meanwhile, Lizzie kept glancing back at Kristina curiously. The other people walked in loose formation around her, and were doing the same, casting glances at Kris and half smiles at one another, as if there were something odd and notable about her, rather than them.

"Why do they keep looking at me like that?" Kristina panted, finally managing to get alongside Lizzie as she crossed 14th and headed toward the Village.

"I'd like to walk with you," Lizzie said, as if she hadn't heard the question. Her voice was clear, with none of the soft edges from when they'd met in Bryant Park. "But we need rules."

"What do you mean?"

The girl strode across Bleecker without appearing to care whether traffic was coming. Kristina almost got taken out by a cyclist and had to jump back onto the curb. Lizzie waited on the other side until Kris reached her, then immediately set off again.

"Look straight ahead," she said. "Instead of saying 'yes' or 'no,' nod or shake your head. If you *do* speak, keep your head down and don't be loud. Okay?"

Kristina started to say yes, then nodded instead.

"Excellent!" Lizzie said, delighted, clapping her hands together like a girl who'd laid out the ground rules for a skipping game and received unexpectedly ready assent. "I worked all that out last night."

"Why are you walking so *fast?*"

"I'm not."

They'd reached the fringes of the Village, heading toward SoHo, and the sidewalks were getting crowded. Kristina noticed the other people with them had spread out, one ahead and two behind, and that one couple had transferred to the other side of the street. They were holding hands, the plump girl and a rail-thin boy who'd dyed his hair pure white too. They were still glancing at her, though, with those odd smiles. It was like . . .

It was how Kristina imagined celebrities must feel. Strangers continually slipping glances your way, drinking you in, clocking and logging you as if it were a big deal to be sharing the same space. Why would they be doing that to her, of all people? She couldn't imagine, but it had the effect of making them seem less threatening, as if she had status in some invisible hierarchy.

Lizzie meanwhile kept surging onward, and Kristina found it increasingly hard to keep up. The girl carved down the street as though on a priority track. Sometimes she overtook other pedestrians, not leaving enough space for Kristina to follow. At others she dodged gracefully out of the way of oncoming walkers at the last second, leaving Kristina to clumsily attempt to do the same.

After glancing collisions with two sets of tourists more interested in gawking in store windows than watching where they were going, Kristina gave up.

"Look, slow *down,* will you? If you want to talk, then —"

Lizzie stopped in her tracks and turned to look at her. Someone banged hard into Kristina's back.

"For Christ's sake," the man snarled. "You have a fucking stroke, or what?"

Still fuming at the idiocy of someone who might pause on a sidewalk, for crying out loud, the man stormed off down the road of his angry little life.

Lizzie remained motionless.

"What?" The girl's eyes stayed on her, blank and dead. Kristina lowered her head and muttered, taking care not to move her lips much, "Okay, I get it," she said. "But slow *down,* okay?"

The others had gathered and were clustered around her and Lizzie. A little too close, in fact, looking at her with their unnervingly steady gaze, as if waiting for her to say something else, or do something.

Lizzie glanced around. "Too crowded," she conceded. "Good for us, difficult for you."

She considered, then pointed diagonally across the street. On the other side was a doorway next to a café that was shut for the evening. The doorway was dark, recessed, and partially obscured by trees on either side. "Shoo, friends."

With that, Kristina and Lizzie were alone.

Kristina assumed the girl would lead her into the building — and was weighing up just how dumb an idea it would be to follow — when she realized the doorway itself was their destination. When they were within its shadow Lizzie turned back and indicated for Kristina to stand at a certain angle, her back up against one side of the recess, facing away from the street.

"This should be okay. For a while."

Kristina realized the woman had positioned her so she could speak normally without being seen by anyone passing by. "Where did the others go?"

Lizzie shrugged, but not in a way that said she didn't know. "I'm glad you got the message."

"Was it you who put the other one there? About leaving you alone?"

"Not me. But one of us."

"Why?"

"You were following me. You and John."

"We weren't. We didn't even know who you are. We were just trying to find out who was stalking a friend of mine. Catherine Warren."

The girl's eyes clouded, and she looked away. Kris pressed it. "Why *are* you following her?"

"I don't want to talk about that."

"So . . . what *do* you want to talk about?"

"I'm not used to this," the girl said, sounding defensive. "I'm so out of practice. I don't know what to say to someone like you anymore."

"What do you mean—someone like me?"

"Someone with things."

"When I asked you what you were, you said—"

"Angels, yes," Lizzie said. "It's just a name. Like Journeyman or Dozeno or Fingerman."

"Okay . . . so what's a Fingerman?"

Lizzie held her hand up and placed index and thumb tips together. "Someone who can do this."

"Well . . . *you* can do it."

"Of course. Most Angels have some fingerskills, but we don't have the precision of someone like Maj."

"Who's Maj?"

Lizzie smiled coyly. "A friend."

"Special friend, by the look of it."

Lizzie wasn't saying. "Did you tell John you were coming out to the park?"

"No."

"Did . . . you mind me asking that?"

Kristina shook her head, but the girl was sharp: answering the question had made her feel awkward, disloyal. She didn't talk about John. Ever. When Catherine nattered about Mark—even a corporate merger as successful as theirs experienced occasional interdepartmental gripes—

Kristina listened without giving back. Her relationship with John was private, reality's core, not a subject for status updates.

"Is everything okay with him?"

Kristina was about to tell the girl to mind her own business, but realized that, strangely, she didn't want her to. The conversation felt appropriate. The usual barriers of embarrassment and caution didn't feel present. It was like being coaxed into overdue utterance by some friend you'd had back in school, before life got complicated, when it was possible to know *everything* about someone, every fact of their short life, to the bottom of their soul.

"We're . . . going through an odd patch," she admitted.

The girl laughed, but not in a way that diminished what Kris had said. "Even if two people stand in the ocean next to each other, the waves hit you at different angles." She put a hand on Kristina's arm. "But it will be okay."

"You think?"

"Definitely."

Kristina realized two of the other people were back, and standing beside her—the couple who'd been walking together. They seemed pleased with themselves.

"For you," the man said.

Kristina couldn't work out what he was talking about. The girl glanced ostentatiously down. Kristina looked too and saw the guy had something cupped in his hand, held low, as if to prevent passersby from seeing.

"Quickly," the girl said. "He can't hold it for long."

Kristina took the object. She kept her hands down low and saw she was holding a silver necklace, modern-looking. And expensive. "What . . . what's this?"

"It's for you," the girl said.

"Where did it come from?"

The man pointed across the street. Kristina saw a jewelry store among the boutiques. Women in expensive clothing stood in front of cabinets, heads reverentially bowed. It looked like the kind of place Catherine might head to pick out what Mark might want to give her for an anniversary.

She glanced at Lizzie. The girl smiled, but it looked guarded, or sad. She seemed resigned rather than disapproving. Turning back to the couple in front of her, Kris saw they now appeared worried.

"Don't you like it?" the girl asked. "We could find something else."

"No, it's lovely. But — did you steal it?"

They nodded like a pair of little dogs. "I can't accept this," Kristina said. "It's sweet of you, but —"

But they were gone. Lizzie too.

Kristina was standing alone in the doorway. She shoved the necklace into her jeans pocket, panicked.

There was a man standing on the other side of the street, looking at her. Two men, in fact — one still, the other wandering up and down among the shoppers, hands in the pockets of an old-fashioned suit. The first was staring directly at her. His face was full of flat planes and he wore an ostentatious coat.

Cops?

Kristina had worked thirty bars and never dipped her fingers in the till, held jobs in stores all over the country and not once exercised a five-finger discount either. Now she was in possession of a piece of jewelry that had to be worth several thousand dollars. It wouldn't matter that she hadn't taken it. Having it stuffed into her jeans didn't make it look like she'd been on the verge of returning it to its rightful owner.

Meanwhile the men watched. One moving, the other motionless. The longer she stayed where she was, the more guilty she would look. But if she started to leave, would they come for her? Would they grab her right there, or wait until she hurried up a side street?

What if they weren't even cops?

Would you really dress like that if you were a policeman? A policeman whose job was trying to bust people for stealing from stores?

"Don't turn around."

Not screaming took all the self-possession Kristina possessed. The voice was quiet, female. Lizzie.

Kristina stared at her feet and hissed: "What the *hell* is going on?"

"Just walk away. They're not looking for you."

"Then why are they staring *at* me?"

"It's us they want, not you. Walk away like there's nothing wrong. But tell me your number."

Kristina muttered her phone number. There was silence. After a moment she glanced behind.

There was no one there.

She stepped out onto the sidewalk. The shorter of the two men had already disappeared. The man in the coat turned on his heel and strode off down the road without looking back.

Kristina willed herself to keep calm, to walk slowly. She strolled with the early-evening shoppers, doing her best to look like she was in the market for a handbag or an iPod. She allowed herself to look back only when she reached the next street corner. She saw no one.

She kept walking until the other side of SoHo.

And *then* she ran.

Chapter 34

Kris was over an hour late getting to the restaurant, and by the time she arrived I was tired of fielding the management's increasingly irritable inquiries as to her whereabouts, not least because I didn't know. I'd sent her a few texts, but she hadn't replied, and there wasn't much more I could do—except be concerned on her behalf and know how pissed she'd be if I let her see it. That's all I'd done at lunch, and it hadn't gone well.

I was dealing with a table of Midwesterners who hadn't been expecting little bits of basil all over their pizzas and were extremely perturbed about them, and so when I saw Kris finally hurry into the restaurant I merely rolled my eyes and nodded in the direction of Mario, and then winked—as complex a nonverbal communication as I'm capable of without straining a muscle.

Kristina sent a smile back, a quick but heartfelt one that said she probably wasn't as annoyed at me as she had been earlier—and carrying something else that I couldn't determine—and went to placate the owners' wrath. Not for the first time it struck me that after six months of being model employees we'd begun to make a habit of not being where we were supposed to be, and that Mario and his sister hadn't lasted so many years in the restaurant business by tolerating flakiness for long.

I didn't see Kristina again until table service was done and I went downstairs to the bar. It was busy at first but gradually settled down to regulars. I perched at the corner of the bar and waited, drinking a line of beers—sent in my direction without need for interaction—until Kristina saw a gap in business and headed my way.

"I saw her again," she said without preamble.

"Who?"

She told me about the message on the window of our apartment, working out what it might mean, and going to Union Square. "And do *not* give me grief about this."

"What do I care?" I said. "I mean, it displeases me as a patriarchal asshole who mistrusts any woman's ability to handle any situation, but otherwise, why would I give a shit?"

She opened her mouth, then closed it. "Sorry."

"So what happened?"

She told me about walking with the girl—Lizzie—into SoHo, and the beginnings of a conversation that had been derailed first by a gift and then by . . . well, she wasn't too clear about what had happened after that.

"You think they were cops?"

"They didn't look it, but what do I know about fashion trends in undercover police?"

She was trying to make light, but I could tell she was unsettled. I put my hand on top of hers. She looked at it. "Is this a public display of affection?"

"No. My hand was cold."

"I hate it when we fight."

"Me too. So let's not do it. Show me the thing."

She pulled it out of her pocket, keeping it hidden in her hand until it had been dropped into mine. An attractive piece of modern jewelry. It didn't look cheap, either. "And they handed this to you, even though they'd met you only an hour before?"

She nodded, then had to go serve someone. I clocked that the person sitting two stools along from me was paying a little too much attention— underground bars in the East Village are exactly the kind of place you'd go to buy something not legally come by—and so I dropped my hands into my lap.

By the time Kristina came back I thought I'd worked out what was going on. "The guys. Describe them again."

She did, and I nodded, feeling excited. "That fits. The man who kept still—he sounds like the one I saw at the church, who had some beef with the priest—Reinhart. He's not a cop. He's a criminal."

"How do you know?"

"Trust me. These people you met in the park, Lizzie and her friends: evidently they're skilled at fading into the background—we've already seen how good *she* is at that. And Lizzie didn't seem surprised that two of her friends had stolen something, right?"

"No. She looked disapproving, but she wasn't surprised."

"So that's what they do. They're an urban tribe, whatever, living between the cracks—and they survive by stealing. So they're going to need someone more plugged into the world than they are, with connections for selling stolen goods. I'm thinking that's Reinhart."

Kristina thought about it, nodded. "Maybe. Though...they didn't seem like thieves."

"Not archetypal assholes who take stuff because they're too lazy or dumb to do anything else, no. But you know what this city's like. There's the normal citizens but then all the other layers. Street people, thousands of them. Others living in the tunnels near Penn Station or crashing under a different bridge every night. What if some of these people got organized?"

"Lizzie mentioned people called 'Fingermen,' and others I don't remember," Kristina said, thoughtfully.

"Fingermen has to be a name for the ones who steal stuff, right? They have some people who are good at remaining unnoticed, slipping into places, and taking things, and specialize at it. The money they get goes into food and clothes and burner phones and whatever else they need. That's why Reinhart was taking an interest. He could have been worried that *you* were a cop, or a competitor. If he's got a lucrative arrangement with these people, he's not going to want others muscling in. Could be that's why he was threatening the priest, too."

"Why?"

"Maybe Jeffers is trying to lead them in a different direction. Stop being bad; walk toward the light. You said Lizzie didn't look happy about the stealing. The guy in the white shirt I saw going into the church — he was with her and the priest in Union Square, right? And he'd taken the scared-looking guy to the church, presumably to introduce him to Jeffers, maybe to start the process of getting him out of the criminal life. When Reinhart turned up the guy bolted — perhaps because he knew Reinhart was going to be pissed at him being there."

"Maybe. But that's a lot of maybes. And . . ." She shook her head.

"What am I missing?"

"I don't know There's something *about* these people. They didn't seem like runaways or homeless people. They had more to them than that."

It seemed to me that one of the things they might have, in Kris's eyes, was a life that didn't involve living in a tiny apartment and serving beers underground, an existence that seemed edgier and desirably off the grid of mundanity. I shrugged. "It's the best I've got."

"And I'm not saying it sucks. But then what's the deal with Lizzie and Catherine?"

"Didn't you ask?"

"Yes. She didn't want to talk about it. I got the sense . . . I don't know, that maybe Catherine did something to her, or something. Let her down."

I had another idea. "Maybe they case people's houses too. Stalk normal citizens, map their schedules and routines and work out when would be a good time to stage a burglary."

"No way," Kris said. "I don't believe she'd be a party to something like that."

"Kris, you only just met her."

"Yeah, and tell me you don't make character assessments just as fast. You pegged this Reinhart guy as a villain in two seconds flat."

"I trust your judgment. But people on the edge will countenance doing things that —"

Kris shook her head firmly and wouldn't talk about it anymore.

When we got back to the apartment the message on the window was gone. That meant someone had been out on our roof again, and while Kris seemed to be becoming comfortable with our window turning into some kind of low-tech Facebook, I was not.

As we lay in bed I asked Kristina if she'd at least talk to me before meeting with Lizzie or any of her friends again. She said she would. I wasn't sure that I believed her, however, and I wasn't sure I understood what this said about the way things stood between us.

Chapter 35

At two in the morning Maj rose from the floorboards where he'd been lying. Sometimes there were others here too, sometimes not. This night, he had lain alone. Sleep had never come easy, but he always made the effort. The Gathered used to say it was as important to them, and their minds, as to anyone else. So he tried. Recently he'd found it harder, however. And tonight, though he'd gone through the motions of returning to the upper floor of a boarded-up ex–digital goods store in Midtown (a recent casualty of online retail dominance; though the upstairs room was messy and pigeons had already made it in through a broken window to start spreading shit and feathers, the roof was in place and at least it wasn't damp) it had not come at all.

He'd suspected it might be that way after meeting with Lizzie earlier. She'd told him about her near encounter with Reinhart in SoHo. She'd done so even though she knew he'd disapprove of what she'd been doing—hanging out with a tourist from the other side. She was open about what she did and thought and had told the truth. What she'd done wasn't what was bothering him, though he'd told her to be careful, both of Reinhart and her new acquaintance.

What was bothering him was the increasing suspicion that . . . *something was going on.*

None of the Angels worked for Reinhart. Several used to in the past, like Flaxon, but all had stopped after coming under Lizzie's influence. So why had Reinhart been watching them tonight? And why had he turned up at the church? The two events so close together had to be connected. So far, the worldviews of Jeffers and Reinhart had coexisted without contact. Both men knew of each other and the competing pulls they represented, but there had been dead space between them.

Last night Reinhart had crossed it.

He was making it personal, and once he'd started down that road it seemed unlikely he'd retreat. It had not been lost on Maj that Reinhart's parting comments had been delivered at him. Why? Golzen kept recycling his pitch that Maj should come and work for Reinhart—a transparent attempt to bind him into Golzen's messianic nonsense about Perfect—but last night was the first time they'd been in the same room.

So why had Reinhart spoken to him directly? As if he felt he had some kind of call on him?

Maj didn't know. He didn't like not knowing.

He slipped out of the building via the broken window, walked across the next roof, and then dropped down into a backstreet.

Though he'd never been to the building on Orchard, it was easy to find. He'd heard tell of its general location, and had to walk the streets for only half an hour—keeping an eye out for surreptitious-looking friends, shadows slipping around street corners—before homing in on a walk-down with a black door at the bottom. A sketchy club, now empty for the night. The door was thick but lighter than it looked, and unlocked.

Maj walked into the large, empty space. There was no one there but for a slight figure sitting slumped at the bar. With a start, Maj realized who it was.

It was the teenager he'd last run into when he'd been walking with David, the girl in the gray hoodie who'd invited him to a party in the Meatpacking District. The change in twenty-four hours was disturbing. Gone was the it's-all-good teen he'd gotten used to bumping into on the streets. Her face was pale now. She'd been crying, and her eyes were ringed with smudged black makeup.

"Are you okay?"

She didn't say anything. She looked like a Missing Person poster, and when someone emerged from the shadows to the side of the bar, Maj put two and two together.

"You asshole," Maj said. "What did you do to her?"

"Provided enlightenment," Golzen said. "My business has always been to help people get where they're going."

Maj turned to the girl. "What did he tell you?"

She looked away. "What I am."

"What—friendly? Fun?"

"No. What I *really* am."

"Then why are you here?"

"He said there was a man who could help me."

"He lied," Maj said. "Reinhart will make you cheat and steal. Ask yourself what Lizzie would say about those things. You like Lizzie, right?"

"She's wonderful."

"Right. And she thinks Reinhart is scum."

"Hey, hey," said a voice. Reinhart came striding toward him from a doorway at the end of the room. "Good to see you, Maj. Glad you made it to the nest at last."

"Leave Jeffers alone," Maj said.

Reinhart grimaced, looked sad, held his hands out, palms up. Play-acting. "*That's* why you're here?"

"He helps people. You don't."

"Wrong, my friend. That is my whole point. That is why I've been trying to get Golzen to put us together for a talk. Which he's apparently now done, for which I'm grateful."

"He's a good dog, right?"

"There's a place in this world for people who do what they're told, Maj. Good things come to them."

"Charity. Exactly the bullshit we've had enough of."

"I agree. I agree. No more handouts. I can help with that, Maj. I can help all of you. Time is running out for the old-school. You need to step up, come enjoy a new way to be. I can get you there."

Meanwhile the girl had slipped down off her stool and was approaching along a curved line, like a cat. She crept closer to Reinhart, looking up at his face.

"Are you Reinhart?"

He frowned at her. "Who are you?"

"Are you going to like me?"

"Get away from me, you freak," Reinhart said, turning to Golzen. "Who the fuck is this?"

"A Dozeno. Just turned her," Golzen said with pride. "She's wide open. Dumb as a sack of rocks, but we could get her eavesdropping PIN numbers or something, once she's got her ditzy head around what she is."

The girl kept staring up at Reinhart's face. "Are you going to be my friend?"

He laughed. "*Friend?* If you were real, you'd be strapped facedown to a bed right now, getting broken in. As it is you're good to me for only one thing and I will get into that later, but right now I'm *busy,* so fuck off."

"I don't understand."

Reinhart sent a backhand blow at the girl's face. It went straight through her head, but she flinched and fell back. He looked at her thoughtfully.

"Actually," he said to Golzen, "there's substance there. She might be able to do basic fingerwork, with training. Make a note."

The girl straightened slowly, hand against her face. "You know?" she said to Maj. "I think you're right. He doesn't seem like a very nice man."

"He's not," Maj said. "Go find Lizzie. Talk to her. She'll help. I can help too."

"Maybe," the girl said. "But the thing is...I don't really know you either. Or Lizzie. Or anybody else."

She turned from him, from everyone, and wandered away into the darkness in the corner of the big, empty basement, crying once more. Reinhart watched her go, as if finding the sight interesting. Or amusing.

Or . . . something.

"You're everything we don't need," Maj said to him. "Stay the hell out of our world."

He walked out and didn't look back.

And that, Golzen felt, was hopefully that. Reinhart turned to him, however.

"I don't see your buddies," he said irritably. "I asked you to stick them to that guy. I think I said 'like glue.' I didn't see any glue. I don't see your guys. Were they outside, waiting? Tell me they're outside."

Golzen shook his head. "It's not hard to keep track of what Maj's up to. I had another idea. I sent them after Maj's friend."

"Sent them? Where?"

"I don't know. Wherever the guy lives. They followed him after you confronted Jeffers in the church last night. They'll watch Maj's friend and return and tell me if there's any leverage we might be able to use on Maj, something from his friend's life. Assuming you think it's worth it, of course, after his attitude tonight."

"Good work," Reinhart said thoughtfully. "I like what you've done there. Let me know."

He nodded, then wandered off into the shadows in the direction the girl had gone, dismissing Golzen as if he'd vanished, or had never been there at all.

Just until we leave for Perfect, Golzen thought as he watched him go. *Then you'll have to find a new dog.*

In a way, he almost hoped it *would* be Maj.

He had a feeling Maj might bite.

Chapter 36

The first thing Talia did when she got home, as always, was take a bath. When you're living in a trailer of significant age and lackluster specifications this is not a quick or simple procedure, but it's hot working behind a coffee machine, and she'd always been a girl who liked to be clean. She supposed there weren't many people in town who thought of Talia Willocks as a girl these days. But she'd been one once. She still was. Mother fucking Teresa herself must have stopped to gawk at the clouds or check out a cute butt once in a while, even after she looked like she'd been exhumed.

When she was done bathing—she never rushed that part, having always believed in marking out her day into sections, like chapters maybe—she wandered back into her home's main area, clad in a pink terry-cloth bathrobe (she needed to replace it soon; it was starting to fray on the sleeves and okay, there was no one to see, but you had to keep on top of that stuff). Her living space was tidy. Keeping a place (or a life) in good order merely meant putting things where they were supposed to go, and if you lived in a trailer and didn't pick up that habit then you were going to be wallowing in a pigsty real fast.

The place gave her everything she needed. She had her sitting area, a pair of two-seater couches in an L shape, the second of which de-marked the space from the kitchenette and the table where she ate and did administrative chores . . . and everything else. The real parts of her life. At present, approximately seven square feet of the horizontal surfaces—a portion of one of the couches, two patches of kitchen, a spot right in the middle of the table, and two apparently random positions on the floor—were home to the sides, paws, or posteriors of cats. Six were currently indoors, the others outside, who knows where, doing stuff, who knows what. A long time ago a man whom Talia had loved used to deliver a stock response to being asked whether he'd had enough pizza yet.

"Is there any left?" he'd say.

"Yes."

"Well, no, then," he'd answer, baffled.

Talia felt the same about cats. She knew people who believed nine was too many. For her the words "too many" didn't compute with cats. Sure, you could be some batty old lady who let the place fill up with fur and uncleaned litter trays, but Talia was not that woman and wasn't ever going to be.

She wandered around, spending time with each of her friends. They craned their heads up into her hand, or rolled over, or sat focused on some interior thought. Once she'd said hello to each she felt like she was really home, and it was time to get on.

She changed into stretch pants and sweatshirt and put the robe back on over it all, then fixed herself a little food. She didn't eat much in the evening. She didn't eat much at *any* time, despite her running gag about stealing the cakes at Roast Me. Either she was falling foul of hidden calories somewhere or her body wanted to be this shape, and she was done pretending she gave a shit. She fixed a vegetable stir-fry with some of the smoked tofu she'd become mildly addicted to, flicking the pan in the way she'd seen that guy do it on television (and that, after some practice, she could replicate without shunting half the contents over the stove). When it was cooked, she reached to the magnetized strip on the left where her cooking implements hung.

Her fingers failed to find what they expected. Her spatula wasn't there.

She frowned, looked around — and spotted it on the magnetic strip on the other side. Well, that wasn't where it was supposed to be. That was for the knives. Huh. How had that happened? Nobody else would have moved it. She couldn't remember the last time someone had been in her home. A long time back it had been a popular destination for those in the county who enjoyed a beer and a smoke while one or more of them played Neil Young songs to varying degrees of recognizability on battered guitars. The younger (and much slimmer) version of Talia Willocks could lay a harmony line on top and, moreover, kept a dependable stock of cold beer in the fridge and made fine brownies too, albeit of the kind that had you staring at the stars and talking all kinds of happy crap by the time you'd finished your second.

Those days were gone, and most of those people had drifted on or gone corporate — George Lofland was the only one she still passed the time of day with. The trailer parties had stopped the day Ed died. The heart had gone out of the town for a few months after the crash in which he was killed along with five other well-liked locals. It was a simple accident, nobody's fault, just one of those things, which somehow made it worse.

The heart had never quite gone out of Talia's life, though for a long time its beating had been quiet indeed, and there had been nights in the first months where she'd worried it might slow to nothing. Then one night, sitting in a chair by herself in front of the trailer and pretty deep in the bag, she'd happened to see a shooting star, cheap and easy though that might seem when the story's told. She'd been seeing them all her life and it wasn't any big deal, but that had the point.

Not everything is somebody's fault.

Magic happens, and shit happens, and neither lasts forever. You have to let the instances burn themselves out, arcing over the time horizon, and then get the fuck back on your feet and reengage the fight.

Ed's dead.

Get over it.

The next day she'd woken up with a vicious hangover but had hauled herself into town and bought a big notebook. That had been the start. She'd written something — and usually a lot — every day since. At first just a diary (which she still kept up, in ordered ranks of identical notebooks on the shelf behind the TV), then the more creative journaling, and finally . . . the novel. Ta-da.

She looked at the spatula hanging on the rail and decided she must have put it there herself.

Hey, girl, still got some wild in you. You put the spatula on a different rail for once. Rock and fucking roll.

She fished the food out of the pan and onto a plate and took it to the table. Four of the cats came and watched while she did this, but in a companionable way, as they knew there was nothing on the plate for cats. Talia chatted with them about her day while she ate, and why not? There was nobody to hear.

Three hours later she sat back from the computer and blew strands of hair off her face. Writing always made her hot—though not that kind of hot, ha-ha. It just fired her up. She sympathized with David for the trouble he was having, but it never got her that way. Whether she was updating her diary or plowing into the sequel to *The Quest of Alegoria* (she knew she shouldn't until she'd heard from David what he thought about the first, but the characters had started doing their song and dance in her head and she couldn't stop herself from hooking up and seeing where they wanted to go next), words had always come easily. She was a relaxed kind of person, didn't care much what people thought, and maybe that helped. David was a nice guy and she still hadn't gotten over how touched she'd been by his offer to read her book (she got the sense that he thought fantasy was beneath him, and that was okay; a lot of people did), but he was kind of . . . *uptight.* Actually, that wasn't the word.

Talia put her elbows on the table and concentrated. Words were like cats (if you thought hard enough about it, pretty much everything was like cats, or unlike them, or whatever). Chase after cats or words and they'll outrun you every time. Sit still, act like you don't care, and they'll be all over you (another lesson that David could benefit from learning).

It wasn't *uptight,* it was...

Guarded. Yeah, that was closer. He was friendly and all, and obviously loved Dawn to death, but it was like his eyes were turned in—as if what happened inside his skull was the realest thing in his world. Talia loved to write, but she knew the difference between inside and out and which was important. She wasn't sure David *did* know this, and she'd been nearly blown out of her panties when he'd blurted out his news about the baby. It was touching as hell but out of character, as if he'd decided that it was worth interacting with real people for once. Of course, with what had happened to his parents, maybe it wasn't so surprising that he took a cautious approach. Maybe that was simply good sense, and one of these days he'd see his own shooting star—or hopefully something less obvious, as Talia believed David might think wake-up calls delivered via shooting star a little beneath him, too—and relax a little.

Clichéd though the star had been, it had worked. You didn't need fancy, not with things that counted. Ed used to say you could play half the songs in the world (and pretty much all of the good ones) with just three chords.

God, she hoped David liked her book.

If he did, surely that was a good sign. In her heart of hearts she knew she wrote for herself, but shit, a little money would come in handy and it would be kind of cool to go into libraries and see her book there, women waiting patiently for their chance to take it out and spend a little time in Talia's world of wonders.

We'll see. No point waiting on it. Not when there's so many more words out there to write.

She had her hands raised to go back to typing when she noticed something was up with the cats. During the time she'd been working, the cast of feline companions had been in flux. Some went out via the flap in the door; others came in. It was getting late now, though, after eleven, and...

she counted, and confirmed what she'd already known (if you love cats, you know if they're around without having to check)—everybody was inside. All present and accounted for. Five spread over the couches. Two underneath them. And two...

It was the two on the table she noticed first. Sandy and Pickles. They'd been curled up at the far end (they were siblings and usually slept together) and then both raised their heads at the same time and stood up.

Talia heard a rustling, looked around, and saw most of the cats on the couches had done the same.

She wasn't fussed by this—they did it all the time, feline senses picking up on small creatures of the night unwisely straying too close outside. A mouse, vole, rat, whatever. At this time of night most of the cats would muse on it for a minute and then settle back down, reasoning that there'd be plenty of opportunity for terrorizing wildlife the following day, and it was late, and really it was pretty comfortable and warm inside.

Only Tilly—who Talia saw was now jumping down from the couch, tail up—would generally elect to make something of it. Though the smallest and one of the oldest of her cat friends, Tilly operated a Zero Tolerance and Nuke From Orbit approach to anything that strayed near her territory, and could be guaranteed to go and chase the living crap out of whatever was outside, sometimes returning with the remains in her mouth as an offering to the big human she lived with.

Now, however, she saw that Tilly had hesitated about halfway to the trailer door. She sat down abruptly. Looked back the way she'd come. Trying to pinpoint the noise from outside, presumably, which Talia hadn't even heard. Pickles and Sandy seemed to be doing the same, and none of the other cats had settled down yet either.

Kind of odd, but cats got ideas into their heads once in a while and just as quickly forgot them. Whatever. It was getting late and she had at least another blank line break in her before it was time for—

Someone knocked on the door.

Talia froze, hands still poised. There was no doubt that's what it had been. There were trees near the trailer, but none of them came close enough for a branch to have made the sound. It had come from the door, too, not the roof—a straightforward *rap rap rap*. Not loud. Like you'd do if you were half expected. But people didn't come visiting Talia, not down this road, and certainly not this late.

"Who's there?"

Her voice was strong. Talia Willocks had never taken any shit, and if some happy asshole had gotten themselves lost then they needed to know right away who they'd be dealing with when and if she opened her trailer door.

The cats were all looking in the same direction. Talia hit the key combination to save her work, strode over to the door, and opened it.

"Who is it?"

There was nobody outside. She looked both ways and plodded down the little metal stairs. From here you could see from her lot (somewhat overgrown; she didn't care much about the outside) down the twenty-foot path to the road. There was no one there either.

A hundred yards up the way was the graveyard. Its proximity had never bothered her. It was where you put dead people, right? Dead people wouldn't do you any harm. Ed lay up there, along with the other people who shared his death day, and hundreds of others who'd passed over the years. The thought had never yielded any comfort but on the other hand, neither did she mind.

She looked in the other direction. The road came to an end forty yards down the way, replaced by the foot-worn path of those who wanted to head down to the high-sided and rocky creek that had given the town its name, generally to make out. Talia's best bet was that some young couple, likely a few brews down, had rapped on her door as a joke—before tearing off down the path.

They'd've had to be quick, though. And it was kind of cold tonight.

Colder than most people would find appealing for al fresco activities of the hot and heavy kind. There was a frisky wind, too. Talia couldn't see a fallen twig or anything obvious lying on the ground, but that didn't mean there wasn't one.

There was a soft feeling against her leg, and she jumped before realizing it was just Tilly cat, come to see. Talia bent down and scratched her head. The cat tolerated this for a moment and then wandered off.

Show's over, I guess.

Talia yawned massively. Maybe she didn't have those extra few paragraphs in her tonight after all. Could be the little fictional people were going to have to stay frozen in place for tonight.

Someone called her name.

She whipped her head around, heart stopping in her throat. She heard the wind moving the branches of the trees behind the trailer and along the road.

Meanwhile, Tilly nosed around in the long grass, not looking like a cat who'd detected any disturbance in the force. She pounced on something — real or imaginary — and then trotted back up the steps and indoors.

The wind kept blowing, then died a little. Either way, the wind hadn't been what Talia had heard. It couldn't be, because it didn't make sense, but it had sounded like someone had called her name.

A man's voice. Soft, somewhere up the road, between here and the church. And yes . . . there it was again.

It hadn't called out "Talia," though. It had sounded like Tally-Anne. Her real name, the one she'd been given at birth, which no one ever used now. No one had called her by it much even in the old days. Her mother and father, when they were still alive . . . and a man long dead, whom she'd once loved.

Talia stayed on the steps, pulling her robe tight but getting colder and colder, for ten more minutes.

She didn't hear anything else.

Chapter 37

Kristina wasn't alarmed when she realized someone was following her—only surprised it had taken so long. Truth be told, she'd been wandering around in the hope it might happen. She would prefer not to be called upon to tell that truth, though. She'd rather stick with what she'd told John, that she was heading over to Swift's to collect the book for next week's reading group. Which she dutifully did before taking a long walk uptown and back, including both Bryant and Union Square Parks and getting nothing for her trouble but feet that were sore enough to be a real pain when it came to working that evening.

She'd been convinced that somewhere along the way she'd have company. Lizzie, hopefully, but if not then one of her friends, who could presumably lead her to Lizzie. Eventually she got bored and headed for home. Well, maybe bored wasn't quite right. It was...

Disappointed.

And more than that.

Back when she was sixteen there'd been this party in Black Ridge. She hadn't really known the girls throwing it—they'd been Ginny's pals—but she'd run into them a couple of times on the street and on nights when Kristina and Ginny and Henna had managed to slip into bars (not an impossible feat in the mountain backwoods of Washington State, if the three of you are tall for your age and, let's face it, somewhat cute). They hung out all the time, at one another's houses, at the Yakima mall when they could get a ride. They did everything as a group back in the days when it was essential to feel people had your back and were walking side by side with you into the strange rooms of adulthood. Henna and

Ginny lived up the road, two houses apart, and the unspoken arrange-ment was they'd come walking down toward town, pick Kristina up, and head together into what passed for the bright lights of Black Ridge, there to behave as badly as possible within the limited options available.

Anyway, this party had been set up and the word was it was going to be *major*. It was even *themed*—everybody had to turn up dressed in black, white, and red. This presented a challenge for Kristina. Her mother was not one of those maternal souls who relished guiding her daughter toward adulthood. She had other things she wanted to inculcate in her, but not that. Kristina was forced to pick up the basics by herself, which frequently left her feeling that she hadn't got stuff quite right. She didn't have many clothes, certainly nothing that would look sufficiently kick-ass at a party that—Kristina was sure—was going to be life-changingly grown-up. Word was a bunch of *boys* were going to be there—new boys, different boys, not the ones who always hung around or who you saw at school.

Kris gathered together what she could. She had a black skirt that she thought she looked kind of okay in. She found some red stockings cheap in town. She had a white blouse. The last wasn't in any way cool and in fact made the whole ensemble look a bit odd, like some waitress who'd got dressed in the dark, but it was the best she could do and if the deal was it had to be black, white, and red, then that's what you had to do.

She showered. She put on makeup—somewhat inexpertly, as she didn't have any good stuff and her mother had never shown any interest in giving her tips. She looked at herself in the mirror and wondered how changed she would be, how many things she would have learned and done, by the end of the night. She dressed in her black, white, and red clothes. She looked in the mirror one more time and wished herself luck.

She went downstairs cautiously. Her mother was in position on the sofa, watching TV. Permission had been granted for Kristina to go to the party. Kristina's mother believed, entirely correctly, that her own reputa-tion within the town would stop anybody from getting fresh with her daughter. That, at any rate, would be a charitable interpretation for her not minding her daughter going out: Kristina knew that not giving a shit also played a part. Ginny's and Henna's parents had been told artfully constructed mistruths about the event—excitement over which was by now causing Kristina to hyperventilate—and believed their daughters were going to a study session at another girl's house, a session that could go on very, very late. The tactical advantages of drinking vodka, assuming it was available (on the grounds that it didn't leave a smell on your breath), had been discussed and agreed upon by all three girls.

Kristina's mother ran her eyes up and down her daughter and grunted. "What *do* you look like?"

She went back to watching her show. Kristina's father would have said something nicer, but he was dead, and he wouldn't have wanted her to go out. Kristina decided she didn't want to wait downstairs. She grabbed an apple from the kitchen—she knew she ought to put *something* in her stomach before all the vodka—and returned to her room. She could wait there. She could see the street corner from her window. As soon as the girls came into sight—and they'd probably be along soon; it was coming up for seven and the party was due to start at eight—she'd race downstairs and leave the house.

She sat on her window seat, gnawing at the apple, forcing herself to eat almost half of it despite the butterflies in her stomach. She waited. And she waited.

And they didn't come.

On Monday the school was full of stories about the party. The shadows cast by stories, anyhow. The people who'd attended only really talked to other people who'd been there. There was a lot of sniggering and implication and innuendo. Ginny had an outrageous hickey on her neck that came close to getting her sent home from school. There was talk of things that had been drunk and whispers of other, even more glittering deeds.

When Kristina diffidently asked Henna what happened, why they hadn't come to pick her up, her friend shrugged.

"You didn't call to make plans," she said.

"But you always pick me up on the way into town," Kristina said falteringly. "I just assumed."

"Yeah, well, maybe you assume too much."

Basically it transpired that, though nothing had ever been said, the other two girls felt Kristina took them for granted. Nothing could have been further from the truth, but that was that.

Kristina didn't stop seeing them. They were her friends until she left town at eighteen and spent the next decade spiraling around the country and the world. They hung out and had some good times.

But sitting by yourself in a window and waiting, watching as the light turns and the night comes in, trying to work out what could have delayed things, whether you should call or if that made you look desperate or uncool, whether it had gotten too late or if it was still possible she would hear the doorbell—as it was now too dark to see them coming down the street... Kristina thought she'd always remember how that felt, and most of all how it had been to finally give up (she lasted until half past nine) and take the dumb fucking clothes off and go downstairs to get something proper to eat. Her mother had still been in her chair, the television off, staring into space.

She looked at Kristina. She didn't say anything, but she smiled. It was a bitter little thing.

If you'd have asked Kris, she would have said that evening was far behind her. But maybe evenings like that never get behind us. When you're young you're very raw, and if the world smacks you it really stings.

And when friends betray and forget you, it *scars*.

When Kristina realized what was going on in her head she laughed at herself, sent up a prayer that Henna had put on even *more* weight than the last time Kris had seen her, and headed home.

Just before she turned onto their street she remembered they were out of milk. And...well, pretty much everything else. She stopped by the Not Very Good Deli and gathered up some organic two percent and random cookies. It was as she was zoning out in front of the dried pasta—a clear indication of having run out of inspiration: if there's one food people who work in an Italian restaurant tend not to crave on nights off, it's pasta—that she felt something. If you asked a scientist about it, he or she would put it down to a glimpse or a reflection, but it wasn't. Kris knew humans aren't confined by their bodies or skulls. They seep. With some strong souls, they can even stretch, sometimes for long distances.

She didn't turn to look.

She walked to the register as if nothing was happening, paid for her purchases, and stepped outside. She dawdled up the street, trying to figure out what to do. Should she head somewhere more private—or find a way to signal John that another meeting could be about to happen, to see if he could get in on it as well?

"Hey," said a voice, suddenly very close.

It wasn't a woman's voice. It was a man's.

Kris turned. It was the man in the coat. The man who'd been watching her in SoHo the night before. "You talking to me?"

"I think so," he said, smiling. He gestured up and down the street. "I don't see anybody else, do you?"

Kristina realized he was right. Something twisted in her stomach. Meanwhile the man took a couple of steps closer to her.

She faced him down. "I don't know you, do I?"

"No. I don't know you either. But I saw you last night with some people I *do* know."

"Yeah, I saw you too. What's your point?"

"What were you doing with them?"

"Look, Mr. ...."

"My name is Reinhart."

"I need to get home. My boyfriend's expecting me."

She hated falling back on the my-boyfriend's-waiting ploy, but something about the man in front of her said this was a situation she needed to exit as quickly and decisively as possible.

"Of course. Someone like you, there will always be a man waiting. But by the time this boyfriend starts thinking 'I wonder where dear Kristina's got to?' it would be too late, you see."

"Look. I don't know who you are —"

"Yes, you do. I told you. Reinhart. I can spell it for you, if you wish. And here's the thing. The people you were talking to last night, they're not important to me. They got their own life; we don't do business. Especially because the girl you were talking to, Lizzie, she doesn't like these guys to steal. That's okay. I respect that. But there are *other* people, friends of theirs, who *do* steal . . . and with them, I *do* have business. It's important to me. Understand?"

Kristina considered running, but dismissed the idea. Something about the heavy poise of the man said he would be able to move hard and fast if the need arose.

"I watch your face," he said, "and I think yes, she understands. This is good. The job of a businessman is taking care of business, right? I got people already trying to make things difficult for me. I don't need more. Your face also tells me you'd like to go now, and that's okay. I have other things I need to attend to. I hope I'll never see you again — especially not near anyone who works for me. You think we can agree to that?"

Kristina nodded.

"That's excellent. Because otherwise I will have to do something about it. And if *that* happens, your boyfriend can look for you all over the city, all over the state, but he's not going to find anything. Which would be a shame, yes? It's an ugly world we live in. It's always sad when something beautiful is destroyed."

He reached up with disconcerting speed and stroked a finger along her left cheekbone. Then he walked away.

Kristina ran along the street and around the corner, and when she saw John at the top of the steps outside their apartment, she called out to him and ran faster still.

Chapter 38

David was thinking about magnets.

He was supposed to be thinking about work, of course, but he wasn't. Of all the things Maj had said, the one that stuck most clearly had been the stuff about magnets. Today David and his desk were behaving like two of the world's strongest, set to repel.

He wanted to work. He *needed* to. Yet there was some portion of his mind—one that held the keys to major muscle groups—that clearly desired otherwise. It was like having two people inhabiting the same body, Siamese twin souls determined to run in opposite directions.

And this morning, not-working David was wiping the floor with the opposition.

Taking a break from the screen and going across the hall into the spare bedroom hadn't helped either. He'd hoped having something to do with his hands might free his mind. It did not. Dawn had done almost everything already. The only job remaining was sorting the boxes David had shipped once he realized he was going to stay in Rockbridge. They held bits from his childhood, mainly books, and mementos of his parents.

David's parents had died in a car accident while he was living in New York City, a flashback he very seldom referred to in his personal narrative. He'd told Talia about it one afternoon because it was similar to what had happened to the guy she used to go out with. Dawn knew about it, of course. Otherwise, if the subject came up—around an inquiry as to whether he was seeing family at Thanksgiving, for example—he'd explain the situation and weather the inevitable sympathy, not volunteering the information that both his parents had been shit-faced drunk at the time, his father moreover high, and they'd been lucky not to take out an innocent family who'd happened to be driving late along the same highway.

His parents' car had gone off the road and smacked into a tree, and that was that. After their death he'd gone home from New York, sold the house and almost everything in it. He'd wandered the country for two years before settling on Rockbridge after meeting and falling in love with Dawn. He'd opened one of the storage boxes when they'd moved into this house — hence his mother's pottery piece downstairs — and then resealed it and never thought about it or the other two again. Reopening them now did not help his mood. He missed his parents, of course. He had loved them. His father's battered typewriter didn't bring him back, however, nor the brooch his mother had been wearing the night of the crash. A pair of their cocktail glasses did, sort of, but not in a good way.

His impulse was to seal the boxes back up again and either heft them up into the attic or take them down to the dump. He knew the former wouldn't play with Dawn, however — she was not someone who tolerated things merely being stowed; it was a miracle they'd lasted this long in the spare room — and the latter didn't seem right.

You can't throw the past away. You have to integrate it into your life or else it sits there just beyond the edge of your vision, dust-gathering, rotting.

The fact that you can't see something doesn't mean it's gone.

After forty minutes he'd given up and left the house, but walking wasn't helping either. His mind was still full of magnets. He knew Maj and the man's relationship to David's life was something he needed to work out — or at least *remember*. He couldn't do that and it scared him.

He knew he ought to talk to Dawn about it, too. He didn't want to sound crazy, however, especially with the news they'd had. The second reason was...harder to put his finger on. The situation made him feel vulnerable and exposed. It felt like a sleeping dog that should be let lie forever. Maybe even fed a little doctored steak, just to make sure.

He slowed as he came in view of Roast Me, considering an afternoon coffee. He couldn't face talking to Talia about her book, however. What you create is like a person, as is the process itself. Talking to someone who's succeeding in writing when you're not is like hearing them describe just how much great and experimental sex they're having with your partner.

He could lie, maybe, saying he'd got to the end of the book and it was great — but then she'd ask him about the climax or something else he'd be supposed to know, and the lie would be exposed.

He got caught out. Talia wasn't inside, for once, but stomping around clearing cups off the benches built into the window. Without running across the road, he couldn't avoid her.

"Hey," she said. Her smile was brief and her voice quiet. She did not ask him about his word count. In fact, that single word of greeting appeared to be all.

"I haven't had a chance to read any more of your book," David said, disconcerted. "Been busy."

"No problemo."

Concerned she might be pissed at him, he checked her face. It was blank. Uncharacteristically so. Usually Talia's weather was right there for everyone to read.

"I'm still loving it. I definitely think you've got something."

She straightened, several cups in each large hand, and blew a strand of hair off her hot face. "That's great, David. Thank you."

"Are you...okay?"

"Sure. Why?"

"I don't know. You just seem..."

Every time he'd seen Talia she'd been extremely Talia-like. Today she wasn't. She seemed older. Old, in fact.

She glanced down the street. When she looked back, it was if something had changed, as if — as when he'd first offered to read her manuscript — many years and an accretion of events had been sanded off her face. "Where do people go, do you think?"

"Go?"

"When they die."

David shrugged. "No idea. Why?"

"I just figured you might have a take. Because of, you know."

David knew she meant his parents, but had never given the matter any thought. He said so.

"I always assumed they went up to heaven," she said. "Or maybe... maybe if there *was* no heaven, then they just stopped, bang, that's the end of it. Or if there *was* anything left, some kernel that doesn't die or fade away because the body starts to rot, then maybe that part was locked away in what's left, under the earth. In the bones and stuff."

David wasn't sure what he could say. He didn't know what she might be hoping for.

"But maybe that's *not* it, huh? Maybe they *do* go somewhere, just not heaven. Or hell, I guess. Maybe it's such a big *thing,* death, that you can wind up out of sync with where you used to be. Like getting thrown clean out through the windshield of a car. But bigger than that. Getting thrown so hard that you wind up miles and miles away." She glanced at him. "You think?"

"Could be," David said. It felt weak, but she didn't seem to be listening to his contribution anyway.

"Saw George this morning," she went on, blindsiding him. "He's having a hard time. He's still sure he saw someone on the road through the forest, and he gave the guy a lift into town and that he vanished when they got here. Weird, huh? Like bringing a ghost home."

David opened his mouth — this *was* something he could contribute to, even if it'd just be the same gentle dismissal he'd given before — but he hesitated, as he finally put two and two together.

The hitchhiker was Maj, of course — Maj on his way to visit him. It must have been.

Talia mistook his silence. "But that's just friend-of-a-friend bullshit, right?" she said, and laughed — looking like herself again. "Anyway, stop bugging me, asshole. There's people waiting inside. I must repair to the counter, my wonders to perform."

She kicked the door and strode back into the coffee shop, bellowing to the people in line that she was coming already; stop your fucking whining for the love of God.

David walked away quickly.

Meanwhile, fresh back from school and sitting in the kitchen, Dawn decided she simply could not face marking any more homework. She was finding it hard to focus. Could be hormones, she supposed. Could also be...

She looked up.

Directly above the kitchen was the spare room — the soon-to-be-nursery. She'd done everything she could, everything possible without David going through his boxes. Until he'd dispersed their contents she couldn't put dust sheets down properly, and that meant she couldn't repaint the room. She knew he was only being slow because he was trying to concentrate on the new book, and understood that meant he had to look inward and found it hard to maintain hooks into the real world. His "Eddie Moscone" phase, she called it, after one of the kids in her class. That was fine, and understandable.

But she wanted *to get on.*

It occurred to her that perhaps she could go up and take a look through his boxes. Make easy calls on what he'd want to keep and what he would not. He'd likely want most of it — he had few enough mementos of his childhood. Weirdly little, in her view, but she was a constitutional hoarder who occasionally took herself in hand. David was the opposite. He seemed to have left his past behind like yesterday's rain.

Going through the boxes would take only fifteen minutes. If she couldn't help, she couldn't help. But if she could presort them into little piles for him, it might finally get the thing done.

Plus . . . it would be a good excuse not to sit getting frustrated about how tough some kids found it to work out what you had left if you took a nickel and six cents away from a quarter, for the love of God.

She made herself a cup of herbal tea and cheerfully took it upstairs.

Chapter 39

It wasn't hard to find Reinhart. Something that might give patrons of the world's restaurants pause for thought, did they but know, is that the staff in the places they drop so much cash in are often one step from the criminal fraternity. Not through character — there are plenty of cooks, waiters, and bar staff whose moral fiber would stand favorable comparison with normal citizens, and walk all over that of the average banker or CEO. There's a degree of recreational drug use, however, and some of the people washing pans and dishes are doing so because their record makes it hard for them to do much else. A lot of the restaurant business happens at night, too, and that's always tended to be when the bad guys ply their ancient trades, or spend time propping up the kind of bars where kitchen workers may also go after work.

Bottom line is, I asked some questions and this led me on to other people in other bars, where I asked more questions, and pretty soon I knew where to go.

It wasn't hard to find him, and I probably should have given that more thought at the time, but I did not.

It was in what you're supposed to call Clinton these days but will always be Hell's Kitchen to anyone but realtors. You don't have to look hard to find vestiges of the pregentrified voice of the area — you can't just line a couple blocks with bistros and expect everything else to disappear. The restaurant was called '. Yes, apostrophe. According to their website, this reflected the executive chef's belief that something was missing from contemporary American cuisine. Personally, I suspected it meant something was missing from the chef's brain, but he certainly didn't lack patrons. From the sidewalk you could see the place was full even on a Wednesday at lunchtime. Everybody looked very nice, and they sat in a space that was light and airy and dotted with round tables accented with linen and single white blooms in delicate little vases in the center. Staff buzzed around in gray slacks and lilac shirts and none of them looked like they'd been within shouting distance of illegal in their life. One of the guys in the kitchen had, though, and he'd told me to look for a table in the middle.

Reinhart sat with two other men. You could tell it was a business meeting and that the other guys were legit. Both wore charcoal suits, though one had removed his jacket to reveal a pale blue shirt. Reinhart was talking in a sober, considered fashion. He looked tamped down, certainly compared to the man I'd seen in the church a couple of nights before.

He finished his presentation. The men nodded, looked at one another, lips pouted, as if whatever proposal had just been made was very hard to argue with.

Reinhart sat back, wiping his mouth with his napkin. Then he looked up and saw me. I took this as my cue to walk in off the street. A woman in a smart pantsuit tried to intercept me, but she was not hard to avoid.

I stood over the table. "Good food?"

Reinhart looked up. "Very good," he said. "The vongole is superb. I take lunch here almost every day. But . . . I suppose you knew that."

"Correct," I said, keeping my voice low so as not to impact on the eating pleasure of other diners, or cause anyone to call the cops just yet. Pantsuit had retreated to her podium but was keeping an eye on me. "A creature of habit. That means either you're dumb or very confident. Unless you got someone at a table somewhere in the room? If so, they're kind of slow to their feet."

I made a show of looking around, though of course I'd done so before I walked in. I'm not a total fool. There had been no male one-tops nor pairs of serious-looking guys casting casual glances across the room. "I guess not. Which means either you *are* dumb, or you don't believe someone would have the balls."

"You still look familiar," Reinhart said, as if I were background music. "Just can't work out where from."

I tried not to clench my fists. "I'm going to become *very* familiar if you don't listen. Last night you had a conversation on the street with a friend of mine."

Reinhart glanced apologetically at his lunch companions. "Are you the boyfriend? That makes sense. Two people popping up in my business, turns out they're together. A pair of problems. I should have figured that out. Maybe I am dumb after all."

"Nah," I said. "Don't think so. What do *you* think?" I asked his companions. "He seem stupid to you?"

One looked away. The other stared at the remains of his veal parmigiana as if wondering whether he should have ordered something else.

"Me neither," I said. "So here's the thing, Reinhart. Come near her again and I'll hurt you. *Threaten* her and that will be the end of you. Understand?"

He looked at me with vague interest, as if trying to work out what language I was speaking in.

"Whatever your business with this man, I'd walk away," I told the guy with the veal. "But finish your food first. Someone worked hard on that."

The encounter did not leave me feeling good. I hadn't understood how angry I was until confronted with Reinhart, and I'd done nothing but embarrass both him and me. People do not like being embarrassed, most of all men like him. Or me—especially when I've done it to myself.

I hailed a cab with no destination in mind, but after a few blocks told the driver to take me down to Chelsea. I got out on 16th, but instead of going to the church went straight to the house next door and rang the buzzer.

"Who is it?"

"John Henderson."

There was a pause. "And?"

"I'd like to talk to you."

"I'm afraid I'm busy right now."

"Then I apologize for the inconvenience. But I just lit a fire under a man and I need you to explain to me what I've done."

"What are you talking about?"

"Reinhart," I said.

There was a pause, and then a click.

The hallway beyond was small and dark. After a moment I heard footsteps coming down the stairs. They stopped before I could see anyone.

"Come upstairs, won't you? It's the only part of the house that ever seems to get any light."

The footsteps went back up again.

I trotted up past a first story with a landing and two closed doors, and onward to the top. Jeffers stood aside to let me into a room at the front of the house. It held a desk, two chairs that looked like they'd been borrowed from the church, and an upright piano. The only personal touch was an armchair, formerly luxurious but now threadbare, by the window. He saw me looking at it.

"My predecessor's. He lived here for thirty years."

"Feel some days like he still is?"

My comment was intended as throwaway empathy, but he looked at me sharply. "What happened with Reinhart?"

"He followed my partner yesterday and threatened her. I'm just back from talking to him."

"You're in better shape than I would have expected."

"I made sure it happened in a public place."

Jeffers shook his head.

"What's that supposed to mean?"

"How did he know who your partner was? Why did even care? Because you were here the other night. Which shows he already *knows* where you live, and that means—"

"He didn't know about her because of me."

"What do you mean?"

"Until I confronted him over lunch, he didn't know there was a connection between us."

I realized with a sinking heart that I'd helped Reinhart draw a line between two people he had reason to have a problem with, and that sometimes men who don't hide are not merely excessively confident. They may also believe that they're well connected enough not to need to care. Sometimes they're right.

"I don't understand."

"Kristina found a cryptic message a couple of days ago," I said, sitting on one of the wooden chairs. "It was written in the dirt on our window."

"An unusual means of communication."

"Right. Especially as we live on the fifth floor. She worked out the message and went to Union Square Park. She met some people there, including the woman I later saw you talking to in Union Square. You know the one. We've been through this. Her name's Lizzie."

The priest listened with an expression I couldn't place at first.

"A couple stole jewelry and presented it to her. Then everyone ran off—leaving her stuck in a doorway still holding the goods...at which point she noticed two men watching. One was Reinhart. Yesterday he accosted her in a backstreet and was not subtle about warning her to stay out of his business."

Jeffers's face had become composed again. I knew now what I'd seen in his features, however. It was the look of a man who has been found out over something personal: a matter that has been on his mind a great deal but not allowed out on show; a load he has been carrying by himself, which at times has felt very heavy indeed.

"Talk to me," I said. "Explain what I've gotten myself into. I may even be able to help."

"No," he said, sitting on the other chair. "You won't. But I'll tell you what you need to know."

He told me he'd been the priest there for three years. When he'd arrived he'd found a community in decline. His predecessor had been in place a long time and was much loved and just about managed to hold the place steady, acting as a bridge between the era when people believed by default and a new one in which they did not. Partly, Jeffers said, this change lay at the hands of science. While he had no personal issue with the objective assessment of verifiable facts, the reductionist agenda could lead in only one direction when it came to the worship of things unseen. Even more important, he believed, was that people just didn't have time for it. In the old days life was simple. You worked and slept and you attempted to reproduce. If you had time in between then what you craved was a sense of wonder, something to keep you reconciled to the drudgery of the day-to-day—and a sense of community, too. For hundreds of years the church was the go-to for both, but the Internet killed that. E-mail and Facebook took interaction and threw it somewhere nonconcrete: up in the cloud, yes, but not one where angels sat jamming on golden harps. You didn't need to catch up outside the church gates on Sunday morning— you were constantly aware of your friends' and neighbors' every deed and thought and meal. If you wanted a glimpse of the lords of your manor, Twitter provided it in a parallel stream: endless updates on how vewwy, vewwy much your hallowed movie star loves the husband who in reality she's enthusiastically cheating on with her personal trainer, among others. Instead of thinking about the nature of the universe, and your life, and wondering what kind of being or circumstance could have given rise to it, you thought "Cool! Ashton Kutcher has tweeted again, just for me!"

After six months Jeffers had started to make do, settling for the status quo like the last Roman living in a far-flung European backwater after the empire had pulled the plug. It wasn't a bad life and there were still a few old people who cared. As a way of serving the Lord and filling in the years until he could take a meeting with Him in person, it would do.

"Then I met Lizzie," the priest said, looking up at me. "And Maj, and some others, and things changed."

"Where did you first meet them?"

"I don't know."

"You can't remember?"

"I can't recall where I first became aware of them."

"I'm not sure I understand the distinction."

"They're not easy to pin down."

"Who are they?"

"People who've been forgotten by the rest of us and have no place in our society. That's a hard life to live. Unlike most, they're doing something about it."

"Stealing, you mean."

He shook his head. "Very few. For most there's no point, or wasn't until Reinhart came along. They're organized, after a fashion. They have places they live and hide; there are roles and ways of being; there's even a kind of hierarchical society. There *was,* anyway. Then a few of the older ones, the people who'd put a lot of this in place, left the picture at the same time."

"Died, you mean?"

I could see him choosing his words. "It would be more accurate to say they stopped exerting an influence. Unfortunately Reinhart arrived during the same period, and he realized he could make criminal use of some of the skills the remaining had acquired."

"Like?"

"Avoiding detection. Very successfully."

"And stealing things."

"Regretfully, yes."

"How does it work?"

"Sometimes simply taking things out of stores—small, expensive goods that are handed on to Reinhart for sale. The thing is, there are very few of them who are skilled at that, and so he's always coming up with new ideas. He has them spying at ATMs, observing PIN numbers. Once the victim is around the corner, Reinhart's other accomplices intercept him or her and detain them until they've had a chance to use the number and the bank card to remove large sums of money."

"Uh-huh," I said, remembering the spate of similar crimes in our neighborhood over the last months. "And what do they get out of it?"

"Shelter. And attention."

"If they want attention, why do they spend their lives in hiding?"

"It's...difficult to explain. I'd become aware of some of these people in the neighborhood. I befriended a few. It's not easy. When I realized how they were being used by Reinhart, I started a program. I tried to help them to see my church as a safe and supportive place. Tried to move them away from criminal acts, too. Partly on moral grounds. Mainly because sooner or later it'd mean exposure for them. Some have responded well."

"Which Reinhart doesn't like. Hence him being here the other night, and also threatening Kristina."

"Yes."

"So why hasn't he just whacked you?"

The priest looked confused. "Whacked?"

"Had you killed. These people tend to think in very straight lines."

"You think someone would kill a priest over something like this? Are you serious?"

I looked into his sober, calm eyes, and tried to figure out how to break the news that people died every day for incomparably less. Then I realized from the corners of his mouth that he knew this fact very well.

"You're a smart man," I said, standing. "And probably a good one. But I'd think seriously about letting these people look after themselves."

"That would not be the Lord's way. Or mine."

"Maybe. But the Lord doesn't live by himself in a house that would be easy to break into. These people exist outside society for a reason. They know the score. They don't get anything out of our world, sure, but that means they also won't feel they have to give in return."

He smiled, and I realized it was like talking to a great big bear, one who found the spectacle of the human in front of him mildly interesting, especially the noises he was making with his mouth, but who would not be altering his behavior on the basis of anything I said.

"Seriously," I tried. "If it comes down to it, these are not people you can trust to get your back."

"They are lost," he said. "It's my job to bring them home."

Chapter 40

Kristina's phone started being weird halfway through the afternoon. It rang, showing a number she didn't recognize—but there was no one there. The first time she didn't think anything of it. It was a Sprint phone and the service sucked. Attempts to discuss this with the company had achieved nothing but rage and the desire to hunt down and kill everyone who worked for them, which apparently you're not allowed to do. Forty minutes later it happened again. She stuffed the phone back in her pocket afterward, prey to the churning in the guts that comes when our inexplicable new tech starts misbehaving. In days of yore you prayed to God to keep the magic working. Now we navigate ritualistic menus, sit in prayer on hold, and pay homage to customer service representatives of indifferent competence and temper. It's a matter of debate which yields the more tangible results.

Then it happened *again*.

This time she didn't even bother to look. John had texted ten minutes before, and she'd replied. The only other person she could think of was Catherine Warren, but her name would have shown on the screen.

Then she pulled the phone back out, prey to a thought. She navigated to the incoming log and confirmed the failed calls had all come from the same number and that the last time had left a message. Maybe it was Catherine after all—calling from another number after a phone fault or loss, perhaps to say she wouldn't be coming to the book club that evening. They hadn't spoken since the fabulously awkward meeting at her house.

Kristina thought she'd better check. Annoyingly, the message had also failed. A ten-second stretch of silence—or the strange, tidal version of it that dead telecommunication equipment sings—and it cut off.

She walked on, more slowly now, keeping the phone in her hand. Five minutes later, it rang again. "Yes?" she said, getting it up to her ear fast. "Who is it?" Silence. "Don't hang up," she said, hurrying into a side street. "I can't hear you."

The line went dead.

Swearing, she flicked back to voice mail. As she waited for the previous message to read back, she wandered down the street, cupping the earpiece with her other hand to cut out extraneous noise—and trying not to remember that it was a street pretty much like this where she'd been cornered and threatened the day before.

She listened to the tidal noise again, the silence that wasn't silence. Except...maybe it wasn't silence. Maybe she could hear...something. Something very faint.

She listened to the sound one more time, hunched next to a stairwell, a finger in her other ear, closing her eyes to hand everything over to a single sense.

It *could* just have been her mind trying to usher random sounds toward meaning, like those recordings people made in houses that were supposed to be haunted, in fact just meaningless white noise.

She didn't think so, however.

brprr, sssnn

That's what it sounded like—someone whispering in your ear before you were awake. The first part sounded a *little* like "Bryant Park," though. Perhaps only because it was in her mind as the first place she'd met Lizzie, but once she'd heard the sounds that way, she couldn't unhear the words. The second part sounded like it meant something, too. In fact, she heard that part first. It sounded like someone saying "Seven."

Bryant Park, seven.

She listened to the recording one more time and couldn't make herself hear it differently. Why it should sound so very faint and strange, she had no idea. Maybe a problem with her phone, or voice mail, or the movement of the spheres. She wasn't tangling with Sprint's asshole version of customer service to find out.

She could think of only one person who might be trying to leave a message—especially one that short, suggesting a meeting in a park. Lizzie had taken her number. If the whole thing wasn't Kristina's imagination, this had to be from her. And if it was an invitation to meet up, Kris wanted to take her up on it.

But what about Reinhart? She'd been *really* scared last night, and scaring Kris wasn't a job for the faint of heart. She'd gone running to John and he'd hugged her and made sure she was all right—and not done what she knew he wanted to, which was run off and try to find the guy. He hadn't said anything about him since, either, which must have taken herculean reserves of self-denial. And if what he'd since told her about his conversation with the priest that afternoon was true, and some of Lizzie's broader circle of friends were working for Reinhart, he wouldn't want that deal messed up by people like Kristina.

He'd warned her, and made the message good and clear.

A stray thought dropped into her head. It struck her that John had been vague about how he'd spent his morning. Just walking, he'd said, winding up in Chelsea with Jeffers more or less by chance. It occurred to her to wonder whether he'd been making inquiries about Reinhart instead, and if so, what he'd found. Not much, presumably, or he would have said.

Presumably.

It was six o'clock. She was a twenty-minute walk from the park. Said park was a ten- or fifteen-minute cab ride back down to Nolita. The reading group didn't start until seven thirty and it wasn't like you got shot for being five minutes late. Eyebrows might be raised—and God knows the raising of educated eyebrows could make you feel small as hell—but no one would actually stand up and point at her.

*   *   *

The park was nowhere near the part of town where Reinhart had caught her. There was no reason to expect him to be in this neighborhood. She wasn't expected at the restaurant for a few hours, but John *would* be working—which gave her a rare window of free will.

If it came right down to it, she didn't need a reason.

She wanted to go.

The park was almost empty. A couple of tourists sat huddled over one of the little tables at the top of the steps at the library end, looking cold and daunted. A few office workers cut down the side paths, heads down, focused on getting to the subway or a working dinner or somewhere to grab a couple of private drinks before getting into the next phase of their existence. If there was anything that working a bar taught you it was that there was a whole lot of parallel living going on—people who presented one way for ninety-five percent of the time but lived somewhere more private in the remaining sliver. Kristina had occasionally wondered what proportion of the city's inhabitants spent the hours between five thirty and eight either drinking or covertly holding the hand of a coworker, but had decided it wasn't a question that led anywhere happy.

She walked to the middle of the grass and looked around. She watched the couple at the top of the steps get up and head wearily to their hotel to shower and regroup for an evening's fun in a foreign city and to try to ignore the fact that if they were honest, simply fabulous though it all was, just for tonight they'd prefer to be back at home watching TV and wearing sweatpants.

She checked her watch. Did she wait a little longer, or get a cab? That's what made sense, of course. Heading down to Swift's, meeting with Catherine and patching things up, an hour's chat about the gentle—and slim—novel they'd enjoyed (or, in Kristina's case, tolerated with growing irritation). Then get to the bar and her job and lover and life. Run along that track. *Her* track.

She didn't want to. Not tonight. She wanted something else. She wanted something *new*.

When she looked up she saw there were now people at all four points of the park. Dark figures, their faces unclear, alone or in pairs.

"Hey," she said. Either it wasn't loud enough, or they chose not to respond. She said it again.

"Hello."

The response came from much closer than she was expecting, and from behind. Kris turned and found Lizzie there. Her heart hit a heavy beat.

"Hey."

"You got the message."

"Just about. Why didn't you talk to me?"

"I can't."

"Why? And why did it sound so weak?"

"It's too boring to explain," Lizzie said. "I'm glad you came."

Kristina found herself tongue-tied, and nodded.

The figures from the corner of the park had moved while she wasn't looking, and congregated at the Sixth Avenue end. Kristina recognized several from the previous meeting, including the plump girl. They were all watching her, as if waiting for something.

Lizzie took Kristina's hand. "Let's have some fun."

Chapter 41

Kristina followed the Angels out of the park and into the streets as lights started to come on, and the mood of the streets shifted from afternoon to evening in a city that prides itself on never sleeping. She crossed the avenue, into a knot of streets lined with restaurants and bars on the other side, feeling—knowing—this was a gang that didn't let outsiders in very often, if at all. Sometimes they walked together, chattering to Kristina, asking her questions about her life. Then they'd be spread out across the street and both sidewalks, as if they had no connection to one another.

She let herself be led, following in their slipstream—sensing that it was kind of a buzz for them, leading someone like her. Sometimes they'd cut through side streets; at others they'd walk down the middle of the road, weaving between the cars with enough grace and timing that they never got honked (though Kris did, more than once), as if they were cold, hard streams of mountain water cutting through forest soil. She found herself being led into a bar. It was noisy and crowded and dark and it seemed to Kristina that her new friends relaxed when they were inside. Lizzie certainly did. When on the street she always seemed watchful. Here in the hectic gloom there was greater freedom in her movement.

Kristina was confused. Was this a stop off for a drink? No one seemed to be heading toward the bar, but if they weren't here for that, then what could it be? Or were they expecting *her* to step up? The idea didn't bother her—it was clear these people wouldn't have money for Midtown prices—but wasn't anyone going to say anything, or even look hopefully at her? It'd been a long time since Kristina felt gauche (except in Catherine Warren's company), but she didn't understand the rules or what was supposed to happen next. It reminded her of being an adolescent, or even younger—of being young enough to long to fit in, desperate to have a friend who'd show you the way and always have your back.

She noticed the plump girl was standing at the corner of the bar, behind a pair of women in business suits perched on stools with big glasses of wine. One was talking hard and fast. The other was listening intently.

The girl was watching them with the focus of a cat waiting for the mouse to stay still . . .

Then her hand whipped out like a frog tongue smacking on a fly. She grabbed the glass of the nearest woman, took a sip, and had it back on the counter within three seconds.

Kristina blinked.

Her male friend then did the same thing, to the other glass. He was even faster. Both only took sips.

The girl looked at Kris and grinned, then nodded her head toward the drink. *Dare ya.*

Kristina glanced at Lizzie, a pocket of calm in the crowd. "I wouldn't," Lizzie said. "It's not a game everyone can play."

The plump girl's head was still cocked with the same expression on her face, however.

Knowing it was dumb and risky, Kristina grabbed the drink, took a sip, and had it back on the counter before its owner looked back. The girl and her boyfriend laughed delightedly, clapping their hands.

A moment later the woman on the stool grabbed a mouthful of her wine, still listening to her companion, no idea of what had just happened—and apparently not noticing the girl standing next to her even though she was clapping and cheering.

Kristina realized the other Angels were grinning at her, too, delighted, as if she'd passed some kind of test. Even Lizzie smiled, though she rolled her eyes.

Then they all seemed to be leaving, slipping through the crowds toward the door like fish swimming against the current. Kristina followed, having a much harder time of it.

At the door she glanced back at the woman still perched on her stool at the bar, drinking her depleted wine. She realized that if you could do something that simple — if you could learn to always be standing where people weren't looking, and pick your moments so they didn't notice you — then there were a lot of gaps between people, and holes, in the city.

There was a whole world to explore, and to live, in the spaces in between.

Another bar, then a couple of restaurants, grabbing a sip here and a gulp there, even a mouthful of someone's neglected tapas. They passed a few stores and Kristina noticed some of the Angels looking in with a professional eye, as if with a mission in mind . . . but nobody did anything except for one time when an Angel slipped into a secondhand record place. Kristina saw the way he moved between the customers flicking through cases of retro vinyl, how he clocked shopping bags left on the floor and handbags hanging open off people's shoulders. The Angel did nothing but look, however, before floating back out toward the street. As far as Kris could tell, no one had noticed that he had been in the store at all.

By then it was full dark and something had begun to change about the quality of the streetlights or the relationship between the Angels and the normal citizens they moved among. It was like tipping over from being drunk to *very* drunk, or the point where recreational drugs that had so far been supporting an evening of good cheer abruptly gained the upper hand and started leading *you* rather than the other way around.

Quite a few covert mouthfuls of wine had been consumed by that time, but that wasn't it. Kristina felt *less* clumsy, rather than more so, and she stopped finding it hard to follow the Angels along the streets. It felt as if she'd started to hit the same rhythm they were following, as if she'd got the knack of stepping away at the correct time and being where people were not looking, breathing out when everyone else on the street—all the normal people, she caught herself thinking—were breathing in. The adaptation didn't happen all at once. It was more as if the tracks they'd been following started to wend closer and closer. She'd lose the knack for a moment and bash into someone, but then be right back in the groove.

Then the Angels all started running.

At first Kris thought they must be must be running *away* from someone, that they'd been spotted stealing drinks in the last bar. Then she realized this was merely her own sense of guilt, and that the Angels were instead running with a kind of joy, or glee.

They ran out of the road and down Eighth Avenue, and it seemed for a time that there were more of them than there had been before, many more. The newcomers weren't dressed in black and rich colors, however, so it was hard to be sure...but there seemed to be other people running alongside them, or walking fast, or waving as they went by. People on street corners and at bus stops. People walking by. People whom you'd never look at twice when you passed. Background people, who for once had turned to look in your direction, revealing themselves not just to be a texture but living things after all.

Animals, too, dogs and cats and a weirdly large fox, and a little girl whose head seemed far too small...

Then it was back to the group in black again, and Kristina—slowing rapidly, by now out of breath—limped after Lizzie as she ducked off the avenue and onto a residential street. The Angels stopped too, laughing and high-fiving one another, as Kris bent over, leaning against the fence until she'd gotten her breath back and lost most of the spots before her eyes. None of the others seemed at all out of breath. Either they were a *lot* fitter than she was, or...

"Oh, look," one of them said quietly—a short, squat guy who'd been on the periphery of the group until now. He was pointing across the street. "Looky there."

Everyone turned. The road was lined with houses. On one of these, three buildings along from where they stood, the front door hung open. Halfway down the street a man was struggling along with a huge and saggy cardboard box in his arms, toward a car.

"Easy as pie," the plump girl said.

"Um, friends," Lizzie said—but the group was already in movement across the street, heading toward the house. Kristina was carried along with them. Part of this was being drawn in their wake. A larger part was not wanting to be left behind.

The Angels ran up the steps in front of the house, but hesitated on the threshold. Though Lizzie had seemed doubtful, when they ceded control to her, she took it.

She glanced across at the man still trudging up the street with his box. Then smiled mischievously.

"Quickly, then," she said, and they all went inside.

Chapter 42

They swarmed into the hallway. The floor was uncarpeted, bare boards. A similarly unclad staircase led up the left side of the hall to the upper floor. The man who'd cased out the record store went loping straight up it.

A corridor led off to a rear area where a small television played quietly, presumably a kitchen. On the right was a door, and Kristina followed Lizzie and the others through it, scarcely able to believe what was happening, knowing what they should be doing — what *she* should be doing, most of all — was getting the hell out before the guy came back and found them there.

What on earth would they say? Yes, of course there were more of them than there were of him, and maybe they could push past him and run away, but that didn't make it okay. This was . . . *a very bad thing to do.*

That awareness didn't stop her from following Lizzie into the middle of the room. The plump girl's boyfriend went to the window and checked back along the street, presumably acting as lookout — though by the time he saw the guy coming they'd have no chance of leaving without being seen. So what *was* the plan — would they just run straight past him, trusting on speed and the fact that the guy would be so freaked out that he wouldn't give chase? *Was* there even a plan? *Would* they retreat, or was she part of some kind of fucked-up home invasion?

A big shabby rug covered most of the floor. On the other side facing the door (and the battered TV next to it) squatted a lumpy sofa. An armchair lurked at one end. Dotted around the walls were unframed posters from gigs and exhibitions of yesteryear, low-rent versions of the artfully positioned look-what-we-do statements regimented over the walls of the homes of people like Catherine Warren thirty blocks downtown. Box-carrying guy evidently didn't spend too much time worrying about housecleaning. You could see the dust on the empty portions of the shelves from halfway across the room, and the whole place looked like it could do with a wipe and then repainting.

Half of the wall under a back window was taken up with a wooden table. This was strewn with books, pens, and the insides of a laptop computer.

And on the floor underneath it was a child's toy.

Kristina stared at it, thinking: *Oh Christ.*

Then there was a noise out in the hallway. Her heart stopped. Someone was coming.

Kristina whirled around, desperately trying to see a way of escape. There was none. She was in the middle of a room with only one exit. Foot-steps were coming along the hallway toward the door—and there was absolutely *no hope* of getting through it without being seen. She had to hide in this room, somewhere, some*how.*

She waited a second too long. A woman walked past the doorway car-rying a baby over one shoulder.

Kristina froze, knowing she was caught.

But the woman walked past and to the front door instead, where she shouted something down the street—to the hapless guy with the big cardboard box, presumably. The guy who, it turned out, *didn't live alone.*

Knowing these extra seconds were all she had, Kristina took four giant steps toward the only thing she could see that might possibly help—the couch—trying to cover the ground as quickly as possible without mak-ing a sound. Halfway through the final lunging step her self-possession deserted her and she dived.

She landed with a thump just around the back of the sofa and yanked her long legs up to her chest. She felt indescribable relief to be behind something, but this was nowhere near as loud as the panicky, yammering part of her mind that knew it was a pathetically insufficient hiding place and the only question was whether she was discovered within minutes or seconds.

This dreadful attempt at hiding would only make things worse. If she'd been discovered standing in the room she could have made an attempt to appear demented, some confused lunatic wandered in off the street. No, she didn't think she could have pulled it off, but to be found hiding behind the sofa was a straight-down-the-line and no-excuses-possible nightmare.

I'm screwed. I'm screwed.

She heard footsteps and this time they didn't recede back down the corridor but came right into the room.

I'm totally . . . screwed.

"Lazy asshole," said a voice — the woman. "Tell him what, five or six *hundred* times before he does the thing, and then tell him one more time how to do it right? Yes?"

There was a chirrup from the baby, responding to the affectionate tone with no understanding of the content. Her mother sat down on the sofa. She landed heavily, in the middle — bang in front of where Kristina lay, eyes wide. Kris felt the air pushed out of the cushions.

The woman sighed — the heavy, brooding exhale of someone who's exhausted, tired of sleepless nights and having to tell someone what to do the whole time and just the whole damned unfairness of it all.

Kristina tried not to breathe.

A minute later she heard feet coming up the steps outside the house and the front door closing.

"Yeah, so it fits, okay?" A man's voice.

"My hero. You rock."

"Why are you being so pissy?" His voice was louder as he walked into the room. How many more steps before he got the angle to see someone was behind the sofa? Two? One?

"I *told* you it would fit," the woman sniped. "I told you when I asked you to do it *three months ago.*"

"Karen, I'm busy, you know?"

"Too busy to pack up a box of your ex-girlfriend's old shit after *two years* and drive it to the crazy bitch's lair? And busy doing *what*? Oh yeah, that's right—all those YouTube videos don't watch themselves."

"I work, remember? I have to leave the house every day and go do shit. To earn money. To *pay for stuff.*"

"I forgot. Because it's not like you go on about it the whole time. And baby girl here looks after herself. Me, I'm just sitting on the couch watching TV and jerking off."

It was the man's turn to sigh.

Trying to ensure she made not a sound, Kristina wriggled a bit closer to the back of the sofa. Doing this altered the angle of her head. She'd been so focused on saving herself that she hadn't even given a thought as to what had happened to the others.

She saw that Lizzie was under the table down at the end. She sat Indian style and looked insanely relaxed. The short guy who'd suggested they come in here in the first place was next to her, arms around his knees, also apparently at ease.

Kristina titled her head down, looked past her own fetal shape, and saw the plump girl's friend was still down at the window overlooking the street, standing behind the curtain. She remembered the friend who'd gone straight upstairs, and was presumably still up there.

So they were all hiding. Sort of. Except...

The plump girl hadn't moved at all. She was leaning against the wall, arms folded, watching the man and woman and child as if they were a television show.

How can that be? Okay, the man was facing away, in fact had his back to her—and the woman was focused on giving him a hard time.

But there was no *way* they would fail to notice a stranger *standing right there in the middle of the room.*

"Okay, well, it's gone now," the man said weakly.

His partner was smartly back in the game. "Not so much. Next time I get in the car it'll be right..."

"By which I meant *tomorrow afternoon.* I'll dump it around her place."

"And have a nice cup of coffee, no doubt. Talk about old times. It's only polite, right?"

"Karen, the old times were crap. You know that. They ended and thank God. This is a box of old random shit she probably doesn't even remember she's missing. You want, I'll go dump it somewhere and be done with it."

"You can't do that. It's her stuff."

"*Right,*" he said exasperatedly. "So you *said.* So I'll drop it on the way home from work and we can get back to enjoying our so-called lives. Okay?"

"Yeah, yeah."

Kristina had settled into a horrified holding pattern—keeping herself rigid, half listening to what was being said, wondering how long it could be before they noticed the girl standing and watching them or before the man happened to glance over the sofa to see Kristina lying there. She was jolted out of this by a sound and looked up. The baby was staring right at her.

Ignored while her parents thrashed over the same old ground, the baby had pulled itself higher on her mother's shoulder—enough to see over the back of the sofa. She was now staring down at what she'd found on the other side.

She blinked. Somewhere, deep in her tiny, unformed mind, a flag had gone up. The baby knew the woman who was holding her. It knew the man. But who was this other person? Who was this tall, skinny person behind the thing her mother was sitting on? The baby didn't know, but she sensed from the deep reaches of its instinct that unknown big people in the cave was not a good thing.

Her face scrunched up. She started to cry. Kristina stared at her, aghast, not knowing whether to smile or try to turn her face away or what.

"Great," the woman said. "Now she's off again."

"Here, let me," the man said.

The woman stood. "Don't bother."

"Climb off the fucking ledge, okay? Give her to me."

"Okay, be my guest."

Please don't turn around, Kristina prayed. *Please . . . just don't turn around.*

After a moment the baby's cries started to wind down. "There you go," the man said to his child, quiet love in his voice. "It's all okay. There you go."

"How do you even *do* that?" the woman muttered with grudging admiration.

"She senses a masterful male."

"What—through the walls, in some other house?"

"Ha-ha."

There was silence, then the sound of a kiss. A sigh, and the woman spoke again, more softly. "At least you're not an asshole all the time."

"Whereas you are a twenty-four-seven bitch."

There was the sound of a man being swatted hard, but not without affection, on the behind. "I'm sorry," he said. "I know Diana's stuff pisses you off and I should have done it long ago. My bad."

"You bad, me bad too."

"Bad as each other."

"No, I wouldn't go that far."

They laughed together, quietly.

"Don't you spend *any* time jerking off? *I* sure as hell would."

"No. I save it up," the woman said. "You get princess here down to sleep, I may even show you."

"Deal. I'll go upstairs and give it a try. You open some wine. Don't start without me."

"Drinking, or the other thing?"

"Either."

And then, praise God, Kristina heard them walk together out of the room. She jerked her head to stare at Lizzie and the other friend under the table. Lizzie was looking right at her, already holding up a finger.

The message was clear — be quiet and ready to move.

Lizzie waited a beat, then quickly came out from under the table. Kristina jumped to her feet, her joints crackling like rifle shots, and the person behind the curtain slipped out at the same time.

"Yeah, so I guess now would be a good time," the plump girl sniggered, making no effort to be quiet. "Though I kinda want to stick around to catch part two of tonight's special presentation."

The others ignored her. Kris followed Lizzie out into the hallway and to the front door.

"Open it," Lizzie whispered. Kristina flipped the latch as gently as possible and the friends flooded past and out onto the steps. She followed, pulling the door closed as quietly as she'd opened it.

By the time that was done the others were on the sidewalk. She ran down to join them as they hurried off down the road...all starting to laugh.

"What the *fuck?*" Kristina shouted, stomping after them. "Are you out of your *minds?* Do you have any *idea* how close we were to being caught?"

"Not very," the plump girl said.

"What about the guy who went upstairs?"

"He'll be fine," Lizzie said. "But that's enough for one night. Let's go find somewhere quiet."

"Screw this," Kristina shouted, all the fear she'd felt spilling over into fury. "I'm *done* here. That was *insane.* I don't understand why I'm not being arrested right now, and how the *hell* did those people not see someone who was standing right in front of them?"

Lizzie put a hand on her arm.

Kris shook it off. "No. Tell me. *Why didn't they see her?*"

Lizzie hesitated, then appeared to make a decision.

Chapter 43

I had an encounter with Lydia on the way to work. Generally she didn't wind up near the restaurant until midevening, following the inexplicable tracks you run along when you have neither job nor house nor friends but for a shifting cast of unpredictable individuals whom life has pushed into the same position. There are a lot of these trails in cities. People like you and me may not know where they run, but they're there all the same, two species sharing the same environment, the only competition for resources coming in the shape of a hand held out and a voice asking diffidently for spare change.

As I came in view of the Adriatico on the way to evening service, however, Lydia was there at the corner.

"S'up, Lyds?"

It was obvious something was different. I don't know what it is about people who stand to the side of what's considered sane, but their energy is wrong — something hectic about their eyes or vague in their movements, a sense of the person being trapped in an invisible corner and struggling to gain voice.

Lydia didn't look so much that way this evening. She simply looked old, and lost, and as if she was sick to death of too many things to start making a list.

She shrugged. "Aw, okay."

"Really?"

"I guess." She looked across the street, biting her lip. "I'll tell you what it is. I ain't seen him."

"Seen who?"

"Frankie, of course."

"Since when?"

"Couple days. Since I saw you that night."

"Does that happen? Gaps?"

She shook her head uncertainly. "Don't see him every day. He hasn't ever been that way. Even way back, when he was...around more. But this seems long."

"Why do you think that is?"

She lifted her shoulders sadly. I realized how bony they were. She'd always been birdlike under the layers of trash can castoffs, but it looked like she'd lost weight. "Wonder if I finally chased him off."

I waited, to give her a chance to go on, but she didn't. I hadn't missed the reference to a time when Frankie had been "around more." I'd never heard her say anything that danced around acknowledging there was something significantly different about her ex-lover's relationship to the world now.

"Is there anything you can do?" I asked.

"Do?"

"Something more likely to make him come around."

She stared at me as if I were the most dumb-ass fool it'd been her misfortune to encounter. "If there was, you think I wouldn't be doing it the whole damned time?"

I laughed. "Yeah okay. Sorry."

"He's alive, you know. I know everybody thinks I'm crazy. That he got kilt in that bar. But it didn't happen. There was some guys after him, that's true. He pissed them off bad. It's why he disappeared. Duh. But he ain't dead. You believe that?"

"You tell me he isn't, Lydia, then he isn't."

"Hmm. I'll tell you something else. He's the last man I did it with. And I used to *like* doing it. Was real good at it, too. You believe *that?*"

I did my best to suggest that I did believe her, and also that it wasn't one of the most wildly uncomfortable questions I'd ever been asked.

"You think I'd have waited if he wasn't still alive?"

"No," I said, "I don't believe that."

She nodded vigorously, and I saw that she was crying. "Damn straight."

I reached in my pocket and got out a scrap of paper. I scribbled a note on one side and an address on the other. "You ever go to church?"

"Hell no," she said. "God's a cunt."

"Okay, but I met a guy recently. He's a priest, but he seems like a good man."

"So?"

"Sometimes it's good to have someone to talk to. A person who isn't going to hassle you about getting into a shelter and when was the last time you had a bath or took your meds, blah blah blah."

Lydia squinted at the paper. "Chelsea? I lived there, long time ago. Well, crashed in a guy's apartment. Was a lot less boring in that neighborhood back then, I'll tell you. The stuff I saw! It's different now."

"You walked that road once; you can do it again."

"And he ain't going to try to get me down on my knees praising God?"

"He might. But I reckon you'd be a match for him, don't you?"

She smiled. "What the fuck you doing here talking to me, anyway? Ain't you got a job?"

Before I went into the restaurant I looked back. I saw Lydia stuff the piece of the paper into one of her pockets. Months ago I'd given her my cell phone number, and she'd done the same then. She'd never called, of course, and I felt sure the paper I'd just given her would be there in two or five or ten years, the day or night when some city employee had the distasteful job of checking for possessions among the clothes of the deceased.

But I was wrong about that.

I went in the back and changed into the black pants and white shirt that Mario insists upon, and got straight out onto the floor. The restaurant was already crowded—like the homeless, tourists and hungry locals have chaotic schedules and routines and it's impossible to predict how busy any given night is going to be, though that hasn't stopped Maria (who believes she harbors some kind of clairvoyant ability) from trying. She's dogged about it, too—making her prediction at precisely noon every day, and scoring herself at the end of every night. She's been doing it for fifteen years, which is a long time, though evidently not enough to read what her meticulous records are telling her, which is that the cat who hangs around the bins at the back of the restaurant would make a better job of it.

By eight thirty she'd thrown up her hands and admitted she'd missed the signs (as usual). We were packed to the point of having an actual freaking line on the sidewalk. I knew Kristina wouldn't turn up at the usual time because it was book club night and she had a standing dispensation to arrive two hours late, and I didn't have the time to give her much thought because tonight, of all nights, Mario had decided to give Paulo a trial on the floor.

It wasn't working out. The restaurant has a strange internal shape due to the position of the pizza oven and the fact that it was carved out of two separate buildings god knows how long ago. There's a big main area covered by two waitresses, and two arms out—one along the window on the right (my domain, alongside Jimmy, a guy in his midfifties who has been on the job longer than he's been alive and can out-waiter any other living being), the other on the opposite side, in the back. The latter is the Adriatico's equivalent of Siberia and gets filled up last, which is why Paulo had been assigned there. Once the area started to fill up, however, it became clear that he wasn't cutting it. Something needed to be done, and fast.

Mario gave me the nod and I ceded control of the front area (and its higher tips) to Jimmy, who was man enough to pick up the slack. I intercepted Paulo where he was quaking by the kitchen pickup, and let him know I was on the case. His relief was so palpable you could have sat it in a chair and given it a glass of wine. I got him to fill me in on which tables' service was most obviously falling apart and settled to placating people and shouting at the kitchen to expedite the orders of those dying of hunger (none of them, of course, but customers can be assholes, especially when they scent weakness in a server). For fifteen minutes I was so focused on all this that I didn't even notice the table in the far corner, whose meal was proceeding in an orderly fashion and thus not on anybody's radar.

I was picking up from a table eight feet away when someone spoke. "See. I was right. I knew that I knew you."

Reinhart was sitting by himself. He'd turned so that his face was visible to me now, and was smiling, knife and fork in his hands over a plate of food.

"I know. I know," he said, shrugging affably. "Two restaurants in one day, right? But I get a lot of exercise. You only get so many meals in your life. You should make the most of them. And I do. I like my food. *Love* it, in fact. I savor all physical things."

"Good for you."

"I've been here before. A few months back. That's where I saw you. You don't remember me from then. Just another customer, right? Busy busy."

"I'm busy now."

"So I see. You got people to serve. That's a waiter's job. I just need to tell you something."

People were watching now. That didn't matter. I could still have done the sensible thing, which was head back to the kitchen with the plates. But I did not.

With a be-there-in-a-minute nod to a four-top who were still waiting for appetizers, I walked over to Reinhart's table. "This needs to be quick."

"It will be."

"So what did you want to say?"

He took one more bite of his steak and put his knife and fork down. "People only embarrass me once."

*   *   *

I spent years in the armed forces and other institutions of violence. I've had training, keep fit, and I've got game. But it wasn't even the plates I was holding that handicapped me. Reinhart was just far too fast.

He was out of his seat like a jump cut, and I didn't have time to step back before the first punch hit me in the face like a cinder block. After that I barely knew what was happening. I was aware of fists crunching into my ribs and stomach with very regular frequency and intensity — fractionally aware, too, that while I was trying to avoid customers and their tables Reinhart was showing no such compunction. I fought back as best I could, but I was starting from way behind.

I staggered, and then fell back another step, managing to keep upright for maybe ten seconds and trying to throw blows back that dead-ended in the punches coming my way. Then I was on the ground, dimly conscious of people shouting and glasses shattering as kicks hammered into my stomach and chest and head so hard it felt like there was no flesh between my bones and his toe, or his heel when he started stomping down on me with that.

Then it stopped.

It was noisy around me but in the way the waves are when you're right in among them — alien, tidal, a cacophony with nothing to help differentiate meaning. I tried to push up off the ground but could not.

A patch of white light moved in front of my right eye, getting bigger. I heard a smeary voice above me.

"Call Kristina," it said, and only then did I realize Kris hadn't turned up yet and it must be late.

Then nothing.

Chapter 44

Kristina was sitting on a bench in a small empty park overlooking the Hudson River. It was cold and dark, silent but for the sound of traffic on the road behind and distant lapping in the water below. The other friends had shaded away on the walk over—either saying goodbye and smiling shyly, or simply reaching a point of not being there anymore—except for the plump girl and her boy, who were sitting on the grass thirty feet away.

"He's half right," Lizzie said.

Once Kristina had calmed down a little and consented to go to the park, Lizzie had asked about John, if things had improved since they'd last met. Kristina surprised herself by answering, slowly starting to talk about their lives in a way she'd never done with Catherine. She even admitted that—despite his tendency to be *incredibly* annoying—she loved John. This was a word she'd never found easy to use. It felt okay, though, and she was glad she'd said it. Like weddings, and funerals, there are times when life needs a witness to feel real.

From this she'd gone on to telling Lizzie about John's theory about Reinhart's role in their world, and this was what Lizzie had responded to, after a long pause. "Which half is right, and which is wrong?"

"Reinhart does have an arrangement," Lizzie confirmed. "He deals with one of us called Golzen. It's his group—they've taken to calling themselves the twelve—who are working most closely with Reinhart. It's not a forced arrangement. They do it freely."

"Why?"

"They receive things in return. Which increases Golzen's status and ego... It's complicated. We've never had a situation like this. I hoped it would sort itself out. But I'm not so sure. I've been trying to get people to stop taking things. This is bringing them back to it."

"But why would you steal in the first place?"

"It made us ... popular. It's hard to describe. But the other part is that it's the most active behavior that most of us are capable of. It ... makes you feel alive."

Kristina guessed she understood. Though she'd never stolen as an adult, like most kids she and girlfriends had lifted things from stores as a dare. Both times she'd thrown away the trinket the same day. Though she had felt bad and compromised, she remembered the anticipation and thrill. Presumably that's what Lizzie was talking about.

She sensed the other woman was not comfortable, however, and turned the conversation to more personal areas. "Do *you* have anybody? I mean, like a boyfriend?"

"There's someone who's more important to me than anyone else."

"The guy you mentioned last time? Maj?"

Lizzie nodded.

"What's he like?"

"He's good-looking and he's smart and I'm happier when I'm with him than when I'm not. But he spends a lot of his time with his mind on other things."

"So, he's a man, then. What the hell is that *about?*"

They laughed quietly together. It'd been a long time since Kris sat talking to anyone about their boyfriends — but for small talk to pass a slow evening with some other bartender, conversations that ran aground after it became obvious the only advice was *dump the asshole, change the locks, and do it now.* With Lizzie it felt different. Lizzie asked questions effortlessly. She was a good listener, too. Kris wasn't sure she knew how to do this kind of thing anymore. It had been too long since she'd had this kind of friend. If a friend was what Lizzie was, or could become. The funny thing was, it felt like she always had been.

"Where is he this evening?"

"Maj comes and he goes. Some of us like to stay in the same place. He's not so much like that. Plus he's got a job. I think he's on call tonight."

"What kind of job?"

"He's a Fingerman."

"You used that word before. What is it?"

"Someone who's good at using their hands."

"Like a craftsman? He makes things?"

"No. We can't make anything, dead or alive. He touches things, when people need him to. Opens them, presses them, you know."

Kristina nodded, though she was not sure what this was supposed to mean. "Do you love him?"

Lizzie laughed. "That's a big question."

"You asked me. I answered it."

"True. Well . . . yes, I suppose I do."

"A lot?"

"As much as I can, given who I am and what he is. That's quite a lot."

Kristina realized that's what she'd meant, too, and that she wasn't even sure what loving someone meant anymore. Yes, attraction of course, and wanting to be with; but it wasn't really about that kind of thing now, was it? It wasn't raised heartbeats and smoldering glances. It was feeling comfortable and secure and valued; it was less about how you felt right now and more about how you might in the future, about the things you might want until the day you died.

"Do you want children someday?"

Lizzie sat looking at her hands, and Kristina realized she had no idea how old the other woman was. Sometimes she seemed older than her — late thirties, maybe even forty. Most of the time, she seemed about the same age. Right now, she looked about thirteen.

"Kristina," she said. "I'm not real."

"I hear you," Kris replied, with feeling. "But everybody feels like that from time to time, right? Doesn't mean you wouldn't make a good parent."

"No," Lizzie said patiently. "I'm *not real.*"

Kristina stared at her, unsure whether to laugh. "Okay. Right. So what are you?"

Lizzie looked distant and ashamed. "I'm imaginary."

"This is . . . some kind of metaphor thing, right?"

"No."

"But . . . *what?*"

"We don't know how it works. There was one of us who had a theory. Every generation there's a few who think harder about things. Lonely Clive was one of those. I knew him, and Maj did too, very well. But Clive's hollow now. Even the strongest lose faith."

"You mean . . . he's dead?"

"No. He's barely there. His idea was that we hollow when we become wholly forgotten by our real friend — when their mind heals over and loses any memory of us even in dreams. And he may have been right, but it can happen in other ways. I've known a few who've deliberately chosen that road. Who elected not to exist anymore. The irony is that you have to be strong to make that choice. The rest of us just fade . . . until the day our friend dies."

Kristina had decided to let Lizzie keep talking until it started making sense. "What . . . happens then?"

"The Bloom. A few hours, sometimes as much as a day, when you're stronger than you've ever been. And then . . ."

She held her hands in a loose ball, as if containing a soul, some energy, an idea; then she gently opened them out, to suggest nothing at all.

"Lizzie, if you guys choose to believe you're not real, if it's some big existential . . . whatever, then that's fine. But . . . *it's not true.*"

"Kris — you saw Flaxon in the house."

"Who's Flaxon?"

Lizzie gestured toward the plump girl on the grass. "She was a Dozeno until six months ago. That's what we call those who don't understand what they are. Some stay like that forever, which is sad. Most get it sooner or later. When Flaxon realized, she kicked *hard*. Took against real people in the worst way. She did some really bad stuff—and worked for Reinhart for a while, until we managed to get her to walk with us instead. She's a lot calmer now, but once in a while she still . . . well, you asked how she could stand there in front of that couple in the house. They didn't see her, did they?"

No, they had not. And Kristina knew that the people in the house should really have been able to see Lizzie and the other guy under the table, too.

"But *I* can see you."

"Yes, you can. John too, evidently. Some people have always been able to see things out of the corner of their eye. And children sometimes, and animals, cats especially. With others it happens when we get drawn to their attention—if something gets knocked over, or someone points us out. Once you've seen one it's easier to see others, apparently. You call these people 'mediums.' Luckily, almost all of them are fake."

"We saw you because we were trying to find out who was following Catherine Warren."

Lizzie nodded.

"And why were you?"

"You can't work it out?" Lizzie's voice was almost too quiet to hear. "I'm her imaginary friend. Or, I was."

"What, like . . . the things that *kids* have?"

Lizzie smiled stiffly. "Yes. Those things that kids have. And then forget. That's what happens. People grow up and forget. Doesn't mean we just *stop*."

She turned to Kristina, looking old and miserable. "You ever have a dream, something you thought you'd do one day, that you fantasized about for hour after hour, and planned to the last degree, and truly believed you'd make part of your future come what may . . . But then life changed, or you did, and you slowly forgot about it?"

"I guess."

"We're like that. Like the guitars that sit in the corner of living rooms, never played. Like plans for the year in Paris that never happens. Like months of unrequited longing that never ends in a kiss. Once that much energy has been poured into something it never completely goes away. It's a part of that person's life forever, something that didn't happen. Negatives shape people too, like white space on a page. A dream doesn't die just because it doesn't come true. And . . . neither do we."

"Do you—"

But then Lizzie was standing, and a second later the plump girl leapt to her feet and was running, fast—the boyfriend not far behind. Lizzie set after them.

Kristina did her best to follow. She saw a woman weaving on the side of the street, fifty yards away, holding the hand of a child—a girl about four or five years old. Traffic was coursing up and down the street—not thickly, but fast.

The little girl seemed to be more aware of this fact than her mother, who was determined to cross the street and to do it right there and now. Flaxon was headed straight toward them. She was fast—eerily fast.

The little girl's mother kept making attempts to cross the road. The girl looked unsure, but this was her mother, and she had a tight grip on her hand. The little girl was not in control. She was going to have to trust that her mother knew what she was doing.

Flaxon got to within twenty feet and decelerated, so abruptly that Kristina had to pull her head back to see her again. She was catching up to Lizzie now but neither of them was going to make it there before whatever was about to happen took place.

The mother finally lost patience with the traffic. You could tell this from the set of her shoulders, from something that communicated itself through the air. She'd decided now was good enough and she was done waiting for the assholes to let her cross.

Her girl had become distracted and was no longer looking at the cars, but frowning...turning to look around her, as if aware something was coming her way.

Flaxon strode right past behind them, grabbing the mother's shoulder just as she started to step out into the road. She pulled it hard—a quick, sharp movement—before carrying on past.

The girl looked up, as if knowing something had passed behind them. Her mother was pulled off balance. With one foot raised to step out into the road, there was no way of keeping herself upright.

She toppled backward awkwardly, kept from crashing outright by her daughter's hold on her, just as a motorcycle came from out of nowhere.

It came so fast and so close that you could smell the leather the driver was wearing and hear the smeared residue of his snarl to get the fuck out of the way.

The woman landed flat on her back on the sidewalk, mouth open, eyes horribly wide. She knew damned well what had just happened and how it would have gone if chance hadn't caused her to slip and fall backward.

"Oh holy Jesus," she said. "Oh Jesus, Jesus."

Her little girl stood blinking down at her. "Mom, are you okay? What happened?"

"I'm okay," the woman said, getting back to her feet. She looked around and saw a pedestrian crossing a hundred feet up the street. She seemed shaken, pulled back out of whatever mental or chemical fugue had brought her so close to being a small, sad item somewhere low down on page seven of tomorrow's newspaper. "Let's use the crosswalk. We should *always* do that, right?"

"Right." The girl reached up and took her mother's hand again.

Her mother gripped it tight and looked down at her, face trembling. "Okay, honey."

They waited at the light until it was safe to cross, and then did so slowly and very carefully. Kristina watched. Behind her she was aware of Lizzie going over to Flaxon and kissing her softly on the cheek.

"Get off," Flaxon muttered. "Weirdo."

But she looked pleased.

As they got to the other side, the little girl looked back at where Kris stood with Lizzie and Flaxon and her guy. Kristina saw the girl looking right at her, didn't want to be a scary adult, and smiled.

The girl registered this, but it hadn't been Kris she was looking for.

Kristina became aware that her phone was ringing. It was the restaurant. For a while she'd forgotten she had a job and that she was now very late for it. Right now, in the midst of this evening and what had just (nearly) happened, she didn't give a crap about serving people more cheap wine than they needed. But she hit the button and prepared to use her charm on Mario one more time.

"I'm sorry," she said. "I got —"

It wasn't Mario, but his sister. She sounded freaked out. "You have to hurry. You have to go there now."

"What? Why?"

"It's John. He's in the hospital."

Chapter 45

Talia sat at her table. Her laptop was in front of her but it was closed. That was okay. A growl in her stomach reminded her she hadn't eaten anything. That was okay too. The hunger was hypothetical. The words... well, she'd written nothing for two days. Nothing in the novel, nothing even into the diary where she'd written at least something every day since the shooting star. The conversation with George had planted a seed in her mind, a seed that had grown, sucking up whatever nutrients the words used to thrive on.

At work it was easier to ignore. There was always stuff going on, somebody to greet and serve, something to clean or refill. Except for her exchange with David — which she'd come out of feeling like a bit of an ass, though she doubted he'd have noticed anything — work just rolled on, lots of business as usual.

But at home...

Of course it was absurd, because not one thing had *changed,* but her home felt different. It was still tidy. It remained pretty full of cats. Everything, as far as she could tell, was in its place.

Her spatula was where it was supposed to be.

In the time since, she'd wondered about that. She'd wondered if maybe it *hadn't* been a case of her breaking the habit of many years by hanging the damned thing up on the other side, but if someone else had been in here, if they'd taken the spatula down to look at it and then put it back up in the wrong place.

Why would somebody do that? No reason.

Unless they'd recognized the spatula, perhaps. It was old and battered.

Talia had owned it a very long time—had used it to lever some of those own brand brownies out of the baking tray back in the mists of yesteryear. *Maybe* someone who'd been around back then might have thought to take a nostalgic look at it.

Maybe.

She'd looked around the trailer, looked *hard,* and hadn't been able to find much else out of place. Everything was shipshape and socked away, as Ed used to say. She'd noticed something about her diaries, though. These were kept in neat rows on the shelves behind the little TV, which she hardly ever watched. Every one was the same, inexpensive red exercise books of the type that didn't cost much at any time of year but you could get even cheaper during back-to-school promotions—which is what she'd always done, buying ten at once and stashing until needed. They stood in orderly ranks, the spines getting more faded as they went back in time, aged by the light that came through the window in the afternoons. She kept them in order. This wasn't some anal-retentive thing or the result of any effort. You finished a book, you put it next to the previous one and did the same the next time and the next. Much like events in the real world, chronology looked after itself.

Except... last night she'd found a couple out of order. Way back— from the early days, on the far left of the top shelf. It could be that she'd put them back in the wrong order; once in a while she'd pull a volume down to remind herself of things that had happened and to convince herself that keeping a diary wasn't a wholly pointless exercise. She made sure to put the book back in its right place, though, which was easy given each was numbered on the spine with the dates it covered and also a sequential number. It'd be hard to imagine messing that up, even if she'd had a beer or two, which (though she'd never again toyed with the too-many-is-not-enough approach from the months after Ed's death) was not unknown. Could also be a cat-related event. Some of the younger ones liked to go nuts midevening, galloping around the place and knocking things down.

A couple of times they'd knocked books off those shelves. She might have been in a hurry to clean up the mess and shoved them back up there without worrying too much about the order.

Did she remember that happening? No.

But then, presumably she wouldn't.

She didn't lock the trailer when she went into town. She took her laptop with her, always. There was nothing else worth stealing.

So somebody *could* have come in here, taken down a volume or two, and looked through. The town's younger element were likely too consistently stoned for a mission of that complexity, though, and lacked the imagination. Anyone who was enough of an asshole to do it would have probably messed the place up, too, and left a turd in the middle of the floor for good measure.

A little mystery, huh. Maybe she should tell David about it, see if he could use it to break through his writer's block. But she doubted she would. She'd seen the way he'd looked when she'd told him about George's hitchhiker. She'd given him enough.

After a while she tired of running the problem around and got up to feed the cats. It was nearly ten already. She should have done it hours before. The entire crew was in attendance, and most stood up with her, knowing it was well past time.

As she squatted down to shell the gunk out of tins into their bowls, Talia found herself noticing the bottom of the kitchen cabinets. Nicks. Little scrapes and rust spots. Her home felt small tonight. And make-do, and old. It'd never felt like that before. It was Talia Willocks's firm, comfortable exterior, the side she showed to the world—or would have, if anyone ever came to see. Now it felt like a bubble had burst, releasing whatever had made it a home and leaving a thin, empty skin.

She straightened. Looked around. A fifty-five-year-old woman living by herself in a trailer with a bunch of cats. Is this what the younger

Tally-Anne thought was coming down the road? No. That hot little number had foreseen a few more years of fun and games and then a marriage day—be it ever so simple and small, catered by friends and served on the finest paper plates Dollar Tree had to offer. A handful of kids. A little house. School concerts. Yard sales. Stuff like that. She didn't miss most of it. By her age she'd be out the other side of those things, probably be cussing about how much free babysitting Grandma was getting hit up for.

But she'd have someone to complain to, someone who'd know she didn't really mean it, a man who'd be by her side for all the stuff coming down the pike, as he'd been there for everything before.

That's what was missing.

The cats snaffled and chomped around their bowls. Talia watched them with love.

And then the knocking came on the door.

As she stood outside the trailer, the wind rose. It had been that way the previous night, too, when the knocking had come a second time—though then she hadn't opened the door, but stayed inside, huddled on the couch. She felt that when someone who wasn't there came knocking, this was the best approach.

Tonight she'd decided differently. That was why, though she'd taken her bath as usual, she wasn't wearing stretch pants and the pink toweling robe. She wore a dress in beige and cream that she'd had a few years, and sure it was very tight around the hips and upper arms and everywhere else and she probably looked like a tank in desert camouflage, but it was the best she had.

There'd been no one there when she opened the door, but Talia had decided you didn't hear knocking on your house three nights running if there was truly nobody outside.

She heard a rustling sound and glanced down to see Tilly by her feet, looking up at her. Probably wondering why the big human was outside the mothership at this time of night.

"Mama's just waiting," she told her, and bent to scratch her ears. "Be back inside in a little while."

Maybe the cat understood, maybe she didn't, but after a few more sniffs of the air she turned and went back in the trailer.

Talia stayed where she was. She wasn't waiting, not really. What could she be waiting for?

But she stayed.

Ten minutes later she heard someone call. It was faint, as it had been on the first night. Very weak, as if the caller had traveled some distance and was weary and that low cry was the best he could muster for now.

This time the sound did not come from up the direction of the graveyard, however. It came from the other direction, past the end of the road, from somewhere along the track that led toward the steep sides of the creek. It was about the same distance away, though, and she could hear what it said at least as clearly as before.

"Tally-Anne."

So faint. As if the moment of death had thrown the person so far away, and into such blackness, that it had taken him twenty years to haul his way back home again. Traveling on foot, for the most part, even on hands and knees, except maybe for that helping hand over the last part, a ride into Rockbridge in the back of George Lofland's battered Toyota SUV — a ride from someone the deceased had known and drunk with, back in the day.

"I'm coming," she said.

She closed the door of the trailer and walked down the road. Skirted the chain at the end and set up along the trail through the long grasses.

It took a few minutes to get to where the track veered left, following the ridge above the rocky sides down to the river. This started off passable but soon became choked with low bushes and tangling brambles. Talia stayed high for the time being, however—until the trees started to gather it'd be easier than finding a way to scramble down the ten-foot slope. It should be easier to spot him from up here, too, whoever he might be.

Who was she kidding? She knew who it was, or who she wanted it to be. Why else would she be out here at night, in her best dress, as the wind gathered above and it started to rain? She walked fast, shoving bushes out of her way. She could feel something, knew there was something up ahead.

"Tally-Anne."

She started moving faster still. About a minute later she heard another sound, however, mixed in with the wind but seeming to come from the same direction.

It was a laugh, she thought. But if so, it had sounded high-pitched, almost like a woman's.

Talia hesitated. What if it *wasn't* Ed's voice she was hearing? What if some dumb-ass kids with evil intent had come in her home when she was at work, flicked through old diaries, and found the name she used to go by set down in some maudlin recollection of how much fuller her life had once been?

What if this was someone's cruel idea of a game?

But then she heard her name again. She started to trot, elbowing branches aside as the ridge started to get into the edges of the forest. She couldn't tell whether the voice was coming from up along the ridge or down from the narrow, jagged path by the creek. It was along here somewhere, though, and she was getting closer, too.

"Tally-Anne. I'm over here."

She started to run in earnest. Her feet caught in the brambles and she nearly tripped, but she kept running faster through the undergrowth, deeper into the trees. She thought maybe he was down there in the cutting, looking for her, too tired to make it all the way back into her arms and trusting her to get to him. She was worthy of that trust.

Then she saw him.

Thirty yards away, down in the dip. A tall man with long hair. She called out his name, again and again, running even faster, telling him she was coming, waiting for a break in the bushes before she could start to make her way down the slope to him.

But then someone stepped out from behind a tree right in front of her. It was a woman. Tall, painfully thin, with terribly red hair.

She started to smile, some dry, stretched movement of her lips away from dark teeth, and then she disappeared.

Talia screamed and lost her footing and started to slip, and when one leg got caught behind the remnants of an old tree stump, she lost her balance altogether and there was nothing to do except fall.

She fell nothing like a star.

Part Three

Dreams are real as long as they last. Can we say more of life?

Havelock Ellis

Chapter 46

"I'm fine," I said.

"John, you are so *not* fine."

I repeated that I was fine. I was aware I was saying it for something like the fourth or fifth time, and groggily, and that neither was helping my case. Being able to make this simple opinion understood seemed very important, however.

"John . . . oh Jesus. *Look* at you."

"I'm fine," I said. Then I passed out.

When I opened my eyes again Kristina was still sitting by the bed. A nurse — the same one who'd been there all along, I believed, though the room was pretty dark and I wasn't entirely sure — was standing to one side.

"And . . . he's back," the nurse said cheerfully, checking her watch. "Barely five minutes that time. Your boy ain't one to take shit lying down, huh?"

"Hey," I said thickly.

"Tell me one more time that you're fine," Kris said in a low, sincere tone, "and I'll punch you myself."

"Okay," I said. "To be honest, it kind of hurts."

"What does?" asked the nurse.

"Pretty much everything."

"That's good."

She gave me a looking over and got me to follow her finger while she moved it across various planes in front of my eyes and then marched out into the corridor to go about her business, evidently satisfied I was no closer to death than I deserved.

The last thing I remembered before waking up in the hospital was seeing—from my floor-level perspective—Reinhart leaving the restaurant. He had not stabbed a warning finger in my face or delivered gritty parting shots. The guys who do that learned their violence from television and their threats are like muscles acquired from the gym—they look good but lack the steel that comes from being tempered by real life. I was now ruefully convinced Reinhart had served his apprenticeship at the knee of people who were not interested in how things looked, but concerned rather with putting their enemies on the ground hard and fast. On it, or underneath. I knew he would have relented only because that kind of man has the sense to stop short of committing actual murder in front of fifty civilian witnesses—and that he would want very much to finish what he'd started, in private.

Mario's sister hadn't waited for an ambulance but drove me the twenty blocks up to Bellevue herself, once Jimmy and Paulo had dragged me out through tables of fascinated diners and laid me across the backseat of her car. She told me this when I woke, briefly, the first time. She also said she'd called Kris and that the nurse believed I wasn't going to die, probably, so she had to get back to work; it was a busy night and now they were down a waiter, for God's sake, and when it came to paying the hospital bills I was on my own, of course.

Kris was there when next I surfaced. And, thankfully, still here this third time.

I pushed myself up in bed. "Where were you?"

"I'll tell you later," she said. "There's . . . there's a guy who wants to talk to you."

From my newly elevated position I could see a man in the doorway. I thought for a moment there was someone else out in the dimly lit corridor beyond, but I didn't get a good look.

"Who are you?" I asked.

The man came and stood at the end of the bed. He pulled out a wallet and showed NYPD ID that said his name was Detective Raul Brooke.

"Okay," I said. "So what do you want?"

"For you to tell me what happened."

"I got beat up."

"That'd be obvious from about thirty feet away, sir. I was hoping for more in the way of detail."

"I don't have any."

"Uh-huh. A witness gave us a name, so I don't need you to volunteer that. I'd simply like you to explain the nature of your encounter with Mr. Reinhart."

"Personal."

"Uh-huh," he said again. "Your assailant is known to us, Mr. Henderson. You are not the first person to undergo an entanglement with him, though actually you came out of it better than some."

"I got in his face over something. He came to the place where I work and got the jump on me. That's all."

"If you know his name," Kristina said, "why can't you just arrest him?"

"Experience has shown that casual witnesses have a pattern of losing their memory when it comes to this man," Brooke said. "I'm wondering whether your boyfriend might be made of stronger stuff."

"It was a private disagreement," I said.

The cop smiled tightly and put his notebook away. "Right," he said. "That's similar to what the other three said, the people we know had 'private disagreements' with him. One has disappeared. The other is in a wheelchair. He lives in a facility in Queens. His son visits him every week, but his dad has no clue who he is."

"I'm sorry to hear that."

"Right," the detective said again. He seemed like a man who'd boiled his vocal responses down to simple units, which he could deploy as and when necessary. He put something on the arm of Kristina's chair and walked toward the door, but stopped as he reached the corridor.

"The third person died. Hard. Of course, we can't tie that to Reinhart, or I wouldn't be here trying to get sense out of the next asshole in line."

I didn't say anything.

"This person was a woman," the cop added, more wearily. "And your friend was smart enough to cut away the parts of her that might have held traces of his DNA. So the bottom line is, we got three people who can't help get this guy what he deserves . . . and one who can. You."

He flicked his thumb at Kristina. "Your friend has my card. She's probably got the smarts to be able to read the words on it, too. If *you* grow a brain anytime soon, Mr. Henderson, give me a call."

He left.

"I'm leaving," I said.

"No, you're not."

I pulled the sheet off the lower half of my body. This triggered ricochets of pains across my chest and back. My first attempt to swing my legs off the bed did not go smoothly and made me feel nauseous. "Yeah, I am."

"Stay *there*."

"Kris, you heard the guy."

"Yes, I *did*. I was worried you hadn't. I was wondering if maybe you'd got hit in the head so often that you lost all ability to hear what the hell people are saying to you, you *asshole*."

Then she had her hands on my shoulder and was either shaking me or trying to push me back down. It wasn't easy to tell which, but I held her until the first rage or fear was spent and eventually got my arms around her back and pulled her in to me. That hurt too, but it was a different kind of pain, and I held her as long as she'd let me, until she'd stopped trying to shout in my ear and was letting me kiss her on the cheek, and then doing the same thing back, reluctantly, and still angrily, but hard.

Finally she pulled away, and I was shocked to see her eyes were wet. I have never seen Kris cry.

"I'm sorry," I said.

"It's not your fault."

"Pushing Reinhart's buttons today was dumb. But that cop sounded serious and that's why I'm out of here. It won't be hard for Reinhart to find out where I am and right now I'm not in a position to—"

"John, you haven't seen what you look like. You haven't talked to the nurse. You're *concussed.*"

"All the more reason to get home."

"He's right," said a voice.

I looked at the door to discover a tall girl in a black coat standing out in the dark corridor, the girl who seemed to have been the catalyst to pull us into all of this, whatever "this" was.

Kristina looked as guilty as hell and I guessed I knew where she'd been that evening. "Lizzie—what are you *doing* here?"

"I followed you," the woman said. "It's what we do."

"John should *stay here.* And talk to that policeman."

Lizzie shook her head. "Those would be mistakes."

Kristina went out into the corridor. They went back and forth for a while, which gave me the opportunity to slide awkwardly out of bed, wrench myself out of the gown, find my clothes, and get dressed. Getting out of the gown revealed how bruised and scuffed my chest was. Climbing into my clothes suggested that in my current state I could probably be knocked over by a toddler, or a boisterous mouse. I stuck to the task, however, moving like a puppet with tangled strings. I picked up the cop's business card and stuffed that in my pocket, too.

"So," I said when I was done and had lurched out into the corridor to join them. "How do we get out of this place? I'm afraid I have no idea."

"John, for God's *sake*..."

"I'm dressed and it hurt and I'm not getting undressed again." I meant to say more but got light-headed and had to lean against the wall.

"Christ," she said. "Okay, let's go."

The corridor was in night mode, periodically lit by dim lights. There was no sign of the nurse. Lizzie held up a hand to tell us to stay where we were. She hurried to the intersection and looked both ways, then gestured for us to follow. I wasn't sure why I was taking direction from her, but if it meant I could get out of the hospital I was prepared to go along with it for now.

At the intersection we found a nurse's station, empty, and a sign pointing down a long corridor toward the elevators. The longest of the corridors, of course.

We started along it, but then Lizzie slowed, twisting her head around in short, abrupt movements, as if listening for something. Whatever it was, she eventually seemed to catch it.

She bit her lip. "Go," she said.

Kris hesitated, caught between wanting to get me out and wanting to know what was going on. "What is it?"

"It's... just go," Lizzie muttered, setting off down the side corridor. "Go somewhere safe."

But Kristina followed the girl as she hurried away, and I limped after her. Every three yards along this corridor was a door to an individual room. All had been left slightly ajar, presumably to allow monitoring staff to poke their heads in during the night. For no obvious reason, Lizzie approached the door about halfway along and then froze outside, hand held up toward the door as if about to push it open.

She was so unnaturally still that for a moment it seemed as if she could never have moved at all, but was something seen as a layer over the world, like a particular vivid memory or daydream. Then she was in movement again, gently pushing.

We reached the doorway as she stepped in. It was dark inside, with only a low glow from a short fluorescent tube halfway up the far wall.

On the left was a bed. In it lay a man, propped up. He was asleep, breathing raggedly. He was pale and bloated and had plastic tubes going into one wrist and one nostril and it did not seem likely that he was in the hospital for something minor. This was a man whose body was at war against him. His body, and time.

I turned to go, feeling bad for intruding on his sickness and while he was asleep, but realized there was someone else in the room. There was a chair in the corner, pointed toward the bed. Another man, younger than the other or in better health and shape, was sitting there. He had his elbows on his knees and his hands clasped tightly together, intently watching the man in the bed. He was rocking back and forth.

"Oh, Billy," Lizzie said.

He didn't answer. Lizzie put her hand on his shoulder. "How long have you been here?"

He licked his lips. "Two days."

"What happened?"

"Heart attack."

"But he's only..."

"I know. I *know*. But it's been coming. I realize that now. I hadn't seen him in years. I didn't understand how he'd become. I thought it was me losing faith, slowly going hollow. But it was him all along."

The figure in the bed pulled in a rasping breath. "No," Billy said, leaning forward. "No..."

After a few seconds the man in the bed breathed out again, and the rhythm of his chest's rise and fall seemed to settle. Lizzie stood by the bed, looking down. "Why isn't anybody here with him?"

"They were. I've been standing at the end of the bed all day, out of their way. The doctors say he's stable, so they've gone home to get some rest and change their clothes and, I don't know, that kind of thing."

"Well, if the doctor says that then... it could all be okay."

The man shook his head. In the weak light his face looked pinched, almost translucent. I don't think he had any idea that Kristina and I were even in the room.

"I felt it. I didn't realize it, but I *felt* it. That's why... that's why. It *wasn't* my fault."

Lizzie looked at us. "Go," she said. She no longer looked elfin, or distant. She looked like if we didn't go then bad things would happen to us.

"Kris," I said... but then the man on the bed made a quiet, terrible sound, as if he'd tried to pull in another breath and found the world withholding it.

He tried again, and this time it sounded like he'd succeeded but the air had gone the wrong way inside his body, as if there was no longer any proper place in there for it. His eyes opened, staring up at the ceiling, and in them was all possible knowledge of what was happening to him. He knew, and because he knew it was impossible for the rest of us not to know too.

"Get a nurse," Kristina said. "John, get a —"

A final exhale, an out breath that seemed to last far longer than it should for a pair of lungs to void themselves of air — as if instead it was clearing out the stale remains of every single inhale, back through thirty years of in-and-outs and sneezes, to childhood breaths in fields and classrooms, breaths sucked in to blow out birthday candles, back even to the first breath scrabbled out of a cold new world, to give the power to wail.

The man on the chair — Billy — was standing now, coming closer to the bed, arms held down and rigid by his sides. He closed his eyes.

"Goodbye, my friend."

The breath finished, or came to a point where it was no longer going on. In the life of the person in the bed, nothing ever happened again.

The man standing next to him seemed to condense. It was as if something had shifted in the lighting, making a shape that had been so inconsequential when we entered that I hadn't even noticed him into something more substantial. Not bigger, exactly, but much more *there*.

He was motionless for a moment, then took in a *huge* jagged breath, his eyes flying open. "Ha," he said.

He breathed out massively, then back in again. "Ha!" He started walking around the room, faster and faster, arms and legs jerking robotically. "Oh, yes," he said, starting to laugh. *"That's* what I'm talking about."

He pulled another monstrous breath in through mouth and nose, and held it down, as if savoring it.

"Billy," Lizzie said. "Billy, slow down."

He paid no attention to her. He completed one more chaotic circuit of the room and nearly knocked me down as he went striding out the door, arms thrashing.

Lizzie ran after him, leaving us in a hospital room with a cooling body and no clue what was going on.

"What the hell just happened?"

"Let's get you home," Kristina said, with a final glance at the dead man in the bed. "There's . . . stuff we need to talk about."

Chapter 47

We didn't go home, however. In the cab we realized that if Reinhart did decide to come back and finish the discussion tonight, then directly after the hospital he'd come hunting where we lived. Both of us believed he'd already have that information or be able to obtain it, and that being trapped up at the top of a five-story building was a bad defensive position.

I hated the feeling of hiding from him, but on the other hand—and perhaps contrary to appearances—I'm not a total fool. If we were going to meet again, it needed to be in circumstances of my choosing, or at least at a time when I could straighten my back and move my limbs without feeling like I was going to pass out. Merely lolling in the back of a yellow cab felt like someone was still hitting me, and my brain was so washy and vague that I wasn't completely convinced of what I thought I'd seen in the private room in the hospital.

Trying to work out where to hide in the middle of the night is a good way to focus the mind on the relationships in your life. The news that came back was not good. The restaurant made no sense and neither did the apartments of any staff members. Even if we'd been close enough to impose upon them, their connection to the Adriatico would rule them out. I'd traced Reinhart to his lunch via this kind of link and I had no doubt he'd be able to do the same in reverse. The only other person we could think of was Catherine, which clearly wasn't an option either. Once we'd run out of ideas and sat in silence for a few minutes, Kristina took my hand.

"We don't really live here, do we?"

"No," I said. "Maybe you're right. Maybe we should move. Live in a neighborhood. Try to hang with some real people for a change."

She shook her head.

"Why? I thought that's what you wanted."

"Throwing money at a more expensive apartment isn't going to solve anything."

"It might help." She shook her head again, with a finality I found unnerving. "Kris, what?"

"How much cash do you have on you now?"

"Not enough for a hotel room, if that's what you're thinking. And I didn't bring any cards out with me."

"How much?"

Wincing, I managed to lever my wallet out of my pocket and check the contents. "About eighty bucks."

She took the bills and shoved them through the slot in the glass toward the driver.

"That's what we have," she said to him.

The driver, an elderly man in a turban, looked surprised — but didn't give the money back. "Where to?"

"Just drive."

"I need a destination."

"Take us to wherever forty bucks gets us, and then come back. In the meantime, shut this slot thing, please, and then turn your radio up."

The guy decided the money was worth the attitude, and did what he'd been asked. Kristina sat back in the seat, and — after a couple of false starts — told me what had happened to her before she turned up at the hospital.

I listened, and tried not to interrupt.

The money bought us half an hour, enough for me to get Kristina to repeat the sections of her story that I found hardest to believe and also to establish that she at least half believed what Lizzie had told her as they sat together in the park. I spent the last five minutes in silence, watching out the window as smeared neon and streetlights flowed across the pane like bright horizontal raindrops. It was hard to push focus past these and other reflections in the glass and out onto the people on the sidewalks, leaning in doorways, sitting on benches, the people who are always out there, on their way somewhere or back, glimpsed from the side or behind, people whose identity and business you'll never know and who really, in your heart of hearts, you afford no more reality than the shadows of birds flying overhead.

Yes, clearly they represent something. But something real? Something as substantial as you and me? I didn't understand how what Kristina had told me could possibly work, but that did not mean it could not be so. There had been a time when I didn't understand how I could live in a world where my eldest son was dead, in which I could look at the woman I married and see someone I didn't recognize, or how I could now be living three thousand miles from Tyler, my remaining boy, and not have seen him in a year or have the faintest idea of what he was like now that he was six years old and older than Scott ever got to be. It had seemed impossible that I could find or take the steps that would lead me from a previous reality to these new ones without breaking apart on the journey. I did not, in fact, handle the events well — except perhaps in that I did ultimately survive, and woke up one morning and understood that this new world I lived in was real, and that therefore I must be real too.

Did that mean that the previous one had been unreal? That reality in which Scott walked the earth, or my mother, come to that — where did it stand now? It did not feel as if it lay back in time, that a mere sequence of events was what had moved it away from me. It felt like it still existed to one side, through a glass wall a hundred feet thick. I could see the land on the other side in my mind's eye, and sometimes in melancholy fantasy or sleeping dream it came closer than that, as if when I poured my soul and all the emotional energy I had into it these shades on the other side of alive/not alive and true/not true remained far more proximal than I'd thought. Close, in fact, to still being real.

If you believe life is worth living, it is. If you believe you are fat, you are. And if you believe for long enough, and strongly enough, that someone imaginary is real, and they were to come to believe it too . . .

Kris waited as patiently as she could, but in the end dug me in the ribs. "Well?"

"*Ow.*"

"Sorry. But . . . *well?* Talk to me. Say something."

I leaned forward and opened the slot to the driver's compartment. "How much we got left?"

He glanced at the meter. "About five bucks."

"Take us to Chelsea," I said.

I leaned against the railing at the bottom of the steps as Kristina hesitated at the door.

"John, it's two o'clock in the morning."

"Push the thing."

She pressed quickly on the door buzzer, trying to make a noise that should be audible to someone already awake, but hopefully not enough to raise the sleeping.

At first nothing seemed to happen, but then we heard the slow tramp of footsteps coming down the staircase inside. There was a pause, then the sound of a bolt and a chain being slid across. The door opened.

Father Jeffers stood in a yellow glow inside. He looked me up and down. "What on earth happened to you?"

"Not what," I said. "Who."

Chapter 48

An hour later, three things had happened. I'd been given several cups of strong coffee, which had helped. I'd seen myself in a mirror, which had not. Though I felt Kristina's and Jeffers's reactions had been extreme, a look at my face would leave you in no doubt that I'd been in a fight and lost. Apart from a few stitches in a cut under my left cheekbone, it was mainly bruising and scrapes, however. I wouldn't want to have to apply for a job in childcare or public relations, but I've seen worse, and the coffee and a fistful of painkillers from the priest's bathroom cabinet had made me feel better.

The third thing was that Kristina had told the priest what she'd told me, and I'd sketched out other events of the last week. Jeffers had listened impassively, as though withstanding a parishioner's doleful recitation of excessive drinking or unwholesome thoughts toward his neighbor's ass, in preparation for trotting out the prescribed means of atoning for such deviations from accepted moral practice. Only at one point did he seem more affected, when Kristina confirmed that Lizzie had been our first point of contact.

"You're absolutely sure she was taking an interest in this friend of yours?"

"Yes," I said. "I told you the time I disturbed your piano practice. It's been going on for some time."

"What do you mean by 'some time'?"

"I'm not sure," I admitted. "Certainly a few weeks, and that's what had been freaking Catherine out. But she also seems to think it happened a long time ago too."

Jeffers didn't appear surprised. We were in his study, dimly lit by a couple of yellow lamps. He and Kristina had insisted that I take the comfortable chair, and were perched on wooden ones.

"I'm sorry to hear that," he said eventually. "Lizzie starting to follow again is a backward step. I shall need to discuss it with her."

Kris was watching him, as if beginning to get an idea about something. "Fine," she said. "But it's not just about Lizzie. There are others, too. Flaxon, the other ones that call themselves Angels. Lizzie's friend Maj, too. And she mentioned another... Golzen?"

Jeffers smiled stiffly. "I'm aware of him, yes."

"How many of these people *are* there?"

"I must have met fifty over the last three years, perhaps closer to a hundred. I suspect there are many, many more. I have been trying to work with some of them."

"Work how?"

"Develop a program of recovery. Help them to move from their current state to a more positive one."

"But who *are* they?" I asked. "They're basically people who've fallen between the cracks, right?"

"No," he said. "It's... more complicated than that, and you're not going to believe it."

"Try us," Kris said.

"You really want to know?"

"Yes."

"They're dead."

Kristina and I stared at him.

"I told you." He sighed. "One of the biggest problems with my job is that 'dead' is a word that startles people."

"It's a big word," I said.

"Of course. Because these days it says a world-changing event has happened. It didn't use to. People had a relationship with those who had gone before. Some believe one of the reasons our species turned from a nomadic lifestyle was we started to bury the departed, housing them before we even housed ourselves. If you have an ongoing dialogue with the dead then you don't want to leave them behind. Heaven was a way of getting around this — a realm that is always 'above' wherever you are and from which the deceased can be benignly looking down even if you keep moving. For thousands of years religion supported people's grief by telling them the dead remained in reach, but now science says that when someone dies they're gone forever except in memory, and that those memories are merely electrical impulses in a bundle of fragile flesh, and so death has become the big divide. The bigger the chasm, the more terrifying it becomes."

"But how does that relate to Lizzie and her friends?"

"They're ghosts," he said. "People who died in the city but haven't moved on."

"Lizzie is *not* a ghost," Kristina said. "She's *there*. Her friends are, too. I spent two hours with them stealing drinks off people in bars, for God's sake."

"Nobody said ghosts can't interact with the physical world," Jeffers said. "There's all the stories about them passing through walls and vanishing at will, but the ability to disappear is just about whether you're *noticed* or not. Real people can do that too. And for every story like those there's another about poltergeists — spirits that *can* manipulate objects, however crudely — or elves or pixies that take things and move them around, or phantoms that run cold fingers across the back of your neck."

"You're saying these are all the same thing?"

"The same *kind* of thing. We're able to see some of these spirits, once in a while, in the right conditions. With others we only experience their effects, but that holds true of normal life too. If someone claps their hands together out of our sight, we still *hear* the event; we don't need to see it or suffer the hand smacking against our own body to prove it. Just as there are many types of human, with different abilities and ways of being, so it is with souls, too."

I couldn't work out whether the guy was serious or if this was some weird priest metaphor that I was too tired to get. "So *why* are these spirits still here?"

"Unfinished business. Or because there's someone still alive, refusing to let go, maintaining a relationship that is too strong for the departed to progress according to the natural order of things."

I remembered giving the priest's address to Lydia earlier that evening—an event that felt like it had taken place about two weeks ago—and wondered if that had been such a smart idea after all. "But how would that *work*?"

"Strange," Jeffers said. "I wouldn't have taken you for a staunch defender of science."

"I'm not. That doesn't mean I'll believe any old crap. Seriously. How *would it work*?"

"Do you know how love works? Or hate? Or hope? Yet you wouldn't deny their existence or power to change human behavior."

"Those are emotions, not states of being."

"I'm aware it's a category error in the minds of a philosopher, but they're seldom the most practical of thinkers and I'm not sure there's a big distinction in the real world. The universe is a different place to someone who's in love than it is to one who is withstanding grief—different worlds that exist side by side, brought into being by emotion. If emotion can structure reality then why shouldn't it enable an individual soul to persist beyond its intended span?"

I shook my head, knowing there were a million flaws in this but not being able to nail them.

"It's not a permanent state," he said. "It's unstable, precisely because it relies upon emotion. Some of their number, the ones they call Hollows, they're closer to moving on. They retreat from the world, often settling in

graveyards, as if they dimly remember the circumstance of their inter-
ment and wish to rejoin the process of transition. There are others who
appear not to even realize they're dead — the Dozenos. On the other side
of the spectrum, the strong and self-actualized dead, there are Fingermen, who possess a poltergeist-style ability to manipulate objects. There
are especially restless spirits called Journeymen, who have no desire to
remain near the person holding them here, and there are Cornermen, who
remain stationary for long periods — as if tied to one particular locale —
and pass messages among the other ghosts. There are more of these souls
on the loose than there ever used to be. The dead have always been with
us. There have always been spirits that lost their way. But now that our
society has taken down the signposts it will happen more and more."

"Surely it doesn't matter if we pull the plug on ways of understanding
death. Doesn't *God* call them home?"

Jeffers looked at me as though I were a member of a Sunday school
class who, having previously shown promise, had revealed himself to have
understood nothing at all.

I wanted a cigarette but couldn't face the four-floor trek downstairs to the
outdoors. I felt exhausted and in pain. But I wanted to understand.

"So according to you, Reinhart has built himself a team of *ghosts* to
help him steal shit?"

"Yes. These souls, or 'friends,' as they tend to call themselves, are in
moral danger. Many may still be here as a result of shortcomings in their
lives. To encourage them to engage in further acts of turpitude is to damn
them forever. I am not prepared to let that happen."

"Speaking as someone with recent experience in the field," I said, "you
may not have a lot of choice over what Reinhart does. Unless you're prepared to get biblical on it in ways different from the ones you're accustomed to."

Jeffers reached to the desk in the corner, opened the drawer, and pulled out an ashtray. "Another leaving from my predecessor. Open the window, please."

I stared at him. "How did you know?"

"People's feelings and desires are often visible, sometimes even tangible," he said. "That's precisely what I've been trying to tell you."

"What I still don't understand," Kristina said, "is why some of the friends work with Reinhart."

"His main contact among them is this Golzen person. Every now and then one of these souls tries to raise themselves above the others. Usually that's been a positive thing. But Golzen has . . . a different take."

"Different how?"

"More militant. There's a widespread misapprehension among the friends about their state of being. This 'imaginary friends' delusion that Lizzie told Kristina about — unfortunately, she believes it. A great many of them do. Golzen has exploited this, along with legends and stories that have gained credence over the years, including one concerning a promised land."

I laughed. "Dead people have their own *myths?*"

"Gather three individuals together and by the end of the evening part of their relationship will rest upon something supposed, rather than demonstrably true."

"But what if they *are* imaginary?" Kristina said. "Are you *sure* they're not?"

The priest stood. "I've told you what I believe. I have a spare room. It's never been used, so I daresay it's rather dusty, but you're welcome to it."

Kris and I looked at each other, and knew that given the chance not to have to go back home, we'd take it.

"Thank you," I said.

"They're dead," he said flatly. "Don't believe it if they tell you differently. Sometimes the dead lie."

Chapter 49

David sat with his back to the wall. He could smell clean carpet—Dawn had gone ahead and vacuumed around the boxes that evening, not pointedly, but the point was still made. He couldn't see much. That wasn't because it was the middle of the night and the spare room was dark. It wasn't that there wasn't much to see in the room even during the day.

He just wasn't seeing anything outside his own head.

When he got back he'd tried to work, of course. Nothing had come of it—of course. He'd read more of Talia's book and glumly accepted that the further she'd gotten into her stride the better it became. Her writing possessed authenticity and directness and a simple pleasure in the act of creation, something he doubted he'd be able to replicate. For him it was always going to be more complicated. Talia was a real person and made things up for fun. For him the act of imagination was more deep-seated. It was who he was, and that made it harder; if you'd made your own self up, written yourself, reality will always seem compromised.

At dinner he and Dawn talked of inconsequential things. She seemed distracted but when asked said she was fine. It could be concerns about the pregnancy, he supposed, or wondering how his book was going but not wanting to ask because she knew it would stress him out to have to admit it wasn't going well. It could more likely be that David was finding it hard to mesh with the world, and as a consequence everything seemed off balance and skewed—even positive things like going to an ATM and knowing there would be money in their account. After such a long time where they'd been scraping by, being solvent made the world strange.

The thing with Maj was the same. He'd tried to forget about it, to run with the idea it was something he didn't need and could thus be excised. It didn't work. It was like trying to put a looming tax bill out of your mind. You keep pretending it'll be okay and think furiously about other things — about anything else at all — but it's there in the twist in your stomach and in the way you hold your shoulders.

As he got into bed with Dawn, David finally decided to try to talk to her about it, tell her about the stranger who'd come to visit and what had happened in New York. He couldn't keep burying it, and he knew himself well enough to realize that when he had something on his mind he behaved awkwardly — and it might be this that was making Dawn quiet.

He lay next to her trying to think of a noncrazy way of bringing the subject up, but took too long; her breathing settled into the rhythms that meant the god of sleep had gathered her in his arms. So he lay there, mind spinning faster and faster, stomach cramping, until he decided he might as well get up.

As he padded out into the hallway, he passed the door to the spare room. Maybe he could use the time to sort through the stuff, if he did it quietly — at least get one positive thing out of the day. He went in and shut the door. He didn't bother to turn on the light. There was enough moonlight coming through the window.

He pulled the lids of the boxes open and took everything out, arranging it around where he sat. It was the same stuff he'd seen before. Nothing surprising. Nothing he'd forgotten about. No big reveals. A few souvenirs of once having had parents, books that a much younger version of himself had loved. The only interesting thing about these was the authors. Ray Bradbury. Philip K. Dick. Stephen King. These were the kind of stories he'd enjoyed and yet he'd gone on to sell a literary novel. He knew why that was — but what next? Did he carry on pretending to be that guy when he had no right, or should he to try to find a route back to who he was? Was there even anything left to return to?

The books felt like they belonged to someone else. The house felt like it did, too.

There was a noise from downstairs.

He walked quietly out onto the landing. The noise had seemed to come from directly beneath the spare room. The kitchen. A scraping sound.

He went to the bedroom and poked his head around the door to check that it wasn't Dawn waking and going downstairs to see what he was up to. She was fast asleep. So what did he do now? Stay where he was, at the top of the stairs, and wait to see if someone came up them?

He started slowly down the staircase, carefully lowering each foot, using years of familiarity with the house to stick to the outside of the treads so as not to set off any creaks. He hesitated before turning the corner at the return, listening as hard as he could. All he could hear was the sound of rushing in his ears.

He quickly took the next step, bending at the waist so as to be able to see down into the hallway right away. Something was off about the light. He couldn't tell what, but he knew now that he hadn't imagined the sound.

He waited, motionless, expecting to see a shape or shadow crossing the hallway. Nothing happened.

Very slowly, holding on to the banister to help him get around the corner soundlessly, he started down the lower flight. By the time he got to the bottom it was obvious what was unusual about the light in the hallway.

The front door was open.

Knowing now that he was dealing with a very real situation, David stopped. The door was open. Only nine inches or so, but open is open.

But did that mean someone *was* inside, or *had* been inside? You had to work on the assumption someone was still inside, surely.

So . . . did he creep back upstairs, use the phone in his study to call the cops? What if the intruder came up the stairs when he was doing that, or before the police arrived? Presumably they'd left the door open to make it easier to escape. Would it be better to make as much noise as possible now, in the hope of scaring them off?

The front door closed.

David blinked at it. It looked like a hand had pulled it shut—from the outside. That's all he'd seen—a hand pulling the handle.

The hand hadn't been there, and then it was.

He waited, poised awkwardly with his feet on two different stairs, strain settling into the muscles in his legs. Nothing else happened.

He walked down the last two steps. He crept over to the tall and narrow window next to the front door. He kept well back in the darkness, craning his neck to see if there was anyone out there on the path.

He couldn't see anyone. He turned his head and checked the sidewalk down on the street. No one there either. He waited and heard nothing.

So he reached out for the door and opened it.

Cold air came in, along with moonlight, the factor that had keyed him in to the door being open in the first place. He went out onto the step. The stone was very cold underfoot. The street was silent, dead, and empty. He looked left and he looked right. He saw no one.

He did not look up, and so he did not see the three tall, thin people lying on the roof, their faces hanging over the edge, grinning down at him.

When he had the door shut behind him again David stood in the hallway. He didn't know for sure that the house was empty, of course. The fact that (he thought) he'd seen a hand pulling the door from the outside didn't prove there was no one left in the interior. It didn't *feel* like it. He realized that while he'd been on the stairs he'd *known* there was someone in the house. He could feel it.

He could *then,* anyhow. Now it felt otherwise. Was he prepared to trust that intuition?

He walked to the sitting room, took a breath, and slipped his head around the door. An empty room, looking staged, as they did in the night, familiar objects and furniture turned into sets.

He didn't think it likely that someone would be in the half bathroom, but he checked anyway. Then he walked toward the kitchen.

It was obvious from the doorway that something was wrong, but in the darkness it took him a moment to work out what. It was something about the color and texture, and it was all over the place.

He turned on the light. The room was covered in pieces of paper. It jumped into his head that it must be Talia's book, but then he remembered that he'd never printed it out. There were sheets on the table, across the floor, on the counters. Literally all over the place.

He bent down and picked up the nearest. It was blank. He pulled another few pieces toward him and saw they were the same. Blank. On both sides.

He moved around the kitchen, gathering up pieces of typing paper until he'd gotten them all.

Chapter 50

Waking the morning after a serious fight is not good. My body felt like it had been dismantled in my sleep and put back together in basically the right shape, but without whatever cushioning substance normally stops the parts from scraping against one another. My head was no better, but I woke up with a resolution fully formed. I was going home. It might be a crappy apartment with barely enough room to swing a cat (soon after we'd moved in, somewhat drunk, Kris and I had established this was technically possible using a cardboard mockup), but it was mine.

I opened my eyes to find I was alone in the narrow bed. Kris was perched on the arm of the comfortable chair, looking out the window.

"What time is it?"

"Just after seven," she said.

"How long have you been awake?"

"Didn't sleep."

"At all? Why?"

"Keeping an eye on the bare-knuckle fighter. I woke you a couple of times to make sure you didn't think you were Napoleon. Don't you remember?"

I shook my head, found the movement hurt, and said no instead. "So am I out of the woods?"

"Search me. I'm a barmaid, not a neurologist. Check this out, though."

I hauled myself over to the window. From there you could see down and across to the church. Father Jeffers was standing there alone.

"What's he doing?"

"Nothing," she said. "I heard him leave the building—about two minutes after the phone downstairs rang. He's been there half an hour."

"Waiting for?"

"That would be the question."

Not sure I needed to know the answer, I went into the bathroom. This showed no sign of recent habitation. It was clean but otherwise could have been in a museum. White tiles, an unsmeared mirror, a neatly folded fawn towel hanging off a rail, and a white sink and shower stall. I established that the last of these functioned, and undressed gingerly. There were a lot of bruises but they were hurting less as my body warmed up, and the sight of each just made me more resolved.

I was out of the shower and halfway back into my clothes when Kristina called out, "Quick—come here!"

We pressed our faces up against the glass. At first I could only see one person coming up the street, intermittently visible through the trees. A slim man, in a suit. He was running up the middle of the road. He ran for a while, at least, then stopped and whirled around. Then he was running again.

"Is that the guy from the hospital?"

"Yes," I said. "And look who else."

Two people were following in his wake, one on either sidewalk as if to shepherd him. A woman in a red dress under a black coat and a man in jeans.

"Lizzie," I said. "I've seen the guy before, too."

"I think that's Maj," Kris said

By the time we stepped out of the house Lizzie and the other guy had managed to corral Billy toward the church. He was still fighting it—not with aggression or ill will, but hectic enthusiasm. He was like a child on a sugar rush, right at the moment when it's all just uncontrollably fantastic and the best possible way to feel and you believe everybody else *must* be finding all this as hilarious as you are. He kept darting toward the other two as if about to make a getaway up the street, but then turning back in a circle, arms held out like a bird. He didn't really want to escape. He was happy where he was. He would, by the look of it, be happy just about anywhere.

As we got closer we realized that wasn't the whole story. He was very pale, with a slick of perspiration over his face. As we got in range, he stopped whirling and stared at me, blinking rapidly.

"I know you," he said. "I know you. I know you."

He laughed loudly before trying to dart off down the road again. Maj moved to put himself in his way, effectively forcing him through the gate and into the church enclosure. Once there, Billy seemed to recognize his surroundings and looked up at the stairs.

"Hey, Father," he called. "Look at me!"

"I see you," Jeffers said. "I've always seen you."

"But not like now, huh?"

"You're certainly very visible this morning."

"Ha!"

"You look a little worn-out, though. Why don't you come inside. Catch your breath."

"Aha, no," Billy said, with a smile of low cunning. "I've been in there *before*. I want to see *new* things."

"Of course you do," the priest said. "I have new things inside."

"What kind of things?" Billy said. "Are they green? Are they sand-papery?"

"Not especially. But I have pastries. And coffee."

"Ooh."

Billy hesitated. When he stopped moving, I realized the damp glow over his face did not look like sweat. It looked like something viscous seeping from the pores. His fingers were twitching. His hair looked like straw, and he was scrawny inside his disheveled suit.

Maj remained outside the gate, ready to bar an escape. Lizzie stood farther back, one hand in front of her mouth. She looked composed in sadness, as if happening upon a photograph of somebody now gone, someone she hadn't realized how much she missed.

Billy was breathing more heavily. The power that had seemed to thrum through him was abating. He blinked, his eyes staying closed for a beat too long.

"I feel silly," he said distractedly. "I . . . I've forgotten something. What is it?"

"Come inside," Jeffers said softly.

Billy seemed to be having second thoughts, but he looked weary now. He didn't look as if he could make it up the stairs, never mind go haring off down the street.

Maj walked into the enclosed area and came up behind him. He leaned forward and said something in Billy's ear. Whatever it was, it seemed to perk the other man up.

"Really?" he said, looking round. The look broke my heart. It was the kind a boy might give his father if, some sunny afternoon, the man had decided to treat his son to an ice cream cone out of the blue.

Maj nodded. Billy smiled, a small boy's grin that changed his face so much it was hard to remember what it had looked like before. He waved to Lizzie before running off up the stairs, past the priest, and into the church.

Maj followed, more slowly. Jeffers walked down the steps past him and over to the gate.

"Thank you, Lizzie," he said.

"You asked," she said. "So I did it. That's all."

She looked upset, as though she wanted no part of whatever was about to happen.

"It's the right thing," Jeffers said. "Will you come by later?"

She walked away without answering. Jeffers watched for a moment, then hurried up the stairs and into the church, closing the door behind him.

"I'm going after her," Kris said. She pecked me on the cheek.

I let myself in through the church gate.

Jeffers was a man of his word. There was a tray on the table by the wall under the lackluster stained-glass windows. Billy was stuffing baked goods into his mouth. Jeffers meanwhile busied himself with moving prayer books from one neat pile into another.

Maj had turned around one of the chairs in the back row and was watching Billy with a complicated expression. There was something of the look Lizzie had given the priest in it, but a touch of envy, too.

Jeffers smiled. "How's that taste, Billy?"

"Great," Billy said, voice indistinct. "Fucking *great*."

"That's good. Would you like some coffee?"

"Hell yes."

Billy reached for a thermos that Jeffers had placed next to the tray. He tried to pick it up but fumbled the handle. He frowned, and tried again.

"It's pretty heavy," Jeffers said. "Why don't you let me help you with it?"

"I can do it." Billy tried again, but he couldn't. Frustrated, he made a growling sound.

"Let the father do it," Maj said. "He's had more practice, that's all."

"Exactly," Jeffers said, picking it up and pouring a careful stream of coffee into a white mug. Billy watched the process avidly, still chewing on a *pain au chocolat*.

The priest glanced at me. "Do you remember John, Billy? He was there in the hospital with you last night."

Billy looked at me. "Yeah. Maybe."

Maj was looking at me too. "What's he doing here now?"

"He's run into problems with someone we know," Jeffers said. He held a pot of cream in front of Billy, who nodded enthusiastically. "Which is why he looks like he got pulled through a hedge backward."

Maj came to look me up and down. Being that close to him made the conversations of last night seem absurd. He was a man in his early thirties, with strong bone structure and stubble across his jawline. His hair was brown, midlength. His eyes were brown too, with a touch of green around the irises. He was there. He took up space. He was substantial, and his presence was strong.

"Yes, you could touch me," he said, as if he knew what I'd been thinking.

He was also, however, wearing exactly the same outfit as when I'd last glimpsed him. Battered jeans and the untucked shirt. Of course, someone living as he did — however that might precisely be — wouldn't change their outfit often. The clothes did not look tired, however, as if at the end of several days' use. There was no hint of sweat. In fact, there was no odor to him at all. We underestimate the importance of that sense, but once you've noticed its absence, you keep noticing it.

It made me wonder whether the clothes he was wearing were independent objects in their own right, or if they were just part of the idea of him.

"I've heard two different theories that say I *shouldn't* be able to touch you."

"I don't know what you've been told," Maj said. "Don't care, either. I'm sorry you've run into Reinhart. He's a bad man. But our world is none of your business. The best thing to do would be to leave."

"I'll do that," I said. "But that doesn't mean Reinhart's going to leave me alone. A cop told me last night that Reinhart tends to finish what he starts. Two days ago he threatened my girlfriend. I don't like that. And I don't like that this mess came from you people."

"No, it didn't."

"Yeah, it did. If we hadn't been trying to find out who was following one of Kristina's friends, we'd never have even seen your friend Lizzie."

His eyes narrowed. This felt strangely noticeable, as if I was admiring the realism of a special effect. "Lizzie was following someone?"

"Catherine Warren. Do you know her?"

I don't know what I'd said, or why it meant something to him, but the man's whole attitude changed.

"It happens," Jeffers said quickly. "Look at you and David. You've even *talked* to him."

"That's different. And I told her about it," Maj said. "She didn't say anything to me about this."

"It's just following," Jeffers said. "Not trying to make contact. I'm sure it's fine."

There was a violent coughing sound.

Billy was still at the table, cup of coffee in one hand and yet another pastry in the other. A mouthful of this had gone down the wrong way. He was trying to clear it, hacking up like a cat with a hairball. At first it didn't seem such a big deal—flaky pastry down the windpipe—but the cough got deeper, wrenching.

"Aren't you going to do something?" I said. "He's choking."

Maj watched. "No, he's not."

Billy turned from the table. His eyes were bulging, his face white. Even through his coughing he was still trying to shove some more of the pastry into his mouth.

"It's too late, Billy," Jeffers said.

Billy didn't seem to hear. He raised the coffee to his mouth, chewing manically. The blockage seemed to clear, and he smiled. "Got it," he said.

As the mug got to his lips, something fell to the floor near his feet. I stared at it. It was brown, damp.

"What the hell is that?"

The others ignored me. I looked closer and saw that it was a mouthful of chewed pastry. Other things were floating down to join it now, flakes, drifting down through the air. Through Billy's body.

He tipped the cup back and poured coffee into his mouth. The liquid fell out and through his face and the length of his body to splatter onto the wooden floor.

Jeffers started murmuring something, a stream of words that sounded formalized. Maj put his hand out to Billy. Billy stared at it and then up at Maj's face.

"Is that *it?*"

"Afraid so."

"But that wasn't . . . Oh, no, that's not *fair.*"

"Your friend was very sick when he died," Maj said. "Maybe there just wasn't that much left to have."

"Not *fair.*" Billy stared wildly around, but not for an escape. He looked as if he were trying to drink things in. "That's not *fair.*"

Jeffers kept up his words, nodding gently.

"Go *fuck yourself,*" Billy shouted. "You don't understand shit." He tried to throw the mug at the priest, but it clattered to the floor and broke. Jeffers didn't flinch.

"Go well," Maj said, and shook Billy's hand.

"I don't want to."

"But you'll see your friend."

Billy hesitated. "Do you think? Am I going home?"

Maj looked awkward. "To be honest, I don't know. But that's what they say. He died last night. So there's a chance he'll be wherever you're going, right?"

"Can you come with me?"

"Not now. But one day."

Jeffers put his hand on my shoulder. "I'd like you to go now."

I didn't feel like fighting a priest, and I didn't feel like I had any place there. But I couldn't help glancing back before I went through the door.

Jeffers had his hand on Billy's head. Billy was trembling, weeping. The words coming out of Jeffers's mouth were soothing.

I left. I have no idea what happened next.

Chapter 51

Lizzie moved fast—faster than Kris had ever seen before. Soon she was having to trot to even keep her in sight. When Lizzie seemed to jump cut to the other side of 14th without crossing the road, Kris shouted the girl's name and ran across the street after her, and kept shouting in the hope that it would embarrass the girl into stopping. At first Lizzie ignored her, but slowly she drew to a halt. She didn't turn.

"What do you want?"

Kris came around the front. Lizzie didn't look friendly. "To *talk* to you."

"What about?"

"What was happening to Billy?"

"What comes to all of us."

"He was dying?"

"The end of the Bloom. What else did you think was on the horizon? Even for you? Did you have some other destination in mind?"

"Jeffers thinks you're already dead, Lizzie."

"He's a nice man. But he's wrong."

"He's kind of sweet on you too, isn't he?"

"Come, come. How could anyone be sweet on a ghost?"

"Because he's lonely and bored and has found something where he believes he can make a difference. And because you're not a ghost."

"So what am I?"

"I don't *know.* I want you to explain. *Properly.*"

Lizzie looked away, seemingly at people walking up and down the street. A middle-aged couple, bickering good-naturedly. A mother smiling down at a child in a stroller. A man standing on the corner and sipping from a coffee, looking vaguely into space as if he'd forgotten what he was supposed to be doing. She breathed out, slow and long, and some of the tension seemed to dissipate.

"You really want to know? What it's like?"

"Yes."

Pretty soon Kristina got an inkling of where they might be headed. The idea didn't make her feel comfortable, and she asked if that's where Lizzie was going. She spoke the question in a low tone, moving her lips as little as possible, sticking to the rules.

Lizzie didn't answer.

Kristina kept following—though she knew the girl's silence probably meant she was right—tucking behind and walking in Lizzie's wake. Nobody looked at the other girl as they cut through the Village, though a few glanced at Kristina, seeing a woman on a mission, striding out, looking neither left nor right—one of the extras that cities and towns are wallpapered with, shadows put on the streets by God to stop everywhere seeming empty.

Five minutes later Lizzie turned onto Greenwich Avenue and headed along the south side, straight toward the café where Kristina had met with Catherine several times and where she'd introduced her to John, for better or worse. For a ten-yard stretch there was no one close by and Kristina spoke at her normal volume.

"I don't know what you've got in mind, Lizzie, but can't you just tell me instead? I've spent a lot of time following you around."

"Telling won't work. You have to walk this life yourself."

Then they were level with the café. Lizzie glanced to the right. Kristina did the same, cringing, and saw Catherine at one of the tables inside with two women she'd never seen before.

She turned her head away quickly, her heart doing a double-thump, hoping to God Catherine hadn't seen her.

But she found herself slowing over her next stride, stealing another glance. The other women looked a lot like Catherine. Not physically—both had dark hair and their weights and heights were distributed along the spectrum of social norms for this time and place—but in every other way. They were well dressed and accessorized. Their hair had been recently cut and styled. They were armed with expensive purses and boutique iPhone cases. There was an ease about the angles at which they sat to one another, too—one leaning forward, the other back, the last turned slightly to the side—that made them look like a matching set.

And there was something about the way they laughed.

As Lizzie and Kristina passed, one of the trio evidently said something uproarious. You couldn't hear the cackling out on the sidewalk, but stripping it of sound merely made it more arresting. The nearest threw her head back. The other sniggered into her hand. Catherine started with a smile but upgraded to a reluctant oh-you-are-bad guffaw. They looked like equals in a warm, shared moment—or, Kristina found herself thinking, like . . . witches. Three hearty, well-groomed witches of the West Village, gathered together where it cost five bucks for a flat white and the dainty cakes and cookies had been fashioned from ingredients so tightly optimized that eating them made you *more* healthy.

When shall we three meet again? Tomorrow, dear sisters, or else the next day, whenever our busy, fulfilling lives allow. Let's synchronize smartphones. Get something in the virtual diary. Let's write the next verse of this everlasting song, the Ballad of the Urban Supermom.

Then Kristina was past the café and it was as if a light had gone out, turning her and Lizzie back into two random women on a shadowy sidewalk with nowhere in particular to go on a cold fall morning.

Lizzie led Kris across the road before coming back along the other side. When she was opposite the café once again she stopped, taking Kristina by surprise. Lizzie was *never* stationary in public. Even when apparently standing in one spot, she constantly turned back and forth, taking a step backward or forward or to the side.

For this moment, however, she was absolutely still.

"What?"

"Wait," Lizzie said.

"For *what?*"

"...this."

At that moment, Catherine glanced up and looked directly at them. Kristina froze.

She *so* did not want to be caught gawking across the street—even though she lived a twenty-minute walk away and could legitimately be taking a stroll through the Village. She could be heading for this very café. She lived in New York City too. It wasn't like she needed a membership card or qualified sponsor to gain access to coffee shops. And if she'd happened to see her book club pal Catherine inside, what could be more natural than to stop—maybe even wave, go in and say hi?

She felt horribly caught out nonetheless, and had no desire to wave, much less walk over and strike up a conversation with Catherine in front of those two other women. Those *better* women.

The women who were more real than she was.

Catherine meanwhile gazed out at the exact spot where they were standing—Kristina could have *sworn* she did, that she looked her right in the eyes—but her gaze floated past, as if she'd glanced up to check whether the sky held sign of rain and found it did not. She turned back to one of her companions and started nodding vigorously at whatever she was saying.

"See?" Lizzie said quietly.

"See what?"

"How do you feel?"

Kristina felt embarrassed, insubstantial. "So what?" she snapped. "She wasn't *looking*. She's got her mind on what's been said or how long it is until school's out or whatever. No big deal."

"That's what you feel?"

"Yes. Because anything else would be dumb."

"Right," Lizzie said, as she turned to head up the street. "Keep telling yourself that."

"I don't want to do this," Kristina said, several hours later. They were outside Catherine's daughters' school. In the meantime they'd walked. Just that. They had gone in no stores or cafés. As Lizzie pointed out, she had no money and no one would serve her anyway. So they walked, an endless communion with the streets. Sometimes Lizzie pointed other people out to Kristina, people on corners, lying in park bushes, standing outside restaurants watching the people inside — usually watching one person in particular, it seemed, like a obsessive fan club of one. She pointed also at a few rooftops, both low and high, where men and women were sometimes to be found perching, looking up at the sky or down at the streets or apparently at nothing at all. She pointed out someone dressed as a clown, riding by on the top of a bus. She pointed out a very large ginger cat wearing striped trousers, sitting in the middle of the street as traffic passed by on either side. They all looked lost and alone.

By the time they got to the school, it was five minutes before dismissal, and the tribe of mothers was swelling in the street. Kristina felt cold and tired and sad. "Seriously. I don't feel comfortable being here."

"That's up to you," Lizzie said. She was under a tree, holding on to the trunk with one hand and slowly circling around. "You can do whatever you like."

"If she spots us, she's going to call the cops."

"Spots *you*, you mean."

"Lizzie, let's go. Let's do something else."

But Lizzie wouldn't leave, and Kristina stayed. She faded back up the street and stuck close to the railings in front of one of the houses, and kept her head down, but she stayed. She saw Catherine stride confidently into the street. Saw her stop to exchange words with other mothers, mostly flybys but one longer conversation, more serious, concluded with mutual smiles. Saw her put her hand on a few arms as she passed through the crowd and saw the owners of those arms turn and acknowledge her passing and her right to be there.

When Catherine got to the gates she was greeted by the teacher on duty, who chatted cheerfully before remembering something and reaching into a folder. She pulled out a piece of colored paper and stood close to Catherine to discuss it. Catherine turned her head to ask a considered question. What was the document about? Probably nothing so important. A concert, school trip, book drive. It was something *they* knew about, however, and you did not. You got that message all the way down the street. That piece of pale blue paper held a world in it, a universe you did not know and never would.

Lizzie still held the tree with one hand but had stopped circling. She was watching Catherine, her face expressionless, absorbing every little thing that happened, every inconsequential thing she did.

Ella and Isabella came running across the playground. As they were released back into the wild, the younger, Isabella, threw herself up at Catherine without checking arms were in place to catch her—as you did, when you were confident your mother loved you and would always be there to halt your fall. Kristina's mother had not been that way. Kristina's mother was dead, and her daughter was broadly content with the arrangement. That didn't mean it wouldn't have been nice for things to have been otherwise.

Still Lizzie watched, silent.

Catherine strolled off up the road with a child holding each hand, turning her head to one side and then the other to listen to their updates and speculations and questions, a woman at the center of her world.

Kristina realized Lizzie was no longer beside her. She followed the girl as she walked up the street.

They eventually stopped at the grassy area beside the Hudson River, past where the Riverwalk ended. They leaned together against the railing, looking out over the water. Kristina had lost count of the times her phone had buzzed. More than four. John, texting to find out where the hell she was; texting again subsequently because he was smart and considerate enough to realize that if she hadn't responded the first time she was busy doing whatever she was doing and wouldn't welcome a call. That was John. He thought things through, even if there came a point when he then decided to *stop* thinking and start acting instead. She could picture him, waiting for her somewhere, wanting to talk about what happened next, and maybe also whether they were going to head over to the restaurant later, given that they still had jobs.

Because Kristina *did* have a place in the world. For a few hours most nights she was a fixture in the firmament of strangers: the woman who made the alcohol happen and kept the banter flowing when a couple hours in the company of intoxicating liquors was all these men (and women) had to look forward to. Many were divorced or notoriously single. Others did apparently have a home to go to, but when someone's ordering another drink at ten thirty you wonder whether the place where they're not is really home, no matter how long and hard they work to keep paying the bills and regardless of who's there waiting for them. Kristina had more than once thought that she'd rather end up like Lydia than one of these banished ghosts, people with homes that were not a home.

In the end they went, however, and she did too, with John. Where is home? Where you're allowed without question, where your right to be is accepted. What must it be like to not have that? To have no direction home because home doesn't exist anywhere; to be like an electrical device with a plug that fits no socket in the entire world.

"What are you going to do?"

Lizzie's face was somewhere between thoughtful and confused. "What do you mean?"

"I get it. I understand what you've been showing me. The question is what you're going to do about it."

"There's nothing I *can* do."

"Really?"

Kristina watched as the girl turned the question over in her mind. She looked thinner this afternoon, less substantial. Just plain unhappy, perhaps.

"I used to think I was the lucky one," Lizzie said. "Compared to Maj. He had nothing. I could watch, at least. Though for a long, long time I stopped myself. When Catherine moved in with Mark I knew it was over between us. I kept away. But then a month or two ago... I fell off the wagon. I started following her again."

"Are you jealous?"

"Of Maj?" Lizzie shook her head. "I'm glad for him. Any good thing that happens is good for everyone. This isn't about him. It's about me. I'm just... I'm tired."

"Of what?"

Lizzie raised her hands in a gesture that meant everything, and the absence of it. She was tired of lack, of making do in the hope of better tomorrows.

"Isn't there *anything* you can do?"

The girl laughed, the first bitter sound Kristina had heard her utter. "Sure. I can go sit against the wall in old St. Pat's or some unpopular park, or in one of the old tunnels where trains don't run anymore. They say it doesn't take long once you've decided to hollow out."

Kris was shocked. "Is that what you *want?*"

"No. I want a home."

"Good. Because if I heard you were even *considering* something like that, I'd come kick your ass."

Lizzie smiled. "You can't kick imaginary ass."

"You'd be surprised what I can do. That solution sucks. It's not happening. What's the alternative?"

Lizzie shrugged, but not in a way that said she didn't know the answer. She knew, all right.

"So do that instead," Kristina said, knowing she was out on a limb and speaking of things she didn't understand well enough. Sometimes you do that, though. Sometimes that's what friends are for: to watch from the outside of your life, and listen, and say the thing you need to hear said.

Lizzie was still, so motionless that she looked like a painting. "Really?"

"I think it's time for a reunion. Don't you?"

Lizzie went back to staring out over the water toward the unknown land and buildings on the other side.

Kristina left her to it, walking off down the street to rejoin life as she knew it.

She saw Lizzie only one more time.

Chapter 52

The first David knew about it was when he went into Roast Me. He got up at the usual hour. He made Dawn breakfast. He almost always did this, but that morning he especially wanted to get to the kitchen before her. In case he'd missed one of the blank sheets of paper. In case something else had happened there, something silent, while he lay unsleeping next to his wife. Just in case.

The kitchen was fine. Which meant everything else was fine, right? Right. Until something else happened, everything was fine.

You bet.

Dawn seemed chirpier than the night before and drove off to school in good humor. David went straight upstairs to the spare room. The contents of his boxes lay on the floor where he'd left them in the night. He decided he was done being bullied by inanimate objects and methodically destroyed the cardboard crates to force himself to do something about the items in them *right now.*

It took only half an hour, as he basically moved almost all of their contents into his study. So what had the fuss been about? Why had it taken him so long to do this?

Why was he not thinking about the paper in the kitchen the night before, and the open door?

He knew at least that he had not imagined or dreamed that incident, because the pile of paper was where he'd left it after gathering the sheets from the kitchen, on the lower shelf on the table in the front hallway. He wasn't sure whether it would have been better to have imagined an inexplicable incident so clearly that it felt real, or for it to have actually happened, and felt rising hysteria when he tried to make the choice.

In daylight it was easier to see that the sheets of paper didn't look like they'd been sold recently. They were dry and slightly yellowed. He knew why that was. That didn't help him understand them any better.

He took one of his childhood books back out of the bookcase where he'd just stacked it, a bookcase that would — six months from now — hold author copies of his own work. This morning that did not feel like anything to be proud of. The book he picked was *I Sing the Body Electric*. It was a paperback, and obviously well read. He didn't remember it, however. He knew it was his, could recall owning it, but it got cloudy after that.

He flicked through the pages, smelling old paper. Old paper in books, old paper in a pile. All he had was old paper and secondhand words.

Something caught his eye near the end of the book. It was another piece of paper, folded over, wedged between the pages. He unfolded it.

Something was written in pencil, faint and scratchy. It wasn't David's handwriting, even as it had been back in his early teens. It wasn't in either of his parents' hands either. It looked like the work of someone struggling to manipulate a physical object.

David held it up and squinted. It said:

Why am I called maj?

He dropped it in the trash and left the house thinking firmly about other things.

He could tell something was off from the moment he walked into the coffeehouse. Dylan was behind the counter, failing to cope. Nobody was tutting or giving him grief, however. Dylan was nineteen and, as Talia put it, "dozy like a fucking mouse" — very much the barista B or C team, drafted in only when one of the main servers was sick. Regulars tended to feel able to give him a certain amount of good-natured ribbing in recompense for the guaranteed inaccuracy and scaldedness of the coffees they'd receive by his hand. This afternoon everyone in line seemed subdued, and silent.

As David got closer to the counter he noticed Dylan wasn't merely being slow. His hands were shaking. Sylvia, the owner, was back there too, turned from the room, on the phone.

"You okay?" David asked. He was reconciled to the idea that his coffee would be completely wrong.

Dylan looked at him. "Shit," he said, after a moment. "You don't know?"

"Don't know what?"

"Talia's dead."

"She's ... *what?*"

"Yeah." Dylan started nodding and swallowing compulsively. "They found her a couple hours ago."

"Where?"

"By the creek. The cops came by a while back to let us know—Sylvia called me in when Talia didn't show and wasn't answering her phone."

"Well, did she fall, or ..."

"I don't know, dude. That's all they told us."

David pushed back from the counter, unable to process this information. He'd stood *right here* and blurted out his and Dawn's news to Talia only two days ago. How could she be ... "Jesus."

"It's fucked up," Dylan agreed.

David walked stiff-legged out of the coffeehouse. When he hit the cold outside he became aware his mouth was hanging open, and shut it. He should call Dawn—she'd known Talia longer, having been born and bred in Rockbridge—but he didn't know what he could say to her. The news would arrive at the school soon enough and probably she'd call him. He wasn't sure what he'd say then either. Quite apart from her having been a friend, he'd spent a lot of the last week buried in her novel. The idea that the mind that had created it was now gone doubled the effect. She'd taken a world with her.

"I want to talk to you," someone said.

It was George Lofland. His face was red and he wasn't wearing a jacket, despite the chill.

"What abou—"

Then George was right in his face. His breath smelled of stale alcohol. He shoved a hand into David's chest, knocking him backward.

"Hey," David said. "What's the—"

"What's the *problem?* Have you heard about Talia?"

"Dylan just told me. But—"

"Someone killed her." George had stopped trying to push David back down the sidewalk and was standing hands on hips. When he was in front of you like that you realized he was kind of a big guy.

"What? What makes you even *say* that?"

"I've just been up to her place," he said. "The cops are there. One of them is Bedloe's son. I've known him since he was a kid."

"Are *they* saying somebody killed her?"

"No. But they didn't know her like I did. Talia was never going to kill herself, and even if she *did,* she'd have left instructions about her cats. And plenty of food. Which she did not. I just fed them myself."

"But no one's *saying* she killed herself, are they? Surely it was an accident."

"An accident she got herself dressed up for, in fancy clothes?"

David was uncomfortably aware that someone would be able to tell that a confrontation was going on from right across the street. "What are you talking about?"

"The Bedloe kid told me how she was found. At the bottom of the creek, neck broken. Wearing a dress smarter than anything else they found in the trailer, something that didn't even fit. That make any sense to you?"

It didn't, but nothing about Talia's death had made sense. He could tell Lofland was one step from taking a swing at him, however, so he tried to speak calmly.

"So...what do you think happened?"

"I don't *know* what happened, David. What I *do* know is she called me on the phone yesterday afternoon, asking questions about that guy I picked up in my car. A guy who disappeared into thin air—just like the guy you were talking with in Kendricks."

"I...was there by myself. I told you that."

"I know that's what you *said*, but it was bullshit. I know I saw a guy sitting opposite you, and then he wasn't there. Talia kept me on the line for twenty minutes trying to get me to remember things about the guy I picked up. Now, why do you think she would do that?"

"I have no idea."

"Me neither. Then that same night she gets dolled up and goes out to meet someone and..." He swallowed. "And she doesn't come back."

David tried to get these pieces to fit together and couldn't. "I don't know what to tell you," he said.

"I can see that. But I'll tell *you* this. If I find your 'friend' had anything to do with what happened to her, anything *at all*, I'm going to come find you. Understand?"

David realized that George meant what he said and that there lurked years of pent-up anger and frustration in the man that would help him carry the job through. Denying anything—everything—wasn't going to help.

He nodded. George stormed away.

David had no desire to go home. Home—the house he owned with Dawn, where they kept their stuff—did not feel like a place he needed to be. If anywhere, he felt he needed to go back to his hometown—something he'd never felt since leaving it years before. He didn't understand why. There was nothing for him there. No closure to be had. Nothing that could be said or done. No parents.

No friends.

He knew this was the reality of Talia's death sinking in. Where you live is not your world. What you own isn't either. The people you know . . . *that's* the world you live in, and that's why living a life is like building a house on an emotional fault line. Places persist, but every living thing is going to die.

Die, or leave you.

He recalled an acquaintance who went on a contract to a country eight hours' time difference away; the guy said living that far out of sync with everyone he knew felt like being a ghost. Maybe that's all being a ghost *is* — finding yourself out of step with everything and everyone you knew. David had never been sociable (total loner geek — thanks, Dad), so the few people he cared about loomed large. Talia had been one, even though they'd never gone for a drink, eaten together, even visited each other's house. Losing her was bad enough. That someone might think he was somehow *involved* or implicated . . . was terrible.

And how *could* he be? He thought back to the last conversation they'd had, outside Roast Me. She'd been talking very strangely, yes.

He'd blown straight past the concern he should probably have felt for her state of mind because of the part where she reprised the story of George and the hitchhiker. Was there something he'd missed, something he could have talked her down from, a difference he could have made?

He tried to remember. There'd been something about how people when they died might not actually have gone, or something . . . Christ.

She'd got it into her head that the guy George picked up on the forest road was a ghost.

Not just any ghost, either. Talia had believed in signs and portents. It was all over her novel — there was even a mawkish and credibility-stretching moment where one of her key characters, the slim and plucky heroine, was given fresh strength to continue life's struggle after seeing a shooting star. Yes, this was fiction, but what people write reflects what they believe—fiction is where you go to tell or read the truth that people will stare or laugh at you for expressing in real life. She'd latched on to George's hitchhiker story right from the start, telling David about it the same day in the coffee shop. It had spoken to her, and maybe something *else* had then happened that had given her some bizarre cause to add two and two together to make seventy-five...

The person George picked up *must* have been Maj, as he'd already realized. But how did that explain what had happened? There was no evidence Maj was in town now, or had been last night. What motive would he have for hassling other people, never mind setting up a situation in which one of them might *die?*

Except...*someone* had been in David's house, hadn't they? That was evidence of *someone* being on his case in however inexplicable a manner, even if it wasn't Maj.

And if Maj or these others were unable to get anywhere with David, what might be the obvious next step?

Lean on his friends.

Isn't that what the crazy or vindictive *did* in these circumstances—bring pressure on their victim in any way they can, threatening him from the outside? Talia wasn't in a position to force David to do anything, though—and Maj had already made contact with David. Why would he resort to doing things secondhand?

What if it hadn't been Maj, but *someone like him?*

It had been clear from the night in the city that Maj had friends, people who lived the same kind of life. Might he have sent some of them to try to lean on David? Or...

Maj also had enemies.

David remembered the people in Bid's. The unfriendly-looking guy in the old-fashioned suit and the fucked-up thin people who'd been with him in the bar. He recalled that, as he'd hurried away from the church later, he'd thought he'd been followed for at least some of the way to the train station. By whom, he wasn't sure. He thought he'd lost them.

But what if he'd been followed all the way home?

When he got to the house he knew at once that someone had been inside again. The paper he'd stowed on the hall table had been thrown all over the hallway. He hurried around, picking it up. He knew where the paper had come from. He'd known last night. It was old stock from one of the boxes he'd unpacked in the study, one of the things he'd kept from the upstairs room in his parents' house, his father's much-discussed "study." Paper his father had never typed anything on. A secondhand blank slate.

He had to get rid of it. He gathered the sheets and went back out the door to the side of the house where the recycling was kept. The paper felt like it was symbolic of everything that needed purging from his life, and he lifted the lid of the container and raised his arm high, ready to hurl the paper into it.

There was something in there.

Something other than tin cans and cardboard and glass bottles that had held organic ice tea. He pulled it out, feeling the skin all over his scalp crawling. It was obvious what it was. He just didn't understand it.

It was a laptop. He turned it over in his hands. It was battered, cheap-looking. He'd never seen it before. So what the hell was it doing in his recycling?

He hurried back indoors. Once inside, he popped the catch on the laptop and opened it. After a pause the screen blinked into life. There was so much unfamiliarity there—smaller screen, Windows instead of Mac, someone else's lunatic idea of how to organize a desktop—that it took him a few moments to spot something he recognized. In the middle of the desktop (a fuzzy picture of a lot of cats) was a file called ALEGO-RIA II.

No no no . . .

Within a minute he'd confirmed it beyond doubt. This was Talia's laptop. He closed the machine and put it on the floor, so hard he probably came close to damaging it, but he had to get it out of his hands.

He felt like vomiting.

He had a dead woman's computer in his house. If he was right and someone *had* followed him home from the city, there could be no doubt that they were now systematically persecuting him.

Coming into the house.

Attacking his friends.

Even trying to implicate him in Talia's death. What else would be the point of putting the computer here?

It had to stop.

He had to deal with it.

He stared at the machine as if it could leap up and bite him — knowing that, for now, job number one was finding somewhere in the house to hide it — and it randomly struck him that he didn't have to finish reading Talia's book now. The idea felt bad. He felt he owed it to her to get to the end, out of respect. Nobody else ever would. He also wanted to know what happened. On that most basic of levels the book worked, and worked well.

As he carried the laptop upstairs another thought dropped into his mind.

Had anybody else seen Talia's book?

Anybody apart from him?

It was only when he straightened from stowing the laptop in his closet that he realized if he *was* right, and someone *was* attacking him through those closest to him, there was one obvious person they would target next.

Chapter 53

Lizzie went downtown first and left a message. After that she kept in movement, spiraling around the deed and building her concentration. If she was going to break her own rules it had to be worth it. She had to get it right.

With the girls it was hard to be specific and bringing something for the sake of it wouldn't work—so she dropped the idea. Catherine was hard too, but in different ways. She had so much already. It seemed hard to believe she could want for more. We do, though. Lizzie understood that. There's always something new to add to the pile. We want more stuff and the comfort that comes with it. We want to surround ourselves with a nest, a cocoon. It's one of the reasons we have friends, and there's nothing necessarily wrong with the arrangement... assuming you can *get* the stuff. If you can't then all you have is no stuff, and after a while the lack of things starts to suffocate you.

She avoided the parks. She might chance upon Maj in one and, though she really wanted to see him, she knew he'd realize something was up. It was too late for her to be dissuaded and she did not want to argue with him.

So she remained in perpetual movement, as throughout her life. Walking, walking, with nowhere to sit down at the end of it. She realized how tired her feet were. Not physically, but emotionally. Her legs were the idea of tired. That's all they really were if you got down to it, ideas and dreams, and while people poured so much time and energy into both they were also liable to drop them at a moment's notice. Most of the time it doesn't matter whether dreams come to fruition. It only matters whether they cheer you up. Except, perhaps, to the dreams themselves, who might yearn to come true, to become more than a comforting pattern of thought that eventually lapses into an emotional line of least resistance.

That's why change sometimes had to come to those who weren't looking for it—who'd done everything they could to *avoid* it. They could squat there in their great big warm houses with their big warm lives, ignoring everything outside their window. You could do that if you had enough stuff inside with you, if you *had* an inside to start off with. That didn't mean the situation couldn't change. Lizzie had tried hard not to need, very hard, but after so many years it still hadn't worked. If Kristina could take Lizzie seriously and seem to want to be her friend, what was to say others could not?

Was there any law that said dreams could not dream too?

Lizzie felt dumb and childish for having followed and watched and been a good girl. For accepting her lot. The time for being dumb and childish was over.

It ended this afternoon.

It ended now.

She was close to settling on Bloomingdale's when she had a better idea. She hurried back down Fifth Avenue. Going to Bloomingdale's would have felt too much like the bad old days. Instead she'd try the street where she'd followed Kristina the first time they'd spoken to each other. That felt appropriate. It was following the signs, and Lizzie was a believer in story-maker events. Why else would she have met Kristina—and come to believe in the possibility of a real friendship there—if not for the idea of today to come into her mind? You put thoughts out into the universe and God gives them form and sets them down. So Father Jeffers said, and on that he might even be right.

She walked along 47th, peering in windows. Within a few minutes she'd found a store that looked like a possibility. It had interesting things in the window and was a little larger than most of the others, which would make it easier too. She picked her moment, moving in a meandering figure eight over a forty-yard radius, waiting until she'd seen a few people enter the store—a couple of men who looked like dealers, a handful of civilians too.

Then she slipped inside.

The interior was lined on three sides by display units filled with tray cases, turned into a U shape by a central island, within which a fat-faced man in an expensive suit prowled. The walls were mirrored to help ricochet light around the space and make the diamonds and other precious stones sparkle, but that was all to the good. Lots of reflections made it harder for people to see, confusing their sense of space.

At the back of the store the two men in homburgs were involved in a voluble price negotiation with another employee, who was listening with the stoic expression of someone who'd been down this road many times and generally ended up receiving a price very close to what he'd originally had in mind. Lizzie drifted past and saw the two men were buying rings in quantity—plain, functional things that would not suit her purpose.

She paused by a pair of German tourists (gawking at thick gold bracelets, also wholly inappropriate), before glancing over the shoulders of a group at the central island: three whip-thin English women giving serious consideration to a tray that Lizzie could immediately tell was far more interesting. It held five pieces of silver jewelry in arts-and-crafts style, each given plenty of space on a cushion to showcase their individuality— and to broadcast the message that they weren't going to be cheap. They looked good. They looked right.

One of them in particular, the brooch in the middle, would be *perfect*.

The fat-faced man was being attentive, having judged the ladies weren't just killing time but could have their interest parlayed up into acquisition. He unlocked the unit and brought the tray up onto the counter.

The women bent at the waist to inspect the treasures a little closer. Lizzie felt her insides start to churn.

It felt like being a teenager again, and not in a good way. It felt dirty.

She kept moving around the U shape. She knew that when she got to the other side she should keep walking, go back out into the world and forget the idea. But she knew also that you go to your god or goddess with offerings, and that she'd been locked on this course from the moment she'd seen Billy's Bloom, and probably before. He wasn't the first she'd seen burn out, but for some reason it had hit her much, much harder.

If she walked out now, what came next? Would her heart heal for the hundredth time, or would it be forever suspended in a moment of blackness?

She ground to a halt, feeling out of practice and drained of hope, fully lost.

One of the men in homburgs turned around.

His colleague was still haggling vigorously, but this man had become distracted, as if he'd smelled something unexpected. He peered peevishly around the store, face creasing into a frown.

Lizzie realized she had to be quick. Sometimes people felt something. You could never predict who, and once they'd done so the atmosphere would change and it would be harder.

The need for speed made the decision for her. She waited until the man had turned back to reengage with the negotiations, and then she coughed.

Two of the English women glanced up — distractedly, minds still on the goodies on the counter. Their eyes skated across the apparently empty space behind them, unable to see Lizzie, and then returned to the matter at hand — the display cushion.

Lizzie moved decisively toward the window. This was constructed of a pair of sliding panels of glass on runners, locked in the middle, protecting the goods in the window from people inside the store.

She placed her hands on the left pane of glass, widely spread apart. The head is the hardest part of your body. It's where all the thinking is. That makes it tough. Fragile, too, of course, the place where all the real and lasting pain is born, and stays—but hard enough for her purposes in the physical world.

Lizzie summoned all her concentration, and smashed her forehead into the glass.

It wasn't anything like the impact Maj or another Fingerman could have achieved, but it was enough. The glass cracked loudly, splintering diagonally across the large pane.

Everyone in the store heard it. The Germans took a defensive step backward. Two of the English ladies did the same, pulling the third—who was still obliviously inspecting jewelry—with them.

The store owner started bellowing in a foreign language, gesturing at the underling in back to come and do something about the situation. He came hurrying, leaving the men in homburgs wide-eyed.

The top half of the window slowly tilted forward, then fell to the ground with a tremendous splintering crash. There was screaming and running.

Lizzie swept past the velvet cushion with her hand out, weaved through the chaos, and ran from the store.

When she got back onto Fifth Avenue she slowed, however, knowing she had to go back. This was a betrayal of everything she'd come to believe, turning the clock back too far and too hard and in a way that could only lead to bad things.

But without it . . .

As she hesitated, she saw a couple coming up the street. Mid-twenties, hand in hand, the man wearing a baby papoose. The child inside it could only be weeks old. The couple looked exhausted but so happy, adrift on the bleary seas of early parenthood, adapting to the changes inaugurated by this new phase in their lives.

Lizzie felt her heart stiffen. She'd been born—as they all had—before their friends had any conception of the process of conception. They were a sterile race. Just one more thing that none of them would ever have.

Unaware that she'd come to a standstill—and that a man in his early thirties and a girl of six had caught split-second glimpses of her, this tall woman wearing a red velvet dress under a black coat, and that trying to discuss the Ghost Lady of Fifth Avenue would earn the child a telling off for making up stories and bring the man a step closer to finally being diagnosed schizophrenic—Lizzie decided the time for sinning had come. It's how we broke out of the cozy prison of the Garden of Eden, after all. Father Jeffers wouldn't approve, but then he didn't really understand anything except dead composers, and death is too safe a haven for those who want to live.

Lizzie clasped the brooch tightly in her hand, where passersby would hopefully not see it, and started to walk quickly down the street. She felt bad. She felt scared. She felt excited.

It was time to go home.

Chapter 54

When Kristina finally answered her phone I told her to meet me at the apartment but didn't go into detail. It took her a long time to get home and I decided in the meantime to get out of the place and wait on the street. With Reinhart at large, I realized, it wouldn't be smart to hang around right outside and so I went forty yards up the sidewalk and sat in a shadowed doorway for nearly three hours and smoked and drank a series of coffees from the deli and watched leaves wandering along the street and didn't try too hard to get everything to line up in my mind. My body and head still hurt, but it was settling into a set of sturdy aches now, rather than urgent yelps. My brain felt clear. I wanted it to stay that way because it was evident my life was changing for good today. You seldom get warnings so obvious, and I figured I'd better be ready for what came next with an open mind.

Kristina eventually came wandering down the street. I whistled and she spotted me in the doorway and came over.

She looked down at me in silence, then held out her hand. I passed her a cigarette. Kristina smokes only about once a month, and it's always a portent of storm clouds.

"So what happened with you and Lizzie?"

She sat on the step next to me and took a light. "How do you know something happened?"

"The way you look, plus the fact that you've been gone a very long time and wouldn't answer the phone. This isn't a time for holding back, Kris."

"I know."

"So what happened?"

"She showed me some things."

"What kind of things?"

She shrugged. "What her life is like. What *all* their lives are like."

"Who *are* these people?"

"Lizzie's adamant she's not dead. I believe her. I don't get why ghosts would attach to other people the way she is with Catherine. It doesn't make sense."

"Make *sense?* You realize we're sitting discussing whether someone we've both spoken to is dead? So, what—are we back to them being imaginary friends?"

"I don't know, John. That's what Lizzie told me. I don't see why she'd lie."

"Did you ever have one? When you were a kid?"

"An imaginary friend? No. At least not that I remember."

"Me neither," I said. "But...I guess that's their whole point."

"What happened back at the church, with Billy?"

Now it was my turn to shrug. "I have no idea."

"Didn't you see?"

"I saw. I just don't know *what* I saw, in that I have no way of explaining or understanding it."

I described what had happened, up to the point where coffee and bits of Danish started falling through Billy's body and splatting on the floor. After I'd left the church I'd stood on the street for a few moments. The guy/ghost/friend/whatever called Maj walked away without saying another word. His head was down. He looked like a person who had a mission in mind.

Kris listened and was silent for a while. "There's only two options here, John. Either we're screwed up in the head or this stuff is real—whatever the explanation is. Sitting with cold sun shining down on us, the first option seems more credible, maybe, but it's not. You know that. If it were *just* me, or just *you,* that'd be one thing. But we've both seen these people, spoken to them."

"How did the conversation with Lizzie end?"

Kris looked uncomfortable. "She's unhappy."

"About what?"

"Everything. She has a friend. Had one, anyway. That relationship is more important to her than anything else in the world — even more than the one with Maj. Maj managed to make contact with his friend.

"They've spoken, even hung out for a few hours. Lizzie's glad for him, but it's brought home how unhappy she is about her own life."

"So?"

"What?"

"So what did you tell her?"

"That maybe she needed to do something about it."

"Kristina, I don't think we want to start interfering in these people's lives."

"I wasn't interfering."

"Okay, bad word. I meant, we understand nowhere near enough about their world to offer advice."

"She's my friend, John."

"Friend? How many times have you even met her?"

"What difference does *that* make?"

"Friend's a big word, Kris."

"It's big because it's a tiny step and the tiny steps are the hardest to understand. The first time you came into the bar in Black Ridge I knew we could be friends — whatever else might happen. Didn't you?"

I thought about it. "Yes."

"That's not shared time. That's not interests in common or dating agency profiling. That's something that passes through the air in an instant, that comes out of people's minds and is real and you have to say yes to."

"I see where you're going, but I don't think it's enough to explain Lizzie, or Maj."

"I'm not trying to explain them," she said, stubbing out her cigarette. "I don't have to. We've had conversations with these people. They exist. We're out the other side of having to explain how or why. The question is what we *do*. That's what I've been trying to work out. I left Lizzie hours ago and I still don't have an answer. I've been alternating between thinking I'm crazy and knowing I'm not. It doesn't make much difference. I still don't know what to do."

She was right. The problem of how something works is of little importance outside laboratories. The question is what happens next.

"I still think it's a mistake to get between Lizzie and Catherine," I said. "Other people's relationships are written in a different language, especially when they're broken."

"You're right," she said reluctantly. "Next time I see her I'll back off on the idea."

"Okay," I said. "Well, the next thing—"

I was interrupted by someone cheerfully shouting my name, and started—suddenly realizing how wrapped up I'd been and that Reinhart could have come strolling up and shot me in the head before I'd known what was happening. Thankfully, it was only Lydia heading down the road.

"Hey, Lyds," I said, standing painfully and trying not to sound tense. "How are you?"

"Well, you know," she said thoughtfully, "I've been better. But, matter of fact, I've been worse."

She looked okay. Certainly better than she had when I'd seen her the night before. "That's good."

"*You* look like shit, though."

"Thanks," I said, as she leaned forward to peer at my face. "I had a disagreement with someone."

"They kicked your ass, by the look of it."

"It may not be over yet."

"Wasn't Krissie here, was it?"

"No."

She cackled merrily for a moment. "I talked to him," she said, for a moment making me think she'd somehow run in to Reinhart. "Thanks for that."

"Frankie? He's back?"

"No. Don't know where that asshole's got to, and today I don't care. Fuck him. I mean, I went and talked to the other guy. This morning. That priest."

Kristina was looking question marks at me. "I gave Lyds his address last night," I muttered. "This was before I knew Jeffers believed in ghosts."

Lydia laughed, completely normally, a sound I'd never heard from her before. "He really does, doesn't he? Good listener, though. I went around thinking I didn't know why I was wasting my time, but I'd been feeling so shitty in my soul lately maybe it was time to try anything. Next thing I know I'm telling him about Frankie and all *manner* of crap, and he's kind of like you are about it. He listens. He heard me out and went with it, and I only had to explain to him about three times that Frankie ain't dead. Didn't ask me to pray with him or nothing either. Gave me a pastry, too."

"That's great," Kristina said thoughtfully. I could see her trying to make something of this, to work out whether Lyds maybe wasn't crazy after all, and if for all these years she'd been trying to make contact with something that actually existed; if perhaps this was a case of a real person trying to reconnect with a friend, one who'd decided he didn't want to play ball.

"Jeffers seems like a good guy," I said, to forestall this. I felt Lydia's world was complicated enough and that if an hour of being taken seriously had made a difference then there was no need to get it tangled up with other stuff.

Lyds sniffed, losing interest, and wandered off down the street. "You put that ugly mug of yours indoors," she yelled back as a parting shot. "You're going to scare people looking like that."

"You need to come upstairs now," I told Kristina, when Lydia had finally turned the corner. Kris was about to crack wise, but then she saw the expression on my face.

She stood in the middle of the room, not saying anything. I think she'd started to guess what was up from the way I double-locked the street door, but there's no substitute for seeing something in the flesh.

The apartment had been destroyed. Not just turned over, not merely vandalized. They—or he—had been extremely thorough. Every drawer had been turned out and its contents broken or torn. Every plate, bowl, and piece of glassware had been smashed. The fridge had been opened and pulled over onto its front, turning the floor into a sea of liquids. Everything from the cupboards had been broken, thrown around. Every lightbulb in the apartment was smashed, along with the mirror in the bathroom and the two wooden chairs we'd bought for good money at a nice store in SoHo in the first flush of living in the city. Cards we'd written to each other, along with a few pieces of cheap art we'd picked up in local thrift stores, had been set fire to. The ashes from these had been thrown onto a pile of Kristina's clothes and the sheets from our bed in the middle of the living room.

It had been meticulous. I'd had plenty of time to go through it in the hours while Kristina wasn't answering her phone, and yet coming back into the apartment after a couple of hours was a shock. The apartment as it had been yesterday was still alive in my mind. It takes a while for your mind to understand something's gone.

Eventually Kris looked at me. Her eyes were dry, but she was blinking rapidly. "Other rooms the same?"

"Yes."

"Guess we did right not coming home last night, huh?"

"Guess so," I said. "And I don't think we should stay here now. He's going to come back. He only did this because he couldn't do it to me."

"Jesus."

"FYI, he didn't tear or burn *everything*, unfortunately. I can't find your diary or that notebook you insist on keeping stuff in. Like your passwords and ATM numbers. And your credit card."

"He's a psycho, isn't he." This was a statement, not a question. "I mean, a real one."

"Yes. An angry man just trashes the place. This is dismantlement. He went back and forth, breaking everything that could be broken, and then he went back through it and broke it some more. I don't want to think what the equivalent would be when committed upon a person. I especially do not want it to happen to us. So let's go."

"Where?"

"I don't know. Not back to Jeffers. He's in deep enough already, and I don't think him being a priest will stay Reinhart's hand."

"Well, then, where?" Kristina said, her voice rising. The reality of what surrounded her was beginning to sink in. There were spots of high color on her cheeks. "Where else can we *go*, John? Are we going to be fucking *street people* now? Should we chase after Lydia and see if she knows some good parks to sleep in?"

"The first thing we should do is leave, Kris. Seriously. Let's talk about this outside."

"Outside? Oh — you mean *where we live*, right?"

I put my arms around her. "We'll find somewhere for tonight. We can sleep in the bar if we have to — Mario's got some serious locks on that place. After that . . ."

I trailed off, not knowing what would happen after that. I'd even wondered if it was excessively insane to consider talking to Lizzie or Maj or one of these other people. They evidently had places to roost at night. Maybe there'd be room for us, maybe not.

Kristina didn't say anything. She was looking past my shoulder, and I figured she'd noticed something else that was broken or missing or was maybe trying to see past all the chaos entirely.

"What times were you in here? From when until when?"

"Don't know," I said. "I got here around ten. Why?"

"Then what? When did you go outside? Right after we spoke on the phone?"

"Yeah, pretty much. I was certainly down there a few hours. Why?"

She disengaged from me and pointed. I turned and looked at the window. There was writing on it, scrawled in the dust and rain dirt on the other side.

"Was that there when you were here?"

"No," I said, going closer. "I remember being amazed he hadn't broken the window too. There was nothing on it then."

We angled our heads to catch the light against the dirt. It was easier to read than the first time, as if whoever had left this had tried a lot harder, pouring all their concentration into it.

It said:

GOING TO TALK TO MY FRIEND
THANKYOU :-)
LXXX

"Oh no," Kristina said. She ran out the door.

Chapter 55

Catherine turned from unlocking the front door to find Ella and Isabella weren't waiting on the steps behind her as she'd assumed, but were still down on the sidewalk. More than that, they were arguing. This had been brewing from the moment she'd picked them up from school. Usually the girls got along as well as you could expect of lifelong competitors for parental attention and resources, but once in a while something (or someone) snapped. It was almost always Isabella. She had stronger opinions than Ella on just about everything, and no compunction about taking incisive action to ensure they were widely understood. Ella took life as it came. Isabella regarded the world as a work in progress and herself as a one-person focus group of infinite power. In that, Catherine privately believed, she took after her mother.

"Hey, hey, *hey,*" she said, as Isa abruptly escalated to shock and awe mode and punched her elder sister in the chest. "Isa—*stop* that!"

The girls turned as one and launched into high-pitched mutual denunciations. Catherine hurried down the steps to sort it out, leaving the door open behind her.

An hour later, homework was done. Pretty much. Isabella had been flogged through memorizing her six spelling words of the week and writing extremely short sentences showcasing them. Ella had done enough work on her project on Chad to feel honor had been served. Catherine was at a loss to understand why her daughter had to do a project on Chad— nobody's idea of an A- or even C-list country—but that wasn't the point, and hers had been the easier ride. Ella, though less sharp, accepted homework as another aspect of the world in the face of which she was essentially powerless. Isa resisted enforced learning with passion, imagination, and a capacity for self-distraction that bordered on genius. Catherine had largely managed to ignore the fact that this was an hour of her life she was never going to get back, for which one daughter's newfound ability to spell "beach" and the other's shadowy understanding of the whereabouts of N'Djamena, Chad's capital (and home of its only cinema, apparently), might never seem sufficient recompense.

There was more to be done, but she sensed none of the team were in the right place for it. Ella appeared listless, Isa closer to the edge than usual. When Catherine ran out of steam as works foreman at the homework mines, both children looked at her with tired and grumpy faces.

"That's enough for today," she said. "Go on; shoo."

"Can we watch television?"

Catherine opened her mouth to say no, of course not, then realized she was feeling pretty listless herself and screw the developmental implications. This was precisely what television had been invented for—or would have been, if women had been allowed to do the inventing back then. "Okay," she said. "For a little while."

"Can we have a cookie?"

"I'll see what I can find."

"Yay!"

Much cheered, the girls ran out of the kitchen and into the family room. Feeling the wash of relief that comes from completing some trivially arduous but potentially volatile session of child-wrangling, Catherine started to gather up the books and papers strewn over the table—but then decided the smarter tactician would get the girls settled with a snack first. As she turned toward the cupboard, her gaze skated across the antique mirror propped up over the mantelpiece.

She frowned and looked back. For a moment it had looked like there was a shadow in the corner, the kind of thing a passing figure might cast on the white walls. A cloud passing outside the window, presumably.

Luckily it turned out there were two oatmeal cookies left. She took these and two glasses of apple juice through to the other room.

When she came back into the kitchen, something felt different. She looked around. Everything was as it should be. A quiet, airy kitchen, the sound of wholesome entertainment from the other room. Catherine had a little time, too — Mark was heading straight from work to a business dinner (again). Except for getting the kids bathed and into bed and read to and asleep, the evening was her own, and amen to that. People drain you — of time, energy, even the will to live sometimes. Being able to ride the rails by yourself for once is a good way to recharge. Catherine thought a cup of Earl Grey tea might be a nice way to start, and reached for the kettle.

She noticed the table and stopped. She put the kettle down.

There was a clamor from the next room, distracting her. She quickly walked through the door to find the girls pointing at the television set.

Catherine saw a blank screen. "Yes, so?"

"It stopped."

"Well, was it the end?"

"No," Isa said firmly. "It was *not* finished yet."

"So press PLAY again. It's probably just a glitch."

Emma got the remote from the end of the sofa, held it out like she was afraid it was going to explode in her face, and pressed the button. Nothing happened.

Isa asked: "What's a glitch?"

Catherine took the remote. "When the world does something odd." She stabbed at the PLAY, STOP and PAUSE buttons. "Well, maybe you've watched enough already."

"No! It's only been on for a second!"

"Well, there's something wrong with it and Daddy's not here so—"

The DVD suddenly came on again, in midscene. The sound was *way* too loud, grotesquely so. Ella let out a squeal of surprise. Isa cackled in strange glee.

Catherine hurriedly wrestled the volume back to a sane level. "Did you mess with the remote? I've *told* you about doing that."

Both girls denied it immediately and in unison. In the face of potential punishment, they deserted the ship of sisterhood faster than the eye could blink, ratting the other out immediately. Taking the same side was a reliable indicator of joint innocence.

"Well, just don't touch it, okay?"

She'd lost them already. Both were munching their cookies, staring at the cartoon. Catherine put the remote out of reach and went back into the kitchen, where she stood and looked at the table.

When she'd stopped to sort out cookies and juice, the table had held two exercise books, seventeen pencils in a rainbow of colors, printouts from Wikipedia, a sharpener, and two erasers. They'd been spread across the artfully distressed Restoration Hardware table with the randomness only children can cause.

Now everything was down at one end.

The papers were in a pile, the exercise books on top. The pencils were lined up next to one another, perfectly aligned at the unsharpened end.

She hadn't done that. She was sure of it.

She noticed what wasn't on the table—a mess—before noticing what *was* there. Something was lying in the middle of the table. A small object, metallic, but not shiny. What the hell was it?

She took cautious steps forward. Was it a *brooch?* Unconsciously her hand reached up to her chest before she remembered that she hadn't put on anything that morning. So it couldn't have fallen off.

Was it even hers? She looked more closely. The piece was two inches wide and one inch tall, a muted pewter. The detailing had the sinuous lines you'd associate with early Tiffany, or Liberty, and with Archibald Knox in particular. It was the kind of thing that, had she seen it in a store, she'd have bought in a flash.

But she didn't recognize it.

An upcoming gift from Mark — stashed in a drawer, found by the girls and played with before being dumped here? They'd been through her jewelry any number of times in the past, despite stern warnings, and one pair of earrings had disappeared never to be seen again.

But this hadn't been on the table when they'd gone into the living room, and neither of the girls had been back in the kitchen since. They wouldn't have tidied the table up, either.

She picked up the brooch. It was heavy. And beautiful. But it shouldn't be here, and the cool weight of it in her hand reminded her of something. Of feelings of guilt and pleasure, inextricably mingled. Of needs and desires that felt personal, rather than domestic, a long time ago. Of being younger.

"I hope you like it," said a voice.

Catherine whirled around.

There was no one there.

She backed away. She realized the brooch was still in her hand and dropped it on the table. Threw it almost. Part of her had been hoping it was some kind of illusion or daydream. It wasn't. Imaginary brooches do not go *thunk*.

There was no one in the kitchen. She could see that. The only other place the voice could have come from was the DVD the kids were watching. The voices on the soundtrack were high-pitched, squeaky. The voice she thought she'd heard was different. Female. Adult.

Familiar?

She went to the hallway and stuck her head out. No one there, of course.

She leaned over to the staircase and peered up and down, seeing nothing but dust-free floorboards, white walls, black-and-white photos, and restrained art.

She turned back to the kitchen but decided now that she was out here she might as well make a proper fool of herself. She trotted upstairs and checked the bedrooms and bathrooms, then back down past the kitchen and into the formal sitting room, before going right down to the lower hallway, which was empty too.

The front door was shut. Catherine stood by it, relieved and yet not relieved. The house was empty. Just her and the girls. She'd demonstrated it.

That should be a good thing. So why had proving it made her feel worse?

She looked around the hallway, realizing how much of being at home was an unspoken contract with the building. It's yours, and you belong to it. There was a bond there, surely. Or maybe not. Maybe it was just a structure that a dead person had built out of insensate materials as cheaply as possible. Maybe it didn't care about you at all, and could be accommodating to the passage of others.

Christ, she thought. *What* others? There were no others. She'd just *proved* it.

She breathed out heavily. Gathered herself.

And that's when the girls began to scream.

Chapter 56

They were huddled tightly together at the end of the sofa in the living room, eyes wide, utterly silent.

Ella leapt up and ran to her mother as soon as she came in the room, nearly knocking her off her feet. The television was showing an innocuous scene from the DVD. There was no sound, however.

"What?" Catherine said. "What's wrong?"

She was freaked out, and spoke too sharply. Ella started crying, clinging to her, burying her face in her stomach. "Ella," she said. "Calm down. What—"

Then the television went off.

The screen went black. Catherine heard the sound of the button being depressed. Not the button on the remote—the actual plastic button on the unit itself.

Isa was motionless on the sofa. She looked very scared but also curious. "There's a lady," she said.

Catherine stared at her. "What?"

Isa lifted her arm and pointed to an area near the television set. There was nothing there.

"Isa—what are you *talking* about?"

"A pretty lady."

"There's no one there, Isa. Stop making up stories."

Isa started to move her arm. She held it up at the same height, moving it slowly to the left as if following something changing position from beside the television to the far end of the room, near the fireplace.

The back of Catherine's neck felt very cold. "Isa...what are you pointing at?"

"For heaven's sake," said a voice. "Can't you see me *at all?*"

It was the voice Catherine had heard in the kitchen. It sounded now as though the speaker was trying to remain cheerful in the face of high odds.

Catherine grabbed the TV remote and stabbed at the off button and the volume button. Nothing happened.

"It's not the television, Cathy. She's pointing at *me*. Why can't you see?"

Ella started to wail, a hitching cry. Isa remained silent, staring avidly at the end of the room, her head moving from left to right, as if watching something. Something large, too—her head was tilted backward—and perhaps something that was pacing up and down. Catherine couldn't see anything at all.

"Catherine."

And then...she could. Down at the far end of the room, in front of the bookcase. A shadow, like the one she thought she'd seen in the kitchen.

She took a step back, pulling Ella with her. "Isa—come here."

"Who is it, Mama?" Isa didn't move. "Who is the lady?"

Then finally Catherine saw her, standing in front of the fireplace.

A tall woman, wearing a red velvet full-length dress under a long black coat. Her face was bone pale. Red lips and dark eyes, thick hair gathered up, like...

"How did you get in here?"

"It's *me,* Catherine."

The woman disappeared again, as though a shutter had come down between them, or as if she was there only when Catherine blinked, painted on the inside of her eyelids.

"What the hell is happening?"

"Who's the lady, Mama?" Isa asked. She could evidently still see the woman. "Why is she so mad at you?"

"Mommy knows," said the voice.

"Who the hell *are* you?"

"Come on, Catherine. It's *Lizzie*."

Catherine's stomach rolled over. All the blood felt like it dropped out of her head, as if she'd been sucked down a snake to being five years old, as if everything she'd ever done had been found out.

Lizzie.

Oh holy God.

"Get . . . get out of my house," Catherine said, trying to keep her voice steady, turning blindly toward the spot the voice had come from.

Suddenly the woman was visible again, stronger and more concrete this time.

Lizzie took a step toward her, hands held out, and finally Isa lost it and started screaming too.

"It's okay," Lizzie said to the children, trying to smile in a reassuring way. "I'm not going to hurt you."

Catherine screamed at her. "*Get out.*"

"But . . . I brought you something."

"What are you *talking* about?"

"The brooch. You like it, don't you?"

"That was *you?*"

"Of course."

"Take it back. Take it and *get out of my house.*"

"But . . . that's what you always wanted," Lizzie said, confused. "I thought . . . I thought you stopped seeing me because I stopped doing what you wanted."

"I didn't want you to steal."

"Yes . . . you *did*. You asked me to. You *told* me to. In school you wanted me to do other stuff, like the Kelly thing, but when we came to the city that's all you ever *talked* about. Things you wanted me to *get* for you."

Catherine was clutched by a vertiginous twist of guilt, so strong it felt like nausea.

She hadn't thought of Kelly Marshall in twenty years, but all it took was hearing the name to take her back to the afternoon when she'd seen the girl who'd been her best friend, talking in class with a boy Catherine had decided she might fall in love with. She didn't want to be taken back there, didn't want to remember how Kelly had lost that boy (to Catherine) after she'd been accused of stealing from other girls, or how she'd wound up losing weight and getting thinner and thinner until she was a full-blown anorexic who got taken out of the school by her parents, never to be seen again.

"Get out of here," she said as firmly as she could, not liking the cracking sound in her voice.

"This was a mistake, wasn't it?" Lizzie said forlornly. "I should have been happy with what we'd had. Or what I thought we'd had."

"You're not real," Catherine shouted. "You've *never* been real."

"I was real from the moment you first saw me," Lizzie shouted, clenching her fists. "I *am* real, and I *was your friend.* I've stayed your friend, keeping an eye, keeping you safe when you walk home at night. I never forgot you. You forgot *me.* You *threw me away.*"

"You can't throw away something that doesn't exist."

"I *do* exist."

"You don't. You're *nothing.*"

"No—I *have* nothing. While you've got *everything.* The house, husband, the daughters. That's you and that's *always* been you. Pretty Cathy's got to have whatever she wants, even if she has to make her friend steal it for her."

Catherine was trying to retreat, drawing the girls with her. Ella seemed to be slipping into a catatonic state, eyes wide, chest rising and falling in silent sobs. Isa was staring at the pretty lady who kept disappearing and coming back, who was saying all these interesting things and advancing toward them.

"*That's* what your lovely mama is like underneath, girls. A thief and a liar and a cheat—and not even brave enough to do it on her own."

Catherine abruptly pushed the kids to one side and swung her hand toward the woman in front of her.

Isa saw the pretty lady's hand whip up and grab her mother's wrist, however, far too fast. Lizzie held on to it with all her might, moving her face closer and closer to Catherine's.

"Remember me," she said. "*Remember how much you loved me.*"

"I never loved you."

"Yes, you did. You *did.*"

Catherine shoved her own face forward until they were nose to nose. "You were *nothing* to me. Ever. You were just me talking to myself, the make-believe of a little girl who didn't have a *real* friend when she needed one and made up a pathetic excuse for one instead."

"You *needed* me."

"No. You were just a game."

"You made me do things."

"And how pathetic is *that?* You were just the bits of me I didn't want festering in my own head. You followed me here to the city and wouldn't let go, *long* after you should have been forgotten. *You* kept stealing on your own because that's *all you knew how to do.*"

Lizzie tried to grip Catherine's wrist harder, tried to hurt her, tried to grind the bones together until they broke—but she couldn't get enough purchase.

Meanwhile the children screamed and cried.

"If you didn't get the message back then," Catherine said, "then get it now. I *don't* remember you, I *don't* want you, and I have to look after my children now—something you'll never have. Why? Oh yeah, that's right—*because you're not real.*"

Catherine shoved out, but the other woman didn't let go and so she found herself off balance. Lizzie discovered she did have further strength of purpose after all, a strength that came out of a mist of outraged hurt and black fury.

She lashed her arm, throwing Catherine sideways to smack into the wall next to the television. Catherine crumpled to the ground.

"Oh, I'll go," Lizzie said. "And I know just the way to make that happen. You ever hear of the Bloom, Cathy? It involves you, I'm afraid. And involves you *giving,* for once. Giving your perfect life."

She started toward Catherine, who was dazedly trying to push herself upright against the wall. She saw a very heavy glass vase on the bookcase above Catherine's head. She knew she had the will left to knock it over, and gravity would do the rest, gravity and time, bringing an end to this prison.

Catherine looked up and saw what Lizzie had seen.

"Mama," Isa said.

Ella was screaming, off in another world. But Isa had stopped and was crawling toward her mother.

Lizzie hesitated, seeing the girl reach her hand out toward Catherine, toward her mother, the shining star at the center of her world. She saw Catherine, who knew Lizzie was coming for her and what might happen if she got to her, decide that it was more important that she reach back and take her daughter's hand.

Lizzie realized that *this* was love, not what she'd thought she'd had from Catherine all the long years ago.

Catherine was right. Lizzie had never been loved.

She'd never been anything at all.

Chapter 57

It began to rain and traffic was crazy all the way through the Village and within minutes of getting in a cab I wished we'd stuck to going on foot. Kristina got on the driver's case about taking some other route, but I knew it wouldn't make any difference and tried to ease her back into the seat. She fought me hard but eventually saw the guy just wasn't paying attention anyway. As soon as we started making headway I called ahead to Jeffers. It rang and rang and I was about to give up when he came on the line, sounding distracted. I told him we were headed in his direction and to be out on the street waiting for us.

"Is it Reinhart?"

"No," I said. "It's Lizzie."

Now I had him. "What's wrong?"

"Nothing, I hope. We're in a cab. Just be outside."

Kristina rocked in the seat next to me, her body rigid, willing the traffic to part.

Five minutes later it'd become clear that it wasn't going to and so we got the guy to let us out on the corner of 14th Street and Seventh Avenue. As we started to run up the avenue, I called Jeffers again.

"I'm here," he said. He sounded freaked out. "I'm standing outside. Where *are* you?"

"Change of plan. We're on foot. Come to the corner of Eighth."

The sidewalks were black and wet, clogged with bad-tempered people with umbrellas and apparently no desire to *get the hell out of other people's way,* and soon I gave up trying to be dignified or polite and simply ran straight at anyone who was in my path.

Kristina was just behind as we reached the end of the stretch of 16th that intersected with Eighth, and I saw Jeffers on the other side looking all around. The street was wall-to-wall traffic, but here it was moving fast.

"Is that Maj with him?"

"Oh thank God," Kristina said. "He'll be able to talk to her."

She shouted across, telling them to run up toward 18th. Jeffers looked confused, but Maj got it right away — he evidently knew where Catherine lived. They started running up the street, and rather than confront the traffic and cross over, we ran up the side we were on. It wasn't as busy as Seventh, but there were plenty of people hurrying home or heading to bars and restaurants or trying to get somewhere out of the rain.

Jeffers was having a hard time trying to follow Maj. Maj was running *fast,* weaving through people far more quickly than I could have done, than anyone should even be able to. He'd seen something up ahead, too.

"No," he shouted. "No!"

He ran faster, shouting Lizzie's name over and over. He went straight past 18th, sprinting now, arms pistoning forward and back. At first I couldn't understand why he hadn't turned in there, gone toward Catherine's house.

Then I realized what he was running toward.

Lizzie was half a block ahead, staggering along the middle of the road, cars flashing past her on either side. Her head was down, hair loose and straggled and wet. Her shoulders were bent.

I don't know why she was heading back toward us. Perhaps she'd gone up the other way first, lost track, found herself coming back down the road by accident.

She was flicker-lit by car headlights and signs, red, white, and yellow. She didn't look like she had any destination in mind. She looked wholly lost. She looked like a child slipping beneath the surface of a lake.

Maj was closer now, still shouting her name. Nobody saw him running past. Nobody cared. They did see Jeffers come up behind and jumped out of the way, but they didn't care about anything except the inconvenience.

Kristina lunged across the next street, nearly getting taken out by a car. I got caught trying to follow her and was forced diagonally against the traffic until I was trapped in the middle of the avenue.

"Lizzie," I shouted. *"Stay where you are."*

She raised her head, but I don't think it was because she'd heard me. Her face was glowing white and dripping wet and it was not from the rain.

Kristina called her name over and over.

Maj ran into the traffic toward her, shouting too. I don't think she heard them either. I don't think she knew where she was, and I don't believe she cared.

She tilted her head back and howled.

Nobody heard. Nobody in the cars streaming past her on either side, no one on the sidewalks. No one but us, and we were too slow, though I don't believe it would have made any difference if we'd been quicker.

At the last moment she did see us, saw Maj at least, and Kristina too. She saw them, but she remained alone. I saw her eyes narrow, saw her summon all the concentration and substance she could muster, using pure force of will to make herself as concrete as possible.

I saw her smile fiercely as she did this, and maybe she *did* see me then, because she was looking at someone — or perhaps she saw through me to some other and better place and time.

There was a beat, and then she became much brighter. That's the wrong word. She became more *there*.

An instant later a cab ran straight into her.

Nothing happened. Nothing flew up into the air. The driver slammed on the brakes and skidded thirty feet, tires fighting the wet surface. Other cars barked and honked and swerved.

The cab came to a juddering halt as I sprinted toward it. A skinny man leapt out. He stared all around, whirling on the spot, terrified, knowing he'd just hit someone — but wherever he looked, he saw exactly the same as I did. Nothing.

When he'd spun around five times he seemed to realize I was ten feet away, doing the same thing. "What the fuck?" he said. "Did you *see* her?"

People honked. People shouted at him, at me.

"There was no one there," I said.

"*Bullshit,* man!"

"Just a trick of the light."

"No fucking way. No *way.* There was a woman. I saw her. There was no one there, and *then there was.* I fucking ran straight into her, man."

"You didn't hit anyone," I said.

Maj stood in the middle of the traffic, frozen, staring at the spot where Lizzie had last been. Kristina had reeled off up the sidewalk, head in hands. Jeffers was motionless, mouth open, face blank.

"I was right here," I told the driver. "I saw everything. You did nothing wrong."

"What the fuck?" he kept saying. "What the *fuck?*"

As I walked back over to the sidewalk, wanting to go to Kristina, I saw something on the side of the road.

A twist of red velvet cloth, something that could once have been a dress. Not recently — it was faded and filthy from years of rain and dirt — but once. It was screwed up into the side of the gutter, and looked like it had been trodden on and rained on and ignored ten thousand times.

When I reached down for it, it had gone.

And when I looked up and tried to find Kristina, she'd gone too.

Chapter 58

Dawn was closing out the day. The last of her kids had just left—Eddie Moscone, who always hung around the school grounds for at least an hour, playing on the climbing frame with focus and concentration while his mother piggybacked school Wi-Fi to send e-mails or update her status or whatever the heck it was people did with their phones the whole damned day. Dawn had a phone, sure. She used it for phone calls, old-school. The rest of the time she preferred to spend with people who were *there*.

Dawn had a guilty secret. She hated the Internet. Sure, it was useful for shopping, but the rest of the time she watched family and friends putting it out there—updating constantly, being passionate and sincere, putting up heartfelt blogs when someone died. And what came back? Nothing. Nobody cared. Your follower count—a more critical indicator of your worth than anything you did in real life—would stay the same, or maybe even dip because you were being too serious, not hip or smart or ironic enough. Followers are not friends. Friends are different and do not come cheap. So why not *forget* the constant attention seeking...and just be?

That was one of the things Dawn liked about her kids—their ability to exist. Most of them, anyway. She paused in tidying books in her classroom's library of battered classics and watched Eddie on the bars. Eddie was a decent kid, intelligent, polite and responsive most of the time. At other times he retreated. Sometimes it took two or three nudges to bring him back to the world. God knows Dawn saw David doing the same thing often enough—and it could take more than two or three prods to recenter her husband if he'd really got his vague on—but when you watched Eddie you realized how much of his universe came out of his own head and how very real it was to him.

Eventually Eddie's mother got serious about hauling her kid away, and they left. A few older children would be wandering about the campus, engaged in projects, some teachers too, but otherwise it had the calm you find only during downtime in places that take hard use during the day. Dawn worked her way around the classroom, putting everything in order. She privately believed this was her key role in the children's lives, whatever the job description might say. Yes, she had to teach them a bunch of stuff, but providing a predictable environment in which to grow a little older — while absorbing all the weird crap the world threw at them — was just as important. And someday in the not so distant future, another woman (or man, possibly, though the lower grades tend to attract the feminine touch) would be doing this for her child, too. Children, of course — part of her still hadn't gotten around that twist.

Container loads of supplements were on the way. A vast bounty of advice about the best ways to maintain your body and mind during pregnancy had been downloaded (okay, the web was good for that stuff), with further hard-copy manuals expected any day in the mail. The attic room was nearly done and . . . would be finished soon.

She shelved the questions that came from that last point, sticking to a decision made as she'd brushed her teeth that morning, and contented herself with the bottom-line declaration that Dawn and David's babies would be born into an orderly world, inside and out.

Of that, my embryonic beings, have no doubt.

She decided she could call the classroom done. All the art equipment was where it was supposed to be, bar a couple of crayons on the counter, which she'd tidy on the way out; chairs were under tables; circle time mats in a neat pile; and there was a picture of a face on the door.

Dawn did a double take.

The door to the classroom was made of wood and painted a cheerful green except for a glass panel in the upper half. A sheet of paper was stuck to this, the kind she handed out many times a day for pupils to inexpertly mark in one way or another.

This one had also been marked, but it didn't look like it had been done by a child. The face was rendered in black crayon—an irregular oval, a few lines inside evoking eyes, nose, and ears, a hooked one below that looked something like a smile.

As she looked more closely, however, she saw the lines were labored and ragged, drawn far more arduously than their freedom implied, as if even holding the crayon had been a struggle.

Dawn had seen a lot of face drawings. One of the first exercises she gave pupils each year was a self-portrait. The amount you could tell about a child—signs ranging from the level of competence and dexterity to the use of color, and even the size of the face relative to the page—was remarkable. She'd never seen one like this, though. Strong, flowing lines suggested long and unkempt hair—whereas children tended to render it either as unfeasibly neat or in wild scribbles. The facial expression, though technically a smile, was not one you'd want to see coming at you. The eyes were too knowing. The line of the mouth seemed cruel.

Dawn knew that any child who'd seen a countenance like this in real life needed an appointment with the school counselor. Urgently. It was horrible.

She took it down. None too gently, either—the top of the sheet tore, leaving a fragment still attached with the blob of tack that had been used to put it up there.

But by whom, and when? Dawn hadn't left the classroom since the end of school. Had somebody sneaked in and stuck it up when she wasn't looking? Would that even have been *possible?*

Dawn went to the window. For a moment the playground was empty, and then she saw Jeff—school handyman, gardener, general factotum—in the distance, going about his endless tasks. He didn't glance over and of course it wouldn't have been him.

Neither could Dawn imagine any of the older kids doing this. It was a good school. Sneaking into a classroom behind a female teacher's back and putting up a picture...that was pretty creepy.

She turned from the window. And let out a shriek.

There were three pictures on the blackboard now.

All were faces. Two obviously female, the other male. One of the women's faces was substantially rounder than the other. The expressions were muted and blank. Whoever had drawn them hadn't been trying to imbue them with life. They'd been trying to say something else.

A threat.

The door was shut. It would have been impossible for anyone to open it without her noticing, much less get to the blackboard and stick pictures up in a neat row.

Dawn looked at the opposite corner of the classroom.

The library was arranged in a four-foot-high bookcase, behind which was an area two feet deep. This was where she left her bag and sweater during the day, the closest she had to a backstage area.

It struck her now that it was also big enough, just about, for someone to hide. For a person—a smallish person—to have lurked, darting out while she'd been looking at Jeff to stick the papers to the board before scurrying back again.

Maybe big enough. Just about.

Dawn knew the sensible thing to do was run to the door, get Jeff, and have him come take a look—but this was her classroom, dammit. If some older kid got away with something like this, then...

She put the drawing in her hand down on the counter and squared up to the opposite corner.

"Okay—who's back there?" Her voice was clear and strong. It was met with silence.

You're going to be a mother, Dawn reminded herself. *Now is the time to start making sure you don't take any shit.* "Seriously, this isn't funny. Come out here."

Still nothing. No quiet, explosive giggling or the intake of breath you might expect from a little prankster who'd realized the game was up.

Abruptly Dawn decided the hell with it and walked over.

There was no one behind the bookcase.

She blinked, not realizing how convinced she'd been that she'd find someone there until she didn't.

Someone tapped her in the middle of the back.

She whirled around. The classroom was empty. Of course. She would have heard the door—it was impossible to open it without a loud click. It must just have been a twitch between her shoulder blades, a reaction to discovering nothing behind the library bookcase.

Except... Dawn knelt and picked the black crayon off the floor.

She straightened and looked over toward the counter near the door. There were two other crayons there now. Hadn't there been three before?

She wasn't sure. She wasn't sure *enough,* anyway.

She saw that there were no longer any pictures on the blackboard. Moving in a calm and sedate manner, and electing to leave any stray crayons wherever they damned well were, Dawn left the classroom.

She locked the door and walked toward the lot without a glance back.

She sat in the car for ten minutes before turning the ignition. By then she'd worked it all out.

She was pregnant. Duh. Everybody knew the hormones screwed with your head. She knew damned well that she'd seen the pictures—but there was seeing and *seeing.* You saw things in daydreams and imagination, too. It didn't mean they'd actually been there. If the pictures were no longer in the classroom, then they could not have been there in the first place.

Weird. Yes. But... explained.

She'd tell David about it, of course—but not right away. He'd been very twitchy since he got back from New York, a lot more Eddie Moscone than usual. Dawn wasn't sure how he'd react to the reveal that pregnancy hormones might be messing with his wife's head more than was probably normal.

Not to mention that when the time came for a big talk, there was something else they needed to discuss, something a lot more concrete. She didn't want that water muddied with this.

She breathed out, a hard and active exhale. She started the car feeling shaken but confident that the world was broadly okay, and hurrah for that.

She didn't realize that all the time she'd been tidying the classroom, three people had been there with her—two men, one woman, all of them thin and very tall, sometimes watching from the edges of the room, sometimes behind her, sometimes right up close, surrounding her, grinning, peeking down her blouse.

And she also didn't know that all three of them were now sitting in the backseat of her car.

Chapter 59

As David sprinted up the road toward the school, he saw Dawn's car coming the other way. He jumped into the street and waved, trying not to look too frantic, trying to make this look like it was a normal thing to do. He could see Dawn through the windshield staring into the middle distance, mind on something else; then he saw her clocking the fact that some idiot was in middle of the road, then finally that the idiot was her husband.

She braked, too hard. The wheels spun and the car skidded toward him. David got his arm out between his body and the car, sidestepping out of the way at the last moment.

He yanked open the passenger door. "Are you okay?"

"What are you *doing,* David?"

He got in. "Has anything weird happened?"

"I could have *killed* you." He kept staring at her. "David . . . what? Why are you here? And why are you looking so weird? You're scaring me."

"Are you *sure* nothing strange has happened to you? Or around you?"

"David — what's this about?"

"Didn't you hear about Talia?"

"Heard *what,* David? I've been in the classroom all day, and the last two hours I've been marking and . . ."

She broke off. David kept trying to work out what was strange about her. The atmosphere in the car felt wrong, as if there was something that wasn't being spoken about.

"What?" he said. "What aren't you telling me?"

"*Nothing.* What's the big deal?"

"Talia's dead."

"*What?*"

He pulled his seat belt tight. "Drive."

"Drive? Where?"

"New York."

"New *York?* Are you *joking?*"

He looked at her. "Dawn, do I look like I'm joking?"

She drove.

He told her everything.

At first, just what had happened in the days after their trip to the city. Bumping into the man outside Bryant Park and in the train station. The matchbook left outside their house in the night, the same day she'd come back from school to find a pile of small change on the step. The meeting in Kendricks.

Dawn kept trying to interrupt, but he pleaded with her to let him speak until he got it all out.

Then it got harder, because he moved into the realm of lies. He had to start telling her about things he'd misled her over, or hidden by omission. The fact that when he'd hooked up with the guy in the city, it hadn't been a simple case of meeting an old friend. That this was the same guy who'd bumped into him and come to their town to talk. That David hadn't come home from the city to make sure he was there in time for the scan, but because *very weird shit* had started happening.

"But..." Dawn interrupted finally. She was piloting the car quickly but with care. That's why David usually let her drive. She possessed a sense of being in control—of a car, of herself, of life—that he'd never felt. "Who *is* this guy? I thought you said he was a friend."

David hesitated. Could he tell her this? Could he tell the woman who was carrying his child—children—that he believed a phantom from his childhood had somehow come back into his life?

"It's difficult to explain," he said.

"Wait." She concentrated for a moment, negotiating the car into the fast-moving traffic on the freeway. Then she glanced at him. "Do you love me?"

"Of course," he said, baffled. "Why do you ask that?"

She told him what had just happened in the classroom. He felt his stomach lurch. He'd known *something* had happened as soon as he opened the car door. That explained the atmosphere, the sense of things unsaid. He hoped it did, anyhow, though her telling it hadn't dissipated what he was feeling.

"So," she said. "Am I going nuts?"

"No," he said. "But what else?"

"What do you mean?"

"Is there something you're not telling me?"

"No." She seemed irritable. "But there's something *you're* not saying."

"I'm getting to it," he snapped. This was going wrong. He could feel it curdling, but he didn't understand why. He felt a nonspecific crankiness, bad temper, a pervading sense of something dark and broken, a desire to nurture conflict out of curiosity, to see how far it could go—or be pushed. It felt like something black and gleefully bad was creeping up behind, something that wanted nothing less than his misery for all time.

"I know about the manuscript," Dawn said.

She had decided to see if there was anything she could do to help, she said. She knew he was busy, caught up in the new book. It was the way their relationship always worked—her marshaling the real world, him standing on the ledge outside the window, bringing home the dreams.

So she'd gone upstairs and had a look through his boxes. Pretty quickly it had become clear that he'd want to keep most of it, and he had to decide where it went (because the obvious and only acceptable answer would be "in your study, dude"). By the time she got to the third box she'd lost focus and was peering into it with little more than mild curiosity.

When she spotted the pile of paper, she'd snapped back to attention.

How cool, she thought—the manuscript for David's novel. That shouldn't be hidden away in a box. That should be... well, not actually on display (a pile of paper was never going to look acceptable in the living room) but at least safely stowed. She pulled it out and leafed through the first few pages, smiling, before realizing there was something strange about it.

Yes, it was the book, but it was different. Not only in the way a first draft will always be different—the raw material, hacked like a block of stone out of the quarry of random words and events, ready to be shaped into meaning by subsequent drafts—but *wholly* different. David's handwriting was all over it, in pencil and ballpoint pen, hundreds of corrections and changes. But the stuff underneath, the typed material, not to mention the very paper it was typed on...

"What was it, David? Where did it come from?"

David had been listening without any attempt to speak, eyes on the growing traffic through the windshield, as they came into Newark. He looked down at his hands. Lying hands, hands that...

"It was my father's," he said.

"What?"

"The place where I grew up wasn't very different from Rockbridge. It was called Palmerston, in Pennsylvania. There was a weird shooting there back in the 1990s, but otherwise it was your regular small town. My parents lived there all their lives. They loved each other, but they argued. A lot. Viciously sometimes. One of the things they used to argue about was a little room my father used as his study. It was a hobby. He..."

David found he couldn't finish. He didn't have to. Dawn already knew, and she said the words for him. "He wrote the book I found."

"Yes."

"But it wasn't finished," she said "There was only half a novel there, and the prose was *terrible*, and..."

"He was still working on it when they died, I guess. He tinkered with it for years. Maybe he would have finished it, maybe not. When I packed up stuff to bring to Rockbridge, I found the manuscript. I didn't think about it for a long time, but one day I wondered whether I should try to do something with it. At first it was supposed to be something for him, a way of getting to know him better, or...But as I worked at it and changed it and added things and took stuff out, I stopped seeing it as his book and started seeing it as mine. And when I finished it and gave it to you and you said you loved it...I didn't want to admit it hadn't been."

"David, you could have told me."

"I know. I fucked up. And...I wonder whether Maj coming back into my life has to do with all of that. He bumped into me on the day I met with my publishers for the first time. That can't be a coincidence, can it?"

"David, who *is* Maj?"

"He was the first thing I ever wrote, my first big make-believe. I just made him up a little too well."

Chapter 60

When Golzen got to the club he found the street door ajar. From that moment he realized that things were running differently, that something was afoot. Maybe he even started to hope tonight was going to be the night. You follow the signs, unclear though they may be.

Follow signs, until Jedburgh appears.

There was no one behind the bar, though cold blue light shone from the bulbs behind the bottles. Chalk up another hint that all was not business as usual. By now tattooed staff would normally be checking that the beer fridges were stocked, racking backup spirits on the high shelves. Golzen walked across the big empty space to the office.

Reinhart was waiting, arms folded, leaning back against the desk. Golzen noticed immediately that the phone was not in its customary place, but lying in six pieces against the wall and over the floor.

"What happened to that?"

"It broke."

Reinhart spoke as if the event had nothing to do with him, as though whatever cataclysm had befallen the device had occurred at its own hands and been its own fault. Though trivial — Golzen had seen the man do far worse to foes both inanimate and animate — he found this disquieting. It reminded him of the kind of thoughts that sometimes needled at him from the cloudy depths of his own mind: the thoughts that said everything was a game, and the darker and bloodier it got, the better. The ones that said there was no responsibility, no fault, no damage, no rules. The thoughts that didn't have the slightest understanding of what those words even meant.

"Who was it?"

"The priest. I don't know how he got this number, but he's crazier than usual tonight. Ratfuck insane."

"Something happened over in Chelsea an hour ago, in the street near his church. One of the friends canceled herself out. She was very popular. A lot of people are upset. He's probably one of them."

Golzen considered mentioning that Lizzie had been very close to Maj, too, but elected not to. Since the encounter the day before, Reinhart had been silent about Maj. Golzen was content to let that remain so.

"Whatever. The priest has gone past the point of no return. He needs dealing with."

"He's not our only problem."

"I'm aware that other people are trying to make our business their business."

"Don't we need to do something about them, too?"

"I will. Have no doubt. But they're no threat."

There was something wrong here. It was as if Reinhart had turned some part of himself up. Some not-good part. "To you, maybe. But to *us*. These people know who we are, *what* we are. They may try to do something."

"Let them. When the enemy comes at you, the smart tactician does not retreat. He doesn't even stand and fight unless absolutely necessary. You know why?"

"Why?"

Reinhart smiled serenely. "The enemy is at their weakest at the moment when they advance. They're off balance, head full of plans and impulses and leaping ahead to their victory...instead of watching what *you're* doing. That makes it the ideal time to vault straight over them in the direction you were already going."

Golzen blinked, feeling caught out, as if he couldn't keep up. "But... what direction is that?"

"You don't get it. That's why I am me and you are you. You don't even realize who the enemy *is*. It's not these new people, the tough guy and his witchy girlfriend. We kill them, they're gone. But that's not the end of it. The enemy is *everyone,* my friend. You must start at your own front door, but after that, there is no end to it. That's who we're fighting all the time, and today is Day Zero of the new deal."

"You mean..."

"Yes. We're doing it. Right now."

Golzen's heart leapt. "We're leaving for Perfect?"

"Not us, no."

"But you said..."

Reinhart shook his head. "I said nothing. You didn't listen properly and so you heard things that were never said. Nobody's going anywhere."

"We're going to Perfect," Golzen said stubbornly.

"Perfect isn't a place. It's a *state.*"

"Like... Colorado?"

"No, you dumb asshole. A state of *being.* You can't change anything by altering where you are. You have to change *what* you are. That option is unavailable to you because of the situation with your own friend. You should have had the presence of mind to do something about that way back in the day. I'm sorry."

He didn't look remotely sorry.

"I'm not *going?*"

"No one's going anywhere. Are you even *listening?*"

"What are you... Perfect is a *place.*"

"Jesus. So tell me—where do you think this place even is? Utah? Texas? Fucking California? You think you were going on some Mormon adventure, prancing off into the wilderness to find the promised fucking land?"

Golzen stared at him. That's exactly what he'd thought would happen, what he'd believed lay in his future and destiny since the night many years ago when he dreamed of a place where they could all live like normal people. Perfect had been Reinhart's name for it. In Golzen's dream it had been announced to him as Jedburgh, and in the confines of his head he still thought of it that way. He'd thought Reinhart believed in it too, but now he was saying something else . . . and Golzen couldn't even work out what it was.

"So . . . what *is* going to happen? When?"

Reinhart bounced off the desk and strode out into the main club room. Golzen hurried after him.

"It's already started," Reinhart said. "A broadcast was passed to all available Cornermen"—he checked his watch—"nearly forty minutes ago. It won't happen all at once. It depends when the chosen happen to get the message. That's okay. That's the *other* secret to success in battle, my friend. No events. Only evolution."

"I don't . . . understand."

"No, you don't. Let's leave it at that."

Golzen became aware of someone coming toward them out of the shadows. "Wait up," said a girl's voice.

"Hey," Reinhart said. "You ready?"

It was the girl Golzen had brought to Reinhart—the ditzy teen he'd turned a few days before. She looked different, though. She was dressed the same, was still the kind of random hoodie girl that no one would look twice at in the street, but there was a new confidence about her. She looked like she had a destination now.

She grinned. "You bet."

Golzen glared at her. "What's *she* doing here?"

"I always liked your idea of there being twelve initial warriors," Reinhart said. "It has a ring to it, you know? Twelve holy ghosts, ha-ha. So she's doing this thing in your place."

"*What?*"

"She's got what it takes. Fingerskills and an accessible friend. You have neither. Maj would have been perfect, of course. He's a weapon already. He took the step long ago. You're no good for this."

"But . . . but she's *nobody*."

"Screw you," the girl said with amusement. "My name's Jessica. Or it's gonna be."

Reinhart laughed. "That's my girl. Go and be."

He tossed something to her. She caught it deftly in one hand and held it up in front of Golzen, taunting him.

A matchbook.

"Later," she said, and walked quickly toward the street. By the time she got through the door, she was running.

Reinhart chuckled. Then he stopped, just like that, as if tiring of doing an impersonation of a normal person. His face darkened. "There's a thing I'm going to do," he said. "Then we need to talk. The fun starts here, but we have much still to do, my friend."

Golzen's head was buzzing. He felt sickened, disgusted with himself. Christmas day had come and there was nothing under the tree. There never had been. There wasn't even a tree. Just lies. Always lies.

"No," he said numbly.

He turned his back on Reinhart and walked out into the twilight.

Chapter 61

I'd run up and down the avenue all the way from 14th to 23rd. I'd searched down it again, this time along every side street to the next avenues. I had the phone to my ear throughout, hitting redial time and again.

I couldn't find Kristina anywhere. After forty minutes I realized this wasn't working and I stopped running around like a fool. I thought it very unlikely she'd have gone to work, but I called the restaurant to eliminate the possibility. Mario's sister answered and tartly said no, she hadn't seen her and she didn't want to either, because we were both fired.

"What? Why?"

"She never here. You a fighting man. Mario, he had enough."

I knew it would have been Maria who made the decision rather than her brother, but I was too wound up to take the problem seriously right now and said fine, but if Kris happened by could they tell her to call me, please. Mario's sister sniffed and said maybe and put the phone down, which I had to hope meant yes.

I went back up to 18th and rang the bell of Catherine Warren's house. There was no response, but I saw the drapes move on the second floor so I put my thumb back on the buzzer and kept it there until I saw a shape in the hallway. Catherine kept the chain on but opened the door, a tear-stained child in her arms.

Catherine's face was hard and set. "Go away."

"Have you seen Kristina?"

"No. Now go, or I'll call the police."

She was so self-possessed, so impregnable, that I couldn't help myself. "So how'd it go with Lizzic? Not well, by the look of it."

Her eyes didn't even flicker. "I don't know anyone by that name," she said. "I never have."

She slammed the door in my face.

Our apartment—or the remains of it—was a possibility, but I believed that however upset Kristina was, she'd have the sense to avoid going back there. I'd seen the look in her eyes as she surveyed the devastation and knew the place was dead to her. She hadn't liked it much before, and whatever we'd built there was gone.

I realized that although I'd spent every day with this woman for six months, we remained separate. I knew where *our* places were—the cafés and delis and bars where we spent time—but there was some whole different Kristina-based map of Manhattan, and I didn't have a copy. I didn't know where she went when I wasn't there. She didn't know where I went, either, and this finally proved to me that we'd never really lived here. Our tracks were faint pencil lines on the city's plan. It was too big and old for us to make lasting marks upon it. We needed to find somewhere we could start to write ourselves in ink, together, a place where our lives would become part of the object itself—otherwise we were just shades, haunting street corners, passing time.

I kept walking fast and running, trying her phone.

She kept not answering.

I spun around like a headless chicken for another hour—checking bars, calling people we knew from late-night drinking sessions—before I had a better idea. I'd gotten myself way up in Midtown and it took another twenty minutes to get back from there to the place I'd thought of.

Union Square Park was empty. It was cold and dark and the drizzle had settled in. No one would have any good reason to be there—no one with a normal life, anyway. But this is where Kris and I had first encountered the friends en masse and where she'd met up with Lizzie and the Angels. Maybe she'd come here to mourn her. I didn't know. I couldn't think of anywhere else.

I finally slowed down—partly because my lungs and legs were aching, and also because I didn't think I'd stand any chance of finding what I was looking for if I came into the area loud and fast.

I walked down the central path. The grass and bushes and trees on either side of it were empty apart from a few sleeping street people on benches. I got to the bottom and there were others in evidence—but just regular humans, striding between wherever they'd been and whoever they were going to. Each looked like they had sensible lives where things were joined with straight lines and everything had a beginning, middle, and an end. I did not feel a part of that world.

It would take only ten minutes to run to the apartment, but I still believed that would be a waste of time. I decided to give the park one more circuit, just in case. This time I forsook the path and stepped over low hedges, looking around the bushes and under trees—even under the benches. By the time I got back up to the northern section I was beginning to lose hope.

Then I spotted something over in the kids' playground. It was closed, but two figures, adult size, were standing in the open area between the slides and climbing frames. One had his back to me. He was wearing a shirt and jeans.

The other was a man with short, ginger hair, wearing an ill-matched suit. As I watched, this second guy reached out and put a hand on the other's shoulder. His face said he knew he ought to be saying something and he had absolutely no idea what it might be. The other guy shook it off and started shouting. I could hear the noise, feel the anger, but couldn't make out the words.

I ran to the wooden fence. "Hey," I said.

They ignored me. The man in jeans was losing it now, shouting louder and louder, arms flailing by his sides. I was close enough that what he was saying should have been audible, but all I got was misery and fury.

I let myself in the gate, aware I could be approaching a drug deal going wrong and setting myself up for another trip to the hospital. I didn't care.

"Turn the fuck around," I shouted, my voice spiraling out of my control.

The man turned. It was Maj, of course. His face was pure white. His eyes were black. He seemed condensed and powerful and yet on the verge of blowing apart, a dark kernel of terrible anger and violence.

"Have you seen Kristina?"

The other man glanced at me but was far more concerned with trying to talk Maj down.

"Do you *know where she is?*"

"Look, I don't know, mate," said the man in the suit. "Never met her. And we've got bigger—"

Maj ran off. The other guy went after him. By the time I got outside the enclosure, they'd become lost in shadows.

"*Assholes,*" I shouted. "She tried to *help.* She tried to stop it happening. Lizzie was her *friend.*"

All I heard in reply were the sounds of leaves in the trees around the park and traffic out on the streets.

As I stormed back toward the road I saw someone standing in the bushes by the side of the playground, however. She might even have been there all along—from the angle I'd approached, I wouldn't have seen her.

She was dressed in black but with a vibrant green skirt. She was plump with pure white hair. She was watching me.

But then she wasn't there.

*   *   *

Two minutes later my phone rang. I yanked it out of my pocket so fast that it spun out of my fingers. I snatched it off the floor and got it to my ear.

"Kris? Where are you?"

"Not her," a voice said — an older, croaky voice. "It's Lydia. You got to come, John."

"Where? Are you with Kris?"

"No, I don't know where your girl is. But you got to come to the church. Right now."

"What? Why?"

"There's a bad man here."

Chapter 62

Streets slick with rain and reflecting lights and blackness a purple-blue oil in puddles. Cars flashing by on their way from nowhere to nowhere else, spraying cold, dirty water. Windows and houses and stores and bars. Distant shouts, honks, half a laugh at some circumstance out of sight. People, real and imagined, standing, walking, turning—still or in movement.

So many strangers, so few friends; among the millions of people in the world, barely a handful you'd rather be with than be alone. You could pass through all this like a shadow and never be a part of it.

You can pass like that, and Kristina did. She walked. Her head was empty but for one thought.

Eventually she ended up somewhere. She had been standing in it for five minutes before she realized where she even was. She became aware of trees and bushes and a dark open space. Bryant Park.

Of course. Her feet had brought her here—her feet and the part of the mind that keeps moving even when the thinking portions have absolved responsibility and dived into a black hole. Her feet had brought her to the first place where she and Lizzie had spoken.

Why would they do that? How could it help?

Kristina had thought she had no more tears. She was wrong. She'd kept finding she was wrong about this, discovering herself doubled up, stomach clenched in the kind of spasm the body resorts to when poisoned. Events can poison, too. If you cry on the streets people will avoid you. They will step past and look the other way. They know the kind of things that cause people to break down in public and are scared it might be contagious. The only times Kris could remember something this huge was the death of her father. A bulletproof world of beings and love had split along a seam, leaving a gap for some force outside to suck someone out of the circle and into permanent darkness beyond.

She was aware her response was out of proportion. As John had pointed out with characteristic bluntness, she hadn't known Lizzie long or well. It was like being knocked sideways by the death of a celebrity. Ridiculous. Self-indulgent. And yet real. People can define your world and emotional space without having sat at the same table. You build your own universe, and if you choose to cover some of its walls with pictures of someone you've never met — patching over your need for love and attention and meaning when there's no real person to fit the bill — then the tearing of their image from reality will uncover cracks just as real as the death of someone you've known all your life.

Somehow, Lizzie's death did exactly that. Not to mention . . . it was Kris's fault.

She knew she needed to talk to John, that he was the only person who might be able to make her feel better, but every time her phone buzzed she let it go. She didn't deserve help. Her dumb speech to Lizzie about how it was time for a reunion — what the hell had she thought she was doing? What had made her think she had the perspective to talk that way?

She slumped onto a bench, mercifully obscured from the rest of the world by an overhanging tree. Her head was splitting, nose dripping, her face a puddle of hot tears and cold drizzle, and still it kept coming, pumped out by the fiercest and most terrible motor of grief — the idea that something could have been done differently and none of this would have happened; that you have been the engine of your own destruction. It's the moment that the smoker with lung cancer realizes they could have gone through with giving up twenty years ago; the moment the sole survivor of a car crash realizes he could have double-checked in the mirror before changing lanes on the interstate; the agonizing moment someone on a rusty fire escape has to think yeah, maybe they could have checked how stable the thing felt before climbing out...and meanwhile the old bolt pulls free of crumbling brick and the entire contraption of life tilts away from the wall of reality on a one-way trip into blackness.

Regret is the poison that kills for all eternity, because no matter how violently the mind and body spasms, it cannot be expelled. Lizzie was dead because of something Kristina had said.

That was a deed that would never be repaired.

"It's not your fault."

Kristina jerked her head up. She had no idea how long she'd been on the bench, lost in silent screams of self-recrimination. For a moment she couldn't see who had spoken. Then she realized the Angel girl, Flaxon, was standing in front of her, body as straight as the rain. It was coming down harder now and the girl looked soaked. This fact cut through Kristina's confusion.

"How...are you wet?"

"The more you feel, the harder you are. A person could break bricks on you right now. I heard you half the way from Union Square."

She came and sat next to Kristina. Kristina sniffed, wiped her nose on her sleeve, unsure how seriously to take what the girl had said.

"For real," Flaxon said, as if in answer. Her face was pinched-looking. She seemed thinner than the night before, and smaller and younger — though also stronger. She held up her hand, and Kristina saw that a few of the raindrops seemed to bounce, rather than passing through. "I can hear what you're thinking, too, a bit. Only because you're loud. And because you think like my friend did. She was a dismal bitch too."

Kristina was surprised into something like a laugh. "What...happened to her?"

"No idea. She dropped me. End of story."

Kristina remembered Lizzie saying how hard it had been for this girl to accept her place in the world, and suspected that *wasn't* the end of the story, but she was done trying to wheedle information out of people.

"I'm sorry."

"I need to talk to you," Flaxon said.

Kristina felt another surge of guilt, certain she was about to be brought to account and that she deserved it. "I'm sorry," she said again.

The girl shook her head curtly. "Get over yourself. Just because you're real doesn't mean everything starts and ends with you. Lizzie was a strong person. She acted. *She* did the thing. Don't try to take that away from her."

"Then . . . what?"

"I was down in Union Square and I overheard something and I see a dark cloud over it."

"What do you mean?"

"Maj was there with that Cornerman buddy of his, Fictitious Bob, and he was losing it. Badly. Not sure if you're aware, but Maj knows where his real friend lives."

"I heard."

"Okay. Well, if you're looking for what pushed Lizzie over the edge this afternoon, that's more likely it than anything you said or did."

"No. She said she was happy for Maj."

"I'm sure she was. She had a lot of good and happy thoughts and she spread them around. That's how she rolled. But it was also like a knife to her."

"Why?"

"Everybody wants to feel they're the center of creation, not just someone's friend. But you get used to it. Kinda. Not everybody gets to be a rock star, right? It's hard for us to love, though. One another, anyway."

"Because of what you feel for your real friend?" .

"It's like a first love, I think. From what I've heard. That sound right?"

Kristina thought about it. That first love, the one that changes you, striking like an arrow or axe into your adolescent heart, the one that will (despite decades of dating and far deeper and more meaningful affairs) define your emotional landscape forever. You won't spend the rest of your life trying to replicate it—you may do just the opposite—but it's there nonetheless, a ghost in your heart. She nodded.

"Maj and Lizzie got close, though," Flaxon said. "He is *very* broken up by what happened and *almighty* pissed at the world of real people right now."

Aware that she was deflecting some of her anger at her own actions, Kristina said: "So maybe him talking to his friend is exactly what needs to happen."

"No," Flaxon said patiently. "No good comes of it. Ever. I don't think it would be his friend he'd be looking for anyway. He was ranting about the priest."

"Jeffers? Why? He's been trying to *help*."

"Maybe. But Maj thinks he screwed with Lizzie's thinking and maybe it was part of what made her...do what she did today. It's a really bad idea for them to talk right now."

"Are you sure? Real people have to *learn*. They have to take responsibility for what they say and do."

"You don't get it. Maj is different."

"I know. He's a Fingerman. A good one."

"Oh, he's that. The best that ever was, people say. But that's not what I'm talking about." Her voice dropped to a whisper, a tangled mixture of distaste, respect, and dark excitement. "He killed someone once. A real person."

Kristina stared. "How would that even be *possible?*"

"I don't know. I don't know who it was or when or how. But they say it's true. It's why Reinhart wanted him to work for him so bad—he'd already crossed that line. My point is, if Maj gets the brush-off from Jeffers then people could get hurt. You think Lizzie would have wanted that? For Maj to do something black because of her?"

"But what can I do?"

"At least talk to Maj. He knows Lizzie dug you. It might make a difference."

"I don't know where he is."

"First place to try would be the church, duh?"

Kristina didn't know what to say. She didn't know whether going after someone she'd barely met would make a difference, or if she even had the courage to try after what had happened.

"Still hearing you, babe," Flaxon said. She shook her head like a dog, spreading rain flying in all directions. "There's something else Lizzie used to say, and it's what stopped me running with the bad guys and made me want to be an Angel instead. She said regret is the only thing that kills forever and also the only poison that you feed yourself."

Kristina blinked at her. This was exactly what she'd thought earlier, almost word for word. It couldn't be coincidence, and she knew Lizzie hadn't said it to her.

Was part of Lizzie here now, in this park?

Was part of her *inside* Kristina now?

"Let's get on this," Flaxon said, standing. "And page your boy-friend, too."

"I don't even know whether he'll come."

"Make him. He seems like a guy who'd be useful in this type of situa-tion." She winked. "Also, he's kind of hot, for a real person."

Flaxon started running. Aware she was stopping the other girl from moving much faster, Kristina did her best to keep up, and ran after Flaxon as fast as she could.

Chapter 63

David kept talking as Dawn drove in through the outskirts of the city. He talked longer than ever before in his life, dredging up out of memory and hidden spaces. He told her everything he could remember from the time he crawled under a kitchen table in the midst of a fight that was breaking his heart, to find a boy there with him. He told her about the hours and days spent in the woods by himself — except for the friend he'd conjured up; the times in his bedroom with him playing the endless made-up games that neither parent could seem to stomach or understand; the long walks they would take together as David — a solitary boy, the total loner geek — explored the small town where he grew up. Told her, too, how Maj was there into his early teens and beyond, long after he'd heard about the idea of imaginary friends and realized most people had forgotten about them by then. How when he was at some other kid's birthday party at a roller-skating rink or bigger house, Maj would be there in the background, giving him a wink every now and then to reassure him he wasn't alone. How the boy kept pace with him in age while always looking and dressing differently, always that bit more daring than David and naughtier *(what nobody sees, nobody knows)* — sometimes lifting a dollar bill from dresser tables or small change from the tips people left in restaurants and putting them where David would find them, dropping them out of the air to be discovered on the floor or on the path outside his parents' house. Money that David saved and eventually used to buy the basic word processor on which he tentatively started to write, in secret, keeping silent about this lest his mother find out and hate the endeavor in him as much as she evidently hated it in his father; also in case his father poured scorn upon it as he did with most everything else his son did, scorn mixed with the pungent jealousy that's born of the realization that too many years have passed without achievement and there's a new generation coming to elbow you aside and take the things you assumed one day would be yours.

Dawn listened in silence apart from when they got close to the bridge over to Manhattan, when she asked him where they were going. He got out the map from the glove compartment and told her to head toward Chelsea.

He told her how Maj had remained a constant into his late teens, well past the point where David had realized this was an abnormal state of affairs and had begun to become embarrassed by seeing his old friend in the background in bars or keg parties or outside the windows of diners in which David was muddling through his first, terrified dates. David had started to fight back against his father's character summation by then, trying to reinvent himself as someone who *could* function sociably, and was making progress, too — to the point where he'd stopped wanting to be reminded of the terribly lonely little boy who'd once hidden under the kitchen table.

You want to be different from everyone else and then you want to be the same, and finally you need to be different again. That means being *you*, and nobody else. Old friends become an encumbrance, a reminder of the buggy beta version of you. The magnets started to repel, and the move to New York turned up the charge a hundredfold. Eventually David pushed hard enough and grew up enough, and the idea of Maj fell out of his head.

"I just didn't remember," David said, as he sat flicker-lit by neon in the passenger seat, eyes glazed with an avalanche of things that had been lost. "I forgot Maj. I have to remember him again now, or he's never going to leave me alone."

Five minutes later Dawn made the turn onto 16th. She drove along the dark, tree-lined street until David indicated for her to pull over to the curb.

"Why are we here?"

"See the church? That's the one Maj brought me to. The priest knows about him and his friends. He may know where Maj is now. I don't know what else to try."

Dawn turned off the engine. She sat in silence with her hands in her lap. Apart from asking directions, she had not spoken for forty minutes. She seemed in no hurry to say anything now.

"Well?"

"Well what?" she said.

"Do you believe me?"

She pursed her lips. "I don't know."

"I'm telling the truth."

"How could you have forgotten all of this?"

"I didn't forget. I just...didn't think about it."

"But how?"

He shrugged. "The way you forget what you did any given afternoon when you were five or ten. The way you lose track of things you used to feel or understand or dream of when you were fourteen. The way you'll find your favorite toy in a drawer and stare at this tired, dusty thing and find it impossible to understand how there were months when you couldn't go to sleep at night without it. You change and you forget and you leave behind. You abandon things."

"I had an imaginary friend too," Dawn said. "It's why I leave a couple of mouthfuls at the end of a meal."

"So you know what I'm talking about."

"No. I was six years old. All this... It's very hard to believe."

"Oh, believe it," said a voice from the backseat.

There was a low chuckle, and David realized, far too late, that this had been the source of the swirling blackness he'd felt from the moment he got into the car.

Then all the doors locked.

Chapter 64

It took ten minutes to get back to Chelsea. On the way, I fumbled a card out of my wallet and made a call to the cops. I got an answering machine on Raul Brooke's number, but I figured leaving a message was better than nothing.

That done, I concentrated on moving fast. Lyds had been insistent that I not go straight to the church but instead meet her at the junction of Eighth Avenue and 13th. There was no sign of her. I'd tried to get her to be more specific about what was going down, but she was both more together and even crazier than usual, and making the call from a phone box in a noisy bar. I didn't know what to do but wait to see if she appeared.

I tried Kristina yet again in the meantime. "Kris," I said, fighting to keep my voice fairly calm. "Please call me back. I'm sorry about what happened. I'm sorry you couldn't stop it. But *we have to talk.*"

I ended the message feeling I'd once again failed to say anything that would make a difference. On an afterthought I called back and added: "Plus I saw Maj and some other guy in Union Square. Maj looks upset and very angry. I don't know whether he'd try to do anything to Catherine, but if you're near where she lives and see him, bear it in mind. And *please call me.*"

Someone emerged from a shadowed doorway. It was Lydia. Her eyes were wide. She was swallowing compulsively. She approached warily.

"Is . . . that you?"

"Of course it's me, Lyds. How long have you been watching?"

She took cautious steps toward me, peering like a mole. "I had to be sure. Lot of liars out tonight."

"A lot of what?"

She swept her hand to indicate the busy avenue. "You see them too, right? I know you do. Mirror people in windows and puddles, and then the assholes aren't even really there. They're always around. But tonight..."

"Lyds..."

She kept looking around suspiciously. "All *over* the place. Liars. Never *seen* so many. I saw a shadow man run away down the street and climb up a wall like a spider. I saw a hefty girl with white hair screaming and punching a store window and it didn't even break. Five minutes ago I saw another guy, running up 16th. You believe me?"

"Yes, probably, whatever. Lyds, I don't know where Kris is and everything is badly fucked up. Can you *just tell me what's going on?*"

"I went to the church a couple hours ago. Wanted to talk to the priest. He wasn't there and I was going to leave, but then he came back. He looked worse than you do. Not beat up, but *fucked* up. Thought he was drunk, he was staggering up the road so bad. Face wet and smeared and like, I don't know what. He gets his shit together and lets me into the church, but he's shaking and so messed up he can't hold his hands steady. There's a thing of coffee on a table and I pour some for him, and even though it's cold he drinks it and drinks some more and he starts pacing around the place and talking to himself."

"About what?"

She started hurrying up the avenue, and I followed. "I have no idea. It's just word and then word and they ain't connected, but he's getting angrier and angrier. All this shit about his life and I don't know what. I mean, Jesus fuck, I ain't so fucking happy about how the dice has rolled for me the last few decades, but this guy has *really* got his hate on. He's hurting bad."

I put together how many times Jeffers had dropped Lizzie's name when he'd been discussing the people he'd been trying to help. I wondered if, while he'd been trying to assist them all toward whatever light he felt beckoned to them, perhaps he'd been reaching out to one in particular—reaching out *for,* even. I didn't know how to reconcile that with what he'd told us he believed, but I was giving up on the idea of things making sense. Maybe things don't *have* to make sense. Maybe we should just let everything be.

"And then what?"

"Suddenly he stops shouting. When he starts talking again, he's calm but in a bad way. Tells me he has done wrong, got distracted. Then he goes downstairs and I hear him yelling on the phone. He's even weirder when he comes back up. I try to talk him down, but he's not hearing. He tells me the whole time he's been there there's been ghosts downstairs under the church. He says it's another priest or some shit like that. The guy never left and is watching him the whole time, watching, watching. He says the ghost's never going to leave unless he steps up and does the thing. The man is . . . this priest has got serious issues, John, is what I'm saying. I left him to it because I don't need this kind of crap in my life right now, but as I'm coming out another guy turns up in the street, heading for the church, and he *reeks* of bad."

"What did he look like?"

"Tough-looking, coat, head like a bullet."

"Shit," I said wearily. We were now at the corner of 16th. "Okay, Lyds, you did the right thing."

"I know. But what are you going to do about it?"

"I'm going to the church. You're going to walk away."

"I hear you."

I started up the street, feeling exhausted and scared. I'll admit I was wondering why I would risk contact with a man who'd already beaten the crap out of me. Because another man had been kind to us and taken us in during the middle of the night, I guess. I hoped that was a good enough reason.

I realized Lydia was trotting along right behind me. "Lyds . . ."

"Said I heard you," she rasped. "Didn't say I was going to do what you fucking said."

Chapter 65

When I got to the church I heard the sound of shouting from inside the building and so I ran through the gates and up the stairs, Lydia close behind.

"More liars," Lydia whispered loudly as I hurried down the corridor toward the sound of pain. "Fake people. You *listen* to me, John."

The hall was barely lit but for a couple of lamps and a row of candles down at the far end and it felt like a damp mausoleum. Reinhart was right in the middle, chairs in chaos all around him. Maj was leaning against the wall, watching, face like thunder.

Jeffers lay in a slumped position against the far wall, near the remains of the altar, blood dripping from his nose. He lifted his head when he saw me, but I didn't see anyone I recognized in his eyes.

"Wow, déjà vu," I said to Reinhart, feeling my fists bunch hard and tight. "You really get a kick out of messing up a church, huh?"

He did a double take. "Jesus, *you're* here? How fucking dumb *are* you, Henderson? Haven't you been back to your shitty little apartment yet?"

"That's what I'm here about. I want my girlfriend's credit card back."

Lydia scuttled around me and toward the priest. Reinhart made a grab for her as she passed, but his attention was on me and she eluded him.

"Actually you don't," he said. "I already used it to buy some pretty funky stuff."

"You and I need to talk sometime," I told Reinhart. "But that's not why I'm here. I want the priest."

"You want . . . the priest?"

"I'm going to get him out of your face, okay?"

Reinhart walked over to me. "I checked you out," he said thoughtfully. "You used to do some intelligence shit for the government, right?"

"Long time ago."

"Must have been. I find it hard to believe intelligence *ever* figured in your life. You honestly think you're walking out of here, with the praise Jesus fuckhead or without? Then you're even dumber than you look. You've saved me time by presenting yourself, though, so thank you. I think it's important to be polite to people, don't you, if they've done a good thing?"

I didn't say anything.

"I really do," he mused. "Because that way they understand that when you kill them, you mean that too."

He pistoned his hand out into my chest, knocking me backward. "You trying to take over my action? You really think you can do that?"

"I just want the priest," I said doggedly. "I don't even understand what these people are."

I heard Lydia bellowing from the end wall, asking me to help. She was trying to keep Jeffers down. He was hauling himself to his feet and in the direction of the broken altar. I wasn't in a position to influence their debate because Reinhart was right up in my face now and thrumming with the desire to hurt.

"You don't?" he sneered. "I'll explain. It's simple. They're children. Without attention they're nothing — like all the other losers in this city, in this whole country. It's *look at me, look at me* all fucking day. If no one's looking then they're just empty space, like ninety-nine percent of people in the world."

"See," I said. "You don't know either. Aren't you even curious?"

"I just told you, asshole."

"No. You just told me about yourself."

The street door slammed open behind me and I turned with relief to see a man I'd been hoping would arrive—the person I'd called on the way from Union Square. Raul, the detective who'd come to see me in the hospital.

"S'up, Mr. Henderson," he said.

He looked alert and ready for action, and my stomach flipped over with relief. Reinhart looked perplexed.

"What the fuck are you doing here?"

The cop came and stood next to him. "Mr. Henderson called for assistance. I'm here to help."

Reinhart laughed. "I love it. I just been telling him how dumb he is."

I realized he was right.

Chapter 66

Things happened fast, and this time I was the first to move. It'd been brewing since I woke up in the hospital smarting with the ego of a man who's been physically dominated by another. The cop just happened to be at the head of the line. I decided to cut the next few exchanges and hammered my fist straight up into his gut as hard as I could. He staggered, reaching into his jacket.

Reinhart was very fast to rotate about the waist and throw a blow up toward my face, but I'd been caught out by his speed before and had already stepped to the side and around the cop in anticipation.

I knew he'd be straight after me and that I couldn't fight them both at once, so I focused on smacking hard on the cop, trying to keep him between me and Reinhart long enough to at least get one of them down.

Raul was sucking breath trying to recover from the first punch at the same time as having to duck from further punches from me, and he messed up pulling his hand out of his coat. I ducked another incoming blow from Reinhart and kicked out to the side, catching him below the knee hard enough to knock him back. I was aware of Maj pushing himself off the wall and heading our way and I didn't know what, if anything, he'd be able to do, but I knew it wouldn't be on my side, so I went for broke and smacked my forehead down into the cop's nose, slashing out with my left elbow and connecting with Reinhart's throat more by luck than judgment.

The cop staggered backward. I grabbed his arm. The hand holding the gun tore free from his inside pocket and I let him drop. He slammed onto the floor semi-sideways, head connecting with the boards, and I stamped on his wrist with all my weight.

The fingers spasmed, letting go of the gun.

Reinhart was too strong, though, and my blow to the face hadn't done more than delay him for a second. He slammed into me from the side as I was reaching for the cop's weapon, throwing me off balance to tumble toward Raul, too twisted to try to roll out of it.

A kick caught me under the arm where he'd hit me time and again in the restaurant, sending a vast bloom of pain across my ribs, unusually sharp and pointed, but in my head it was like being winged on the leg by the hood of a car while running across a highway — I knew I absolutely could not stop driving forward, no matter how much it hurt, or Reinhart would tag me time and again until I couldn't move anymore... and this time he'd leave me dead on the floor.

I scrabbled out with my fingers and got ahold of the gun while Reinhart pulled back for another kick, and as I rolled onto my back I could see in his face that this one was coming at my head and would stop me cold. His eyes were already seeing a world in which I was deceased and all that remained was finding a chainsaw.

I swung my arm around to the front and pulled the trigger. I saw his eyes fly open.

Then he was gone.

Not run, not ducked, not sidestepped. He disappeared.

I jumped up, gun gripped in both hands, raking it around in a shaky circle. I panned past Jeffers, who'd finally made it to his feet and was heading to the end of the hall, shambling like an old man.

"Where'd he go?"

Maj looked dumbfounded.

"Where did he go?"

"He's one of us," he said, slowly, as the penny dropped.

"What do you mean? How *can* he be?"

"Well, what did you think?" the cop muttered. He'd pushed himself up onto his elbows. There was blood on his face and his eyes looked groggy but were refocusing fast.

I pointed the gun at him. "Are you one too?"

"Me? I'm just a regular guy."

"So . . . are you Reinhart's friend? His real person?"

"Hell no. Way he tells it, he killed that guy years ago, before he came to the city. Whacked him in a motel room in the back of beyond, somewhere out west. He's killed a lot of people since, like I tried to tell you in the hospital, but you wouldn't fucking listen. Every one has made him stronger. I did *try* to warn you, asshole."

Maj looked like a person whose world had sheared apart in front of his eyes. "But . . . how can he have killed his friend and still . . . be?"

"Search me. You're the freaks. You figure it out. All I know is he's got a dozen of you people heading into the streets tonight to do the same thing."

Maj walked quickly away toward the door. I shouted to him, "What does this mean?"

The cop took his chance and started to get up. He looked like a man who knew he'd been playing the wrong side of the fence for a long time and if he didn't get rid of me, he was about to pay for it.

"Stay the fuck down," I said, bearing down on him. "Where's Reinhart now?"

"I have no idea. He comes and goes. I did start out trying to nail the guy, you know, like a real policeman. I worked out that wasn't going to be possible, and well, you know how the song goes. If you can't beat them . . ."

I realized I'd read him wrong. "Why aren't you scared I'm going to call you in?"

"Because you've got a girlfriend and you have no idea where Reinhart is right now. Or where he'll be tomorrow night when you're sleeping."

"If he wants to hurt us he'll do it anyway."

"That's true," the cop said cheerfully. "You've made some bad life choices recently, huh."

"Where *is* he?"

"Downstairs," Jeffers said.

Keeping the gun on the cop, I stepped back to widen the angle and saw Jeffers reemerging from the door at the end of the hall. He shut it behind him and set off toward the street door, limping. His nose was at an angle, there was blood at the corners of his mouth, and his breathing was ragged. Reinhart had hurt him badly, inside, and he needed a hospital — and yet the priest looked lighter than I'd ever seen him before.

"How do you know? Did you see him down there?"

"I don't need to."

Jeffers got to the end of the hall and pulled the main door shut. He gave it a tug to make sure — a man trying to set in order the parts of the world over which he feels he has control. "He won't have run. The devil never does. He bides his time; he entreats and entices. He'll wait until you're off guard and then reappear, and this time he'll kill you."

"What's downstairs?"

"Don't go down there."

"What's downstairs?"

"Cellars. They stretch under the church and the houses on each side. Full of chairs that need repairing and Bibles and prayer books that seem to be surplus to requirements these days. And dead people."

"What?"

"The previous father knew about the ghosts too. He allowed some to rest here, as they waited for the call home. I didn't work that out until today. I thought it was just *his* spirit down there, restless, unsatisfied with my work. In a way it's a relief to know it's not."

"Excuse me — *who's* downstairs?"

He ignored me. "It's not working, though. They do not fade and will not leave. Either God isn't calling them loudly enough or they're just not listening. It's my job to lead them home. To lead you all."

With a great deal of effort he fumbled something out of his trouser pocket. It was a key. He locked the door, then started doggedly back the other way.

"Jeffers — what are you doing?"

"Don't worry. I don't think any of them will aid Reinhart. They're Hollows. You can feel their presence but they don't move much anymore and they don't care enough about anything to help. He wants *you* to go down there, though. Can't you feel that?"

I could. I didn't know whether it was merely my desire to finish the business with Reinhart, or something else, but there was an undeniable draw to go downstairs.

"You must not," the priest said. "In the darkness he will win. Evil always thrives in the dark, whether it is literal lack of light, or mere ignorance."

"John," Lydia said. She was bending down, her hand on the floor. "You getting this?"

I didn't understand what she meant and ignored her, focusing on the cop — who showed every sign of wanting to get back into it — and trying to make sense of what the priest was saying. "We can't leave Reinhart down there," I said. "I'm not going to just let him go."

"Oh, neither am I. There's only one thing that has always worked," Jeffers said, as he got to the remains of the altar. "It purges and transforms."

"Jeffers — what the fuck are you doing?"

"John," Lydia said more insistently, but by then I'd already realized what she was talking about. The floor was getting hot under foot.

The priest opened the door in the wall behind the altar and threw the key through it, threw it hard, as smoke came billowing out.

Chapter 67

David and Dawn sat with their arms wrapped around each other's heads. Of course they'd tried to unlock the doors and smash the windows, but cars aren't designed to allow this. The designers of modern automobiles do not realize that someday you may have to try to escape from things you cannot touch and can barely see. David had tried talking to the people in the back. The more he talked, the clearer they became, though this was not a good thing. There were two men, one woman. He recognized them.

The woman in back giggled, and the car locks went back up. "You can get out now," she said.

Her voice sounded like the strange friend of your mother's who one night said, "Go on, try it, just this one time; you may even like it."

Dawn kept her head buried in David's shoulder. She couldn't see the people in the back. She'd tried, but all that happened was that her vision went blurry and she felt twists of fury and vicious misery, like tiny arrows of premenstrual tension. She could make out their voices, like snatches of a radio in the next street, but she didn't try to hear what they were saying. Dawn wasn't having any of this. It wasn't lack of strength, and her husband understood that. It was a simple refusal to deal.

David envied her that. He'd always accommodated, always had his doors open too wide. Things had come in. Things had gone out, too — and stayed alive. "No," he said, however. "I'm not opening anything."

"This is our whole problem, you see," the girl in the back muttered. "All your heavy, heavy things. And *Christ* does it piss us off. *Open the door.*"

"No," David said. "You can't do anything to us."

"You're very wrong. As your fat friend Talia would tell you, assuming she could still talk."

"You...What did you do to her?"

"A little game. Real people play in make-believe. *We* get to play with real life—so *much* more fun. Dreams can bite—and they draw real blood. Now open that door or I'm going to slip into your wife's head and scare her so badly she'll abort right here and now."

Dawn jerked her head off David's shoulder. "Who said that?" she whispered. "Who's *back* there?"

"See?" The thin woman laughed. "She can hear *some* things. She'll hear enough when I tell her secrets about what people do to other people sometimes. And especially to little children."

"What do you *want?*" David pleaded, knowing he was fighting a losing battle. "We've done nothing to you."

"You all do something to *all* of us. And we're done putting up with it."

"Open the door," one of the men in the backseat said, the one with straggly hair.

"Open it. Open it," chanted the man with the shaved head, leaning to put his face next to the woman's, "or I'll take the ride into your wife's tidy little soul too. It'll be some trip, dude. I've always been the most imaginative when it comes to breaking things."

"Oh, nonsense," said the woman. "Though impersonating the trailer whale's dead beau *was* your idea, I'll admit. Open the door, David."

Then her expression changed. She hissed: "*Quickly.*"

David heard shouting and saw Maj running up the street. It was like feeling every lie you've ever told and every mistake you've made coming bubbling up out of your subconscious at once, as if someone had found the hidden notebook in which you've written your worst deeds and thoughts and started to read it out loud.

And David realized things had gotten even worse.

*   *   *

Maj stopped at the car. He took a deep breath. Then he reached out and opened the door. David stared up at him: caught, guilty, powerless.

"David," Maj said, years of hurt and loneliness starting to burn. "We really need to talk."

Dawn turned to see a man in jeans and an untucked shirt. His hair was tousled and his jaw stubbled. It was a look she knew David could pull off, though she'd given up trying to lead him toward it.

"I can see you," she said.

"Makes sense," the man said. "You probably know him better than anyone but me."

"No," Dawn said, pushing herself away from David and getting out of the car. "I know him *better.*"

"Dawn . . ." David said, getting out the other side.

Maj stared her down. "You don't even know who I am."

"You're Maj. He just told me everything."

"I doubt it."

"So you're his friend — I get that. You were kids together. I get that too. But he's not yours anymore. He's my *husband.*"

David came around the front. "Dawn, let me —"

"No!" she shouted. "I'm *not* going to let you handle this. That's not the way it's going to be, sunshine."

Maj wasn't getting drawn into the discussion. When he'd seen the car, he'd known this was meant to be, that David arriving in town so soon after Lizzie had gone — and moments after realizing Reinhart had never been real — meant it was time for this joke to be put to bed. Either David was going to put him back into his rightful place in his life, or Maj would take it from him.

Dawn saw this in his eyes, or felt it, and stepped in front of David, keeping him back with her arm.

"I don't want to hurt you," Maj said, taking a step toward them. "So get out of the way."

"No," Dawn said. "Not doing it."

"He's mine."

"Mine."

"I *deserve his life*. I was always the one who made things happen. He's a liar and a taker. You *all* are."

"He's not," Dawn shouted.

"If you don't know that about him," Maj said, in wonder, "then you don't know him at all."

"I know who he is. You just know who he was. People change and friendships end. Deal with it."

David kept trying to pull Dawn away, but she was strong, and furious like he'd never seen her before. Meanwhile, the three skinny people had slipped out of the car and were crowding around, laughing at him in the way he'd always suspected people did when he wasn't looking.

"I'm having a real life," Maj said. "It's time."

He pushed Dawn aside. David backed up, trying to get away around the side of the car. He couldn't get past the skinny people. They blocked him, rubbing their bodies against him. They possessed no substance except for the disgust they made you feel, but that was enough.

Maybe he shouldn't *try* to get away.

Maybe this had been coming all his life, or at least since he got a phone call in the middle of the night a decade ago telling him that his mother and father were dead. If it had *always* felt like a struggle to live, to make friends, to write, to be alive, perhaps it would be easier to let it all go.

"Yes," a voice said, close to his ear. The red-haired woman had pushed even closer to him, letting the front of her dress fall open. It smelled bad in there. "You're right, Davey. It would be *so* much easier that way. You won't be lonely anymore. Do it. Just let go."

David's mind filled with a flash image seen through some other boy's eyes, a scene from many years ago. It was so brief that he couldn't register what it showed—only that the boy in question had been broken into pieces one dark winter's afternoon in a house somewhere up in Wisconsin twenty years ago, and that this woman and her three brothers had been that boy's attempt to surround himself with something he could understand—though it turned out that even the people out of his own head were not his friends. It all got very badly away from him, and there arrived the week when he murdered his family, slowly, one at a time, along with several other people he'd never admitted to and whose bodies have never been found.

David lost the strength in his legs and crashed down to his knees.

"No!" Dawn shouted. "David—*get up.*"

But...why would he? Would it be worth it? Yes, he was going to be a father, probably. So what? He'd screw that up too, carrying on the genetic line. A bad father and a bad writer, a thief and a cheat. Was it worth slogging through the next forty years to prove the fact? If a character was destined to mess up every plotline you tried to put him in, why not let him go, cut him out?

"Do it, then," he mumbled, looking up to see Maj standing over him. "Have my life, if you want."

Dawn tried to get to David but couldn't get past the end of the car. There was something in her way, or someone, *more* than one—she could feel their unpleasant pressure forcing against her like a field of anxiety and temptation, though she couldn't see anyone but Maj. She tried to shout out, to call for help—surely there would be *someone* in the houses on the street who would hear—but blank despair strangled the noise in her throat.

Then, thank God, she heard someone else shouting.

She pulled her eyes from the sight of David on his knees in the gutter next to the car (her car, *their* car, the car she'd already pictured with two little carseats in the back and, years from now, the sound of singing and are-we-there-yet and I-Spy games) and saw two people running down the road.

At least . . . for a moment she thought it was two, but then it was only one — a woman, skinny and tall.

Kristina knew right away what Maj had in mind.

"Maj, *no*," she shouted. Maj was pulling in long, deep breaths and punching them back out again. Each time this happened it seemed like the hairs on his head were more visible. "You think Lizzie can't see you?"

"Don't try to —"

"Oh, shut up," she snapped. "Lizzie's dead. That doesn't mean she's gone. And she *loved* you."

"She didn't love me," he said. "She loved Catherine. Which is how it should —"

"Catherine was her friend and that never goes away. But Lizzie loved *you*. She told me so."

"Listen to her, Maj," Flaxon said.

Kristina saw a great flatness in Maj's eyes that said he knew he should care about what was being said but didn't understand it. "It doesn't matter. She's gone."

"Don't do it, Maj," another voice said, urgently. A squat man in a strange suit was hurrying toward them — the man Kristina had seen in SoHo with Reinhart the first time she went for a walk with Lizzie.

Flaxon snarled at him. "Fuck off, Golzen."

"No, listen to him," Kristina said. "He's trying to stop —"

"It'll just be some trick," Flaxon said. "This is the asshole who told me I wasn't real and got me into a whole load of shit that I only escaped because Lizzie showed me another way. Him and his putridass brothers and sister are groomer slime."

"Brothers?" Kristina said.

Flaxon pointed at the three tall, thin people looming over the man who was on his knees in the gutter. "They've all got the same real person — a world-class sicko called Simon Jedburgh, who's been locked in a psych ward twenty years for...what was it? Oh yeah—dismembering his entire fucking family."

"I've made mistakes," Golzen said. "I'm trying to put them right."

"I don't believe you," Flaxon spat. "There's no promised land either, FYI. That's more bullshit, probably the crazy crap your psycho friend is screaming in his padded cell."

Golzen turned from her and focused on Maj. "Don't harm your friend," he said. "No good will come of it."

"Reinhart's one of us," Maj said.

Golzen stared at him. *"What?"*

"He killed his friend. Look what it did for *him*."

Golzen looked like he was putting ten things together at once. "That's what he's been planning," he said quietly. "That's what he meant by 'Perfect' all along. Evolving to another state. Getting us to kill our real people, to become more like him."

"Suits me," Maj said. "Bring it on."

But Flaxon threw herself at him and started ranting in his face, and then all of them were shouting at once.

Dawn meanwhile kept trying to get through to David, to get his eyes to refocus on her. "Please, David," she said. "Please get up. These things aren't real. They can't do this to you."

The woman called Kristina turned her head. "What the hell is that?"

Dawn realized she could smell something, and heard a crackling sound. "Is that from the church?"

The others turned to look. "Who's in there?" Kristina screamed at Maj. *"Who's in there?"*

"The priest and Reinhart," Maj said. "Some old woman. And...your man."

Kristina grabbed David by the scruff of the neck. She hauled him to his feet, shoving him toward Dawn. "Get him out of here," she said, and then sprinted up the street toward the church.

After a beat, Maj and the others followed.

Chapter 68

Some people are always going to look after themselves—first, foremost, and always. The cop was one of them. He latched on to what Lydia and I had realized—that the priest had set fire to the building, for *the love of Christ*—and that my attention was drawn. He threw himself into me, clattering us into a pile of overturned chairs. He wasn't in Reinhart's league, but he was desperate and focused on one task—getting his gun back.

I got tangled in a mess of broken wood and was finding it impossible to strike back. After ten seconds I started to be afraid that he was going to win. He got his hands around my wrist and began smacking it against anything he could find, sticking terrier-like to the task despite me kicking and kneeing him as hard as I could. Then there was a crunching blow that took us both on the shoulders and smacked us down onto the ground.

"Jesus," Lydia said.

I crawled away to see her holding the remains of the chair she'd brought down on us. "Men are all the same," she muttered. "Get us *out* of here, you assholes. Then you can beat each other to death for all I care."

The cop had taken more of the impact and was still on hands and knees, trying to raise his head. Smoke was billowing in through the door at the end. Jeffers sat on the chair facing the congregation. He looked composed.

"Jeffers," I said. "What have you done?"

He smiled with the maddening peacefulness of someone who is so far out the other side of present circumstances that he finds it hard to understand what you're saying.

I pulled out my phone, but the screen was blank and cracked, and I knew there'd be a phone-shaped bruise on my ribs where Reinhart's shoe had connected with it before I pulled the gun on him. I pressed buttons and nothing happened.

"Call 911," I shouted to the cop, who was getting back to his feet.

"Left it in the car," he muttered.

I ran to the main door and yanked at the handle. It was locked. I knew that. I'd stood and watched Jeffers do it but had been too caught up in Reinhart's disappearance and keeping the gun on the cop that I hadn't processed the implications.

I looked up at the big glass windows, knowing I'd noticed the first time I'd been in the room that they were covered with wire. I jumped onto the table with the scattered remains of Billy's last meal, and tried to see if the wire could be gotten off. Maybe — if you had a few hours and a selection of tools. Some very thorough person had bedded it into the sides of the window frames. There were no other windows in the church because there were buildings on both sides. The roof was thirty feet above my head.

I got down and went back to the front door. I kicked it. Banged my shoulder against it. I realized the cop was heading toward me again and rounded on him.

"Fuck with me and I'll shoot you," I said. "We don't have time for this."

"I know," he said — and threw his own shoulder against the door. Nothing happened. He did it again.

I left him to it and headed back to where Jeffers was sitting. "Is there any way out through the basement?"

"There's no way out of anywhere."

"Listen to me," I said. "I understand that you're in pain of various kinds and have things you feel you need to do. You've got three other people in here with you, though. You don't get to make that call."

"A bad cop, a crazy lady, and a man trying to find his path," the priest said.

"Is that supposed to be me, or you?"

"Oh, both, don't you think?"

The cop had given up on battering the door. "Look, you fucking whacko—"

"If Reinhart's a ghost," I said, holding my hand out to keep the cop back, "then how is this going to help?"

"He's not a ghost. I thought we covered that. He's the reason these souls are trapped in the city."

I could hear the crackling of wood and old paper from below. Smoke was pouring out of the basement door. "At least shut that," I yelled at the cop.

Meanwhile Lyds had come closer. She seemed the calmest person in the room. "But why us?" she asked.

"I had to move quickly," the priest said. "The battle always turns on a moment of decisive action. History shows this. Any one of you could decide to help him. It's better this way."

"Reinhart's just one of these...people," I said. "Somehow he's found a way of getting to the other side of the Bloom and surviving, that's all. How do you know he didn't put the idea for this into your head? How do you know he can't just flip himself out of here, leaving us to burn to death?"

"He can't."

"How do you know?"

"He's right," the cop said. "Reinhart can't do that. He can hide himself in plain sight, but he can't magic himself through walls. He's too solid."

I hesitated, trying to stop myself from doing the wrong thing. When there's a fire, you want to run. Senses shriek with how crucial it is that you get yourself away as fast as possible. I knew there was no point just running around the room. I knew also that Jeffers wouldn't help us even if he could.

So I grabbed a chair and went back to the street end of the room for one last try.

I gathered all my strength and smashed the chair into the bottom of the lowest window. The chair shattered into pieces that rained all around me. The window didn't even crack. Not just covered with wire, it turned out, but reinforced. It wouldn't break until the temperature in here got high enough to override the pressure treatment, by which time we'd be a charred memory.

I pulled out the gun and pointed it at the door. I emptied it into the frame and around the handle. Afterward the door looked like shit, but neither tugging nor kicking made anything move.

I became aware that Lydia was standing right next to me. She looked scared but also brave.

"Come on," she said, holding out her hand. "I'll go with you."

"Go where?"

"Where the key is."

Jeffers got to his feet. "Turn your face from her," he commanded, his voice low and hard. "She lies. He is inside her now."

"You should do it," the cop said to me. "She's right. That's where the key is. That's the only chance."

"So why don't *you* go down there?" Lydia said. "You're the cop, right?"

He went back to banging on the front door. He started shouting, too, to make it look more like he was doing something of substance rather than turning away from the only road that went anywhere but death.

Lydia took my hand, and I let her lead me toward the far end of the room. Jeffers got there first. He positioned himself in front of the doorway.

"Every second you screw around just makes it more likely that people are going to die," I said. "I know very little about your God and his value system, but I don't see how that's ever going to be a good thing."

"You will not pass," he said.

I grabbed his head and threw him aside. I pulled open the door to the basement. "You've done enough," I told Lydia, and put her gently to one side.

Then I went through the door.

Chapter 69

Kristina had her phone out and was on with 911.

"Fire at a church on 16th," she said, struggling to keep her voice calm and intelligible. "There are people inside. Please be fast." The woman on the other end kept trying to get her to stay on the line, but once Kris knew she'd communicated the information and the urgency she hung up and ran with Flaxon to the church.

The smell was strong and smoke was curling out of ventilation gaps in the brickwork down near the floor inside the gates.

"*Shit,*" Flaxon wailed. "What are we going to do?"

Maj vaulted straight over the gate. He ran up the stairs to the door on the right, then came back and over to the other side. "Locked," he said.

Kris ran back into the street, listening for the sound of sirens and hoping to see a truck — but saw nothing other than the couple that had been at the car down the street, hurrying toward her. With early-evening traffic there was no knowing how long it would take for help to arrive. Could be five minutes. Could be twenty.

Could be long enough for everyone to die.

The guy called David seemed to have gotten himself together now, a little. "What's happening?"

"The church is on fire," Kris said, feeling dreamlike. "And my boyfriend is inside."

There was a muted crash as a shadow came and went against the lowest of the colored panes of glass on the upper floor. John was throwing something against it, Kristina guessed, and though it made her feel sick to realize that whatever he'd tried had failed, at least he was still trying things.

"Can you get inside?" she shouted to Flaxon, who was hopping from foot to foot, desperate to do something.

"No," she said. "We climb well. But we can't just go through walls."

Smoke was billowing out of the lower grills; then heat from below started to build and build. Then there was the sound of eight shots. It sounded like they were coming from close to the right doorway.

Dawn screamed. Kris listened and heard something being struck near the same position. And a shout of frustration that she *knew* was John.

"Has somebody been shot?"

"I don't think so," she said, but she wasn't sure and she could feel herself panicking.

Maj turned to David. "Tell me," he said.

"Tell you what?"

"What to do."

David had no idea what he meant. Maj leaned forward and tapped his finger in the middle of David's forehead. "*Focus.* What do you do now? What do *we* do?"

"I don't *know.*"

"So *make it up,* David. You know the question."

"What question?"

"The only one that ever mattered to you. *What happens next?*"

David looked up at the church, thinking furiously. The doors were locked and too tough to break. The windows on the second story were too high and reinforced and someone had just tried to break through them from the inside and failed. Obviously there was an air route into a basement where the smoke was coming from, but they didn't have the tools to break through, and anyway *that was where the fire was.* "I don't know," he said. "I can't..."

Then he stopped, let himself out of the gate and stepped out onto the sidewalk, looking back at the church. He felt something coming at him, opening the door in the back of his mind.

"What?" Maj came after him, followed by Flaxon. "What have you seen?"

"It's the only thing I can think of."

Flaxon saw where he was looking. "The roof."

Kristina looked up at the shallow-pitched roof, and then downward, tracing a route down the wall. Ornamental bricks stuck out at irregular intervals. *Maybe* you could climb that way, if you scrambled up the head-height columns either side of the doorway and then onto the roof above it. Maybe. And maybe you'd fall and die.

"It's all I've got," David said. "I'm sorry."

Maj ran back into the courtyard. Flaxon followed, looking dubious. Smoke from the basement was curling up the front of the building now. Kris heard more shouting from inside. Maj reached for the column on the left side of the door and pulled himself up, then used both hands to haul himself up onto the roof.

"But we won't be able to break through the roof when we get there," Flaxon said as she scaled the other column, bracing her toes on the outcrop at the bottom and pulling herself up onto the little roof, moving more quickly and with greater surety than Maj. "Even you don't have the fingerskills for that, do you?"

Maj shook his head. "There's nothing else to try. We have to get up there and then see what we can do."

"I can do it," David said.

"No, David," Dawn said firmly.

David turned to Kris. "Keep her back," he said. "She's pregnant."

He reached for the column by the side of the doorway and started pulling himself up.

"No!" Dawn screamed. She started to run up the stairs, but Kristina held her arms tight. "Don't!"

"Come back and I'll go," Kris said, but David had already hauled himself up onto the roof above the doorway and was reaching for the brickwork above.

Maj climbed quickly, but Flaxon was faster. She moved up the upper face of the church like a lizard, hands and feet reaching out for the bricks that poked out. She was up and over onto the roof while Maj was still ten feet down and David had barely made it halfway.

Dawn shook Kristina off. "But then what?" she shouted.

The same thing had just occurred to Kristina. It was all very well getting up there and maybe even breaking through the roof, but unless there happened to be a thirty-foot ladder in the church all this would achieve was a bird's-eye view of people being burned alive.

She knew also that John wouldn't be waiting for the fates to step in on his behalf. He'd be trying to break down the walls of the reality he found himself in, kicking toward some better place on the other side, even if that place didn't exist, and even if running toward it might bring the end upon him quicker than it might otherwise have done.

"Please, John," she prayed, silently, but as deep and loud as she could. "I love you. Please don't do something brave."

David nearly fell, twice. The bricks were cold and wet and he'd realized before he was halfway to the roof that this was an insane thing to try and he just wasn't strong enough for it. He knew also that he wasn't strong enough to spend the rest of his life aware that he'd stood on the sidewalk and done nothing, however. He already had too much guilt and regret socked away.

He reached up with hand after hand and scrabbled for enough purchase under his fingers to feel he stood a chance. He was terrified. His insides were twisted so tightly that he could barely breathe. But when he felt he'd gotten enough traction with his fingertips he pushed carefully up with his right leg, straightening it, until his head was poking up over the roof.

Maj and Flaxon were standing halfway down, as if being up here was the most natural thing in the world.

Somehow this made David realize it was only the *idea* of standing on a roof that was frightening. Apart from the knowledge of what will happen to you if you fall, it's no different from being on a slope a couple of feet off the ground. The idea felt precarious in his mind, but it was enough to get him moving again.

He brought his left arm over and reached as far as he could, pushing up with the other leg at the same time . . . until he could start to haul himself up onto the tiles.

Maj was stamping at the roof, but nothing was happening. As David pulled himself up far enough that the balance of his weight was over the roof, he realized that wasn't going to change. He could barely feel the vibration of the other man's foot striking the tiles, even though he was doing it time after time with all his force.

Which meant it was down to David. He hauled himself up using his left hand to grab on to the capstone at the peak of the gable. The pitch of the roof was thankfully shallow, designed to make the space inside seem as big and impressive as possible.

He pulled himself along the tiles toward Maj and Flaxon, using his other hand to scoot himself across the wet tiles. They were slippery and a few were missing. The second time he came across a hole he lowered his head and looked into the gap beyond.

"Need more than that," Maj said, shouting against the wind. David saw that he was right. Beyond the hole was a narrow space, then beams and tight-fitting planks of wood.

Making sure he had a good hold on the capstone, he used his other hand to bang against the boards. They were very solid. Levering off tiles wasn't going to be enough.

"*Now* what?" the girl asked. She'd come over and was squatted down beside him, looking into the hole.

"What about the other end?" Maj said. "Maybe there's a window on the other side of the church."

"So what? We're not going to be able to get to it—and even if we can, it's obviously too high for whoever's in there to get to, or they'd have tried it already."

Maj looked down at David. "This was a crap idea," he said, not unkindly.

Then his foot slipped on a broken tile, and he started to fall.

From below all they saw was a shadow standing at the apex of the roof, right at the end. The sound of flames in the basement was now clearly audible, and the smoke coming out had turned black and choking. There had been no more noises from inside the building itself.

Dawn heard sirens and turned to look up the street. She missed the moment where Maj lost his footing, slipped, and started to topple over the edge of the roof.

She also missed seeing David's hand lash out.

Chapter 70

The other side of the door was a space barely big enough to turn around in, a narrow set of stairs leading down on the left. Within seconds of starting down it was almost impossible to see anything through the smoke.

I didn't want to go down there.

I didn't see any choice.

I held my arm up against my nose and mouth, trying not to breathe deeply despite my lungs' panicky insistence that they needed more air. I felt out with my foot, taking one step at a time. I'd seen the priest throw the key. Surely it couldn't have gone far.

Each time I went down a step I carefully swept my other foot across it, listening for the sound of something small and metal moving against wood.

There was a split-second breeze or change of wind direction and for a moment I could see a little more of where I was — a staircase with a second landing leading down, and below that, reflections of fire on a wall. I thought that I glimpsed something down there, small and dark on the bigger step, and that it *might* be a key.

It was enough to keep me going. But for how long and how far? Could I keep going if it got hotter and if I couldn't see anything?

I had a heavy urge to give up and turn around. It felt as if there was a voice in my head, pleading with me to stop, to turn around — not a bad voice, I didn't think it was Reinhart; it felt like someone who had only love for me and wanted me out of harm's way and for me not to do something dumb.

But if I *didn't* do this, what then?

I made it down to the landing and dropped to a crouch, feeling around on the wooden floor with my hand, trying to stay calm. I couldn't find anything, though I was sure this was the right step. Then my fingers caught on something and by leaning right over and squinting through the smoke I realized it was just a knot in the old wood. That's all I'd seen.

I coughed so hard I went dizzy, caught in a chain of retching spasms that threatened to knock me off balance.

I had to keep going. If Jeffers had thrown the key straight down from the door above, it would have hit the wall over my head and bounced down the next landing. After that it couldn't have gone far. It had to be within twenty feet of where I was. In the growing heat and blackness, that was a long way, but if it meant the difference between living and dying it was close enough.

I lowered myself to a sitting position and started to shuffle down the final set of stairs one at a time.

I heard something ahead. Something new, that is. The crackle of flames from the corner was ever-present. The smoke around me was shot with light from the burning. Some other sound was growing. I got down to the lower level.

Then I saw it. I saw the key.

It was only ten feet away. I dropped onto my hands and knees and felt my way through smoke that had redoubled in thickness. There were splinters in the wood under my hand, but I kept sweeping it back and forth, side to side, reaching out as far ahead of me as I could, until finally they banged into something.

It was hot, the key—the air had heated up to the point where grabbing hold of it made me wince, and then cough again.

I was reaching out too far. The wrenching cough cost me my balance and I tipped onto my face and shoulder, falling to lie halfway around the corner.

My face immediately felt like someone had turned a blowtorch on it. My eyes clamped against the heat, shocked into closure. I was paralyzed, body going into seizure, unable to move in any direction at all.

Above the roar of flames the new noise was getting louder and louder. I'd never heard anything like it in my life before.

Holding my hand out as a block, I cracked open my eyes. All I could see was flame and smoke, alternately black and searing bright, and maybe that's what caused patterns to spark across my brain, as if my eyes were trying to make sense of the insensible.

I felt Reinhart coming toward the corner from the other side. He was at ease. He was glad I'd come. He was happy there was fire. It held no fear for him. He knew it's what you need to transform.

Between us there was the smoke and it was full of people now. It seemed like the flames were highlighting things that lay and sat along this stretch of corridor, scrunched into fetal balls or standing with their faces against the walls. There was a figure with a grotesquely large head and a woman dressed like a dolly, her hair in braids. There were children, or things shaped like them. There was a lion with golden eyes.

The sound...I don't know what it was. I will never know. I couldn't tell whether it was the noise of beings dying, or being born, of horror or a fierce and mindless kind of joy, of a huge dark door being slammed shut forever, or a white one being opened as fifty souls woke from dusty sleep together and moved their fading limbs.

It was horrible. It was beautiful. It held my attention a moment too long.

When I coughed again it didn't feel like all of it came back out. Certainly not enough. My chest locked, full of smoke and heat and unable to expel.

My mind filled with a face, nothing to do with anything down here. It was the face of my remaining son, Tyler, as I'd last seen him, and I realized with terrible sadness that I had abandoned him like some imaginary boy, presenting my back as I walked out of his life. I'd turned my back on him in pain, and to keep myself sane, but he wasn't to understand that. All he knew was that he'd been forgotten and left behind.

The shapes in the smoke still moved. I couldn't get up. My cheek was flat against the boards and I could feel the heat rising from them and hear the sound of whatever beings lined the corridor ahead.

I could also feel Reinhart getting closer to where I lay sprawled, my mind fluttering, splitting into black and white and heat. It did not feel like a single person coming toward me, but I couldn't tell whether that was because of all the others around the corridor or if Reinhart's power and concentration came from a gathering of the people he'd caused to die, lost souls corralled into one vessel and bent now to a single will. Each one of us contains multitudes, after all: who we are and who we've been, and perhaps also who we love or kill.

He squatted down in front of me. His clothes were on fire. He put a finger under my chin and lifted my head.

"I got plans," he said. "I don't need you running around my head like some big black dog without a home. You...can just die. It's my gift to you."

He looked up, as if hearing something. He smiled and stood back up and backed away into the flames and smoke until he became part of them.

I knew that getting the key wasn't enough.

I had to get him, too.

I tried to push myself up. Nothing happened. Once again I heard that other voice, the one deep in my mind, telling me not to do anything rash, not to be a hero. I realized it was Kristina.

"It's okay," I whispered. "I'll be fine." I'm not sure if the words made it out of my head.

I pulled my arm around and tried to get it in front of my face before pulling in another breath. This time I got just enough air into my lungs to experience a moment of jagged clarity, and knew I had to get out of here, *right now,* or Reinhart was going to get what he wanted.

I tried to shift all my limbs at once, hoping to get at least one of them to achieve concerted movement. Nothing happened, again, and I realized that's all I had left. It had been my last shot.

I coughed and I coughed and I coughed, each time with less and less strength.

Then someone yanked my arm, hard—so hard that I felt my chest pulled off the floor and my body dragged up into a slumped position, and beyond.

I heard a voice in my ear, speaking with extraordinary calm. Strong hands hauled me up onto my knees, and this time I knew the hands were real.

I looked up through the smoke, as the hands shoved me back along the corridor, and saw Jeffers's face.

"Go," he said.

The priest stepped over me to walk into the smoke and down through the slowly moving shapes and toward the turning at the end, beyond which lay the fire and whatever now waited there for him, the man or being or thing that called itself Reinhart.

As I crawled toward the stairs I heard the sound of breakage from above, as though a door had been smashed into pieces. Then a lot of shouting.

I made it halfway up.

Chapter 71

What happened in the next hour is patchy. I remember sitting on the curb with an oxygen mask on my face and a blanket around my shoulders, Kristina perched alongside and holding me so tightly she was making it harder to breathe than all the smoke I'd inhaled. I didn't hold that against her, not least because she'd saved my life.

I remember watching a stream of the firefighters she'd summoned going in and out of the church. At first it seemed they'd got it under control, but then something new caught fire in the basement and it started to get away from them. There was a lot of shouting and running. Eventually it died back.

I had told them about seeing the priest in the cellar. I heard one later saying to a colleague that he'd tried to make his way through the blaze down there and thought he saw two people in the distance at the far end before the heat forced him to retreat, though according to the papers the next morning the remains of only one body were eventually retrieved from the wreckage. The piece took the line that Father Robert Jeffers had died in defense of his church, trying to save something he believed in. I think that is a fair assessment.

In the meantime I saw Lydia being loaded into the back of an ambulance on a stretcher, deathly pale but alive. A portion of the floor in the church had given way while I was downstairs, and she and the cop got it almost as bad as I did. The cop ran, fleeing the scene the moment the door was opened. He was standing there waiting for his chance, and had been since the moment he realized help had arrived outside. He did nothing to aid the old woman who'd been trapped with him.

I know his name. There will come a reckoning for him. It may arrive via official channels. It may not.

As my head started to clear I became aware of other people in the street. I saw the guy David standing with a woman Kristina explained to me was his wife. Maj came walking diffidently toward David, and Dawn stepped away, coming to where we sat, to give them space.

There was a pause, long and full, as if between two people who'd known each other a long time ago meeting again, people trying to bridge a gulf a hundred years wide but only a couple of feet deep.

"It was short for 'imaginary,'" David said, as if he'd been asked a question.

Maj nodded. "Okay."

"I'm sorry. I was just a kid, but I should have come up with a better name. You deserved more than that."

"I'm used to it," Maj said. "And it's better than having no name at all."

They stood awkwardly for a moment.

"You didn't have to do that up there," Maj said. "Grabbing my hand."

"I know."

"No. I mean I wouldn't have died if I fell."

"That doesn't mean you let people fall."

Maj nodded, and they looked each other full in the face for the first time. "Goodbye, David."

"What are you going to do?"

"Don't know. May try being a Journeyman for a while. There's a great big world outside the city. None of it's perfect. But it's there."

"Will I see you again?"

"Do you want to?"

"Yes."

"Then maybe."

David watched as Maj walked away up the street. He passed the three siblings who had been in Dawn's car. Maj paused, then suddenly lunged at them, for a moment seeming bigger or brighter. They disappeared. Then at the corner he saw Maj pause once more, to exchange words with a squat man in a striped suit.

He started off again and turned the corner, the other man walking by his side, as though they had decided to travel together for now.

Kristina glanced up at Dawn. "So David's a writer, huh?"

"Yes," she said proudly. "He's got a novel coming out soon."

"Any good?"

"He's awesome. And he'll get even better, too."

"When's the baby due?"

"Bab*ies*. Not for a while. I can't wait. It'll be so good for David to have a family again. He needs roots to keep him from floating away."

"Isn't there anyone else but you?"

She shook her head. "He's an only child, and his parents died in an accident years ago. It was awful for him. It was their fault, too. Well, the people in the car coming up the other side said they thought they *maybe* saw someone stepping into the road before it happened. That David's father swerved to avoid him and lost control. But they never found anyone, and David's always been very sure it was his father's fault."

"Where was David at the time?"

"Here in the city."

I saw Kris thinking about this. I knew her well enough to know she could see a door in her mind, one that would open onto things that hadn't been known before; I knew she wanted to ask questions about how far a friend would be prepared to go for their real person if they feared they were losing them, and whether that real person might even have known what had been done on his behalf, and have been living with it ever since.

"Let's go," I said, pushing myself up to my feet. "Bad things happen. Leave it at that."

Some guy from the ambulance shouted at us as we left, but they were sufficiently busy dealing with Lydia — who was trying to sit and cussing up a storm—that we were able to walk away without someone dragging me off to the hospital.

When we got to the corner I looked back at David and Dawn. They were standing with their foreheads touching, hands together. He loved her—I could see that—and she loved him. Sometimes that's all you need to know.

We spent the night at a hotel. I let Kristina do the talking at reception and stood well out of the way and tried not to smell of wood smoke. I had a long shower and we sat in bathrobes on a balcony fifteen floors up and watched the lights and listened to the cars below. You could see people down on the sidewalks, too, walking up and down, back and forth, standing, waiting, living. I've no doubt that some of them were real. I'm unsure now how to tell which, or of how much difference it makes.

Reinhart was still in the city somewhere, alive. I could feel it. I don't know whether I truly believe he killed his friend and became something new, or that he is like the rest of them, or ever was. It could be that Jeffers was right. Reinhart might simply be the unholy ghost, the shadow in our minds, that thing that has always existed wherever humans congregate, something born out of our behaviors and desires and yet which takes on a life of its own. We try to find words to cage this thing, to help us understand, but it is beyond comprehension. All you can do is fight, wherever you find it, and hope that someday your kind will win—the kind that does the best it can, rather than the worst it is capable of.

The next morning we didn't have to discuss what to do. We left the hotel and walked down to Penn Station and bought two tickets for the first long-distance service due to leave. We sat together as the train started to whir and chug, ready to start out toward the countryside, where there are fewer people, wider spaces, and it's easier to work out who you are. In the fullness of time we may get all the way to the other side of the country, and when that happens I will try to see my ex-wife and my boy. He may never view me as his father. I may always be just some guy. But he needs to know that I did not forget him and never will.

Out of the corner of my eye, as we pulled up out of the tunnels and light flooded into the carriage through the windows, I saw a girl slip into an empty seat six rows behind us. White hair, tough-looking.

Kristina told me her name is Flaxon. I didn't turn and stare. If need be, we'll work out what to do about it somewhere down the line. And she's welcome, anyhow.

We have no idea where we're going. I've got no problem with a friend coming along for the ride.

The church was not the only thing that burned that night. It appears from news reports that there were twelve arson attacks at other locations in the city. Twenty-seven people died, including one in a house on the Upper West Side, where a girl called Jessica Markham suffocated in her bed. Her parents survived. The fire was apparently started by a lit matchbook pushed through the letterbox.

A witness claimed to have seen a teenage girl wearing a gray hoodie standing in the street and watching the flames, before running away into the city.

She was laughing.

She looked very alive.

Epilogue

Ten days later a woman found herself wandering the city in the early afternoon, walking streets she knew and streets she did not, walking because it felt like the only thing to do. Eventually she came to rest in a grassed area at the end of the Riverwalk, overlooking the Hudson. Despite living only ten or fifteen minutes from this little park, she'd never stood on this spot and didn't know what might have drawn her to it now.

Catherine Warren had found herself feeling unaccountably lonely over the last few days. She'd discovered that meeting with friends in the Village, keeping up her end at dinner parties, or chatting with other mothers outside the school gate had started to feel flat. Nothing had changed about these people or about the structures of her existence...and yet something had. There was a lack. A hole, even if she'd long ago stopped being aware of what had filled it.

It felt specific.

It was like someone was missing in her life.

But she supposed everybody feels that way sometimes. You enter adulthood on the promise of becoming full, of achieving one hundred percent and three-sixty degrees and 24-7/365—but slowly come to accept there'll always be a gap somewhere. She knew this intellectually but still couldn't shake the feeling of melancholy. She was old enough to know it would pass, however. The world keeps serving up stuff and you deal with it and sooner or later it's either okay or overlaid with something else—like adding layer after layer of paint onto a canvas until one day you have the finished picture. It may not be what you had in mind when you started. But it is what it is.

She couldn't seem to leave the spot, this park, though she knew she needed to get back to Chelsea and her life. She had to be in good form tonight, too. Mark would be tired. He was busy at work. He was always busy. Work stood behind him, hands on his shoulders, holding him down. He would need nurturing and looking after, and probably—if he had a glass of wine too many again—a great deal of reassurance that everything was okay.

Catherine actually had no idea if everything was okay. She didn't recall being promised it would be, either. She remembered coming to the city convinced she was going to be a journalist, that one day people would pick up *The New York Times* and her byline would be there, fighting the good fight and pulling aside the veil. It didn't happen. She worked hard at it for a while, but the world fought back, with its good-natured persistence and slow but constant cavalcade of events and demands: in the battle between you and reality—as she'd once read somewhere—you should always offer to hold reality's coat.

One day she woke up to realize that she was a mother, not a Pulitzer hopeful, and so she'd decided that she would be the best damned mother she could instead.

These days she barely remembered the other things she'd wanted, and she didn't care. What would be the point? Dreams are supposed to support and succor us, not to make us feel bad. Catherine had always been good at pushing aside things that no longer worked. It was the best way, the adult way, the sensible way—and she had wanted to be adult and sensible since she was a little girl.

She remembered that, at least. She would never remember, because it was buried too deeply, the evenings back then during which someone who should have loved her in better ways had done inappropriate things. She would never recall—except in the shape of the formless but very strong distaste she now held for the work of certain artists from the turn of the previous century—the way in which during these events she had fastened her attention on a reproduction picture on the wall in this man's house, a pre-Raphaelite painting of a young woman standing alone and drinking out of a glass bowl the color of irises, in front of a window showing sailing ships in the distance; a tall, slim girl with thick dark hair and pale skin, wearing a red velvet dress. The girl had looked thoughtful, and kind, the sort of friend that would not allow what was happening to be happening.

But happen it did.

And so what? What matters in life is what *you* do, not what's done to you by someone else.

Catherine frowned, finding herself remembering Thomas Clark, the guy she'd dated before Mark. Though he would never be anything more than part of a superseded past, she found herself wondering how he was and how he dealt with the dreams that had faded around them. He'd had big plans once, too. Maybe she should try to get in touch, say sorry, or hi, or something like that.

She put a pin in the idea.

Eventually she pushed away from the railing and started the walk down to Chelsea. It was time to pick up the girls. She walked slowly at first, then gradually with more enthusiasm, finding that her mood, if not cured, was a little lighter. She thought of her two little girls, happy to have them, and glimpsing for a moment the road that lay in front of these young women—the road of school and college, of living in apartments and having good sex and bad hangovers and working hard and goofing off and meeting a guy (or girl, whatever) and eventually starting to settle, moving in smaller circles like balls rattling around a pinball table, before finally finding the place they were meant to land. Maybe they'd be housewives. Maybe one would be president.

Dreams are dreams and real is real. Somewhere in between is what you get, and that's good enough.

Catherine picked up her step and strode down into the bustle and noise. If she got a move on she might even have time to pick up a tub of shrimp salad. The fact that Mark liked it wasn't the point, and never had been.

The point was this was her life.

Acknowledgments

Thanks to Jon Wood, Malcolm Edwards and Chris Schelling for advice and direction; to Lisa Milton and Susan Lamb for their support; to Jacks Thomas and Midas, and Jemima Forrester; to my father and sister and Stephen Jones and Patrick Goss for bolstering; to Kim Cupp for providing a home while I wrote, and to her and to Karen Hovecamp and Lisa Jenson for making us feel at home — and as always to Paula and Nate. Most of all thank you this time to Uncle Ralph, for getting me where I am now, before going on to wherever it is he has gone.

About the Author

Michael Marshall was born in England but spent his early years in the United States, South Africa, and Australia. He read philosophy and social and political science at King's College, Cambridge, before publishing his first novel in 1994. His critically acclaimed works have won a string of awards, and his breakout novel, *The Straw Men,* was an international bestseller. Marshall has also worked extensively as a screenwriter for clients in both Los Angeles and London. He lives in Santa Cruz, California, and Brighton, England, with his wife and son.

MULHOLLAND BOOKS

You won't be able to put down these Mulholland books.